W9-BLD-101

PRISONER OF PASSION

Molly groped for the door latch. Behind her, she heard Ballenrose ask, "How long are you going to listen to what Buckingham says instead of to your heart?"

"They're the same," she told him.

"I'll believe that when you walk out that door."

Molly raised the latch, held it, heard the blood surging in her veins, coursing round her bones, pulsing in her head . . . "Oh, God," she cried, turning back. "Oh, God—I don't know what to do!"

The Duke of Buckingham had saved Molly from a fate worse than death in Fleet Prison. But now she was a prisoner again—a prisoner of her own passion for . . .

BALLENROSE

SURRENDER TO LOVE

☐ **DEARLY BELOVED by Mary Jo Putney.** Beautiful Diana Brandelin enters into a daring masquerade when she comes to London posing as a dazzling courtesan. But try as she may to weave a web of desire, passion teares away her disguises and her defenses. A Golden Leaf Award Winner. "Wonderfully crafted!" —Romantic Times. (401859—$4.50)

☐ **BLAZE WYNDHAM by Bertrice Small.** A ravishing beauty came to the lavish and lustful court of Henry VIII to become the mistress and confidante of the most powerful man in England. But when he commanded she marry a man she professed to hate—she dared not refuse. "A breathtaking tale." —Romantic Times (401603—$4.95)

☐ **WHERE PASSION LEADS by Lisa Kleypas.** Only the flames of love could melt the brrier between them. Beautiful Rosalie Belleau was swept up in the aristocratic world of luxury when handsome Lord Randall Berkely abducted her. Now, she was awakening into womanhood, as Sir Randall lit the flames of passion and sent her to dizzying heights of ecstasy.... (400496—$3.95)

☐ **GIVE ME TONIGHT by Lisa Kleypas, author of *Love, Come to Me*.** Addie was drawn to Ben Hunter from the moment she met him. This strong, handsome man was different from the other ranch hands on her father's vast Texas spread, as different as Addie was from the meek and mild women around her. But they both had a secret—a secret they would reveal only when the white heat of their passion burned away all barriers between them.... (401239—$4.50)

☐ **DEVIL'S DAUGHTER by Catherine Coulter.** She had never dreamed that Kamal, the savage sultan who dared make her a harem slave, would look so like a blond Nordic god.... He was aflame with urgent desire, and he knew he would take by force what he longed to win by love. (158636—$4.50)

Prices slightly higher in Canada

Buy them at your local bookstore or use this convenient coupon for ordering.

NEW AMERICAN LIBRARY
P.O. Box 999, Bergenfield, New Jersey 07621

Please send me the books I have checked above. I am enclosing $_____ (please add $1.00 to this order to cover postage and handling). Send check or money order—no cash or C.O.D.'s. Prices and numbers are subject to change without notice.

Name_____

Address_____

City _____ State _____ Zip Code _____

Allow 4-6 weeks for delivery.
This offer is subject to withdrawal without notice.

BALLENROSE

by
Mallory Burgess

AN ONYX BOOK

ONYX
Published by the Penguin Group
Penguin Books USA Inc., 375 Hudson Street,
New York, New York 10014, U.S.A.
Penguin Books Ltd, 27 Wrights Lane,
London W8 5TZ, England
Penguin Books Australia Ltd, Ringwood,
Victoria, Australia
Penguin Books Canada Ltd, 2801 John Street,
Markham, Ontario, Canada L3R 1B4
Penguin Books (N.Z.) Ltd, 182–190 Wairau Road,
Auckland 10, New Zealand

Penguin Books Ltd, Registered Offices:
Harmondsworth, Middlesex, England

First published by Onyx, an imprint of New American Library, a division of
Penguin Books USA Inc.

First Printing, March, 1991
10 9 8 7 6 5 4 3 2 1

Copyright © Mallory Burgess, 1991
All rights reserved

 REGISTERED TRADEMARK—MARCA REGISTRADA

Printed in the United States of America

Without limiting the rights under copyright reserved above, no part of this
publication may be reproduced, stored in or introduced into a retrieval system,
or transmitted, in any form, or by any means (electronic, mechanical,
photocopying, recording, or otherwise), without the prior written permission of
both the copyright owner and the above publisher of this book.

BOOKS ARE AVAILABLE AT QUANTITY DISCOUNTS WHEN USED TO PROMOTE
PRODUCTS OR SERVICES. FOR INFORMATION PLEASE WRITE TO PREMIUM
MARKETING DIVISION, PENGUIN BOOKS USA INC., 375 HUDSON STREET, NEW
YORK, NEW YORK 10014.

For Paige and Stan
with love,
on your first anniversary.

I wonder by my troth, what thou,
and I
Did, till we lov'd?

—John Donne,
The Good Morrow

PROLOGUE

*Smithfield Market, London,
September 1669*

"YARROW, FRESH YARROW, a farthing the bunch!" Molly
Willoughby sang in the voice that Billy Buttons swore was
sweeter than her flowers. "I've got yarrow, good for the
bowels, 'n' nice sharp clary t' cleanse yer stomach, 'n'
celandine for the eyes! Come buy my yarrow!" The sour-
faced little woman who'd paused by her stall, blinking in
the bright sun, looked as though she'd start moving again,
and Molly made a quick mental catalog of her wares. If it
wasn't her belly or bowels that had brought her here, or
her bad eyesight, what else could it be?

"I've lady's mantle," she sang, "for pains o' the womb!
Coltsfoot for rheum!" The woman cleared her throat.
"Mullein for cough o' the lungs!" cried Molly, and cursed
beneath her breath as she saw a girl in a gay blue bonnet
approaching from the opposite direction. It was tansy and
eyebright she'd be wanting, to catch her a lover—not to
hear an old woman's list of woes. She shot a sharp glance
at the short, sour customer. "Sneesewort for yer tooth-
ache!" she ventured, and then, as the woman's face turned
even more puckered, "Dillweed for wind!"

And at long last the customer brightened. "Oy, ye must
be one o' them wot reads minds," she whispered, edging
close. "I'm troubled something awful with wind."

"Ye don't say." Molly plucked a bunch of yellow-headed dillweed from one of her pitchers. "Well, if ye boil this up and drink it, the wind do pass freer."

"Does it really work?" the woman wanted to know.

"Why, ye'd best believe it!" Billy Buttons called from the next stall over. "Use it myself, I do, once a week, 'n' I ain't bothered by wind even when the good wife serves up cabbage 'n' broth!"

The woman's eyes had widened. "Ooh, 'twould be fine to eat a bite o' cabbage again," she said longingly.

"Try it," Molly urged, expertly twisting the stems into a knot. "If it don't help ye, come back 'n' tell me. It don't cost but a farthing."

"Oy, it'll work," Billy assured the woman as she pulled a coin from her purse. "Mark my word on it."

"If it don't, I'll be back!"

" 'N' I'll be right here," Molly promised, handing over her change. The woman stuck the bundle in her basket and trotted away. "I owe ye one," Molly hissed to Billy as the girl in the blue bonnet drew nigh.

"So ye do," he said placidly, and boomed out his own song, working the pedal to his whetstone wheel: "Knives honed 'n' scissors sharpened! I'll hone yer knives here!" Molly's voice rang in sweet high counterpoint marked by the wheel's steady thumping:

"Tansy t' make yer skin lovely 'n' pale! Eyebright for bloodshot! Daisies, St. Margaret's daisies t' keep yer love true!"

The girl in the blue hat bought two bunches of those and another of lavender, spending tuppence in all. Molly flipped a farthing to Billy. "Thanks, mate."

He caught the coin on the fly, the edge of the ax he was grinding gleaming, and winked. "Ye're welcome, I'm sure."

By high noon Molly had served six more customers, and her hyssop was wilting. Billy kept an eye on her stall while she refilled the water pitchers. " 'N' another five minutes while I pop back t' see t' Aunt May?" she asked hopefully.

"Faith, pet, go on; ye know ye doesn't have t' keep askin'."

"Yes I do, Billy. 'Tis a big favor ye do me, 'n' I want ye t' know I don't take it for granted."

Billy hooked his thumbs into the loops on his breeches that would have held his belt, if he could have found one to go all the way around his huge stomach. " 'Tis a bigger favor ye do for May, lookin' after her the way ye do. Most girls yer age wouldn't be bothered. Most girls yer ago got nothin' in their empty heads but chasin' after the fellows, like that little chit in the blue bonnet."

Molly laughed at his disdainful expression. "I don't do anythin' for Aunt May that she ain't done for me."

"Hmph," said Billy, sighting along the edge of a lethal pair of shears. " 'Tis God's truth, ain't it? Life's a big circle. When ye're wee, ye need someone to feed ye 'n' change yer nappies, 'n' ye need it again when ye're old."

"So says the philosophic tinker o' Smithfield," Molly said, grinning.

"Get on wi' ye, then." He grinned back. "May as well take yer time. Ain't no one daft enough t' come t' market at noon on a day so bloody hot as this."

"Shall I bring ye back a pint, then?"

He grimaced at the shears, his shirt already soaked with sweat, then flipped her the farthing. "Make it two, there's a pet."

"Right, then." She tucked it into her purse, casting a last glance at the tin pitchers that held her bright wares. "I'm pushin' purple loosestrife, if any do come while I'm gone."

"Which is that?" She pointed out the tall stalks to him. "Hmph. Wot's it good for?"

"Excess o' sweatin'. Ye ought t' try some." She giggled and, when he growled at her and flourished the shears, skipped away from her stall toward Farringdon Street.

"Molly!" Michael Fishman called as she sailed past him. "Come 'n' have a word, then!"

"Not till the sun goes down, mate!" she called back, holding her nose against the stink of his mackerel and cod.

"Molly! Molly Flowers!" That was old Sam Cummings, that sold the ribbons and lace she used to make up her nosegays. "See wot I've got here, all the way from Flanders!" She paused for a moment to admire the length of ivory lace he displayed.

"Oy, 'tis right lovely, Sam. How much, then?"

"For ye, luv?" He considered, mouth pursed up tight. "Two shillings the piece."

"Gor, too rich for my blood. Ye'll have to sell it to King Charles's mistress."

"Will I? To which one, then?" he asked, and laughed toothlessly.

"Yoo-hoo! Is that ye, Molly Flowers?" Sarah Stiles was beckoning from her fruit stand. "I'd have a word wi' ye!"

"Oh, Lord." Molly ducked behind Sam's wagon.

"Still sore at ye for brushin' off that boy o' hers, is she?" Sam asked. Molly nodded. "Well, he's a right bloody rutter, that Andrew is, 'n' if she weren't his mother, she'd see it. Taken up wi' one o' them Campbell girls, he has."

"No! Has he really?" Eben Campbell and his daughters had the bottom stories of the house where Molly and her Aunt May rented a room.

"That's wot I hear, anyways," Sam confirmed. "Oy, ye're well quit o' him." He patted her shoulder. "Ye take yer time, then. Keep lookin' till ye finds the right one. That's wot I did."

"How old were ye when ye got married, Sam?"

"Never did. I'm still lookin'. Though if ye was to take it into yer head ye couldn't live without me—"

"Why, ye old lecher!" Molly pinched him, then escaped from behind the wagon as she saw that Sarah's back was turned.

She scooted past the Dog and Feathers, where she'd fetch Billy's pints on her way back, dodged two carters hurling insults at one another, waved to fat Betty Anders in the door to the baker's, and turned the corner onto Farringdon Street to take advantage of the shade thrown by the tall gray hulk of the Fleet prison. A crowd of urchins with hoops and sticks ran toward her, and she stepped onto the curb even as she marveled at their energy. It had been hot, miserable bloody hot for the past three days, and she felt as wilted as a week-old gillyflower. If the weather doesn't break soon, she thought, wiping her forehead on her sleeve, there'll be trouble in the market. There always was when it got this way.

A whisper of breeze beneath the tall linden that hung over the graveyard wall of St. Etheldreda's offered some relief once she turned onto Fetters Lane, and Molly paused to roll up her left stocking, which had been creeping lower and lower all morning long. She'd been sorely tempted not to wear any leggings when she rose at dawn and felt the air no less stifling than it had been at sundown; after all, Aunt May couldn't see what she had on. But sixteen years of having it drummed into her head that decent girls wore stockings whatever the weather won out in the end. And anyway, she thought ruefully, Aunt May would have sensed she was trying to get away with something. She always did.

The gate to the graveyard opened with a grinding squeak that made Molly jump. She relaxed as she saw it was just Tom Peabody on one of his ramblings, bundled up in his nest of rags. "Jesu, Tom, aren't you hot?" she asked, awed by his fortitude. How could he bear to wear all those clothes? He interrupted his conversation with himself long enough to tip his hat to her; it was newly crowned, she saw, with a tattered chicken feather.

"Molly, ain't it? Molly Flowers?"

"Aye, Tom. How are ye?"

"Passin' fine, passin' fine." Despite his excess of clothing, not a speck of sweat showed on his aged face; there was about him, Molly thought, something of the blithe insouciance of the boys with their hoops.

"Visitin' someone?" she asked, nodding toward the graveyard.

That made him laugh. "Faith, girl, they're all dead!"

Molly smiled into his excited eyes; they were blue and clear as a country mile. "Aye, so I hear." She started to walk on, but he caught her sleeve.

"If a dog barks at night," he hissed, leaning close, "can ye hear that?"

" 'Course I can."

His breath was oddly sweet, as though he'd been sucking peppermints all morning. "Then see that ye do, 'n' move out o' the way."

"Out o' the way o' what?" Molly asked curiously, and suppressed a shiver as he glanced back at the gravestones behind him.

"Out o' the way o' the Stalker, lest he snatch ye off!"

"Oh, honestly, Tom." The poor old bugger was always running on about dogs and someone called the Stalker who haunted his dreams. There in the bright sunlight, Molly giggled. "Why would ye try t' scare me on such a fine day?"

He looked highly offended. "I ain't scarin' ye, girl. Just tryin' t' warn ye."

"Well, consider me warned." She eyed the tattered feather in his hat. "Come down to the stall later 'n' I'll give ye a bachelor's button to stick in there."

"Will ye? Ah, ye're a good girl, ye is. Not that that will save ye."

"Ye're probably right," she told him, smiling into his bright eyes. "Fare thee well, Tom!" She skipped on down the street, leaving the madman to his mutterings.

At Number 10 Gospel Square, Charity Campbell was coming out of her father's butcher shop on the ground floor. Molly was about to call a greeting, but stopped when she saw the burly young man following after her. It was Sarah Stiles's son Andrew, in the black-and-gold jacket of the city watch. Molly ducked under the eaves of the baker's, waiting while they went by. Nearly two months had passed since she'd told Andrew once and for all she wouldn't walk out with him, but he still hadn't forgiven her for the blow to his pride. She hadn't heard he'd joined the watch, but it didn't surprise her. Now he'd be able to bully and harass folk as he always had and call it the law.

Some of his bonus for signing up must have gone to the new dress Charity had on. With her red hair and pale skin, she looked cool as cucumber slices. Of course, she hadn't got stockings on—nor a chemise neither. Molly gave hers a tug, then ran up the three flights of stairs to her room.

"Hallo!" Aunt May called, hearing her coming. "Wot're ye thinkin'?" It was her usual greeting. Molly went to the window to kiss her.

"That only harlots 'n' fools keep cool in such weather."

"Well, if ye're thinkin' of becomin' one or t'other, it had best be a fool. Who'd ye see, Charity Campbell?"

"Now, how did ye know that?" Molly asked, hands on hips.

"I can smell that cheap scent she uses every time she steps out the door. I heard boots too. Who's she with?"

"Andrew Stiles, of all folk." Molly fetched bread and cheese from the cupboard. "Got up like a parrot in a watch uniform. He must o' joined up."

Aunt May shook her head. "Gor, I feel for her poor father. She'll be in the same way as those sisters o' hers before spring. Well, he was asking for trouble, Eben Campbell was, giving 'em such names."

"I don't know why ye say that. Faith had great faith her fellow'd marry her. Hope hoped hers would."

" 'N' Charity?"

"Givin' it away to Andy Stiles, ain't she?"

Aunt May snorted, turning from the window. "I don't know where ye got yer sass, Mary Catherine Willoughby."

"From ye, o' course." Molly set the bread and cheese on the table and drew two mugs of small beer from the cask under the cupboard. Her aunt's long crooked fingers snaked across the surface of the table till she found the cheese, then the knife. Molly waited patiently, though she could have done the serving in two seconds. It was good for her aunt, she knew, to feel there were still some things she could accomplish herself.

"I didn't hear ye givin' 'em good day," Aunt May noted.

"Ye don't miss a thing, do ye?"

"Well, why didn't ye?"

"They were goin' the other way."

"That don't mean ye don't greet yer neighbors. Did somethin' go on betwixt ye 'n' Andrew?"

"I told ye months ago; he asked me walkin' 'n' I said no."

"Well, I hope ye had the sense t' do it delicate-like. That lad'll have a mean streak t' him if he's aught like his mother."

Molly winced, remembering the scene he'd made when she turned him down, and was glad her aunt couldn't see her. "He is."

"He could give ye trouble, in the watch."

"I'll keep out o' his way."

Aunt May seemed on the verge of saying something more, but instead passed Molly sliced bread and cheese.

"I saw Tom Peabody too," Molly offered, glad to change the subject. "Comin' out o' the graveyard at St. Etheldreda's. Gave me an awful start." Surreptitiously she switched the pieces of cheese so her aunt had the bigger one.

"Talkin' t' himself, was he? Give me back my cheese."

"Ye need yer strength, Aunt May."

"For wot? For sittin' by the window? Ye're the one runs about all day." Beneath the old woman's sightless gaze, Molly switched back the cheese. "*Was* he talking t' himself?"

"Aye, right enough. What d'ye reckon makes a soul go off like that?"

Aunt May shrugged her fragile shoulders. "Who knows? Mind ye, I recall a time when he was sharp as the next man, or sharper. And wild—ooh, but he was always up to somethin'! Well, there's been water 'neath the bridge since those days." She paused for a sip of beer. "I recall, if I'm not mistaken, he had lovely eyes."

"Still does," Molly confirmed. "Clear 'n' blue 'n' bright as the autumn sky."

"Well," her aunt said briskly, "ye see the good they did him. How's business?"

"No better'n fair."

"Well, wot can ye expect, in this damned bloody heat?"

"Speaking of this damned bloody heat, ye're not eating."

"Nag," Aunt May said, and took a bite. "How's Billy?"

"Fatter than ever."

"Hmph. Ye may not believe it, but Billy Buttons was a fine figure of a man once upon a time." The hard lines life had carved around her eyes went soft. "I damned near married him. I wonder if he remembers?"

"O' course he does. Why d'ye think he looks after my stall every noontime?"

She laughed. "Because ye brings him his beer." Her fingers pried apart a piece of bread. "Ye know, pet, ye'll have to think o' marryin' sometime."

"Why? Ye never did."

Her aunt laughed. "Oh, I thought about it; I just never did it."

"And neither shall I. At least, not for a long time. Why should I? I've got my stall, 'n' ye, 'n' Bubby. Here, Bubby." She swung round on her stool and fed a bit of bread to the brown sparrow that had lighted on the windowsill. The bird let out a chirp and preened.

"Bubby!" Aunt May scraped the crumbs she'd been making into her palm and held them out to the sparrow, who flew onto her hand and began to peck. "There's my bright boy! Fetch him some water, pet, so I can hear him splash."

Molly did so, filling up a saucer and setting it on the sill. "Don't give him all yer bread, now; he's already the fattest sparrow in London. I've got to get back. Billy's waitin' on his pints." She chewed her lip, watching as Aunt May fed the bird another inch of crust. It grew harder and harder to get her to eat each day, and she had grown so frail. "Anythin' I could fetch home that might strike yer fancy? Some fruit, or a sweet?"

"Nay, thank ye kindly."

"Please, Aunt. Somethin' good for yer supper."

"Well—" Aunt May considered, fingers stroking the sparrow's tail. "Some green grapes, maybe. But not if they're too dear. Mind ye don't spend more'n a penny the pound."

"Right," Molly promised, relieved. So what if grapes hadn't been a penny the pound for a good five years? Anything that might make her go on clinging to a life grown increasingly dim. . . . "I'll give Billy a kiss for ye, shall I? Need that chamber pot emptied?"

"There's naught in't."

"That's because ye're not eating." Molly pressed a kiss to her aunt's crepey cheek.

"That's why ye should marry. So ye'll have someone else to nag."

"I'm happy just naggin' ye. See ye for supper. 'Bye, Bubby." The bird blew a short, sharp note as Molly ran out and back down the three flights of stairs.

If I could only find a room at ground level, she thought longingly, cramming bread and cheese into her mouth as she hurried back to the market. Then Aunt May could talk to the folk as they passed, and hear more of what went on. It had to be horrible drear, not being able to see. And now her deafness was growing too. Why, six months past she'd never have missed Bubby landing for his noontime meal.

But a room would cost money, and that was something Molly was lacking. Seemed like every time she got a bit tucked away, the growers she bought her flowers from raised their prices, or the man who owned the ground the stall sat on hiked the rent, or taxes got raised to pay for King Charles's shenanigans. Eben Campbell hadn't increased the rent he charged for the room he let them in nearly two years, but Molly knew that was only because he felt sorry for them. His pity galled her; she'd rather have paid an extra shilling instead.

Still, she ought to be grateful, she thought, pushing damp wisps of long straw-blond hair off her neck. Eben could have used the extra money, what with Faith and Hope unmarried, and their two children as well. And now it looked as though Charity was following right in her sisters' footsteps. What possessed girls, she wondered for the thousandth time, to get in trouble that way?

Though it was true, there wasn't much else to look forward to in Smithfield. And it would be right lovely to have babies someday. She smiled as she passed Prissy Wingate, dangling her new son over her knees. There'd be time enough for that, though, once Aunt May had gone on to her reward. In the meantime, Molly owed the old woman too much to think about such things.

"Oy, Bart Connor!" she called into the Dog and Feathers. "Put me up two pints for Billy, will ye?"

"Bloody hot, ain't it?" asked the sweating barman.

"Aye," said Molly, taking the cool, beaded mugs he gave her. "A very hot day."

It was still hot come evening, as Molly consolidated her unsold bunches of hollyhock and hyssop and mugwort and emptied the dank water from her pitchers into the gutter, holding her nose against its stench. The buyers had gone home to their suppers, but her work wasn't done. She checked the mental list of tasks that remained: rinse the pitchers at the fountain, sponge down the cart and roll it back to the storage shed, return Billy's mugs to the tavern for him—

"Oh, damn," she muttered, remembering Aunt May's grapes.

"Wot now?" asked Billy, washing down his whetstone.

"I meant t' get Aunt May some fruit. Is Sarah still there, can ye see?"

Billy peered toward Farringdon Street in the gray haze of twilight. "Aye, right enough. Go on, then; I'll mind yer stuff."

"Ye're a poppet, Billy." Molly hiked up her skirts and ran to the fruit seller's stall. "Any green grapes left, Sarah?"

"Molly! Din't ye hear me callin' to ye at noontime, then?" the woman demanded.

"Callin' me?" Molly echoed, her green eyes wide.

"Aye, when ye was talkin' t' Sam!"

"Not a bit," Molly lied. "How about those grapes?"

"Got one bunch left." She slipped them onto her scale. "Just half, at sixpence the pound."

"Jesu, are they so high as that?"

"Got to make me costs, don't I? Times is hard," the fruit seller whined, reminding Molly why she didn't like her. "I'm barely coverin' as 'tis. D'ye want 'em or not?"

"Aye," Molly sighed, almost sure the woman had her thumb on the scale. She could see skinting strangers now and again, but a fellow trader? That really was low.

The woman twisted the grapes in paper, then looked up with a simper. "Seen my Andrew round, have ye?"

"Not lately," said Molly.

"Doin' right well by himself, he is." Sarah fairly glowed with pride. "Ridin' wi' the city watch."

"Aye, so I hear."

"Don't he look dashin', too, in that uniform they gave him."

"I'm sure he does. Well, I've got t' finish my work."

"Ye know," said Sarah, "I told him he was makin' a mistake wantin' t' take up wi' ye. No sense hankerin' after that 'un, I told him. Just like that old aunt o' hers, I said, all high-'n'-mighty. It runs in the blood.''

"Aunt May's no blood kin to me," said Molly, who'd long since learned there was little profit in wrangling. "Still, I'm flattered t' be likened to her. I'm sure Charity Campbell and Andrew have a lot more in common; she's such a generous girl. Looks t' me like yer scale's tipping heavy; ye'd best have it checked before the weight-man catches ye. 'Night, Sarah." She waved cheerily and headed back to her stall.

"Wot kept ye?" Billy called as she trotted up.

"Sarah, wot else? Here, look who's comin'. Tom!" She waved at Tom Peabody, who was meandering along the street in his rags and old hat. "I promised him a flower for his cap," she explained to Billy. "I'm surprised he remembered."

"Oh, he ain't always daft," said the tinker. "I've had conversations with him some days when he seemed as sane as ye 'n' me. Hallo, Tom. Hot, ain't it?"

"Lovely, lovely weather," Tom crooned, looking up at the sky.

" 'Course," Billy told Molly, winking as he mopped his brow, "this ain't one o' those days. How's life treatin' ye, Tom?"

"No sense in complainin'," Tom said, and turned his blue gaze on Molly. "Ye mentioned a flower."

"Aye, so I did. White or red?"

Tom considered it gravely. "Red, I think, don't ye, Billy Buttons?"

"Red suits ye well," Billy told him, equally grave.

"Red it is." Molly plucked one from its bunch and presented it to the madman, who took the feather from his hat, tucked it away in the recesses of his ragged coat, and stuck the flower in its place.

"Thank ye kindly, Molly."

"I'm sure ye're quite welcome."

"Mind that dog barkin' o' nights."

"Don't worry, I will."

Tom put the flower at a jauntier angle and ambled off across the marketplace. "Wot's that dog he's always runnin' on about, then?" Billy asked.

"Oy—" Molly made circles with her hand at her head. "Just more o' his cockle. Give me them mugs, then, 'n' I'll run 'em back."

When she came out of the tavern, Billy was dragging his wheel to the shed. Half a dozen pitchers clenched in each hand, she crossed the cobbles to the fountain and began the rinsing. It was a nuisance washing them each day, but Aunt May had taught her that clean water made the wares last longer, and her few experiments at shortcutting the system the old woman had perfected over forty years of flower-selling only proved its worth. She'd just finished the last of the lot when she heard hoofbeats pounding toward the square from the High Street. Recognizing the approach of the watch, she hurried back to her stall. That was another thing Aunt May had taught her: to steer clear of watchmen. "Best way t' keep out o' trouble is t' keep from makin' trouble," that's what Aunt May said.

Head down, she heard them clatter through the street and stop by the fountain. "Ye, there! Draw us some water," a loud voice cried, and she pitied whatever poor soul had caught the soldiers' eye. "Draw it yerself, can't ye see I'm busy?" another voice answered, and Molly looked up, recognizing it as Tom Peabody's.

"Gor help us," she muttered. Billy had paused on his way back from the shed, seeing Tom perched on the edge of the fountain wall in his nest of rags, trying to piece together a lace that had unraveled from his boot.

"Ye don't look busy t' me, old man," said one of the half-dozen soldiers.

"Then ye're a damn fool. Can't ye see me bootlace is broken?"

"That won't be all that's broken," warned the soldier, "unless ye draw us somewot to drink."

Tom glanced up from his work, his blue gaze steady

and clear. "If 'tis drink ye want, why, there's the Dog 'n' Feathers. Bart'll draw ye a pint o' his best—though between ye 'n' me, his mugs is none too clean."

Another of the uniformed men rode up beside his mate. Molly nibbled her lip as beneath his black hat she recognized the broad, blunt features of Andrew Stiles. "Leave it be, girl," warned Billy, who'd come up behind her. " 'Tis none o' yer worry."

Andrew Stiles prodded Tom with the tip of his crop. "Ye, there. Draw us up some water, 'n' don't give us no sass."

Tom looked him up and down from beneath the tattered brim of his hat. Then his mouth creased in a wide guileless smile. "Why, as I live 'n' breathe. 'Tis little Andy Stiles, all growed up 'n' vaunty."

"Is't a friend o' yers, Andrew?" another of the soldiers asked, grinning.

"Oh, aye," Tom said eagerly. "Many's the time I seen him without his nappies when he were a wee lad."

The soldiers—all but Andrew—snickered, making Tom beam. "Shut up, old man," Andrew snarled.

"Nay, tell us more!" cried one of his mates.

"I'll tell 'em 'bout the time ye 'n' yer brother Todd stole the offerin' plate from St. Etheldreda's, shall I?"

"Ye'll shut yer bloody mouth, old bugger, or I'll have yer hide!"

"La, 'tis a fine sort we have keepin' the peace, ain't it, now?" another watchman teased.

"Oy, that ain't the worst he done! D'ye ken that girl he's sweet on? Eben Campbell's daughter?"

"I'm warnin' ye, old man—"

"Aye, wot about her?" Andrew's mates led Tom on.

All around the market, vendors had stopped their work to watch the entertainment. Tom was blissfully unaware of his audience, but Andrew was not. As the old man opened his mouth again, Andrew's crop stung his cheek.

There was keeping clear of trouble, Molly reflected, but

then there was also looking after those who couldn't see to themselves. "Oy!" she cried, grabbing a fistful of flowers and sashaying out to the well, ignoring a loud groan from Billy. "Leave him be, Andrew; ye know right well he ain't got all his sails t' the wind."

The burly watchman turned to her with something of the look in his eyes a wild pig had when cornered. "Why don't ye just stay the hell out o' this, eh? It ain't none o' yer pie."

"Fair enough, fair enough. But here, then, ain't none o' ye fine gentlemen got sweethearts wot'd be wantin' flowers? I've got nice fresh cockscomb here."

"How much?" one of the guards asked, grinning.

"For ye, mate?" She grinned back at him and tucked one of the stems in his saddle. "No charge, seein' as ye're so handsome."

"Wot about me, then?" another demanded.

Molly smiled saucily and gave him a flower. "No charge for ye, neither, 'cause ye're ugly as sin."

The guards laughed and wheeled their horses around her, vying for her attention. From the edge of the well Tom spoke up again. "I seen *his* cockscomb," he announced, nodding toward Andrew. "There in St. Etheldreda's graveyard, Stickin' it t' Eben Campbell's—"

"Shut up, Tom," Molly said evenly as Andrew's face turned red as a gillyflower. "Billy! Come and take Tom out o' here, so he won't bother the gentlemen."

But Andrew was climbing down from his horse, the whip clenched in his hand. "By God, I'll teach ye t' keep a civil tongue in yer head," he spat, advancing on Tom.

"Billy!" Molly called again, rather desperately.

He came forward at last. "Come on, Andrew, wot's t' get all hct up about?" he asked, tugging at Tom's sleeve. "Everyone knows ye're sweet on Charity."

"Oy, 'tweren't Charity he were with," Tom said helpfully. " 'Twere the older one. Faith, I think. Or was it Hope?"

From the edge of the gathering crowd came a gasp, and then Charity's voice, high and outraged: "Andrew Stiles! Why, ye filthy rotten—"

"Oy!" Sarah Stiles pushed her way forward. "Mind wot ye call me boy!"

"I'll call him wot he is, the no-good two-timin'—"

"Well, maybe 'tis them sisters o' yers," Sarah snapped, "that ye ought t' call names."

"Who's callin' my girls names?" bellowed Eben Campbell, still wearing his bloodstained apron; news of the row had made it all the way to Gospel Square.

"Well, 'tis God's truth, ain't it?" Sarah shrilled. "They didn't get them there bastards by no immaculate conception!"

"Yer son ain't good enough for no girl o' mine, not by half!" Eben shot back.

"He were good enough for Faith at least one time," Tom said with a giggle. "Or were it Hope?"

"Shut *up*, Tom," Billy muttered, trying to lead him away.

The crowd was growing; Charity was sobbing and clinging to her father. Molly felt a harsh hand on her shoulder, whirled around, and looked into Andrew's angry pig's eyes. "All o' this is yer fault," he snarled.

"My fault? Are ye daft?"

"If ye'd let me shut that old man up when I tried—"

"Oh, for God's sake, Andrew." Molly's patience was frayed. "Maybe ye shouldn't have been jumpin' all three o' the virtues at once, eh? Maybe that's wot began it."

"Jealous?" He sneered.

She snorted. "Not likely. I'd sooner be jumped by old mad Tom than ye."

Sarah Stiles had just hurled a ripe plum at Eben. "Oy, break it up!" one of the watchmen shouted, riding to the butcher's rescue.

"My mum's right about ye—ye do think ye're high-'n'-mighty, don't ye?" Andrew's pig's eyes were mean and narrowed. Molly realized that he truly hated her. She began to edge away.

"O' course I don't—"

"Oy, but ye do. D'ye think ye're the bloody queen or somethin'?"

Molly laughed nervously, looking behind her for Billy. "That's a good one, Andr—"

He gave her arm a sharp twist. "Don't ye talk down to me."

She stopped moving back, looking up into his cruel little eyes. "All right, then, I'll tell ye why. Because ye pick on fools like Tom t' make yerself feel big. Because ye're a bully." The fight between Sarah and Eben was escalating; she had to raise her voice. "I know why ye joined the watch—because ye like for folks t' be afraid o' ye. Well, I ain't afraid o' ye, and I never will be." The end of her small speech came out to sudden silence. The people close by her began to applaud.

"Bitch," said Andrew very quietly.

Molly thumbed her nose at him.

"Ye're under arrest," Andrew said.

She laughed. "I'm wot?"

"Under arrest," he repeated.

"On wot bloody charge?" Molly demanded, astonished.

"Disturbin' the peace."

"Oy, go to hell."

"*And* for floutin' the authority of an officer o' the watch."

"Ye can't be serious."

"Oy, I'm dead serious. Here, Tucker!" he called to one of his mates. "Give us a hand with this 'un. I'm runnin' her in."

"Ye're more daft than Tom is!" Molly protested, twisting away as he grabbed her arms. "Ye can't run me in!"

"Just watch me."

"Billy!" Molly searched the crowd for the tinker, saw him, sighed with relief. "Billy, come 'n' talk some sense int' this ruddy fool; he's tryin' t' arrest me!"

"Ye keep back," Andrew warned Billy, "or I'll take ye too!" The tinker hesitated; beside him Molly saw the red gillyflower bobbing atop Tom's hat, and then the pinched face of Sarah Stiles, who'd stopped screeching at Eben to watch her son.

"Here, now, wot's goin' on?" Bart Connor had come out of the Dog and Feathers, wiping his hands on a towel.

"The Stiles boy's arrestin' Molly Flowers," Betty Anders told him.

"There must be some mistake."

"It's no mistake," Andrew said belligerently.

"Why, wot for?"

"Disturbin' the peace."

"That ain't why," old Sam Cummings told Andrew, " 'n' ye know it. 'Tis because she had the good sense t' spurn yer advances!"

"Shut up, old man, or I'll run ye in too! Tucker, come here!"

Tucker was the watchman Molly had called handsome. He got down from his horse and came toward Andrew. "Look here, mate, don't ye think ye're makin' much ado about nothin' 'Tis a hot day. Let's be on our way."

"She's under arrest," Andrew said between clenched teeth. Molly felt a flutter of fear. He was just stupid enough not to back down.

"Look here, Andrew, I didn't mean those things I said," she apologized quickly. "Let's shake 'n' call it quits, eh? No hard feelings."

"There, Stiles, she's said she's sorry," Bart from the Dog and Feathers noted.

"Ye leave him be," Andrew's mother snapped. "He's just doin' his job."

Molly turned to plead her case to Tucker. "Please, ye can't let this happen! I've my Aunt May at home; she's old 'n' blind and there's no one else t' look after her!"

"She should've thought o' that before she started makin' trouble," Andrew said implacably.

"I wasn't makin'—" Molly's voice was lost in the sudden sharp shriek of a whistle. The crowd grew silent, then parted before the tall black horse of the captain of the watch. Resplendent in his huge hat, he scowled down at Andrew and Molly.

"Wot the devil's goin' on here?"

"I'm makin' an arrest, sir," said Andrew.

"Then make it and be done!"

"Yes, sir!" Andrew yanked Molly's arm, triumph in his small eyes. "Ye're under arrest for disturbin' the peace."

"Hold on, mate!" cried Bart. "There weren't no riot or nothin'!"

"Nay, 'n' there won't be now," Andrew said.

Molly looked up at the grim captain. "Please, sir, there's been a misunderstanding! I only—"

"Tell it t' the judge," he barked, and snapped his long whip at the gawking crowd. "Clear out, all o' ye! Back to yer business!"

"Oh, God," Molly whispered with the sudden sense that this was all a dream. But the rope Andrew looped around her wrists and pulled tight had a very real pinch. She searched the wide-eyed faces around her. "Billy—"

"Don't worry, pet," the tinker said nervously. "The charges won't stick."

Andrew tied the rope to his saddle and mounted his horse. "But Aunt May—" Molly began.

"I'll see t' her," Billy promised.

"But wot if—ooh!" She gasped; Andrew had dug his spurs in and started off at a trot. As she ran to keep from being dragged, he turned in the saddle and grinned.

"We'll see if ye're so high-'n'-mighty, Molly Flowers," he hissed, "once ye're in the Fleet."

"The Fleet!" Clutching his rags, Tom Peabody darted out from the throng and ran after Molly. "Ye can't take her there! Not t' the Fleet!" Molly glanced back and saw his blue eyes blank with terror. "Jesu save us, not t' the Fleet! No!"

"Ye know, sir," Tucker told the captain of the watch,

nodding toward Tom, "he's the one's behind it all. Shall I arrest him too?"

"Ye must be jestin'," the captain said briskly, watching the flower in Tom's hat bob as he ran. "Can't ye see he's mad?"

I

1

MEG CALLOWAY HAD red hair, red eyes, not a tooth in her head, and as foul a mouth as any shipman at St. Katherine's docks. Molly liked her. Of the fifteen women who shared Molly's cell, in fact, Meg was the only one she liked at all. Oh, Lizzie Cutler wasn't so bad, at least when she hadn't been drinking the beer she bribed the guard to bring her, and there were one or two others who were decent at times. But most of her fellow prisoners were hard, angry souls with chips on their shoulders the size of the stones that made up the cell walls, and Molly had suffered too much at their hands in the early days of her incarceration to practice forgiveness. Six months in the Fleet had taught her two basic tenets of survival: keep yourself to yourself and don't make trouble.

Six months, one week, and four days, to be exact, she calculated, returning Meg's grin as they lined up with their bowls for supper. That left only five months, two weeks, and six days to go. It was hard to believe she was halfway through. Sometimes it seemed she'd never had any home but this cell, no companions but Meg and Lizzie and the surly women queuing with their wooden bowls and spoons for the evening meal.

There were mornings that she'd wake at dawn, while the cell was still quiet, and, with her eyes shut, cling to the last shreds of sleep, pretending she was back home in Gospel Square again. Aunt May was dozing just across the room, by the open window where Bubby would be coming to wake them with his chirping song. There'd be yesterday's bread sopped in milk for breakfast, and maybe, if business had been good, a nibble of bacon. Gor, those homely meals that she used to despair of! You can keep the fried eggs and sausages and crumpets that I envied the rich for, Molly thought longingly, just give me bread and milk instead of more horrible—

"Gruel!" sang the guard who swung open the door, pail and ladle in hand. Close behind him, squelching any notion of trying to slip by, was the huge black-clad figure of Hugh Stalker. Molly glanced at him and then quickly away. The bearded giant, with his blank eyes and expressionless features, always gave her a chill. She wondered again if it were true what Meg had whispered to her—that he was silent because he'd had his tongue cut out for some unspeakable crime years ago. It wouldn't have surprised her at all. In the nightmares from which she'd suffered ever since she came to the prison, evil always bore Hugh Stalker's empty face.

Just ahead of Meg in the queue was Hannah Crandall— Canny Hannah, the other women called her, with respect in their voices. Molly had heard her boast she'd been in the Fleet fifteen years. She looked it too, Molly thought, listening as the woman wheedled the guard to put more in her bowl. Molly's hand crept up to touch her own tangled hair and feel the flesh stretched tight over her cheekbones. Was she starting to get that look too, like a half-starved street cat, all bones and eyes?

"Don't fret, luv," Meg whispered at her elbow. "Ye're as bonny as the day ye walked in, though a mite more skinny. Jest see how he's lookin' at ye." She nodded toward the guard doling out the gruel.

Molly fought off a shiver as she held out her bowl beneath the guard's randy stare. It would be easy enough to get her bowl filled to brimful; plenty of the others did it, trading their favors for food and drink, for warmer clothes in winter, or a bit of bedstraw. The guards didn't even take them out of the cell; they copulated in corners, up against the wall, fully dressed. Before she came to the Fleet, Molly never really understood what went on between a man and woman. Now she lived for the day when she'd never have to witness it again.

The guard leaned down. His breath was rank with beer and cheese, and his hair reeked of cheap pomade. "Look here," he hissed, opening his doublet to Molly. "An apple. It's yers, luv, for two minutes o' yer time."

"Hmph! Yer wastin' yers." Hannah sneered, miffed that the guard had turned her down for her younger, fairer cellmate. "Don't ye know that's the grand Virgin Molly?" Molly shot her a look of pure hate. She lived in constant terror she'd be raped; only one thing had kept the men in check so far.

"She ain't really no virgin," the guard scoffed, but with a gleam in his eye as he looked back at Molly. "Is ye?"

"Hardly," she told him, reaching for the apple. "I'd be glad t' pass the time o' day wi' a fine lad like ye."

" 'Old on," Meg cried, "don't do it! Got the French pox, she 'as!"

"Oy!" The guard jumped back as though he'd been burned.

"She's crazy," Molly said of Meg, even as she scratched herself through her dress. " 'Tain't no French pox; 'tis just my monthly flux."

"I've 'eard her screamin' nights o' the pain," Meg told the guard. Molly whirled on her, hands up, nails at the ready.

"Filthy liar, I'll scratch out yer eyes!"

" 'Tis God's truth! I'll not stand idle by while ye give such a bonny lad yer filthy disease!"

The guard, who'd been weighing the potential pleasures of Molly against the consequences if she truly did have

syphilis—blindness, insanity, death—decided not to push
his luck, and beckoned to Meg. "How 'bout ye, then?"

"Not for no apple," said Meg, "I can't eat it." She
gave him her toothless grin.

He searched his pockets. "I've a farthing—"

"Sold!" Meg said quickly, snatching it away. The rest
of the women in the cell slurped their gruel and Hugh
Stalker waited in the doorway, taking it all in with his
blank gray eyes. Meg finished with the guard, got her
bowl of gruel, and brought it over beside Molly. The guard
went off, locking the door.

"Thanks," Molly murmured.

"No need," said Meg. "My pleasure."

"Someone's goin' t' catch on t' ye two someday,"
Canny Hannah muttered, still disgruntled.

"Oy, leave 'em be, Hannah," Lizzie Cutler put in.
"Jest because he didn't want an old bag such as ye—"

"Ye're lucky that Stalker can't talk," Hannah told
Molly, scowling," or he'd tell wot ye're up t'."

"No skin off yer nose, is it, now?" Meg demanded,
and went back to her gruel.

"I've a mind t' tell on ye myself," said Hannah.

"If ye do, I'll kill ye," Molly replied with the cool,
utter calm that had served her so well in that hellhole. She
was still younger and stronger than anyone else in the cell.
Hannah closed her mouth.

From the single barred window high in the outer wall
came a long, sharp whistle. "There she goes," Nan Wiggins muttered as Molly leapt to her feet, her supper forgotten.

"Give him a kiss for me," Hannah said nastily, while
the other women jeered. Molly ignored them, scaling the
wall with the toe and finger holds she knew as well as
the cracks in the floor by now, hauling herself up until
she could lean on the stone sill. There he stood, in the
shadows of the outer gate, wrapped in the same bundles
of rags. Even the hat on his head was the same one he'd
worn six months ago: Tom Peabody, clear blue eyes

searching the dark hulk of the prison until he saw her wave her hand.

"Molly Flowers!" He waved back, relief creasing his face in a smile.

"How's Aunt May?" she called to him.

" 'How's Aunt May?' " Hannah mimicked behind her. "Christ, the same bloody question every day."

"Shut up, ye old hag," Meg told her. "Just because nobody cares if you live or die—"

"I'd rather have no one than an old bag o' rags such as he."

"D'ye reckon he's the fellow she's savin' her precious maid's head for?" Nan Wiggins asked, and laughed.

Molly paid no mind to the bickering women; she was too relieved to see Tom hold up his thumb to show Aunt May was well. Every night in the cell she prayed the same prayer, anxious and fervent: God, let her live till I get out of here. Billy was looking after her, she knew, but what if something happened to Billy? Her fear for the frail old woman who'd raised her was far and away the worst part of her imprisonment. She didn't know what she'd have done if mad, muddled Tom hadn't taken it into his head to come each day to the gate and report on Aunt May's welfare. He seemed to understand in some dim way that it was his fault Molly was in the Fleet.

She clung to the bars and saw him glance about as he always did, checking for who knew what danger, before he cupped his hands and shouted up at her: "Mind the dog when it barks!" Molly nodded and waved again, acknowledging the meaningless warning, and he ducked his head and vanished into the shadows.

She let herself down slowly, as comforted by the evening ritual of Tom's visit as a nun might be by vespers. Her cellmates, egged by Hannah, were still jeering at her ragtag beau, but Molly didn't care. As she reclaimed the bowl of gruel Meg had been guarding for her, she thanked God for his mercy in letting Aunt May make it through another day.

"Whist!" Hannah left off her insults and cocked her head at the door. "Someone's comin'! Wot d'ye reckon?"

"Some horny bastard," Lizzie Cutler sighed, "back for a bit o' tail."

"No it ain't," Nan Wiggins hissed. "Listen to them bootheels!" The sharp click, click, click came closer.

"Oy, Lord help us," somebody murmured, " 'tis Warden Fell." Everyone sighed.

If Hugh Stalker was the villain in the daily drama of the Fleet, Warden Abraham Fell served as its buffoon: a man so venal, so corrupt, so puffed with his own importance that he was laughable. In his own way, though, he was every bit as dangerous as Hugh, for to give in to the urge to laugh was to risk the consequences of a temper unchecked by conscience. Warden Fell didn't give a hang for sexual favors; he was out for money, and since no one in Molly's cell had any to speak of, he didn't give a hang about them. He'd just as lief, she was sure, see them all dead.

The key grated in its lock, and the heavy door swung open. The warden stood on the threshold with Hugh Stalker behind him, the torches in the passage outside making unholy halos around their heads.

"His lordship, the Earl o' Ballenrose," Fell announced in his flat little voice, reading from a paper—he was a small man, with a small man's ways—"has convinced His Majesty King Charles and the Parliament t' launch an investigation int' conditions at the Fleet. A board o' inquiry will arrive tomorrow t' interview prisoners regarding mistreatment by the staff." He paused, looking around the cell. "Anyone wot's thinkin' o' complainin' would be wise t' think twice." He turned; Hugh Stalker stepped aside to let him pass. The door closed, the key turned, and they were gone, the warden's high bootheels beating a smart click-click-click in retreat.

No one said anything for a moment. Then one of the younger women in the cell whispered, "D' ye really think—'' Her question, with its tremulous hopefulness, was interrupted by Nan:

"Don't be a damned fool, girl. Anyone wot dared say anythin' to them inquirers would be good as dead. Didn't ye hear Warden Fell?''

"But—''

"She's right, lass,'' Hannah put in. "When ye've been in this dungheap long as I have, ye'll know. Any soul mad enough to complain would be dancin' with Hugh Stalker ere the day is through.'' Everyone knew what that meant; they'd all heard that the tongueless giant took away those prisoners who grew too sick or feeble. Nobody knew what became of them, but once he came for you, you were never heard from again.

"Mebbe not,'' Lou Sutton said slowly. "I heard o' this Ballenrose; they say he's a good sort. Put up money for that new buildin' at St. Bart's Hospital, didn't he?''

"Oy, ye're right; that were Ballenrose,'' somebody said. " 'N' weren't it he spoke up in Parliament when all them landlords down in Shoreditch hiked their rents up at once?''

Hannah snorted. "Gor, if ye could judge a man by wot he said in Parliament, all them peers'd be bloody saints.''

"Wot's that got t' do wi' it?''

"There's never yet been a nobleman born gave a cat's damn for thee 'n' me.'' There was no bitterness in Hannah's voice, just the conviction of a hard, weary lifetime.

"If there's t' be an investigation, though,'' Lou ventured, "then somebody must care.''

"Don't fool yerself,'' Meg Calloway told her, not unkindly. "All it means is that this here Ballenrose fellow sees a chance t' help himself out 'n' lick the boots o' the king.''

"Why—how could investigatin' us do that?''

"How should I know? But ye mark my word. This month 'tis the Fleet; next month 'twill be St. Katherine's docks they're investigatin', 'n' 'twill be char'ty homes the month after that. They do as they please, but naught ever changes. Naught ever will.''

Molly sat spooning up gruel, taking no part in the conversation. If she had, she'd have agreed with Meg. Any illusions she'd once had about her English justice had been dispelled by her day in court, by the coarse, drunken magistrate who'd heard Andrew Stiles's testimony against her, slammed down his gavel, and sentenced her to three months for disturbing the peace. It was when she'd tried to protest, tried to tell her side, that he'd tacked on nine months more.

Night had fallen. Through the window she could see two stars and a corner of moon. The women shifted on the stone floor, settling for sleep.

Meg nestled close to her; the night was cold for April. Molly kept her eyes on that corner of moon until it slid out of sight. She'd no sooner have complained to the Earl of Ballenrose on the morrow than let one of the guards get her against the wall. She was halfway through her sentence, she reminded herself, holding tight to that thought like a promise. Ye'll make it out o' here yet. Keep yerself t' yerself, 'n' don't make trouble.

''Next!'' Hannah Crandall announced, sailing into the cell ahead of Hugh Stalker. The women gathered around her, asking eager questions:

''Wot was it like, then?'' ''How many are there?'' ''Wot did ye say?''

''Ye'll just have to take yer own turns to find out,'' she answered, smug that she'd been the first volunteer. Stalker was waiting, silent and menacing, in the doorway.

''May as well get it bloody done with,'' Lizzie said with a sigh, and went to join him. She was back in a matter of minutes, looking cheerful enough.

''Well?'' Lou Sutton demanded.

''Oy, they're ever such grand gentlemen,'' Lizzie said, primping her hair. Hannah laughed, and Lizzie shot a glance at Molly. "There's a part ye'll like especially, Miss High 'n' Mighty."

"Leave her be," Meg said sharply, moving toward the door. It closed and locked behind her. Molly shimmied up to the window, looking out to pass the time until her turn came. The day was gray and gloomy; a chill rain spattered in through the bars. Victual carts trundled in and out of the yard below, bringing meat and ale for those prisoners who could afford such luxuries. The usual crowd of curious onlookers was gathered at the front gates, peering in to see what was happening. Someone was being flogged; his screams mingled with the thudding hammers of the prison carpenters, building a gallows for some helpless soul.

She slid down again when the door opened. Meg sought her gaze and smiled reassuringly. "Nothin' t' it," she said gaily. "Bunch o' bloody sots, if ye ask me, though one or two ain't bad lookers."

"I'll go next, then, if no one minds," Molly said. No one did.

It was good just to be out of the cell, she thought as she followed silent, towering Hugh Stalker down the torchlit passageway—good to stretch her legs, to walk with some purpose instead of up and down that squalid room. For a moment, as they passed a stairway, the thought of fleeing crossed her mind. But, "Halfway through," she muttered, "don't make trouble." Stalker glanced back at her; there was clearly nothing wrong with his ears.

He stopped in front of a low doorway; from within there came a rumble of men's voices. Molly stepped through and blinked; to her eyes, long accustomed to semidarkness, the bank of candles before her seemed bright as the sun. The door closed at her back.

The men, half a dozen of them, were still talking. Only one, dressed all in black like a priest and sitting in the back of the chamber, looked up when she came in. Her gaze glanced off him and was drawn irresistibly toward the figure directly before her. The Earl of Ballenrose, she thought, and drew a dazzled breath. He was the handsomest man she had ever seen. Nearly as tall as Hugh Stalker, broad-shouldered, slim-hipped, golden-haired—in his midnight-blue robes emblazoned with gold wheels, he looked like a bloody god. Oy, thought Molly, ain't that life for ye, to make a man like that and give him wealth and power too?

The one in the back of the room cleared his throat, and the others glanced toward him. He nodded at Molly, and the rest took their seats. Her eyes still riveted on Ballenrose, Molly caught the last snatch of his conversation with a thin, long-nosed fellow in spectacles: ". . . and then the drab said, 'Oh, your majesty, no! The pleasure's been all *mine!*'" The men laughed. Even his voice was beautiful, Molly thought as Ballenrose looked toward her. She smiled tremulously.

"Name," said the man in spectacles, sounding exceedingly bored.

"Molly Flowers."

"Molly Flowers, milord," the Earl of Ballenrose said. Enchanted by the way her name came out when he spoke it, she smiled again.

"Aye, that's right."

"I meant," said the earl, looking pained, "you must address the members of the board as 'milord.'"

"Oh!" Molly flushed, eager to please this extraordinary man. "Very well." His pale brows knit together. "I mean—very well, m'lord."

The man in spectacles tapped his quill against the table. "And have you any—"

"I beg your pardon." That was the one in black, all the way in the back of the room. "There's no Molly Flowers on the list. Only a Molly Willoughby."

"That's me too," Molly said helpfully. "Mary Catherine Willoughby, that's my real name. Well, not my real name; I don't know that, as I'm an orphan. But Willoughby's my Aunt May's name that I took, 'n' they calls me

Molly Flowers on account o' I runs a stall in Smithfield Mar—"

"That's enough," said the man with the quill, and rolled his eyes. "She's likely got half a dozen aliases, Strakhan. What difference can it make?"

"Just trying to keep matters straight," the one in black said amiably. Ballenrose leaned over and muttered something to a short, bald fellow that made him laugh so hard he spilled wine on his breeches. They were velvet, Molly noticed, and hoped he'd ruined them for good.

"Let's get on with it," said old Spectacles-Face. "Have you any complaints, chit?"

"No, m'lord," Molly told him.

The man in black spoke up again. "You mustn't be intimidated, lass—"

"Good God, Strakhan," the Earl of Ballenrose interrupted him, "you may as well speak Hindi as use words like that!"

"—mustn't be afraid," Strakhan went on, ignoring him, though the others all laughed. "If you've anything to tell us, anything at all about the conditions here, rest assured we'll keep your confidence." Molly looked at him. He had black hair and a rough, craggy face that was the sort that always needed shaving. His eyes were wide-spaced, blue or gray, she couldn't tell which. In any other company he'd have looked quite handsome, though he paled beside the splendor of Ballenrose. As Molly watched, he smiled at her. He had a very nice smile.

"She said there wasn't anything, Strakhan," Spectacles said impatiently.

"I just want to be sure, Dr. Collett, that the young lady understands." He turned to Molly again. "If anyone here has hurt you or mistreated you, you must tell us."

"Would you have them coddled like babies, Strakhan?" Ballenrose demanded. "They *are* criminals, you know."

"I'd have them treated decently, like fellow human beings," Strakhan replied, his deep voice perfectly mild. Molly wondered if perhaps he might be a priest after all.

His clothes were so plain compared to the others, and he seemed to keep himself a little apart. There was something priestlike, too, about his straightforward gaze. "Mistress Willoughby, if you do have anything to say, about the guards or the women in your cell, or even Warden Fell, please do. You needn't be afraid. We'll protect you."

He was so solemn and earnest, Molly might have believed him, if not for the voice in her head that reminded her: *Halfway through . . .*

"I've no complaints, m'lord," she told him briskly.

"Jesu," sighed the Earl of Ballenrose, stretching out his long silk-clad legs. "What a colossal waste of time."

The man called Strakhan looked at Molly with those clear gray-blue eyes. "Are you absolutely sure you've nothing to say?"

She nodded. Dr. Collett tapped his quill again. "Very well, girl, take off your clothes."

Molly jerked her head to stare at him. "Do wot?"

"Do what, *milord,*" Ballenrose murmured. The others laughed, all except for Strakhan.

Dr. Collett pushed his spectacles up to the bridge of his long skinny nose. "Take—off—your—clothes," he repeated as though she were dull-witted, a child.

"I will not," said Molly. "Who the bloody hell d'ye think ye are?"

"I am Dr. John Collett of the Royal Society," old Spectacles said tersely. "These other gentlemen are peers of the realm, charged by His Majesty King Charles to report on conditions here at this jail. We intend to examine you for evidence of mistreatment."

"The bloody hell ye do," Molly snapped, all vows not to make trouble forgotten. "Ye're out t' see a bit o' flesh on the cheap!"

"She has a right to refuse," the man called Strakhan began.

Collett interrupted him: "I don't need you to tell me how to do my job, Strakhan. As for you, young lady, I assure you no one here has any prurient interest in a common doxy.''

"I am *not* a doxy!" Molly told him, eyes flashing green fire. "Just because I'm in prison doesn't give ye the right—"

"It most certainly does," said another of the men.

"The docket here says Mistress Willoughby's crime was disturbing the peace." For the first time there was amusement in Strakhan's deep voice. "Somehow that doesn't surprise me. Leave her be, Collett. Send for the next one."

"If you think I looked at those toothless crones," the little bald fellow said, leering at Molly, "and intend to miss this one—"

"You disgust me, Lord Phipps," Strakhan growled.

"He's quite right, though, you know," someone else said, and chuckled. "Off with her clothes!"

Molly turned in desperation to the resplendent earl in his gold-threaded doublet, holding out her hands. "Lou said ye was a good sort, m'lord Ballenrose—" She stopped, for he'd recoiled from her, his dark eyes hooded.

"Good God," fat Lord Phipps muttered.

"Fool girl," Dr. Collett hissed.

The man dressed in black, the one they called Strakhan, let out a snort. "Mistress Willoughby appears to have confused us, milord Buckingham."

"Buckingham!" Molly stared in awe. Even she knew that George Villiers, the second Duke of Buckingham, was the mightiest man in all England next to the king. "Forgive me, m'lord," she stammered, with an awkward curtsy. Who would ever have believed that someday she'd stand in the same room, breathe the same air, as the great Buckingham? Talk about something to tell one's grandchildren!

The duke seemed to have recovered from his repugnance at being mistaken for a mere earl. "I suppose the question, Strakhan," he said very softly, "is whether she will strip for me though not for thee.'' A look passed between the two lords, one Molly could not read.

"You're a bastard, George," the Earl of Ballenrose said, equally softly.

Buckingham laughed. "Not according to the peerage rolls." He smiled at Molly, a warm, glorious smile. "Come, then, girl, and disrobe. No one will touch you. Just down to your shift."

"I haven't any shift on," Molly confessed shyly. "I had t' trade it t' Hannah Crandall for stockings when it got cold."

"What happened to your stockings?" asked the Earl of Ballenrose.

"Hannah stole them back again when her own wore out." She blushed, looking down at her bare toes.

A chair scraped the floor in the back of the room; Ballenrose had gotten to his feet. "I've had enough of this damned bloody farce."

"Come, come, Anthony," the duke said blandly, "this inquiry was your idea."

"I never meant it to become a cheap show for you and your cronies."

"His Majesty King Charles appointed the members of the board." Buckingham's lovely voice was like silk. "If you've some quibble, take it up with him. Meanwhile, if you'll sit down, we can get on with this task."

Ballenrose stalked to the front of the room. He was nearly as tall as Buckingham, Molly saw, but built quite differently, with more meat on his bones, so he lacked the duke's languid grace. "What's the sense of it? 'Tis plain as day that tyrant of a warden has them all frightened to speak out against him."

"I'll have you know, Strakhan," Dr. Collett said huffily, "I've been acquainted with Warden Fell for a good many years, and there's no finer, more honorable—"

"You would know him, Collett, you snake."

"Gentlemen, gentlemen!" The duke clucked his tongue, wagged a finger, then looked at Molly. "Well, girl, are you afraid to say what's on your mind? You hardly seem the timid sort to me."

While the men wrangled, Molly had come to the disquieting realization that she'd already been in that room twice as long as either Meg or Hannah. If Warden Fell found that out, he'd never believe she hadn't been telling tales to the lords. All she wanted now was to get back to her cell. "Nay, m'lord," she told him quickly. "If I'd anything to say, I'd tell ye." She began to unbutton her smock.

At her side, the Earl of Ballenrose swore beneath his breath. "You're a fine lot of lechers," he told Buckingham and the rest, and left them, clanging the door.

Molly let the smock slide to the floor and stood before the men in just her drawers, arms crossed to hide her breasts. Someone whistled. Lord Phipps said, "Oh, my," and giggled.

"Honestly, Henry," Buckingham rebuked him, leaning back in his chair, considering Molly from beneath his heavy, black-lashed lids. "I see no evidence of beatings, John, do you?"

Dr. Collett shook his head, dipping his quill. "Turn around," he directed Molly. She did so. "Here, what's that?"

"Wot?" she asked, craning her head about. He was looking at the back of her right thigh. "Oh. My birthmark."

"Not a bruise."

"No."

The quill scratched across parchment. "You may go," Dr. Collett told her. She yanked the smock up and wriggled into it, then turned round to curtsy. The Duke of Buckingham was sitting up straight now, leaning his elbows on the table, fingertips pressed together, and staring at her with the strangest glimmer in his dark eyes. For a moment she stared back at him, transfixed. Then, "Go on, get out!" the doctor ordered her impatiently.

She slipped through the door. On the other side, Hugh Stalker was waiting. He crooked a finger at her.

Well, that's that, she thought. It could have been worse. Now, if Stalker didn't manage somehow to tell Warden Fell how long she'd been there . . .

"One of the lords took ill," she told Stalker's back. "He had to leave. You saw him. That's wot kept me."

Hugh Stalker, tongueless, said nothing. Nibbling her lip, Molly followed the silent giant back to the cell.

2

"WOT TOOK *YE* so long?" Hannah Crandall demanded upon Molly's return.

"One o' the gentlemen took ill," she said shortly, taking her place against the wall again.

"Hah, I'll bet." The older woman confronted her, hands on hips. "Tellin' secrets, that's wot ye was doin'. Tattlin' on yer mates."

"Mebbe," said Meg, coming to Molly's rescue, "they were jest in a hurry t' get ye out o' there, Hannah, ye old bag."

"Ye think ye're so smart, ye two, don't ye?" Hannah turned to Stalker. "Mind ye make sure Warden Fell finds out about her takin' so long!" She leaned close to Molly, her breath hot and stinking. "The warden'll see ye get yers, missy-miss."

"Shut up, Hannah," Molly said wearily. "I didn't tell 'em anything." Hugh Stalker, grown impatient, pounded his fist against the door and yanked his thumb at Lou to show that she should be next. She cast a frightened glance at Molly. "Don't worry, pet," she assured her. "Ballenrose—he's the one that caused the trouble—he's left. And who d'ye think is in there? The Duke o' Buckingham, that's who."

"No!" said Lou, wide-eyed.

"Aye, that it is," Meg assured her. "I knew him by the wheels on his coat."

Lou perked up, raking her fingers through her matted hair. "Well! I beg yer pardon, ladies, but I'm off t' call upon his grace!"

Within the space of an hour, the rest of the interviews had been completed. But all the remainder of the day was taken up with talk of the inquiry board, with gossip and comparisons. They discussed the men's hair, their accents, everything they'd worn, right down to their bootlaces, and whenever the conversation wound down, someone would sigh and say, "Did ye ever in all yer life see anythin' so handsome as that Buckingham?"

"How old d'ye reckon he is?" Tillie Hitchens asked dreamily.

"Too young fer ye," Nan snickered.

"Forty-two," Lou said.

"Oy, how would ye know?" Hannah jeered.

"He 'n' my first son shared the same birthdate," Lou announced with a hint of hauteur. "The thirtieth o' January, 1628, that's when he was borned. I recall the way the bells rang; I thought they was for my own bonny boy. 'N' then my Jack weren't even weaned yet afore the first duke got stabbed t' death by that there madman."

"Aye, that's so," Meg confirmed. " 'Twas a soldier had been in his comp'ny that hadn't got paid. Stabbed him right through the heart as he left his breakfast one mornin'. Oy, 'twas a dreadful tragedy."

Molly listened with only one ear; what had happened in 1628 was ancient history to her. The sky outside the window was darkening, and she was waiting for Tom Peabody's whistle, waiting for the day's reassurance about Aunt May.

"Forty-two—Gor, he don't look that old, do he?" one of the women marveled.

"That's how it is when ye're rich," Nan said darkly. "Wot's he got t' make lines on his face, I'd like t' know."

"If *I* was rich," Lou began, and Molly stopped listening completely. It was one of their favorite ways to while away the time, imagining days full of hot raisin crumpets, gowns of satin, and jewels on their hands and hair.

From outside the window came a long sharp whistle. Molly clambered for the wall, just as a whisper of footsteps sounded from the passageway.

"Whist!" Meg hissed, grabbing Molly's smock. "Don't risk it."

"But I've got t' see Tom!"

"The time t' supper passed mighty quick today, didn't it, though?" Tillie noted with wonder.

"That's because it ain't time fer supper," said Hannah. "Them's Hugh Stalker's footsteps; hear how soft 'n' quiet they is?" Her mean eyes found Molly's, and she laughed. "Guess Warden Fell found out wot ye was up to wi' the gentlemen this mornin'. He's sent the Stalker t' fetch ye away!"

Outside the window, Tom whistled again.

"Don't be a ninny," Molly told Hannah. "I didn't do anythin'."

The iron door swung open. Hugh Stalker's huge black shadow fell across the floor. Silently he searched the dim cell, his gaze flickering from one woman's face to another. When he found Molly, he stopped and crooked a finger at her.

"M-me?" she stammered, all the dreadful rumors she had heard of the giant flooding into her mind.

"Hah! Din't I tell ye?" Hannah cackled.

Meg shot her a look of pure venom. "Shut up, old cow!" She patted Molly's hand. "Ye'll be all right, lass. Likely 'tis some kind o' mistake."

Nan had begun to blubber in the corner. "She'll never come back! He'll skin 'n' bone 'n' eat her—"

"Don't believe everythin' ye hear, ye silly fool!" Meg snapped.

Molly looked at Hugh Stalker and shuddered, fear coiling her insides, making her neck hairs prickle. What if it was true, what if this was her doom? Oh, God, it isn't fair, she thought wildly, not when I was halfway through!

Down at the gate, Tom Peabody let out another whistle, long and desperate-sounding. Stalker gestured to Molly again. She glanced at Meg and saw her friend was crying. Molly tried to walk forward, tripped, and was jerked upright by Hannah.

"Fare thee well, darlin'," the crone said, and winked. Stalker grasped Molly's elbow, tugged her through the door and locked it, then dragged her down the passageway.

Struggling to keep on her feet, keep her head, she stumbled along beside him. There was a strange odor clinging to him, she noticed, something metallic and strong, familiar somehow. The torches flared as they passed; her bare feet slapped against the stones. She glanced down and saw Stalker's feet clad in boots of rich soft leather, so buttery-soft that he scarcely made a sound. Jesu, help me, she prayed, shaking all over as she thought of the warden, his flat expression as he'd promised trouble to anyone who complained.

Stalker stopped so abruptly that Molly went skidding past him. He yanked her back like a fish on a line, and she looked up, startled, into his face. In the glow of the torchlight, in that instant, she understood how the tales of his cannibal nature had arisen, for there was in his gaze the most terrible craving, like a hunger that never had been satisfied. "Christ have mercy," Molly gasped.

Just ahead in the passage, Warden Fell loomed up in a doorway. "Come, Hugh, don't dawdle. His grace is waiting," he said.

His grace? thought Molly. Stalker steered her through the door as Warden Fell stepped aside, and she blinked in the sudden blaze of a bank of candles and the dazzling smile of the Duke of Buckingham.

"This is the one?" Warden Fell, voice colorless as always, asked at her back. "Mary Catherine Willoughby, also known as Molly Flowers?"

"That's the one," another man said. Molly saw it was

Dr. Collett, spectacles perched on his long thin nose. He was standing behind Buckingham's chair, frowning slightly. "Thank you, Abraham, you may go."

"Yer servant, m'lords, as always." The door closed with a click.

Molly glanced behind her, realized the warden and Stalker were gone, and began to tremble. "I already told ye, m'lord, I had naught to complain of! Why'd ye bring me back here?"

"My dear girl." The duke's smile was meltingly tender. "You mustn't be afraid. We simply have some questions—"

"I ain't answerin' no questions!"

"John." Buckingham waved a graceful hand. "A cup of wine for Mistress Willoughby, if you please. And you might fetch her a chair."

There was only one reason Molly could think of why a man like him would offer wine to a girl like her. She stiffened, green eyes narrowing. "Listen here, sir. I already told ye, I ain't nobody's doxy, not even yers."

The doctor slid a chair behind her knees, pressed a pewter goblet into her hand. "Keep a civil tongue, young lady. You should be grateful his grace has seen fit to take an interest in your case."

"Take an interest in me?" Molly eyed the great lord even more suspiciously. "Why the devil should ye?"

"We'll get to that in a bit, Mistress Willoughby," he told her. "For now, won't you indulge me by answering a few questions?"

"Wot sort o' questions?"

"My, just look how your hand is clenched around that cup!" He laughed gaily, winningly. "Take a few sips, my dear girl, please. It will relax you."

"Wot sort o' questions?" Molly asked again, not at all sure she wanted to relax.

"Well—where are you from, for instance? Let's begin with that."

"Smithfield," she said briefly.

"Ah. Smithfield. Not a part of the city with which I'm familiar, I'm afraid. How about you, John?"

"Nor I, milord."

"And has your family lived long in Smithfield?" the duke inquired.

"I've got no family. I'm a foundling."

"Forgive me, that's right; you did mention you were an orphan. You've no one at all, no mother or father or sisters or brothers, even?" Molly shook her head. "Well, who looked after you, then?"

"My Aunt May, when I was little. Now I look after her." She grimaced. "Or did, before I ended up here."

"Ah, your Aunt May. And would that be your father's sister or your mother's?"

"She's no kin at all," Molly told the duke somewhat impatiently. "I haven't got any kin. Aunt May said she found me one mornin' down by St. Katherine's docks when she went t' buy her flowers."

"By the docks?" Buckingham cocked a brow. "How extraordinary! How old were you?"

"Aunt May thinks nearly two."

"I see. You know, Mistress Willoughby, I really would be pleased if you'd try that wine. I brought it here myself, from my own cellars. That stuff Warden Fell served us this morning was swill."

"That don't surprise me," Molly muttered, and felt flattered when he laughed. To return the favor she took a sip from the cup, and her own eyebrows arched. She'd never tasted anything so fine in her life.

"You like it?" he asked, seeing her expression.

"It tastes like—" Molly sought the words. "Like melted money."

Buckingham laughed again, a lovely low chuckle. "Do you know, that's exactly what I thought when I first tried it! John, don't you agree?" Dr. Collett made some indeterminate noise. The duke threw him a glance of distinct displeasure, then shrugged at Molly as though to say: Well, what would he know? She smiled back at him and took another sip of the wine.

"If you were two," he went on, "or nearly, you must remember something of your own mother."

Molly hesitated, felt the wine slide into her empty belly like a warm silk ribbon. "I don't know," she said finally, softly. "Sometimes I think I see her in my mind, but I ain't sure."

"What do you think you see?" asked the duke, leaning toward her across the table. Molly blushed, dropping her gaze. "Please tell me," he coaxed her.

"A beautiful lady," she whispered shyly. "Like a princess. When I see her, she is always laughing. And her hair is shining like the sun."

The Duke of Buckingham reached into the folds of his doublet, drawing something out and passing it toward her. "Like this?"

"Milord," Dr. Collett said sharply, "I hardly think—"

"Hush, John! I have got to know. Go on," he told Molly. She picked up the object he'd passed her. It was a little flat locket of silver, hinged like a book. "Open it," the duke said. Molly did so, and drew in her breath. Inside was a tiny painting, no bigger than her thumb, of a woman with long golden hair.

"Oh, my, how lovely!"

"But does it resemble the woman you remember, child?"

Molly shrugged, studying the portrait. "Aye, it does, I reckon. The mouth 'n' the hair 'n' the eyes—" She pushed it back to him. "Who is it of, then?"

"La Comtesse de Angoumois et Poitou," he told her, a sudden tremor in his voice. "My sister, Frances." Molly stared at him blankly. "Your mother, my dear."

"Good God, George!" Dr. Collett burst out. "Are you mad? You can't be certain!"

"I know it, John," Buckingham told him, dark gaze not leaving Molly. "I feel it—here." He tapped his doublet front, over his heart. "You *are* Frances' daughter, my niece, aren't you?"

Molly laughed in disbelief. "Ye're out o' yer mind. Me, yer niece? Aye, 'n' Meg Calloway's the Queen o' France."

The duke didn't seem the least offended. "I know it sounds unlikely, my dear—"

"Impossible's more like it," Dr. Collett muttered.

"But look here." Buckingham stood up and began to unbutton his breeches.

"Jesu in heaven!" Molly whirled for the door. It was locked; she jiggled the handle. "Help! Help, he's goin' t' rape me!"

Someone grabbed her from behind—the duke, his grip tight as iron. "Calm down, Molly! No one is going to hurt you."

"Get yer bloody hands off me!" She aimed a kick backward at his shin.

He let out a yelp. "John! Help me hold her, for God's sake!"

"I must tell you, George, I find this whole thing most—"

"Just help me hold her!"

"Come near me 'n' I'll scratch yer eyes out!" Molly screeched, breaking free of the duke's grasp. She ran to the far side of the room and crouched there, panting, shielded by a chair. Buckingham had his breeches pulled down to his ankles.

"Just look at me, Mary Catherine!" he pleaded.

"Wot are ye, some kind o' pervert? Help!" she shouted again. "Help! Get me out of he—" In the middle of the word she stopped, her mouth still wide open, as the duke turned around, put his back to her and Collett.

"As I live and breathe," the doctor whispered. "George, you never told me—"

Molly stared at the hindside of the Duke of Buckingham's right leg, at the stain spread across it that was the color of the wine she'd been drinking: a stain in the shape of a bird with its wings outspread. "Why, it's the same as—"

He looked at her over his shoulder. "Aye. The same as yours, exactly. That's how I know who you are, Mary Catherine. My niece—my heir." His dark eyes were gleaming. "The future Duchess of Buckingham."

3

MOLLY LET GO of the chair she'd been clutching and sat in it. Then she picked up her goblet from the table and drained it, to the last drop. She'd thought the wine would help her find her tongue, but it didn't. She not only couldn't speak; she couldn't seem to breathe.

"George." Dr. Collett's thin voice was conciliatory as he eyed the duke's leg. "If you'd let me know about the birthmarks—"

"I didn't dare tell you. I didn't dare tell anyone. Not until I could be sure." He pulled up his breeches and buttoned them, then turned around. "I thought, from the first moment I saw you, Mary Catherine, that you were the spit and image of Frances. And I felt something too—a link, a bond between us. Surely you felt it as well."

Molly tried to remember—what *had* she felt when she first saw him? It was no use; she couldn't think clearly. She was so light-headed, her heart was beating so fast . . . "I don't understand," she whispered. "It can't be. How could it be?"

"A miracle of God," the duke told her, his voice hushed and solemn. "The answer to my thousands of prayers." He saw her dubious expression and smiled. "But you still don't believe it."

"Perhaps, George, if you told her the whole story, from the beginning," Dr. Collett suggested.

"Of course, of course. My dear, do you know anything of my family—your family? The house of Buckingham?"

"Not—not really." Something she'd heard earlier that day popped into Molly's head. "Your father—he was killed by a madman. Stabbed to death."

The duke nodded. "Your grandfather. George Villiers, the first duke. He was a great man, Mary Catherine. The best and dearest friend to old King James, and to King Charles the First. I was but a few months old when he was killed." He crossed himself piously. "Frances, my sister, was a scant year older. My father had been educated in France, and made many friends there, among them the Comte de Angoumois et Poitou." The foreign words were so many meaningless syllables to Molly. "After Father died, my mother affianced Frances, according to Father's wishes, to the comte's son Philippe. In 1649, Frances sailed for Paris to be wedded. She was my favorite of all my siblings. How sorry I was to see her go!"

Dr. Collett had refilled Molly's cup, and she drank from it now, not even tasting the wine that had so pleased her before. I'm dreaming, she kept thinking, I must be dreaming. The duke went on talking in his beautiful voice, so lulling and low:

"It was a happy marriage, Frances', but marked by stillbirths—three altogether. That's why we were so happy when at long last she wrote that she had had a child, a daughter she called Mary Catherine. You were born in your grandfather's birth month, my dear, in August 1653. Frances wrote that she longed to visit, but the kingdom was in turmoil then; the second Civil War had broken out. I myself was in exile in Holland."

"Those were terrible days," Dr. Collett put in, "terrible dark days."

"That they were," the duke agreed. "When I returned to England, in 1657, I discovered, to my horror, that Frances had set sail from Poitou the year before, with her infant daughter. A storm came up in the Channel, a terrible tempest. The ship broke apart.'' He hung his head. "No survivors were found."

"Dear God," Molly breathed. "But then how—"

He looked up eagerly. "Another ship was in the Channel on that awful day. Too far away to come to the vessel's aid, but close enough to see that a little boat, a fishing skiff, had made it through. I searched for word of that skiff for years, hoping against hope that somehow, some way, Frances or her babe had been saved. Years ago, in a tavern in Cheapside, I found a fisherman, a great drunken brute, who thought he remembered the storm, remembered rescuing a little girl from the waters. He got her safe to shore. But what became of her after that, I never did learn. Until now."

Across the table he reached for Molly's hand. It bothered him not at all that she was filthy dirty, ridden with lice and fleas, that she stank of her months in that hellish cell. "The birthmark that we bear, Mary Catherine, that we share, is passed down in my family from generation to generation. It's the mark of the house of Buckingham, as indelible and sure as the grace of God. And by God's grace, I've found you." He pressed her hand to his cheek; she felt his tears against her palm. "After all these years," he whispered brokenly. "After all these years, I have found you at last!"

Molly didn't know what to say. What could she say? She still felt she was dreaming. "Please, m'lord," she mumbled, "please, ye mustn't cry. Hush, now, m'lord."

He raised his head, smiled tremulously, though his dark eyes were shining bright with his tears. "Nay, no more 'milord,' my child. You must call me 'Uncle George' from now on."

"And I would be honored, milady," Dr. Collett put in, "if you would consider me your servant, and call me John." He made a handsome bow to her, and that, more than anything else, pierced through Molly's dazed fog. Milady, she thought—why, he means me! He bowed to *me!* Unconsciously she sat up a little straighter, drew her hand away from the duke—from her *uncle* to run it through her tangled hair.

Buckingham pushed her wineglass toward her, still smiling. "I daresay this is a dreadful shock to you."

She laughed, a little shakily. " 'Shock' hardly describes it!"

Dr. Collett took his seat and leaned toward her. "Can you remember anything more of your mother, milady? Do you recall the storm? Try very hard."

Molly clenched her eyes tight shut, pressed her fists to them, concentrating. Through the glow the wine had made in her head, she tried to see it: a ship, a big one like those at St. Katherine's docks, and a storm. Waves rising and falling. Lightning crackling in the sky, thunder rumbling through the air . . . her mother bending down beside her, gold hair wild with wind, whispering, *Hush, my darling. . . .*

"I don't know," she said hesitantly, helplessly. "It's all so much to take in . . . perhaps if ye was to come back tomorrow?"

"Tomorrow!" Buckingham looked aghast. "You can't think, my dear child, that I intend to let you stay another night, nay, another minute in this dreadful place!"

"I should say not!" Dr. Collett affirmed.

"But . . . but where am I to go?"

"Why, home with me, of course!" said the duke. "Home to Cliveden, my estate in Buckinghamshire. To the estate that will be yours someday."

"Oy, I couldn't ever!" Molly shook her head. "Ye see, I don't *know* yet. I can't be certain."

"That's to be expected," Dr. Collett told her soothingly. "You were so very young. It's possible that you may never remember."

"Never!" Molly looked at them, these two strangers, with wide frightened eyes. "Oh, I couldn't bear that!"

"John." The duke gave him a reproachful glance. "You mustn't say that. I'm sure the past will all come back to her, in time." Then he smiled at Molly, that dazzling smile. "For the nonce, what matters is to get you away from here, get you cleaned up and rested and ready to begin your new life."

Molly nibbled her lip. Whether it was true or not, whether she really was related to him, if he could get her out of this prison . . . "Will Warden Fell let me go?"

Dr. Collett laughed at that. "Milady, do you jest? You're the Duke of Buckingham's niece!"

"Rank does have its privileges," Buckingham said, dark eyes twinkling. "We've already talked to Warden Fell. There's a carriage at the gate waiting to take you to Cliveden—to take you home."

"I can scarce believe it." Molly giggled, giddy with wonder. "It's like the fairy stories Aunt May used t' tell!" That thought brought on another. "Gor, wot about Aunt May?"

"What about her?" Dr. Collett echoed.

"Why, I'll have to go straight off and tell her! I don't know how she'll take it. She's ever so old, ye see, 'n' not well at all. She's gone completely blind. When last I saw her, she could hardly hear. Billy Buttons, he was lookin' after her for me. I meant to pay him back in pints o' ale once I got out. 'N'—"

"Whoa!" said the duke, laughing as he held up his hand. "Slow down, child! One thing at a time."

"Ye will let me go see her, though, right away?"

"I'll do better than that. John, suppose you go in your carriage and fetch her to Cliveden, and we'll meet you there."

Molly's gaze went even wider. "Ye . . . ye'd do that? Take Aunt May in?"

"My dear Mary Catherine, could I do any less for the woman who took *you* in—who saved your life?"

"Oh, m'lord—"

"Please! Uncle George."

"Uncle George," she said shyly, and beamed at him. "Ye're a kind, kind man. I don't suppose . . ."

"Go on," he said encouragingly.

"It's just—well, I've missed her so, ye see. D'ye reckon we might stop ourselves, in our carriage, to get her?"

"I'm not sure that would be wise, George," Dr. Collett put in. "If she's so frail as milady says, the vapors of the prison, the diseases—"

"I'm afraid he's quite right, my dear," said the duke. "It would be far safer not to expose her to you just now."

"Oh." Molly thought. "She may not want to go wi' ye, Dr. Collett. After all, she don't know ye."

"Don't fret about that. I'm a physician, after all. I've plenty of experience with recalcitrant patients." Seeing Molly's blank look, he smiled. "Patients who are afraid."

His use of that long unfamiliar word brought home to Molly what a great gap there was between herself and them. "Oy," she whispered, hands pulling at her filthy smock, "I'm sure I don't understand why ye should want t' take *me* in. I'm no credit t' ye, ignorant 'n' foolish as I am."

"Dear girl." The duke reached out his hand, stroked her long tangled hair. "You've got Frances' looks; I've no doubt you've got her mind as well. There's no shame in being ignorant of what you've had no chance to learn. You shall be a *tabula rasa*—an empty slate on which we shall imprint the future of the house of Buckingham." He stood up abruptly. "But first—first we must get you a bath!"

"Can you tell me, milady, where I might find your Aunt May?" Dr. Collett asked.

" 'M'lady.' " Molly winced. "I wish ye wouldn't call me that. It sounds so bloody strange!"

Buckingham smiled. "I'm afraid you'll have to get used to it, my dear. Now, where is Aunt May's house?"

"Oy, it ain't no house. Just one room, that's all, up atop the butcher's shop on Gospel Square, off Fetters Lane in Smithfield. The butcher's name is Eben Campbell." Suddenly she laughed. "Gor, wot I wouldn't give t' see that Charity's face when a carriage comes round for Aunt May! She's Eben's daughter," she explained as the duke arched a brow. "It's on account o' her 'n' Andrew Stiles that I wound up here. Wot happened, ye see—"

He put a finger to his lips, helping her up from her chair. "Hush, my dear. None of that matters now. You must forget the past, think only of the future." Bending down, he kissed her cheek with gentle tenderness, then turned to Dr. Collett. "Did you get that, John? Gospel Square, Smithfield, above the butcher's shop."

"Here," Molly spoke up, inspired, "tell Aunt May that Bubby says it's all right to go wi' ye."

"Bubby?" asked the doctor.

"That's the sparrow we feed at the window. It'll be like a password. Nobody but Aunt May 'n' me knows about Bubby."

"Ah," said the doctor. "I see."

Molly smiled at the duke. "Well, then, all that's left is for me t' say good-bye t' Meg, I reckon. That's my friend back in the cell. Gor, she won't believe wot's happened!"

"My dear, don't you think . . ." he began, then paused.
"Wot?"

"Just that it might be—well, unkind of you to let her know of your good fortune. Rather like rubbing salt in a wound, perhaps?"

"Oy. I didn't look at it that way." How sensitive he was! "But if I don't see her, if I just disappear, she'll worry over me. Why—" She laughed. "She'll think the Stalker ate me!"

"What's that?" asked Dr. Collett.

"Oh—just a story they tell about that great big gloomy fellow Hugh Stalker, that showed me in here. Once he comes for ye, they say, ye never come back again."

"How droll," said the duke. "But in this instance, true. Suppose, Mary Catherine, that instead of your saying good-bye to Meg, I write to Warden Fell and ask she be released? For what crime is she incarcerated?"

"Stabbin' her husband t' death," she said, then, seeing his small shudder, added quickly, "He came at her drunk wi' a pickax; it was self-defense!"

"I cannot *imagine*," he said with great feeling, "how you ever survived your life so far, my dear. You must truly be blessed by God."

"Oy, well," said Molly, "ye can get used t' most anythin', when it comes to that."

"I suppose one can. Well, then, that takes care of Meg." He offered her his arm. "Shall we go?" When she hesitated, he tucked her hand firmly around his elbow, giving it a pat. "You've nothing to be afraid of, Mary Catherine," he said softly, looking down at her. "You need never, ever be afraid again. Now, chin up!" She returned his smile. Dr. Collett opened the door, and side by side they walked out, walked right past Hugh Stalker, past the flickering torches, down a staircase, and straight out of the Fleet.

The hour was late; they'd been longer in that room than she'd realized. She stared up at the sky, drawing in a deep breath, and saw the moon, the *whole* moon, not just a corner, shining far above her. Freedom, she thought, and tasted it, sweet as honeysuckle blossoms, on the wind. Two servants dressed in deep blue cloaks leapt down from the seat and boot of the biggest carriage she had ever seen as the duke emerged. Molly began to laugh. "It won't turn into a squash, will it?"

In the light of the carriage lamps, the duke turned to her questioningly. "It won't what?

"Ye know—like in the story. Cinderella's coach, that turned into a squash at the stroke o' midnight."

He squeezed her hand as he passed her to the footman. "Nay. I promise it won't turn into a squash. John, you'll make sure—"

"Molleee!" The name was a drawn-out scream. Molly whipped around toward the gates, saw the hunched rag-clad figure of a man who clung to the bars in the moonlight. "Molly Flowers! No!"

"Why, it's Tom Peabody!"

"Who?" asked the duke.

"Don't go with 'em, Molly!" Tom screeched, rattling

the bars, setting up such a racket that the carriage horses neighed and shied. Somewhere beyond the gates a dog began to howl.

"Hush, Tom!" she called, and added for the duke's benefit, in a low voice, "He's a little bit off, if ye get my drift. But he's been ever so good about checkin' on me. Here, Tom, look! I'm free!" She waved her unshackled hands.

"Run! Run fer yer life, girl!" he screamed at her. "Run, in the name o' Jesu!"

"It's all right, Tom," she tried to reassure him. "Here, Dr. Collett, I've got an idea. Tom knows right where Aunt May lives; he can take ye there!" Seeing his appalled expression, she laughed. "Oh, don't worry; he's perfectly harmless."

"Perhaps, John," the duke said slowly, "it would be wise for you to take him . . . as a guide."

"As you wish, milord," Dr. Collett said in resignation.

"Thanks ever so much! Oy, Tom, stop yer bawlin'!" Molly shouted as the doctor started toward the gates. "This here is Dr. Collett! He's comin' t' take ye—" Tom let out an unearthly screech, then turned and ran off into the darkness like a man pursued by every demon in hell.

"T' Aunt May," Molly finished lamely, staring in the ragged madman's wake. "Wot d'ye reckon set him off?"

"You might ask Dr. Collett," Buckingham suggested. "You're presenting a paper to the Royal Society later this month, aren't you, John, on the criminally insane?"

"Oy, Tom's no criminal," Molly scoffed.

"No, I daresay not," said Dr. Collett. "Still, it would be intriguing to examine him."

"Ye'd have to find him first," Molly told him with a laugh that turned into a shiver. The moon had sailed behind a cloud, and without its cheery light her worn smock seemed even more thin.

Buckingham had felt her frisson of cold; he pulled off his own cloak and wrapped it round her shoulders. "Into that coach, now!" he ordered briskly. "I didn't find you after all these years to have you die of ague on me. John, you know what you're to do?'' The doctor nodded.

"Gospel Square, Smithfield!'' Molly told him as the footman passed her into the carriage. Buckingham climbed up after her; she stuck her head back out past him. "Tell her about Bubby, don't forget!''

"I won't!'' Collett promised, with a wave. The footman closed the door. Molly felt the carriage shake as he leapt onto the box with the driver. Buckingham reached up and rapped the wood above his head.

"Oy!'' Molly cried, tumbled back among the cushions on the bench as the carriage lurched away. Something with fringe on it was tickling her nose; she laughed, sunk deep into a nest of feathers and velvet.

"Are you all right, Mary Catherine?'' the Duke of Buckingham asked anxiously.

"All right?'' Molly gasped, and began to laugh even harder. "All right?'' The gates to the prison flashed by. She pinched herself on the back of the hand, felt the reassuring nibble of pain. "Oh, m'lord—''

"Uncle George,'' he reminded her again.

"Uncle George.'' Molly could not stop laughing. " 'All right' don't begin t' describe it! I'm . . . I'm . . .''

"Happy?'' he suggested, reaching for her hand.

Molly squeezed his tight. "Happy,'' she agreed.

4

THE CARRIAGE ROLLED on through the dark, silent city. Molly leaned forward to stare from the narrow opening in the window panel, fascinated. Everything looked so different from the height of her seat! Why, she could see straight into people's houses, see a couple kissing by their hearth, a woman washing dishes, a fat man in a nightcap coming to fasten the shutters. "Would ye mind terribly, Uncle George," she asked shyly, "if I opened this just a little bit more?"

"Not at all, my dear. In fact, I was about to suggest it." He fiddled with a latch, and the panel slid back, letting in a rush of night wind. "And perhaps you won't mind if I sprinkle some of this about." In the winking light of the carriage lanterns, Molly saw him pull a little vial from his doublet, uncork it, and shake it over the cushions. The sweet, heavy smell of roses came pouring out, so strong it made her cough. "Too much?" the duke asked.

"Oh, no," she lied, aware of how the prison stench she bore must offend his senses. "Just how long a ride is it t'—where did ye say we was goin'?"

"To Cliveden, in Buckinghamshire. I've built a fine manor there—the finest in all England." He said this without a hint of boastfulness, just a statement of fact—which it probably was, Molly realized, with a little shiver. She tried to imagine herself saying someday, in that same confident tone, "Of course, we live at Cliveden, the finest manor in England." Just the idea threatened to start her giggling again. Not wanting her uncle to think her some sort of flibbertigibbet, she bit off her laughter and said quickly, "I know I'm horribly stupid, but I'm not even sure where Buckinghamshire is."

"My dear child, no one who has managed to survive on the streets of London for a decade and a half could possibly be stupid. You are uneducated, that is all. I expect that in a matter of a few years you will be more than ready to take your place in the world as my heir."

Molly wouldn't have put money on that, but she was touched by his faith in her. She made a silent vow to try her very best not to disappoint him. Nonetheless, there was something that puzzled her. "Ain't ye—ain't ye married?"

The Duke of Buckingham laughed. "You surely don't lack for straightforwardness, do you?"

"I didn't mean no impertinence!" Molly said quickly. "It's just that—well, ye bein' so rich 'n' handsome 'n' all, I should be surprised if some lucky woman hadn't snatched ye up."

"One did." The duke's tone was dryly amused. "I've been wedded for twelve years. Alas, my duchess, Lady Katherine, is barren."

"Oy, how dreadful," Molly breathed. "I'm so very sorry."

"So am I." He paused. "More for my Kate than for myself, in troth. I fear her plight has taken a wretched toll on her mind."

"D'ye mean she's daft?"

"Not in the sense your friend Tom is," he assured her. "But she is most unhappy, and in her unhappiness she blames me, says I neglect and maltreat her."

"Oy." Molly nodded. "D'ye know, there was a couple on Gospel Square that was just the same way. Bob Hinton 'n' his wife, Sally, it were. Ooh, she treated him somethin' dreadful, the poor man; we all felt sorry for him. And Aunt May always said 'twas on account o' Sally couldn't bear. I guess it just goes t' show there ain't no difference 'twixt the rich 'n' the poor after all, 'cept education, like ye says.''

"I suppose it does.''

"And, o' course, money,'' Molly added as an afterthought.

"Aye,'' said the duke. "There is always that. At any rate, I hope you won't put too much store in Kate's complaints. She is not a well woman.''

"They'll just go in one ear 'n' out the other,'' she told him cheerfully. "That's wot we always did wi' Sally, poor soul.''

"It's odd,'' the duke mused. "When we were first married, Kate and I were the happiest couple in Christendom. We were young and in love—why, the world was our oyster, as Shakespeare said.''

"Who?''

"William Shakespeare. The playwright. Have you never heard of him?''

"Nay,'' said Molly. "But I had oysters once. Didn't care for 'em a bit.''

"Really? They're one of my favorites. Well, Shakespeare was before your time. To tell you the truth, Kate's unhappiness was one of the reasons I went on searching for you so long. I thought that if she had a child to raise, even one that wasn't her own, she might reconcile herself to her inability to conceive.''

Molly nodded again. "Aunt May always said she'd o' minded never marryin' more if she hadn't had me to raise. 'N' she had the stall to run 'n' all. I reckon 'tis even harder not to have bairns if ye're rich. 'Twould make the time hang right heavy on yer hands.''

"Exactly,'' Buckingham said, sounding grateful. "I'm so glad that you understand.''

"Pity I'm all grown up now,'' she went on. "Still, I've

got lots to learn, like ye said. Maybe the teachin' will help her.''

"I'm afraid Kate's in no state by now to play the governess," he said with regret. "You will have to rely on the Countess of Shrewsbury for that."

"The Countess o' Shrewsbury?"

"Aye. Lady Agnes. A widow who's been living with us ever since her husband met with an unfortunate accident. I can think of no one better suited to overseeing your education."

"I've got no book learning at all," Molly felt dutybound to confess. "Wot if I'm horribly backward?"

"If volubility is any indication, you're not," the duke told her wryly.

"I don't know wot that word means."

"Ah. 'Voluble,' from the Latin *volubilis*, from *volvere*, meaning 'to roll'—in particular, to roll the tongue."

"Ye mean I talks too much." Molly blushed in the darkness. "Aunt May always said so too."

"Don't apologize, my dear child! The questions you ask are a sign of good, healthy curiosity, and nothing is more important to learning than that."

How kind he was, Molly thought, to turn even her faults into virtues! Nonetheless, she resolved to try to keep a rein on her inquisitiveness. She kept her vow for a full two minutes, until the carriage turned a corner onto a wide avenue. Standing back behind an iron gate, just off the road, was a huge house, the windows of the lower stories ablaze with candles. "Is that the king's palace?" Molly asked in wonder, craning her neck as they rolled by.

"Hardly," said the duke. "Charles has better taste. It's the Earl of Ballenrose's town house." There was more than a hint of disdain to his tone; Molly was reminded of the spat between the two men at the Fleet.

"Don't ye like it?" she asked.

"Like it? I find it a monstrosity. As a matter of fact, I had Cliveden built as my answer to the earl's architectural pretensions." He waved a hand toward the house. "Look at the lines, my dear child! So vulgar and harsh—why, it might have been built a hundred years ago, it is so old-fashioned. No one of note has put up a half-timbered house since the death of Queen Elizabeth, for God's sake."

"I see," said Molly, who didn't. It looked a grand place indeed to her; she liked the way the moonlight shone on the whitewashed walls between the dark staves of wood. Still, that only showed how ignorant she was, she supposed, and tried to imagine what Cliveden must be like if it were even grander. The effort was too much for her; she yawned, and to her embarrassment, her uncle caught her.

"But perhaps architecture bores you, my dear," he said, and when she stammered an apology, he laughed. "I was only teasing. You must be exhausted; this has been rather an extraordinary day for you."

"Ye can say that again," she agreed.

He patted her knee. "Try to get some sleep. When you wake up, we shall be at Cliveden. Your new home."

"I'm afraid t' go t' sleep," she admitted shyly. "I can't help thinkin' that I'm only dreamin'. That if I close my eyes, it'll all be gone—ye, 'n' the carriage, 'n' these here furs 'n' robes . . ." She snuggled into their softness, drew them tight around her as though that might help her to believe in them.

"My dear Mary Catherine." The carriage lamps caught the glint of his beautiful smile. "I assure you I'm quite real—all except for two teeth in the back." She giggled. "And I'm not going anywhere, except to Cliveden. Didn't I tell you that you mustn't be afraid anymore?"

"Aye, but—"

"Hush. No buts. I intend to take very special care of you from now on."

Molly leaned back against the cushions, breathing in the scent of roses, lulled by the clatter and clack of the wheels. One final question occurred to her: "Ye don't think Dr. Collett will have any trouble wi' Aunt May, do ye?"

"I'm quite sure he won't. Go to sleep, Mary Catherine."

"All right. Good night, m'lord." This time Molly caught herself. "I mean, good night, Uncle George."

Molly woke to the feel of sunlight on her face and the loud buzz of snoring. Without opening her eyes, she reached over beside her to shake Meg's shoulder, hoping that would make her stop. But Meg wasn't there. Instead her hand alighted on soft fur. "Jesu! A rat!" she cried, bolting upright.

The snoring stopped; on the other side of the carriage the Duke of Buckingham lunged to his feet, grappled for his sword, and drew it, all in one swift flow of movement that left Molly staring in awe. The carriage driver, hearing Molly's cry, reined in abruptly, and the coach halted with a jolt that sent Buckingham sprawling atop Molly, his blade within a hairbreadth of sticking her through. "M'lord!" The footman yanked open the door to a squealing, heaving mass of lap robes and pillows and hands and feet. "M'lord, wot's happened?"

The duke pushed himself upright, withdrawing his sword from the cushions he'd impaled in a flurry of feathers. "I'm ever so sorry," Molly gasped, disentangling herself from the ermine she'd mistaken for vermin. "I didn't know where I was—"

"It's all right," the duke assured his servants. "We're all right. It's just a mistake."

"I heard milady cry out," the driver tried to explain.

"Aye, as did I," his master said wryly. "I can see, Mary Catherine, that life with you shall never be dull!"

She put a hand to her fast-beating heart. "I've never in all my days seen anybody pull a sword so quick!"

"His majesty's foreign campaigns taught me the worth of light slumber—and of a quick parry. Perkins, where are we?"

"The river road, m'lord," the driver told him, "nearly t' Rawnleigh."

"So close as that?" He peered at the morning sun,

looking pleased. "We'll be in time for breakfast, then. Christ, I've an appetite on."

So did Molly. She also had an exceedingly urgent bladder. "Excuse me, Uncle George." The name still came hesitantly. "I've got t'—" She blushed; all three men were eyeing her expectantly. "Ye know," she mumbled.

"Ah." The duke frowned. "Can't it wait, my dear? We're nearly home, and I'm afraid there's no suitable place nearby."

Molly looked past him through the door. "Wot's wrong wi' them there bushes?"

The footman tittered. The duke shot him a look that could have frozen hell. "Get back to your places," he told the servants, and when they'd gone, he turned to Molly. "I'm afraid, my dear child, that a lady doesn't simply relieve herself in the nearest clump of shrubbery. If there were an inn, or a manor, or even a farmhouse—"

"Oh," said Molly. It had never occurred to her that being grand might have its disadvantages. Longingly she considered the bushes. "D'ye suppose we might forget I'm a lady, jest for a minute or two?"

Her uncle shook his head. "Of all the lessons you must learn, Mary Catherine, I suspect that one will prove the hardest. A true lady must never, ever forget her place in the world, not even for a minute. Just as a footman mustn't; that young man out there will lose his post for having laughed at you."

"Oh, no!" Molly cried in dismay.

"Oh, yes. You see, my dear, the fabric of our society is woven most precariously, as Cromwell's execrable revolution proved." Molly didn't know what "execrable" meant, but it wasn't hard to guess from his tone. "Each link in the chain has its divine order, decreed by God. He is at the top, then the angels, the king, nobles, clergy, peasantry, animals, plants, and rocks. Disturb a single link, and the entire chain is broken." Molly supposed that was true. She'd heard folk talk of Cromwell's Puritan experiment with horror: the battles, the beheadings, burnings at the stake. It was scarcely ten years now since the Great Protector's worthless son and his military cronies has been tossed out and the monarchy restored. Still, it had always seemed like antique history to her; she had never thought about such notions as the fabric of society, much less her place in it. *I never had to,* she realized, with a sudden premonition that being the Duke of Buckingham's niece would prove trickier than she'd thought. There wasn't any question who she was in Smithfield, or of where she belonged.

"So you can understand, Mary Catherine," the duke concluded, "how important it is to be aware at every moment of your station in life."

"Yes, Uncle George," Molly murmured, and crossed her legs tight. "But—"

"Yes, my dear?"

She took a deep breath. "Surely then ye must excuse the footman, for if I'd known my place he would not have forgotten his." Though she feared the duke would be angry with her, she could not bear for the poor footman to lose his post on her account.

Her uncle considered her for a minute, his fine dark eyes inscrutable. "My dear Mary Catherine," he said softly, "you delight me. Had you been born a man, you might have had a fine career in the Parliament." Molly glowed with pleasure at the compliment, and he smiled. "Besides, we must always allow in our schema for the quality of mercy, mustn't we? Very well. The footman shall be spared."

"Thank ye," Molly said.

"You're most welcome." The carriage slowed, then rolled through a vast stone-and-iron gate. The Duke of Buckingham leaned forward in his seat, and his dark eyes glinted as he threw the window panel back as far as it would go. "There," he said, gesturing toward the horizon. "Tell me now how grand you think Ballenrose's house to be."

Molly forgot the footman, forgot even her urgent need

to relieve herself as she stared through the window. "Oh, Uncle George! It looks—" She groped for a comparison. "It looks like heaven!"

He smiled in satisfaction. "How very apt. I modeled it after the villa of the pope outside Rome—with improvements, of course." Molly scarcely heard him; she was gaping at the huge structure that crowned a rolling green hill. Its pale stone gleamed in the sunlight; columns and towers and gables soared toward the sky; staircases topped with urns and statues wound hither and thither. Balconies sprouted from the upper stories, friezes ran round the corners, and the deep-set windows bore great peaked lintels painted blue and gold. As the carriage rumbled closer, she leaned out further, trying to take it all in.

"All right, Mary Catherine." Her uncle tugged her back. "No need to present a spectacle to the servants."

"Ye made this yerself? *Ye* built it?" she asked in awe.

"Well—" He coughed modestly. "I had Sir Christopher Wren look over the plans. But basically, yes."

"Ye're a true genius," Molly said solemnly.

The duke tweaked her chin. "And *you* know the way to a man's heart is flattery."

"No, I mean it!" she insisted. "Why, I'll wager the king himself ain't got a palace this grand."

"As it happens, he hasn't. But then, neither has poor Charles got as much cause to erect a monument to his accomplishments as I have." He grinned wickedly. Molly laughed, less because she understood the jest than out of delight in his good humor. Was this what having a father would have been like? she wondered. She'd never realized how much she might have missed in lacking one before.

The carriage rolled to a stop before the stairs of the imposing portico. Young men in the same blue suits as Perkins, the driver, came running; Molly watched in wonder as they spread a gold-colored cloth along the gravel drive from the carriage to the steps. The footman opened the coach door, head lowered, looking much abashed. "Milady," he said hoarsely, holding out his arms to help her to the ground. She gave him a smile, just to let him know there weren't any hard feelings on her part. He lifted her up, set her down, and her bare feet touched the golden cloth. It was oddly scratchy. The duke climbed out beside her and took her hand.

"Welcome, Mary Catherine. Welcome to Cliveden." There were tears in his eyes; he bent and kissed her cheek. Then he straightened up; the servants fell back. "Shall we?" he asked, and arm in arm they mounted the steep stairs. The great carved wood doors swung open before them. Molly walked into Cliveden, into the magical palace that was her new home.

The hall within was very dark after the morning sunlight. She paused, blinking, on the threshold, and took in vague impressions of a patterned stone floor, arched windows hung with heavy draperies, a soaring ceiling, and an immense double staircase curving upward at the far end of the room. She saw a woman standing in the center of the floor before them—a beautiful woman, breathtaking, with skin as pale as white wheat flour, burnished auburn hair, and heavy ivory breasts that swelled above the wasp waist of her magnificent gown. Its beaded skirts were so wide that Molly could not fathom how she got through doorways.

"Mary Catherine," the duke began, leading her forward. Molly fell to her knees before the ravishing duchess.

"M'lady, I can't begin to tell ye how kind yer husband's been! Why, he—"

"He is not—her—husband," said a low, angry voice that seemed to come from the sky. Molly glanced upward toward the staircase, and at the far end of the hall was another woman. She came down the steps slowly, as though movement pained her: a drab figure, rail-thin, clad in what looked like gray sacking. On the last stair she paused, looking at Molly and then at the duke. "Who is that?"

"My dear Kate." Buckingham crossed to her side. With her on the stair, they were nearly of a height as he kissed her, a little peck meant for her cheek that fell on her hair as she swiveled her head. "This is Mary Catherine. Did the messenger I sent not arrive?"

"Mary Catherine who?" the duchess demanded.

Buckingham glanced back at Molly and shrugged his shoulders, almost imperceptibly. "My sister Frances' long-lost daughter, Kate, my heart."

"Your sister Frances'—" The duchess looked Molly over again, her pinched mouth twisting in a sneer. "What devilry is this, George? What are you up to? Frances' daughter?"

"Aye, Kate. Surely you remember. All these years we feared that she'd been lost at sea—"

"If she'd been lost at sea, she'd at least be clean. Get her up off my floor." Molly scrambled to her feet. "Get her out of my house!" shrilled the duchess. "I'll not have another of your stinking whores under this roof!" Molly stumbled backward, frightened by the woman's bitter vitriol, and felt a hand clasp hers.

"Stand your ground," the auburn-haired beauty whispered, squeezing Molly's fingers. "She doesn't know what she's saying, poor soul."

"Don't you whisper about me, you vile strumpet!" the duchess screamed, grabbing a vase that stood handy, rearing back to hurl it.

"Kate!" The duke caught her arm, held it tightly. "Let go."

"Go to hell," she spat.

"Let—go—the—vase," he repeated sternly but softly. As Molly watched, wide-eyed, the duchess's taut, thin body went limp against her husband. The vase slipped from her hand, crashed to the floor unheeded; Lady Katherine's pale gaze was all for Buckingham.

"Why, George?" she whimpered, and Molly didn't know which was worse, her shouting or this pitiful pleading. "Why do you torment me? Why do you hate me so?"

"Oh, Kate." The duke smoothed back her bedraggled

hair, pressed a kiss to her forehead. "I don't hate thee, Kate. Where are your women?"

"She sent them away," the one beside Molly told him. "She said they were stealing from her."

"Tattletale," the duchess hissed in fury.

"Stealing?" The duke laughed. "Kate, love, what would they steal?"

"My thoughts," she whispered. "They were stealing my thoughts, stealing them for you!"

"What would I want with your thoughts, pet?" The duchess had relaxed again, but Molly saw that the duke still gripped her arm. "Anyway," he added rather ruefully, "you've never made them a secret."

"Don't you jest at me!" She whipped away from him, stumbling back up the stairs. On the landing she paused, turning and finding Molly with her wild, hollow eyes. "Get away from here," she warned. "He eats folk alive, swallows them up whole. He will eat you too, unless you get away!"

"Kate, please," said the duke, starting after her.

"Don't you touch me! Don't come near me!" the madwoman cried, fleeing higher on the stairs and then vanishing down the corridor. Molly heard her swift running footsteps, and the slam of a door that reverberated through the vast stone hall. The echoes died away; the duke stood at the bottom of the stairs, his broad shoulders bent, head lowered in shame.

"George," the auburn-haired woman said softly, taking a step toward him. He shook his head, holding his palm out to stop her, and took a deep breath before he looked up.

"Mary Catherine. I'm so terribly sorry . . ." He breathed out in a sigh. "It appears the duchess is having . . . one of her days." Molly stood in awkward silence, longing to comfort him but not knowing what to say. After a moment he squared his shoulders, even managed a faint smile. "But forgive my Kate—and my manners. Mary

Catherine, allow me to present Lady Agnes, the Countess of Shrewsbury.''

Molly made a curtsy of sorts, still shaken by the scene she'd witnessed. ''Lady Agnes . . .''

''Mary Catherine.'' The beautiful woman smiled reassuringly. ''When milord's messenger arrived to tell us you had been found, the duchess cried for joy. It is only since then that she—well, that she's had one of her spells.''

''What could have brought it on?'' the duke asked, mystified. ''She didn't get into the wine cellars again, did she? I'll have that steward's ears—''

''Nay, milord, I know she did not.'' The countess's bosom rose and fell as she shrugged. ''Who knows? 'I am but mad north-northwest; when the wind is southerly I know a hawk from a handsaw.' ''

Molly looked at her in utter bewilderment. The duke chuckled. ''That, dear Mary Catherine, is Shakespeare too. From a play called *Hamlet.*''

The Countess of Shrewsbury took Molly's chin in her hand, tilting it toward her. ''How lovely she is,'' she murmured.

''The very picture of Frances, don't you think?'' the duke asked, and she nodded agreement.

''But the duchess was right about one thing—she is dreadfully dirty! Suppose we get you straight into a nice warm tub, Mary Catherine.''

''If ye please—'' Molly had been meaning to speak to her uncle about this. ''D'ye suppose that instead of Mary Catherine, ye might call me Molly? 'Tis wot I'm used t', ye see.''

Lady Agnes and her uncle exchanged glances. ''I'm afraid, my dear child,'' the duke said gently, '' 'Molly' is hardly suitable.''

''But it's my name.''

''Not anymore!'' the countess said brightly. ''Don't you think you ought to have a new name to go with your new life?''

Molly bit back a frown. When the woman wasn't talking

as if Molly wasn't even there, she was treating her as though she were five years old. "Wot's wrong wi' 'Molly,' then?"

"Nothing," the duke assured her, his voice soothing. "It's just that all these years I've thought of you as Mary Catherine. That was the name Frances gave you, after all, after your father's good friends, the Queen and Princess of France."

"Ye don't say. Named for a queen 'n' princess, was I?" She pondered that a moment. "Aunt May only called me Mary Catherine when she was cross. She can still call me Molly, can't she?"

"Of course. She can call you anything she pleases."

Molly was much relieved. "Ye know, I'll wager Aunt May'll be right good wi' the duchess. She's got a way wi' folk wot're sickly; she always has had. Speakin' o' which—shouldn't Dr. Collett be here with her by now? I hope there ain't been no trouble."

"I'm sure John would have sent a rider with a message if there were." The duke cocked his head. "I believe I hear a coach now."

"That must be them!" Molly darted toward the doors, only to feel herself yanked backward by the countess's bejeweled hand on her smock.

"Dr. Collett is a distinguished physician," Lady Agnes said, "but the fact remains he is only of the lesser nobility. He must wait, Mary Catherine, upon those like you and me. We will receive him in the solarium after you have bathed and changed."

"But—" Molly turned pleading eyes on her uncle. "But it wouldn't be fair t' make Aunt May wait! She's so old, 'n' she's bound t' be upset and confused!"

"She's quite right, Agnes," he said, to her relief. "I think that we can bend the rules this time, and receive John and Aunt May here." Molly beamed at him, then turned toward the doors as they opened wide. Dr. Collett came in, handing his hat to the butler. "John!" the duke called loudly. "Here you are at last! Is Aunt May outside?"

The doctor blinked at them; Molly was reminded of how dim the hall had seemed when she first entered. "Your grace," he said, coming toward them. "Lady Agnes." He bowed. "Lady Mary Catherine." There was something odd about his voice; Molly looked at him more closely.

"Wot's wrong?" she cried, a sudden tremor chilling her heart. "Wot's happened, where's Aunt May?"

Dr. Collett swallowed. "I'm so terribly sorry to be the bearer of bad news, child. Your Aunt May is dead."

"Dead?" Molly blanched, staring at him. "When? How?"

"Some two months past. The man downstairs, the butcher—"

"Eben," Molly breathed.

"Aye, that's it, Eben Campbell. He said she died in her sleep way back in February. It was very peaceful, he—"

"Nay!" Molly protested. "Nay, it can't be! Tom would've told me!"

"Tom?" asked the duke as Lady Agnes put her arm around Molly's trembling shoulders. "You mean the madman at the gate?"

"Aye, he came every day t' see me, told me how Aunt May was doin'!"

"My dear child." Her uncle cleared his throat. "From what I saw of him, that poor man could no more be relied on as a source of information than could my Kate. John, wouldn't you agree?"

"I'm afraid so. In such a deeply disturbed mind, the lines between truth and falsehood are utterly blurred. He may have gone on telling you that Aunt May was well, milady, simply because he knew that was what you wanted to hear."

"Oh, God." Molly's knees collapsed as the news sank in; only Lady Agnes's arm kept her from falling to the floor. "Oh, God, no! Aunt May . . ."

"Courage, dear," the countess whispered. "Not in front of the servants."

"Hang the servants! I want my Aunt May!"

"John," the duke said worriedly, "have you a sedative? Laudanum, perhaps?"

"Of course. Right here." The doctor rummaged in the bag he carried, then came toward Molly with a little vial. "Drink this, milady, it will make you feel—" She shrank back from him, pointed, screamed:

"There is blood on yer clothes!"

He looked down, saw the dark stain on the lace of his sleeve. "So there is. While I was speaking with that butcher—"

"Eben Campbell," the duke supplied.

"Aye. By the most astonishing coincidence, his daughter went into labor. I delivered the child."

"Well," said the countess, "it just goes to show, does it not, that every cloud has a silver lining! What did she have?"

"I beg your pardon?"

"What did she have—a boy or a girl?"

"Oh. A little girl."

Molly began to laugh in the midst of her crying. "Charity, was it? Charity Campbell?"

"I think that was her name."

"And Andrew's the father. Oy!" She smashed her fists into her forehead, tore at her hair. "It's his bloody fault Aunt May's dead; I'd have kept her alive if I hadn't been in jail! Oh, dammit all, it's so bloody unfair!"

"So it is," her uncle agreed, taking her hands to keep her from doing any further damage. "But think, Mary Catherine, my dear. If you hadn't been in jail, I never would have found you."

"That's right," said the countess. "And you wouldn't have your Uncle George to console you in this time of woe. Just as I said, every cloud—"

"That's enough, Agnes." The duke gathered Molly into his arms. "I know how hard it is to lose someone you loved so much. But you must be brave, must look to the future.'' She laid her cheek against the lacy ruffles on his chest, tears streaming down her face. ''Just imagine how happy Aunt May must be, looking down from heaven and seeing you here in the bosom of your own family at last.''

''I don't want for her t' be in heaven,'' Molly sobbed. ''I want her t' be here!''

''Of course you do. John, where's that laudanum?''

''Right here.''

The shirt ruffles rustled; Molly felt the little bottle pressed to her lips. ''Drink this, my dear,'' her uncle urged. ''It will make you feel better, I promise.'' Dutifully, like a child, Molly opened her mouth and felt a trickle of warm liquid course down her throat. It was syrupy sweet, but the aftertaste was bitter as gall. ''There, there,'' the duke murmured, stroking her tangled hair.

Lady Agnes squealed. ''Good God, George, are those lice?''

''Hush up, Agnes.'' Molly felt herself lifted into the air, into his strong, sure arms just in time, for her head was spinning, and the floor had tilted crazily under her feet. ''I'll put you to bed, Mary Catherine.''

''Not anywhere near *my* rooms, you don't,'' said the countess.

''Speaking of your rooms, Agnes, why don't you go there?'' the duke suggested in a tone that made Molly want to giggle. But she mustn't giggle. Aunt May was dead, her beloved Aunt May. Why, then, did she feel so giddy?''

''Well!'' Lady Agnes huffed. ''I must say, George, I never expected you to take this business so to heart! She is only a—''

''She can hear you,'' Dr. Collett said.

The duke's grip on Molly tightened. ''Only a tired, frightened child, Agnes, who has just lost her dearest friend in the world. *And* she is my niece. I'll thank you to remember that.'' The countess muttered something else that Molly couldn't quite catch. Their voices were growing all murky, as though her head were underwater. She snuggled closer to her uncle's chest, heard him say one last thing:

"You had damned well better remember it, Agnes."

Then a wave of darkness closed over Molly's head, and on its soft crest she drifted, unresisting, weightless as goosedown, into a deep sleep.

II

5

"YOUR UNCLE IS coming," said the Countess of Shrewsbury, folding the letter she'd been reading into a square.

"No!" Molly looked up from her dinner. "I thought he was still in France, treating with King Louis!"

"He expected to land in Dover on the eleventh of April—that would be three days past." It was four, actually, but Molly didn't bother to correct her. The countess had a blithe disregard for most times and dates. "He writes that the negotiations have been completed."

"Really." Molly plucked a leaf from her artichoke and dipped it in the little silver boat of *sauce béarnaise* beside her plate. "Successfully, I trust?"

"I should say so. King Louis has granted me a pension of ten thousand *livres* a year. Mary Catherine, you're dripping."

"I beg your pardon." Molly used her napkin to sop the bit of *béarnaise* that had slid off the leaf. "You took me by surprise, milady; I had no idea that you had ties to Louis."

"A lady never shows surprise, in either her speech or her actions," the countess intoned, and it was all Molly could do not to parrot her words, so often had she heard them in the past year. According to Lady Agnes, the hallmark of *gentillesse* was a self-assured equanimity. "As it happens, I am not acquainted with his majesty; the pen-

sion was presented as a favor to your uncle. By and by,
how much is a *livre* worth?''

Molly forbore to remind her that a lady never mentions
money—another of the countess's favorite adages. ''Twenty
sols, or two hundred and forty *deniers.* ''

''Please, Mary Catherine. You know perfectly well I
haven't your head for figures.''

''About ten shillings.''

''Ah,'' said the countess. ''Pity. I'd have thought
more.''

Molly couldn't imagine what the woman needed money
for, unless to add to her enormous closet of clothes. It was
true she had a son by her late husband, but he was in the
care of guardians, and she rarely spoke of him; Molly
didn't even know his name. ''What else does Uncle
write?''

Lady Agnes consulted the letter again. '' 'In troth,' he
says, 'I believe I've had more honors done me here than
ever any subject.' I like the sound of that. Then a bit about
the treaty between Louis and Charles—how exceedingly
dull are these affairs of state.''

''Quite,'' Molly agreed, knowing it to be the proper
response. Matters politic were no concern of women. ''Is
there no message for me?''

''He sends you his best love, and says he has a present
for you.'' Molly brightened; her uncle always brought the
most wonderful presents when he visited Cliveden. Once
it had been the emerald ear-drops she was wearing, once
a length of gorgeous Venice silk, and once, when he had
been to Brussels, lace for a *fichu,* milk-white and intricate
as snowflakes. The gifts took some of the sting from his
frequent absences; Molly had not expected him to be so
often away. But as the countess told her often enough, a
man's true life lay in his work: home and family were but
adjuncts. And as King Charles' most trusted adviser, the
Duke of Buckingham's work was vital indeed.

''Does he say when he will come?'' she asked. The
countess looked at her across the table.

"Mary Catherine," she said, sounding appalled, "you have cleared your plate."

Molly glanced down and saw it was true. "I'm so very sorry. I was distracted by our conversation."

Lady Agnes sniffed. "Is that what you will tell Queen Catherine when you go to dine at the palace and make such a pig of yourself?"

"I doubt that I shall ever dine with the queen," Molly said longingly. How she wished that she might go to London with her uncle!

"No so long as your table manners are so frightful," the countess agreed. "How many times have I told you, you must pay attention when you eat? When I was at court—"

Molly didn't know how to explain to her that after a lifetime of deprivation, the custom of leaving food on one's plate came hard. Why, a family in Gospel Square could have lived for a week on the scraps the countess fed her little yapping dogs every day. Instead she began to gather up the artichoke leaves from her scrap plate and poke them at the stripped stem. "Mary Catherine," said the countess, "what *are* you doing?"

"I thought perhaps if I reconstructed it—"

"Oh, honestly!" But Lady Agnes had smiled. Having successfully forestalled another lecture, Molly repeated her question:

"Does Uncle say when he'll be home?"

"Aye, on the fifteenth. What is that, the day after tomorrow?"

"The fifteenth!" Molly shoved back her chair. "That's today!"

"Mary Catherine, sit down!"

"But I'm not ready!" Molly said desperately. "I meant to finish reading *The Tempest*, and I've got to learn the sarabande, and I promised him I would know the dates of all the English kings!"

"None of which is any excuse for leaving the table without asking permission."

Molly rolled her eyes. "May I please leave the table?"

"Certainly not. You can hardly accomplish all that before he arrives anyway. And don't make faces at me." The countess frowned at the letter. "Dammit all, had I known George was coming today, I'd have waited dinner. Well, we've only had the first course. And I don't suppose *you* will mind eating again. Still, my hair is a sight. Are you sure today is the fifteenth?"

"Quite sure." Molly moved uneasily in her seat. The way the countess always primped and fussed before her uncle's arrival made her uncomfortable, though she couldn't put her finger on why. After all, an estate like Cliveden needed a mistress, what with the duke's wife's condition, and Molly herself certainly needed a governess. Who better to fill those posts than the widowed Lady Agnes? Still—

"Do stop squirming, child, and go change your clothes," the countess ordered, disregarding the fact that she'd only just told Molly to stay put. "The green *mousseline,* I think. I shall wear the bronze taffeta. No, the oyster damask. Or should it be the turquoise brocade? He hasn't seen that."

Molly had already dropped a deep, graceful curtsy. "If it please milady, pray excuse me," she murmured, and made her escape from the dining hall.

She was in such a rush that she forgot to take her usual precaution of scouting the front hall before entering; she cursed beneath her breath as she heard the duchess cry out, "You there!" Molly halted reluctantly. Lady Agnes just ignored Lady Katherine when she wandered onto the scene, but Molly never felt right doing so, and thought she ought at least to acknowledge the woman's presence. After all, she was Molly's aunt.

"Lady Katherine." Molly curtsied again, smoothly and effortlessly, glancing up from beneath her lashes to try to gauge the duchess's mood. "I hope you are well."

"Oh, I doubt that," the woman said dryly, and Molly's spirits sank. Even more disturbing than Lady Katherine's spells of ranting and raving were her occasional bouts of apparent lucidity. One could be discussing something as innocuous as the weather with her when suddenly those watery blue eyes would go sharp and clear as ice shards, and then it would be devil-take-care.

"I'm sure I don't know what milady means," Molly said cautiously.

" 'I'm sure I don't know what milady means,' " the duchess mimicked adroitly, and laughed. "You're two of a kind, aren't you, you and the Lady Agnus Dei? 'O Lamb of God'—but it will need more than water, won't it, to take her sins away? I hear that you are reading Shakespeare. Have you read *Macbeth?*" Molly nodded, edging away. " 'Out, out, damned spot!' " the duchess quoted. "My husband fancies himself a playwright, did you know that?"

"Aye, of course." Molly had read a work her uncle had written with Dr. Collett and some other friends from the Royal Society, called *The Rehearsal;* it was very witty.

" 'All the world's a stage,' " the duchess said dreamily, " 'and all the men and women merely players . . . and one man in his time plays many parts.' It was Claudius, wasn't it, that played the loving uncle to Hamlet?"

"I—"

"Look to thine uncle," the woman said with a ludicrous wink, and Molly wasn't sure whether that was a quotation or not.

"If you'll excuse me, milady, I must go get ready. His grace is coming home today," she said quickly, curtsying again and hurrying toward the stairs. The duchess's singsong voice followed her as she went:

"There was a time when I adorned myself for him each night like a new bride, shining and anointed . . . well, there was an end to that; all things have their ending. I wonder, has the cook got any strawberries?" She drifted from the great hall, still chattering away.

Molly's footsteps slowed as she reached the staircase. She never climbed those polished marble steps without being struck anew by a sense of wonder at the turns her life had taken since that night a year ago in the Fleet. Somehow seeing the toes of her slippers against the stone, hearing the echo her heels made in the vast space below brought home as nothing else did the incredible extent of her good fortune. If she'd not been in jail, if Uncle George had not come there with the board of inquiry, if that man Ballenrose had prevailed in arguing that she need not undress, she would be back in Smithfield by now, listening to Eben Campbell shout at his daughters in the shop below while she climbed the worn staircase that led to the room she shared with Aunt May.

Poor Aunt May. Molly's heart folded inward with a pang as it always did when she thought of her dying alone in that room, blind and feeble and bereft even of Bubby in that lonely winter. How tickled she would have been by Molly's unlikely luck! And had she just held on a little longer, she might have ended her days here at Cliveden, coddled and cosseted, in the very lap of luxury. But perhaps the shock of the change would have been too much for her; older people were not so resilient as the young. That was what Uncle George suggested, anyway, once when she'd poured out her regrets to him.

He would be pleased with her, even if she had not gotten to *The Tempest* and the sarabande. Molly had never in her life worked so hard as she had this past year, learning to read and write, practicing manners and dancing, memorizing her family's history, even picking up a *soupçon* of French—she, who hadn't even known where France was, who'd never handled a fork or seen a *pâté* knife. It was for Uncle George that she'd stayed up nights poring over her alphabet until her eyes were bleary, for him that she'd endured Lady Agnes' lectures, made ten thousand curtsies until the countess finally declared one fit. But she would have gone through it all again, aye, a million times over, just to see him smile his enchanting smile and declare, "Well done!" He was her mentor, her judge, the father she had never known. But most important, he believed in her, believed in her to his heart's core, in a way no one had ever done before.

Parker was tidying her rooms when she entered—not that they were ever terribly untidy. Sixteen years of cramped living had instilled in Molly a habit for order that made Parker the envy of the other maids, especially the countess's beleaguered Potts. Molly found it passing strange at first to call the servants, most much older than she was, by their last names, but she knew by now that they expected it, would have found anything else offensive. It was just as Uncle George had told her: everyone had his place in the world according to the divine order. That was what held society together, and the order mustn't be disturbed.

"M'lady!" Parker curtsied, feather duster in hand, when she saw her mistress. "I thought ye'd be at dinner for another hour; everythin's awry!"

"It doesn't matter, Parker. I must hurry and change; Uncle George is coming home today!"

"Wot? Wi' no more warnin' than that?" the wiry little maid demanded. Molly knew she ought to reprimand her for the implied criticism of the duke, but let it pass. That was one reason she was glad she'd got Parker for her personal maid instead of Potts or Jenkins or Smith—because she had a bit of spirit. And she didn't seem to begrudge Molly her good luck the way she sensed the others did.

"He wrote," Molly explained, "but the messenger must have been delayed, and then the countess got her dates confused."

Parker giggled at that. "Wot dress would ye be wantin'?"

"Lady Agnes says the green *mousseline.* But I'll wear the blue moiré." The maid nodded approval. It was she who'd pointed out to Molly that the gowns the countess chose for her weren't especially becoming. "Jealous, that's wot she is," she'd confided, "on account o' ye're bein' so much younger 'n' prettier than she."

"Me prettier than Lady Agnes?" Molly laughed at that.

But alone in her rooms one night she'd tried on the gowns the countess's seamstress had made for her, and had to admit the colors and styles didn't flatter her the way Lady Agnes' own did. After that, she chose her fabrics herself from the clothier's swatch, and didn't let the countess dictate what neckline or sleeves she should have.

" 'N' yer jewels?''

Her jewels. Molly glanced at the burlwood chest on her dressing table. Who would ever have believed that someday she would have a whole boxful to choose from, could say casually, "The topazes, Parker," or, "The sapphire necklace, I think," or, "The Cathay pearls"? "Just the ear-drops Uncle gave me," she decided.

Parker frowned. "The countess'll be all decked out in her diamonds 'n' opals, I'll wager."

"Aye, I know. But the blue gown's so simple, I don't want to overwhelm it."

"P'raps ye're right. Besides, 'twill go to show an old house needs more gildin' than a new one." The maid grinned wickedly.

"Parker, you're dreadful," Molly said, even as she wondered whether all maids engaged in such catty rivalries on behalf of their mistresses. "Lady Agnes isn't old."

"She's comin' up thirty."

"Do you really think so?" Thirty did seem elderly, Molly had to admit.

"I'd lay wages on it." Parker lifted Molly's day gown over her head and lowered the blue moiré in its stead. "She'd be wise to look to herself; his grace don't like his ladies long in the tooth."

"If you ask me, Lady Agnes already spends an inordinate amount of time and money dressing. Anyway, why should Uncle care what my governess looks like?" As the blue silk settled onto her shoulders, she saw Parker's brief expression of disbelief, just before the maid arranged her features noncommittally again.

"Troth, there's just some folk born frivolous 'n' others not," she said. "Turn about, if ye please, 'n' suck in."

Molly held her breath while the maid did up the long row of hooks at her back. She'd put on weight since she came here, mostly in her hips and chest. Her bosom wasn't so different now from the countess's magnificent *décolletage,* only suppler and firmer. Of course, she hadn't borne a child, as Lady Agnes had.

With the dress fastened, Parker let down Molly's hair and began to brush it. "Gor, wot I wouldn't give for hair like this," she said, just as she always did. "So smooth 'n' straight, 'n' the color o' sunshine—"

"I'd rather it were curly like yours," Molly said, just as *she* always did.

"Oy, ye're daft." Parker tugged one of the wayward brown ringlets that showed beneath her starched cap. "If I had hair like yers, I'd never in me life ask God for nothin' else. I'd go to market wi' it hangin' loose down me back, 'n' all the boys'd want to marry me."

"I used to wear it that way sometimes to market." Molly smiled, remembering.

" 'Tis a fair crime to do't all up in snoods 'n' wires 'n' whatnot, so nobody can see it," Parker said wistfully.

Molly's gaze, pure leaf green in the late-day sun, slanted toward the maid. "Let's leave it down, then."

"Oy!" Parker's own eyes widened. "Lady Agnes'd have yer ears! 'Twouldn't be half-proper."

"Who cares? There's no one to see except her and Uncle George."

"Ye truly is daft, ye know." The maid scratched her chin with the hairbrush. "Still, I'd love to see her face if ye dared. I bet she'd be green with envy. She has to color hers, ye know, to keep out the gray."

"You're jesting!"

"God's truth. Ain't I seen Potts myself, makin' up the dye? If ye ever tell I told ye, though, I'd lose me place."

"You know I never would. Let's do it, Parker."

"Ye'd be riskin' a lot." The maid frowned. "I'd be riskin' a beatin'."

"I'll swear it was all my idea, that I made you do it.

Come on, what do you say?'' Molly wasn't sure herself why the breach of etiquette was so appealing.

''Well . . .''

''Oh, Parker, you're wonderful, truly you are.'' Impulsively Molly kissed her. ''Now, take the very front and pull it back in a braid—aye, that's the way.''

''I hope ye knows wot ye're doin','' said the maid, nimbly plaiting three strands of Molly's heavy tresses, fastening the ends with a twist of gold filigree.

''We'll soon find out—there's Uncle coming!'' Through the window Molly could see him on his big bay, galloping up the drive. ''Hurry, get the ear-drops!'' Parker brought them from the chest, and Molly fastened them with eager fingers. ''Wish me luck!''

''Good luck,'' said Parker, sounding dubious.

''It'll be fine, you'll see,'' Molly promised, and flew out the door.

In the passageway, she could hear voices from the great hall below—Uncle George, saying, ''Agnes, dear. You look splendid.'' And Lady Agnes murmuring something, and then Uncle George again: ''John's coming straightaway; that nag of his is bloody slow. Have a room made up for him, won't you?'' Molly nibbled her lip. It wasn't fair to Dr. Collett, but she disliked him—she supposed because he'd been the one to bring her news of Aunt May's death. No matter how kind and polite he was—and he was, very—she still felt ill-at-ease in his company. If he was coming, perhaps she ought to put up her hair. . . .

''Mary Catherine, is that you?''

''Uncle George.'' She came out of the shadows of the passage to the top of the staircase that was bathed in the last slanting rays of the dying sun's light. There he was, looking impossibly handsome even in his dusty riding clothes, and staring up at her as though she were a chimera, a vision. Molly paused on the top stair, the blue silk coming to rest with a delicious rustle, her hair a sunlit fall of pale gold satin hanging straight to her knees.

Lady Agnes broke the moment's spell. "Good God, child, your *hair!*"

The duke was shaking his head. "No, Agnes. Not child, not any longer. Come here, my dear." He held out his arms, and Molly ran to him in triumph. The admiration in his eyes had been worth any punishment the countess might devise.

"Your grace." She curtsied gracefully, let him raise her up on his fingertips.

"Let me look at you." She spun about slowly, saw he was laughing. "Holy Christ in heaven, I swear you're the most beautiful thing I have ever seen."

"The most brazen, rather," Lady Agnes said curtly. "Get upstairs this minute and put up your hair; you look a common tart."

"Oh, there's nothing common about her, Agnes, nothing at all!"

"Loose hair," said the tight-mouthed countess, "is hardly the fashion!"

"But Mary Catherine could make it so, no doubt." Molly smiled as her uncle kissed her. "Have you been hard at work? Done your lessons? Minded the countess?"

"Aye, aye, and . . . more or less."

"Minx." He touched her sparkling ear-drop. "Wearing the last present I gave you, I see."

"So am I, George," Lady Agnes pointed out, fingering one of her strands of jewels.

"Aye, and half a dozen more. Do you know, Mary Catherine, you have a most remarkable eye; one gold chain, one single collar of pearls, would have ruined the simplicity of that dress."

"It must be in the blood," she said happily, "for I do ever pattern my taste after yours."

"*And* a deft turning of a compliment." He nodded approval. "You have been hard at work, in troth."

"She cleared her plate at dinner," the countess reported mutinously.

"That would explain how she's put on that most delectable figure."

"Uncle George!" Molly blushed.

"Are we discussing feminine pulchritude?" That was Dr. Collett, coming through the front doors. He stopped on the threshold, stared. "Lady Mary Catherine! Your hair—"

"Just what *I* said," Lady Agnes noted smugly.

"—is absolutely breathtaking! I had no idea."

Molly was experiencing the most enjoyable sensation of having stopped two men dead in their tracks in the last two minutes. She found herself warming to Dr. Collett. "Thank you, sir," she said, and curtsied.

Her uncle was looking at her again, his dark eyes narrowed—nearly the way, Molly thought, a man might appraise a cow or pig at market. She dismissed the notion in her excitement at what he said then: "I think she's ready, John, don't you?"

"Ready for what?" she asked eagerly.

Dr. Collett was nodding. "I should say so!"

"Well, I don't," Lady Agnes snapped, "and I should know far better than either of you! She's cheeky and lax—"

"Ready for *what*, Uncle?" Molly asked again.

"Aye, Agnes," the duke acknowledged, "perhaps. But she has a natural exuberance it would be a pity to stifle." He put his hand to the countess's cheek. "She is a credit to your talents, my dear. I owe you a very great debt."

"So you do," Lady Agnes agreed, scarcely mollified. "See you remember that."

"Oh, he will." Dr. Collett chuckled. "Don't you know we all jest at court that that is what George should have carved on his headstone—'He always paid his debts'?"

"What am I ready for?" asked Molly, feeling like a magpie.

Uncle George smiled mysteriously. "After John and I have had our supper." Then he added, as her chin came up, "No arguments! Don't you know the duty of a lady is—"

"Always to obey her lord and master," Molly finished with him, and sighed.

"Quite so," said the countess. "Come alone, Mary Catherine, and we'll see to the wines."

The meal was a merry one, for Uncle George was in high spirits, and Lady Agnes warmed with each glass of Bordeaux she drank. Dr. Collett was very droll, telling about an experiment one of his colleagues in the Royal Society had presented to the members having to do with sulfur and phosphorus and borax that left everyone in the room with singed eyebrows. Molly thought the whole notion of a bunch of men getting together to witness such experiments rather silly, but her uncle took the study of science seriously—to the point that he had built a laboratory in Cliveden, where he devoted spare moments to a search for the philosopher's stone, which would turn lead or tin to gold. And the doctor hoped to be elected president of the Royal Society at the next referendum, two years hence, with the valuable backing of the Duke of Buckingham.

This night Molly had little patience for talk of elements and spirits and the distillation of the baser metals; she was too preoccupied with wondering what her uncle had meant when he said that she was ready. Since she knew that pestering would only annoy him, she took care that her manners and behavior should be so proper that even the countess couldn't fault her, was at pains to seem interested in the discussion, flattered Dr. Collett by laughing and asking questions, and bided her time.

When the cheese and biscuits and fruit had been served and the moment came for her and Lady Agnes to withdraw, leaving the men to drink their port in peace, Uncle George stood up. "It's such a fine night, I think I'll take my pipe in the gardens. Mary Catherine, why don't you walk with me? If you'll excuse us, Agnes, John . . ."

"If you wish." The countess sounded none too gracious as she rose from her chair, and she nearly tripped over one of her spaniels. Molly wondered how much wine she'd drunk. But there wasn't much time to ponder the matter, for the steward opened the doors to the garden at a signal from the duke; he offered her his arm, and they strolled out onto the parterre.

"Mmm!" Molly raised her face to the night sky. "Smell the hawthorn blossoms! We never got them so sweet as this for our stall." Her uncle had stopped beneath an arbor of eglantine; she turned to him questioningly. "Is something wrong?"

He shook his head. "I was only trying to decide whether you look more lovely in sunlight or moonlight."

"Everyone is so full of kind words today." She laughed, knowing it wouldn't be proper to show him how much she was touched. "I shall have to leave my hair down more often!"

"At least for special occasions," he agreed. "Such as . . . your presentation to his majesty."

"Oh, Uncle George!" Propriety forgotten, she threw her arms around his neck. "Do you truly mean it?"

"I don't see why not. You've more than mastered all you need to make your debut at court. I'm very proud of you, Mary Catherine. You do the family honor." He kissed her forehead. She stepped away, suddenly seized by doubt.

"I'm not sure. There's still so much I don't know, so much I haven't learned . . ."

Her uncle laughed. "You've learned more this past year than most young ladies do in a decade of schooling. Believe me, I know."

"But if I do something wrong, make a mistake—I couldn't bear that, couldn't stand to bring disgrace on you."

"You'll find a girl with looks like yours can be forgiven almost any breach of etiquette," the duke said wryly.

"Well . . ." This was, after all, what Molly had worked so hard for. "I suppose, so long as Lady Agnes is there—"

"She won't be," he broke in. "Regrettably, the countess is not welcome at court."

Molly felt as though he'd just told her grass wasn't green. "Why ever not?"

"Because she is my mistress." He smiled at her look of shock. "Come, child, surely you knew."

Molly supposed she had, but that didn't conquer her surprise at hearing him say it. He'd never spoken to her this way before, as though she were grown-up, like woman and man. "I wanted to explain," he went on, "because it is inevitable that you will hear things at court, that folk will bring you gossip. And I do not want you to be at a disadvantage when they do. One must always deal with one's enemies from a position of strength."

"You have no enemies, surely," Molly protested.

"On the contrary, I have at least as many enemies as friends," he told her ruefully. "That is one of the drawbacks of being in Charles's favor. There are always those who envy intimates of the king. At any rate, Agnes has been my mistress since shortly after her husband's death. Some people at court—most notably, Queen Catherine—feel the countess was overhasty in coming to my bed. But the Earl of Shrewsbury was a difficult man to live with—as difficult, though in different ways, as my poor Kate. The queen also blames me for installing Agnes here at Cliveden. Of course, the queen has never met my wife."

"Uncle George." Molly was embarrassed by his disclosures, yet pleased and flattered that he would take her into his confidence. "You need not justify yourself to me. I of all people know how good and kind you are to Lady Katherine, and how little it gains you."

"Thank you, my dear." He smiled again. "You might try to recall that when the wolves come howling at you at St. James's. Remember, a lady—"

"I know. A lady never shows surprise, either by word or action. I won't. Thank you for warning me."

"While we are in this arena of discussion, Mary Catherine—you do know about the birds and bees and flowers, don't you?"

"I am very fond of gardens, in troth, sir."

He burst out laughing at that. "Agnes has taught you well, by Jove! But honestly—"

"Honestly, I didn't spend sixteen years living upstairs from the Campbell girls without learning what goes on between a woman and a man." She didn't mention the encounters she'd been witness to in prison; he'd only be distressed. "Don't worry, Uncle George. I don't intend to make a gift of my virtue to the first good-looking fellow I meet."

"Which, then, the second or third?" Then he turned serious. "Charles's court has a deserved reputation for lax morals, but believe me, nothing is more frowned upon than an unwed pregnancy. And that *would* disgrace this family."

"I would never, ever do anything that would hurt you, Uncle George."

"Young courtiers can be most persuasive. I know; I was once one myself."

"You speak as though you have one foot in the grave," Molly scoffed. "I think if I managed to fend off the guards at the Fleet, I can deal with Sir Tom and Dick and Harry. But tell me, when do we leave?"

"The king is giving a ball on William Shakespeare's birthday. I think that would make a fit occasion for your presentation."

"April twenty-third—Good Lord, Uncle George, that's only one week hence! I've got a million things to do before then; I'd better go get started!" She stood on tiptoe to kiss him. "This is the finest present you could ever give me. You won't be sorry, I swear it!"

As she whirled toward the house, he called her back: "Mary Catherine. There is . . . one thing more."

"Aye?"

"It's about your past. I've spoken of you to the king already, told him you were brought up in a convent in France. That the convent's records were destroyed in a fire some years past, and that I only recently became aware of your existence and brought you here."

Molly was quiet for a moment. Then, "Why did you tell him that?" she asked. "Surely it is more to your credit that you took me in from the Fleet than from some comfortable convent."

"I'm afraid, my dear girl, there are those who would not see it that way. My enemies are always ready to seize upon any excuse to try to ruin me. The fact that my niece is a convicted felon could play right into their hands." He shrugged. "It's unfortunate, but information is power. Your background is information I'd prefer they not have."

"Very well, if you think—"

"I'd very much like it if you were to swear it to me."

Privately Molly thought he was being a bit overdramatic. But, "Of course I will," she told him. "I swear on all that's holy not to tell anyone where I came from. How's that?"

"Excellent," said the duke. "Now you may go in."

Something occurred to Molly. "What if somebody recognizes me, though? One of the men who was on that inquiry board, perhaps?"

"Come here, Mary Catherine," he told her, smiling, taking her hand. In the center of the parterre was a lily pond, its waters black and smooth like glass; he led her there. "Look," he said, pointing down. She stared at her reflection in wonder. Was that really she, Molly Willoughby, that exquisite, shimmering girl?

"I would wager all I have in the world," said her uncle, sounding bemused, "no one will ever connect the Lady Mary Catherine with a flower girl from Smithfield Market. As a matter of fact, I'd stake my life on it. Now, go on, get on with whatever it is you must get on with to be ready."

"Uncle, what frightful syntax!" Molly blew him a kiss as she ran across the paving stones. At her back she heard him murmuring to himself:

"Moonlight. Definitely moonlight," he said.

6

"HIS GRACE THE Duke of Buckingham and the Lady Mary Catherine Villiers!"

Right foot first, Molly reminded herself, stepping forward. Back straight, head up high. Hand curled just so over Uncle George's arm. Let him lead, follow his rhythm *exactly*. Toes out ever so slightly. And step, slide, pause; step, slide pause . . . it was one hundred steps exactly, Uncle George had said, across the great receiving room of St. James's Palace to the dais where the king was waiting. Lady Agnes' caution rang in her head: "Don't look to either side, not if you think you see St. Peter himself in all his glory. *Float*, Mary Catherine, float like a feather on wind! Don't you want to make your uncle proud?" Molly did, devoutly; nothing in the world could have made her turn aside. Step, slide, pause; step, slide, pause . . . All the way across the great blocks of pale green marble, beneath the arching domed ceiling with its portraits of King Charles and whoever his latest mistress might be. Lady Agnes had described the room to a T, and taught Molly a trick, to look up through her lashes and follow the third row of chandeliers with her nose—"That way you'll stay on line no matter whom he has painted up there now," the countess had said with a sniff. Really, thought Molly, when you came right down to it, it seemed rather unfair that Charles should plaster his mistresses all over the ceiling and not let Uncle George even bring his to—

Stop it! she told herself sternly. That's just the sort of thing to get you into trouble; once you let your mind go wandering, you'll never get it back again. And what if you should lose count? Step, slide, pause; step, slide, pause . . . ninety-eight. Ninety-nine. One hundred. And stop, bend at the knee, head all the way down till your nose hits the floor, keep your skirts spread wide, palms down, fingers together, and *freeze!* "Don't you dare even *breathe,"* Lady Agnes had warned in a terrible voice, "until the king holds out his hand!" There it was now, right in front of her chin, and the heavy gold ring of state—"Kiss it," Lady Agnes had told her, "only don't really touch it, or your teeth might clink." Then, and only then, was she allowed to raise her head to his majesty to hear him say:

"Perfection itself!" Uncle George beamed at her from the chair he'd set up as a throne and pulled her to her feet with the hand she'd just kissed—or almost kissed, rather. "Don't you think so, John?"

"I daresay the queen herself couldn't do any better," Dr. Collett agreed from Molly's side, where he'd been standing in for the duke.

"It was truly all right?" Molly asked anxiously, straightening up from her curtsy.

"If it weren't, believe me, I would let you know. First impressions are so critical," said the duke, "and this is, after all, the first impression the court is to have of you. Now, then. It will probably be very loud, remember, with the musicians and all those people, so you will have to attend very closely to hear what his majesty . . . Mary Catherine, are you listening?"

"I'm sorry, Uncle George. It's just that every time I think about the king actually speaking to me, I come over all faint!"

"More red meat in your diet will cure that," Dr. Collett said briskly.

"Really? Aunt May always said borage for courage," Molly told him, her latent interest pricked.

"Mary Catherine." Her uncle was frowning. "Kindly remember your promise to me. What will cure your faint-headedness is realizing that the king is a man the same as any other—a man with the devil's own eye for the ladies, when it comes to that. He'll likely flirt with you."

"If he does, I shall die."

"If he does, you'll flirt back. But not too adroitly, please. The last thing I need is for Charles to decide to make a conquest of you." Molly tried to imagine becoming the king's mistress and failed; it was just too farfetched. "And after that?" he challenged her.

"You and I shall dance."

He nodded. "I've made arrangements with the musicians for a sarabande."

"Oh, Uncle George, no! I've only just learned that one. Why not the pavane?"

"The sarabande sets you off better; it's younger, more sprightly. If you feel you need more practice, I'll send for the lutist."

"George," Dr. Collett said gently, "it's past midnight now. Don't you think we ought to let her get some sleep?" Molly flashed him a grateful smile.

"If she needs practice, she must have it. Tomorrow *is* the most important day of her life."

"All the more reason she should be rested. You've been over every blessed thing fifty times. Let her go to bed!"

The duke beckoned Molly closer, turned her face to the light, searched her eyes. "Perhaps he's right. You do look weary."

"I'll keep going so long as you want me to," she told him gamely.

"You would, too, wouldn't you?" He smiled, kissed her cheek. "You're a good girl. But run along to bed."

"Are you certain?" Molly knew he'd worked as hard for this as she had, didn't want him to think she was shirking.

"Of course I am. You won't disappoint me, I'm sure of that. Good night, my dear. Sweet dreams."

"Good night, Uncle. Good night, Dr. Collett."

"Good night, Mary Catherine. If you think that you'll have trouble sleeping, I could make you a draft—"

"As tired as I am? No, thank you!" She laughed and left them there in the receiving room.

They were staying at Buckingham House, the duke's home in the city, and it took Molly several tries to find her rooms in the unfamiliar maze of passageways. Parker was snoring on her pallet in the antechamber; Molly tiptoed past the maid to her bedroom, seeing no reason to disturb her sleep.

Despite her exhaustion, Molly's mind was racing, filled with reminders and instructions, and as she undressed, she wondered if perhaps she should have taken Dr. Collett up on his offer of a sleeping draft. She'd found, though, that the drugs he made were nothing like Aunt May's gentle decoctions of flowers and herbs; that cup of laudanum he'd given her the night that she arrived at Cliveden had made her groggy for three whole days. Better just to have some warmed hippocras, get into bed, and hope for the best.

The blue moiré gown she would wear on the morrow was in the clothes press, sprinkled with lavender, bergamot, vanilla, and dried rosebuds; Uncle George had chosen the combination himself. He had chosen, too, the character she was to represent, for the king's ball had a theme: in honor of Will Shakespeare's birthday, everyone was to dress as a character from one of his plays. Molly was Juliet Capulet, half of the great bard's pair of star-crossed lovers; the duke had had made a little silver filigree cap set with lapis lazuli stones for her to wear on her head, and she was to leave her hair unbound.

Wouldn't it be marvelous, she thought, pulling on her nightdress, if she were to meet someone tomorrow the way Juliet had met Romeo at her father's ball? That was her favorite scene in all the plays she'd read. Love at first sight . . .

" 'Oh, she doth teach the torches to burn bright,' " she quoted in a whisper, not wanting to wake Parker: " 'It seems she hangs upon the cheek of night/ As a rich jewel in an Ethiop's ear—/ Beauty too rich for use, for earth too dear!' "

Would any man ever feel thus about her? Would she ever feel thus about a man, so wild and passionate that she would sooner die than live without his love?

Molly had never had much leisure for thinking about love when she lived in Smithfield, but she'd made up for that in the past year. Of course, the notion of falling head over heels in love with a handsome young nobleman, a marquess or perhaps even an earl, was far more appealing than being wedded to the likes of Andrew Stiles. Naturally, she'd have to have Uncle George's approval of whomever she married, but after everything he'd done so far to ensure her happiness, she felt sure he'd take care to see her happily wedded.

"His grace the Duke of Buckingham and the Lady Mary Catherine Villiers!"

After all the time spent preparing for that long walk through the receiving room at St. James's Palace, Molly couldn't believe how quickly it passed. It seemed the steward had no sooner called her name than she was kissing his majesty's ring. "God's troth, George, she is a beauty!" someone said, and it was the king, pulling her to her feet and smiling; he looked, she thought, rather like one of Lady Agnes's amiable spaniels, with two great waves of curling dark hair falling over his ears. "How do you do, my dear?"

Molly didn't trip, didn't freeze, didn't choke or cough or pass wind—"Low-pitched voice, Mary Catherine!" "Make a man feel, when he speaks to you, as though he is the only man in the world!"—but simply said, "Very well, thank your majesty."

He had merry blue eyes that crinkled up at the corners when he laughed; he was laughing now. "Well worth the trouble you put your uncle to in finding you, I'd say! How old are you, Lady Mary Catherine?"

"Seventeen, milord."

"Drat, far too young for an old fogy like me."

"I've always found, milord, that a crown makes a man look considerably younger."

"Hah!" He pinched her cheek, delighted. "They bring 'em up right, the French, don't they, George? Not like those gloomy Spaniards or the Portuguese. Aye, give me a Frenchwoman every time." Queen Catherine, who was from Portugal, was sitting right beside him, but didn't seem to be paying him or anybody else any mind. A tall, thin woman whose shallow skin and plain features were ovewhelmed by the jewels she wore, she was crooning over a little dog in her lap. "Tell me truly, what think you of this newfound uncle of yours?" the king demanded.

"I think him the most wonderful man in the world," Molly told him, smiling at the duke—"excepting your majesty, of course."

"And politic too!" Charles laughed again; Molly found it easy to see why he was called the Merry Monarch. "I apprehend, George, that since you have arrived with your usual fashion for lateness, the dancing is set to begin. Perhaps you might lend me your niece for the first round, while you escort the queen?"

"If your majesty please . . ." That was the queen, in queer, heavily accented English. "We do not care to dance this evening. If you will excuse us, we will retire." She stood, still holding to the little dog.

"Certainly," the king said with scarce-concealed pleasure. "Good night." She had barely stepped from the dais before he beckoned to a lovely blond waiting close at hand. "Louise, will you settle for a duke for your escort, while I further my acquaintance with the charming Lady Mary Catherine?"

Louise Keroualle smiled at Molly even as her sharp blue eyes seemed to size her up, judging whether she posed a threat to her position as the king's favorite mistress. Molly curtsied to her, held her gaze. "How could I refuse," the French-born woman said, "when the partner you propose for me is the most wonderful man in the world—excepting your majesty, of course?" Charles chuckled and pinched her.

"These saucy French wenches!" He gave Molly his arm, then signaled to the musicians. "Let the dancing begin!"

Molly was beyond nervousness at the prospect of the sarabande the duke had arranged; she was already dancing on air. She'd glimpsed the startled approval on her uncle's face when the king proposed he squire her. This was an honor beyond what he'd expected; he could not have asked for more. Knowing that she'd pleased him freed her to relax, observe the faces around her as the king paraded her down to the marble floor. Everyone looked curious; some of the women were openly envious, whispering behind their fans.

"I detect the merest flaw in your education, Lady Mary Catherine," Charles said dryly as they took their places at the head of the line. "Didn't those French nuns teach you that the key to holding a man's interest is to make him believe he is the only fellow in the room?"

Chastened, Molly met his bemused gaze, searching for a suitable reply. "Actually, the nuns taught me the Lord Jesus should be the sole man in my life. I was looking to see if perhaps he might be here."

"Hah! No fear of finding him at my court," he said, grinning. "You'd as lief look for the devil! While we are speaking of things holy, I may as well tell you you dance like an angel."

"Can your majesty keep a secret?" He nodded. "It is the first time I have ever danced in public. Were it not for your divine guidance, I should fall on my face."

"That would be a pity; 'tis a lovely face. I can guess that you're the Lady Juliet—Shakespeare had no fairer heroine—but who, pray tell, is your uncle?"

Molly glanced over her shoulder at the duke in his

midnight-blue cloak emblazoned with stars and planets and suns. "Why, Prospero, milord."

"Ah-hah! The great magician." Charles nodded. "In troth, he never seems to lack for tricks up his sleeve. I distinctly recall instructing my musicians to begin this evening's revelry with a stately pavane. And yet we seem to be tripping to a sarabande."

"Were your majesty to delve the matter deeper, you might find my uncle has managed to make a bit of gold appear in your musicians' purses," Molly told him. Charles burst out laughing.

"Well, I don't begrudge George his sleight-of-hand; a rare jewel deserves a perfect setting. And you, Lady Mary Catherine, are a rare jewel indeed."

"Thank you, your majesty. Prithee, whose costume do you wear?"

"A king. Guess which by my leer," he challenged her. Molly giggled so, she nearly missed a turn.

The dance was over before she knew it. Louise Keroualle appeared at Charles's side to reclaim him, and he kissed Molly's hand, gave her a wink and a pinch, and set her back to her uncle with the loud command that they should share another sarabande soon. Uncle George's dark eyes glowed as he reclaimed her; it was all the sign she needed that she had done well.

After that, the night became a blur of pleasure. A constant stream of men both young and old applied to the duke, eager for introductions and dances. Molly made conversation, sipped from the glasses of sparkling wine her suitors scurried to fetch her, and reveled in the sweet taste of her success. Any number of the courtiers were gallant and handsome, and though she did not feel the instant spark of love that she'd been hoping for, she was kept far too busy to bemoan its lack. She was so busy, in fact, that all the wine she'd been drinking caught up to her in a rush, and she had to excuse herself from the company of the persistent young Marquess of Dorset to inquire of her uncle where a privy might be found.

"Not feeling ill, I hope?" he asked anxiously.

"Oh, no. Just full to bursting," she confessed.

"Ah. Come with me." He led her from the noisy, crowded hall into a lengthy empty passageway. "Where are the bloody servants when you need them, anyway?" he wondered aloud, glancing about. "Well, never mind; I could use a respite myself from your incessant admirers! Do any strike your fancy?"

"They have all been very kind," Molly said, blushing.

"That means no. Never fear, my dear, you've only worked your way through half the peerage so far." He stopped before a gilded door. "Here you are. There are doors to the gardens just around that corner. I think I'll wait for you outside."

"You needn't wait; I can find my way back myself."

"What, and run the risk some love-crazed swain might abduct you?" He shook his head, kissed her temple. "Take your time. I imagine you could use a respite too!"

He strode off toward the gardens. Molly turned the crystal knob of the door and paused, hearing a sharp female voice from within:

". . . a *tad* suspicious, Jess, even you must admit! She shows up out of nowhere claiming to be a niece no one has ever heard of, after all these years? If you ask me, 'niece' is nothing but a fiction; she's another of his lovers."

Molly had been about to retreat, since it was perfectly clear the unseen speaker was talking about her, but this calumny of Uncle George raised her hackles. Cheeks flaming, she stalked into the privy and saw two ladies not much older than she sitting before a looking glass. She gave them a long stare, then said icily, "Oh, I beg your pardon; from the gossip I assumed this was the servants' quarters." She turned on her heel, then stopped short as she heard a flutter of laughter.

"*Touché*, Clare, you deserved that. Don't go, please! We're the next best thing to servants—we're family! Say hello to your cousin Mary Catherine, Clare."

Molly spun around. "Cousin?"

"Aye," the smaller of the girls said cheerily. "Clare and Jessica Fairfax. Our grandmother—"

"And mine were sisters. I know."

"You must excuse Clare," Jessica went on. "Her nose is out of joint because she's spent the last fortnight looking forward to seeing the man she's in love with, and now it turns out he's not even here."

"Shut up, Jess," Clare Fairfax snapped. Molly eyed the two of them more closely. They didn't look a bit like sisters. Jessica was blond and soft, with pale eyes and a wide mouth used to laughter; Clare was dark and sharp-edged, with an angular beauty Molly found extraordinary.

"Of course, you're not helping matters one bit by being such a *grand succès*," the unsquelchable Jessica burbled happily. "If you want to please Clare, you shall have to make a stab at tripping, or spill food on your gown."

Molly had never had cousins before, and saw no reason not to make an effort to get off on the right foot with these despite their rocky beginning. "If you want to know the truth, I'm astounded I haven't done both or worse so far."

"Oh, I'm sure," Clare said coolly. "You looked so ill-at-ease making eyes at the king."

"Isn't she splendidly catty?" Jessica asked fondly. "The only one who can take the edge off her tongue is Uncle George. She's scared to death of him; we both are. And, of course . . ." She paused, sighed, rolling her eyes, hand patting her heart. "Anthony Strakhan, the man of her dreams."

"Shut *up*, Jess!" Clare said again, and hurled her fan at her.

"Anthony Strakhan?" Molly echoed. The name seemed familiar.

"His manly gracefulness, the Earl of Ballenrose," Jessica told her. "His impeccable heart-stirring-ness. His imperial passion-ness. His thrilling long-legged, black-haired, blue-eyed, I'd-adore-you-forever-if-you'd-just-notice-me-ness." Her sister came at her, nails bared, and she ducked. "What's wrong, Clare, did I leave something out?"

"You're a shrew, Jess, did you know that? I swear, I am never in my life telling you anything ever again."

"She will, though," Jessica told Molly. "She'll have to. Because she's such a shrew herself that she hasn't any other friends."

Molly laughed. She liked this irrepressible blond; the girl reminded her of Meg Calloway from the Fleet Jail, though Jessica would have been appalled by the comparison if she'd heard it. As for Clare, well, that sort was the same whether she wore silk or sackcloth; *she* reminded Molly of Charity Campbell. She remembered the Earl of Ballenrose now; he'd been the man in prison that she'd thought was a priest, the one with the intriguing eyes. "I'm pleased to meet you both," she said. "I'm *not* Uncle George's lover."

"Ooh, such straight talk! There, Clare, you've had it from the horse's mouth. Can you guess, Mary Catherine, who Clare came as?"

"Kate in *The Taming of the Shrew?*"

Jessica giggled. "No—though that *was* my suggestion. Try again."

Molly considered Clare's low-cut gold dress, the scarabs at her ears and throat. "Of course—Cleopatra!"

"You see, Jess?" Clare preened. "I told you it was a good costume. You're Juliet, I suppose." She shrugged, an elegantly dismissive gesture. "How awfully *ingénue.*"

"Don't pay her any mind; you look lovely," her sister said. "I, of course, am Jessica, the poor put-upon daughter of Shylock." She examined her arm where Clare had clawed her. "Not a pound, Clare, but I'd say you'd got an ounce of flesh."

"I'd love to stay and talk," Molly said truthfully, "but Uncle George is waiting for me. He didn't tell me you'd be here tonight."

"Not surprising," Clare said with a sniff. "We're the black sheep of the family, you know; our mother married a commoner. What has dear Uncle George in mind for you—replacing *la belle Louise* in the king's affections?"

"Hardly. I don't think he has anything particular in mind at all."

Clare let out a most unladylike snort. "Uncle George without a scheme? That would be the day."

"Ignore her," Jessica said, "everyone else does—including Anthony Strakhan, which is what has got her in a dither. Come on, Clare, we don't dare linger; you've made a bad enough impression as 'tis. I'm so glad to have met you, Mary Catherine! Perhaps we'll screw up our courage and call on Uncle George while he's in town."

"I wish you would," said Molly. "Your costume is magnificent, Clare." Experience had taught her it was wiser to have women like her cousin Clare as friends.

"Thank you. Yours is . . . well, what can I say?"

Then again, thought Molly, having an enemy wasn't the end of the world.

"Dear sister, what a truly wretched human being you are," Jessica said, wagging her blond head. "Good-bye, Mary Catherine!"

"Goodbye, Jessica. Goodbye, Clare."

Well, that was certainly interesting, Molly thought as she made her toilette. She hoped they would call at Buckingham House; it would be lovely to have someone her own age to talk to. Clare's catty comments had shaken her confidence just a tad, but when she checked in the long plate mirror, she was reassured. The blue gown was perfection, and despite the dancing, her hair hadn't gotten mussed; it still flowed straight down her back like a sheet of pale gold. Suddenly she realized how long she had kept poor Uncle George waiting in the gardens. He must think I've forgotten him completely, she thought with chagrin, and hurried from the privy to rescue him.

She had no trouble finding the doors to the gardens; two of the king's purple-coated footmen were standing guard there. They snapped to attention when she appeared, and one offered to accompany her, as it wouldn't have been proper for her to go out walking alone. But she assured them her uncle was waiting for her, and they stood back respectfully to let her pass. The one who'd spoken to her had a broad nose and freckles, and Molly found him quite good-looking. How odd, she thought. *A year ago I'd never have aspired so high as to have a palace guard as my beau, and now it is considered beneath me even to have noticed him!*

As she stepped out onto the terrace, a veil of warm spring air wrapped her in its silken folds. She breathed its fragrance, mingled scents of hawthorn blossoms and musky narcissus and sweet intangible lilac. The sky overhead was a quilt of rich black stitched with stars. In the east a great pellucid moon was rising in the bright cresset of the Pleiades. Molly stood transfixed on the terrace, remembering how she'd once watched that same moon rise through the narrow embrasure in the wall of her jail cell, marked the passing of each tedious day by its passage against her little slice of sky. . . .

And now the whole wide universe was laid out for her taking. Impulsively she put her arms out to embrace it, gather it in, and laughed for sheer gladness at the wonder of it all.

A bit of movement on the path below her caught her eye. "Uncle," she cried, "isn't it splendid? The moon and the stars—"

"I'm not your uncle," a low voice spoke out of the shadows, "but I do agree." Molly dropped her arms abruptly to her sides, feeling exceedingly foolish, a hot blush stealing over her cheeks. The tall man on the path below laughed, compounding her confusion. She bundled up her skirts and hurried down the garden stairs.

"I beg your pardon," she murmured as she passed him, not looking up. It was bad enough he'd caught her acting so silly; now she felt compelled to speak to him, offer that apology even though they'd not been introduced—a cardinal sin, according to Lady Agnes. "I thought that you were someone else."

"I rather wish I were." He touched her sleeve as she went by him, very lightly. "Surely we have met before?"

Reluctantly Molly turned back, found herself looking up into the unmistakable eyes of the Earl of Ballenrose. Fear froze her tongue—had he recognized her? Uncle George had promised no one would. Fear and something more, something she had not felt for a long, long time, not since those far-off spring nights when she would hear Aunt May call from the window of Number 10 Gospel Square and run, fast as her bare feet and child's legs would take her, run across Fetters Lane toward cool milk and apples roasted over the fire, run—

Home. That was what she felt as she stood and gazed at him in the moonlight. Home, haven, rest—all were there in the depths of his world-weary eyes.

He shook his head now, faintly, withdrew his hand from her arm to run it back through his hair. "No, I see. I'm sorry. I thought for a moment . . ." Those extraordinary eyes, so far-seeing; little wonder she'd fancied him a priest the first time they met. "Or . . . have we?"

"No," Molly told him; the word came out a breathless whisper. "No, we never have." She had to think of something to say, something to keep him from remembering her. She tore her eyes from his face, saw the plain black doublet he wore, seized on that. "Who are you supposed to be?"

"Supposed to . . ." He followed her gaze, looked down, laughed. "Oh. The ball. I nearly forgot—the fool, I suppose, from *King Lear,* for coming at all. I've been to the Fleet with the inquiry board; I hadn't time to change."

"Is that still going on?" Molly asked, astonished, before she remembered that a lady never showed surprise in either actions or words.

"Aye." He looked as much surprised as she. "You know about it?"

"Well, I'd heard talk, naturally, but a long time ago."

"Aye—it was a three-day wonder last spring." He gave her a smile that was nearly a grimace. "But I thought everyone else had forgotten."

Molly knew the ice beneath her feet was exceedingly thin, but couldn't resist asking: "Have you learned anything?"

"That the warden is a bloody scoundrel. Our progress is especially slow since everyone but myself and Lord FitzGerald dropped off the board. His majesty's interest in the project waned quickly, as it always does, and the other members took their cues from him."

Molly bristled at that, knowing her uncle had only given it up to devote his time to her. "No doubt they found other projects equally worthy of their attention."

'Oh, no doubt," he said dryly. "Such as deciding what to wear to this evening's affair. But it's rather odd someone like you should take an interest in our prisons. Perhaps you know someone incarcerated at the Fleet?"

Molly experienced a moment's panic, until she realized he'd only meant to make a jest. It was high time she left this dangerous conversation and found her uncle. "Cry you mercy, sir, I must be going."

"Wait! You haven't told me who you are."

"Me? Mary Catherine Villiers, the Duke of Buckingham's niece." He raised a brow, as though he didn't believe it, and she rushed on nervously: "A long-lost niece. His sister Frances' daughter. I was brought up in France, in a convent, by nuns. And then my mother was lost in a shipwreck, and a fire burned the convent records, and—"

"I meant," he interrupted bemusedly, "what character from what play?"

"Oh," said Molly. "The . . . the Lady Juliet."

"Really? Do you know the rhyme at the end of the scene where she and Romeo first meet?" He quoted it in his rich deep voice: " 'My only love, sprung from my only hate!/ Too early seen unknown, and known too late!/ Prodigious birth of love it is to me/ That I must love a loathed enemy.' "

She looked at him with wide eyes. "The Earl of Ballenrose, milady, forever at your service." He bowed low over her hand.

"Mary Catherine!" the duke called to her from the doors to the terrace. "Mary Catherine, are you out there?"

" 'I would not for the world they saw thee here,' " Ballenrose quoted again. His mouth brushed her fingertips; he turned and walked deeper into the garden, into the shadows of the hawthorn trees.

"Mary Catherine!"

"Coming!" she called, and hurried toward the palace.

"I waited and waited," her uncle said with feigned crossness, "and then I came back inside and still I couldn't find you. Why is it that women never are where they're supposed to be?" he appealed to the footmen, who laughed. "Supper's being served," he went on. "What were you doing out here?"

"Nothing," said Molly, driven to lie by some impulse she did not understand. "Looking for you."

"Well, now that we have found each other, may we please go eat? I'm starved."

"Forgive me," she apologized. "The gardens were so lovely, I lingered—"

"Moonstruck, were you?"

"A little, I think." The touch of his fingers on her sleeve, his mouth on her hand . . .

"No matter. Do you know, you've made a conquest."

Her head jerked up. "I have?"

"Aye. The king has asked that you sit by him." Her uncle was smiling complacently.

"Oh."

" 'Oh'?" He laughed. " 'Oh'? That's all that you can say?"

Molly squared her shoulders, shook moonlight from the folds of her gown. "I mean, how marvelous! Shall I ask him to make me duchess of something now, do you think, or wait till after we eat?"

"Minx." He smiled at her fondly. "Let's go in."

7

"AND ANOTHER," PARKER said proudly, bearing an armload of full-blown yellow roses into the drawing room of Buckingham House. "Where d'ye want 'em?"

"More?" Molly groaned, looking up from her breakfast. "Good heavens I hardly know." The mantelpiece, the table, the bookshelves, even the top of the spinet were already crowned with bouquets. "Roses! They must have come from Holland; do you know what the brokers charge for them this early in the year?"

"I'm sure I ain't got no idea. There's a card." Parker managed to find it in among the long thorny stems. "Here. Who're these ones from?"

" 'For the fairest rose in the kingdom,' Molly read, " 'Yours ever, Charles Sackett, Earl of Dorset.' "

"Hmph. Not terribly original, is he?" the maid sniffed.

"No, but still it's sweet. I wonder which he was?"

"I like the verse that one wrote ye," Parker said, searching the room for a spare space in which to set the roses.

"What, Lord Ossory? Well, he's Irish, they've an uncommon gift for words. The man that ran the Dog and Feathers, he was Irish, and oh, the drivel he'd spin out! He could have charmed the sun from the sky." Molly smiled, remembering Bart Connor and his apron, always soaked in ale.

"Mind yer tongue, miss," Parker said as she always did when Molly spoke of her old life. "If yer uncle catches—There's the bloody door again. Hold these." She thrust the roses at Molly and hurried off to answer the bell.

Molly laughed when she trotted back a moment later empty-handed. "What, no flowers?"

"Not this time." Parker took back the roses and handed her mistress a card.

" 'The Misses Clare and Jessica Fairfax,' " Molly read. "Oh, good! Is it all right to receive them without Uncle here?" The duke had gone out early that morning to breakfast at a coffeehouse.

"Don't see why ye'd want t'. That Lady Clare, she's the biggest harpy in London."

"I know; I met her at the palace last night. But her sister seemed ever so nice. Have Thompkins show them in, Parker, and then bring us some cakes and tea."

"Ye've only just finished breakfast," the maid pointed out.

"Aye, and I'm hungry still. I was too full of nerves last night to touch my supper, what with sitting next to the king."

"Hmph. Don't blame me when ye gets fat," said Parker, and marched out again with the breakfast tray.

"My Lord!" Jessica Fairfax said breathlessly a moment later as the butler announced her and her sister to Molly. "Look at all your flowers!"

"Rather like a funeral," Clare said, sinking languidly into a chair. "Your man said we missed Uncle. What a dreadful pity."

"Aye, he's gone out to gather the morning gossip," Molly said, laughing.

"More than likely it's all about you!" Jessica sniffed a huge bunch of fleurs-de-lis appreciatively, then noticed the card. "Do you mind?"

"Oh—that one's particularly treacly . . ."

"Then I *must* read it!" Blue eyes dancing, she unfolded the note. " 'Lady Juliet, I stand ready to lay down my life for you. Your doting Romeo, James Scott, Duke of Monmouth.' Why, I think that's sweet!''

"He's married," Clare said blandly, *"and* fat."

"Don't mind her; she's just jealous," her sister told Molly. "All she got were some droopy old monkshood from a knight."

"It happens I like monkshood; they make a lovely poison. And Robert Porret stands a good chance of being made Earl of Crecy when his tedious old uncle dies."

"Try not to sound too eager for the poor soul to drop off, dearest Clare." Jessica winked at Molly, then continued on her rounds, examining the flowers. "Viscount Melbourne, Dorset, Philip de Beers, the Duke of Chester—even Lord Ossory; what a nice poem he's written! Why, only the king himself is missing."

"M'lady." As if on cue, Parker appeared in the doorway with a bundle of huge nodding peonies. "The fellow wot brought 'em had on the royal livery."

"Sure enough, there's Charles's seal!" Jessica clapped with delight.

"I can't abide peonies; they're so vulgar," Clare drawled. "Is there any chance of getting tea?"

Parker shot her a dangerous look. "Would you bring some, Parker?" Molly asked mildly.

"It'd be here already," the little maid said, " 'cept I been too busy, wot with all yer flowers."

"If a maid talked back like that to me, I'd sack her," Clare announced, examining her long fingernails.

"Clare never gets the chance to sack a maid; they always give notice first," Jessica said dryly. Parker snorted, then hurried away.

"What a peculiar little creature," Clare observed, looking after her. "You really ought to make her stay upstairs."

"Oh, Clare, do make an effort to find something pleasant to say," her sister chastised her. "Here is Mary Catherine on the morning after her grand success, with flowers from every eligible man in the kingdom—and a few who aren't—and—"

"Not from Ballenrose," Clare interrupted.

Jessica stuck out her tongue at her. "Only because he wasn't there. Anyway, the last thing she needs in the world is to catch Anthony Strakhan's eye."

"Why do you say that?" Molly asked, curious.

"Because he's mine," Clare said as Parker brought in tea. "Haven't you any cream cakes? I can't stand those wretched Banbury tarts."

Molly saw Parker's outraged look, shook her head in warning. "Would you go ask Cook, Parker, please? And make sure you thank her for the splendid tray."

"Cream and sugar, please," Jessica said, taking a seat beside Molly. "I *love* Banbury tarts. Anyway, Clare, you had better not let Uncle George find out you've set your cap for Anthony Strakhan either."

"Uncle George be damned," Clare said, to Molly's shock. "No sugar for me."

"Would Uncle George care?" she asked, handing them their cups.

"He'd have apoplexy. They can't stand each other." Clare frowned at her tea. "I see you like it weak."

"I'll pour it back," Molly offered, and did. "Do you know why?"

"Why they don't like each other?" Jessica shrugged prettily. "I suppose Uncle thinks him an upstart."

"Uncle George is only the second duke when it comes to that," Clare pointed out. "The Strakhans were earls under the Edwards; they just lost the title when the Tudors came in."

"Whatever for?" asked Molly.

"Refusing the oath of allegiance to Henry the Eighth. The fifth earl was executed, I think." Clare waved away the plate of cream cakes Parker proffered. "I'm not hungry after all."

"I'll have one, thank you kindly," Jessica said. Molly wondered briefly how she liked always having to make up for her sister's rudeness. "It seems the Ballenrose line had an affinity for lost causes. The title wasn't revived until Charles bestowed the earldom on Anthony a few years ago in recognition of his efforts to restore the monarchy. I've heard he fought with Charles's forces against Cromwell at Dunbar and Worcester when he was just a boy; he couldn't have been more than twelve or thirteen."

"What is he like?" Molly asked.

"That's right, you haven't met him. Let's see. Brave, noble, kind." Jessica ticked off on her fingers. "Intelligent, polite—that's why Clare likes him; opposites attract. Dashing, stalwart—"

"Virile," Clare put in.

"As if you knew," her sister sniffed.

"I intend to find out."

"Oh, honestly, Clare. To hear you talk, one would think you'd bedded all the bachelors at court."

"How do you know I haven't?"

"Because I never let you out of my sight, for fear you'll open your big mouth at the wrong moment and get us both banned from court."

Clare's sloe eyes were narrowed. "I'm not so stupid as you think me, little sister."

"I don't think you're stupid at all, Clare. If you were, you wouldn't worry me so."

They glared at each other, while Molly nibbled a tart, bemused by their bickering. Then Jessica said, "At any rate, I needn't fret about your offending Uncle George by taking up with Ballenrose, so long as he stays away from the palace as he did last night. Lady Tavistock says he has got a mistress, you know, in some hovel in the city. An actress, like the king's moll."

Molly had heard of Charles's affair with the famed Nell Gwyn, a commoner from Drury Lane. "Do you suppose he does?"

Jessica laughed, shaking her head. "Not a bit. He told me once he doesn't even care for the theater."

"He has better taste, anyway," said Clare, pursing her

exquisite mouth, "than to take up with a whore from the gutter."

"Just because she's from the gutter," Molly said, "doesn't mean she's a whore."

Jessica choked on her tea. "If Nell Gwyn's not a whore, then I don't know who is!"

"Why would the king take up with her, then?" Molly asked, puzzled.

Jessica shrugged. "Men like a bit o' rough, as our nurse used to say, on the side. No one looks askance. It's not as though they marry such women. Now, that *would* cause a fuss!"

Clare's dark gaze skewered Molly. "You surprise me, cousin dear. I should think you'd know all about whores, having passed so much time in the company of the Countess of Shrewsbury."

"Clare," Jessica warned.

Molly silently thanked Uncle George for preparing her for that. "The Lady Agnes has been very kind to me. Frankly, I find it unfair that she's unwelcome at court for the same sin that finds Louise Keroualle seated beside the king."

"Madame de Keroualle never instigated the murder of her own husband—"

"Clare! You're quite right, Mary Catherine, it isn't—"

"Or went herself to the duel in which he died."

"Shut up, Clare; you know perfectly well that is only a vicious rumor." Jessica glared at her. Molly was saying to herself, over and over: A lady never shows surprise in either words or actions. . . .

Making sure her hand was steady, she reached for Clare's cup. "I think you'll find this strong enough now. I must say, knowing the countess as I do, I find it impossible to credit such a rumor."

"Well, it's no rumor, is it, that Uncle George shot her husband dead and then moved her into his house?"

"Clare," said her sister, "hadn't you better remember whose house *you're* in right now?"

"I think that would be wise."

All three girls spun round to face the doorway at the sound of the male voice. "Uncle George." Molly stood and curtsied, just a beat ahead of her cousins. "We were having some tea; will you join us?"

"Thank you, no. How are you, Jessica?"

"W-well, thank you, Uncle George," she said rather uncertainly.

"And you, Clare?"

Molly had to admire her cousin's brazenness; she gave the duke a blazing smile that, oddly enough, pointed up a family resemblance Molly hadn't noticed before. "Absolutely splendid; how kind of you to ask. We took the liberty of coming to call on the newest addition to the Villiers clan."

"So I see. You've gotten in the habit of taking liberties, Clare; you did so with the truth just now. I only wounded the Earl of Shrewsbury in our duel; he died of a gangrene. Your flowers are lovely, Mary Catherine. Jessica, I was just at Simpson's coffeehouse and Lord Wallingford was remarking how attractively you danced last evening. I must say I agree. Do give my regards to your mother. Good day, ladies."

"Good day, Uncle George," the sisters chorused. He turned and went out; Molly heard the tapping of his boot-heels as he mounted the stairs.

"Holy Jesu, Clare!" Jessica collapsed into her chair, white-faced and shaken. "One of these days you'll get your right comeuppance, mark my words!"

"Don't be such a simpleton, Jess. Uncle George is a man of the world; he knows what's said about him."

"But to repeat such gossip under his own roof—"

"What difference does that make? What do you think men do when they sit about in coffeehouses all morning? They gossip, that's what." Clare sat with a fluff of her skirts; if she'd been shaken at all by the duke's chilly reception, Molly couldn't see it. "You'll notice he didn't dispute the basic facts of the matter. And if he hadn't been carrying on with Lady Agnes, the earl wouldn't have challenged him.''

"When he explained the *facts* to me,'' Molly said pointedly, "he said they didn't become lovers until after the earl's death.''

"Well, if you believe that, you're as simple as Jess.'' Clare bit into a tart with perfect sangfroid. Molly looked down at her hands. Of course, he also hadn't mentioned the duel . . .

"M'lady.'' Parker stood in the doorway. "There's been another deliv'ry.''

"Lilies of the valley!'' Jessica cried, clearly as glad as Molly for the interruption. "My absolute favorite; they're ever so much nicer than those great huge bundles of irises or roses.''

"And so much less costly,'' said Clare. "Who are they from, somebody's footman?''

"They smell heavenly,'' Jessica went on, ignoring her sister as the maid brought her mistress the small neat bouquet. Molly opened the card. "Well? Who's your latest admirer?''

Molly stared at it for a moment, felt a little hitch in her heartbeat. "I don't know . . .''

"Don't know?''

"He didn't sign his name.''

"Anonymous flowers? How quaint. What did he write?'' Clare leaned over, snatched the card from Molly's hand, read it. "Hmph,'' she sniffed. "I'll say.''

"Here, let me see.'' Jessica scanned the note and looked up at Molly. "Who in the world—''

"I can't imagine,'' said Molly, taking back the card, folding it in fourths and slipping it surreptitiously into the sleeve of her gown.

"Your poor fool,'' it read.

8

"THE MOST REMARKABLE thing," Jessica Fairfax told Molly as Madame LaFarge, her mouth filled with pins, adjusted the waistline of her gown, "is that you seem so unaffected by it all. Why, if suitors were flocking to my sister the way they flock to you, she'd be unbearable!" She paused. "Of course, she already is." Madame LaFarge choked, spraying a small cascade of pins onto the carpet. "Are you all right, Madame?" Jessica asked anxiously.

"Oui, oui. Ce n'est rien," said the seamstress, gathering them up again.

Molly laughed; she could guess why Madame had coughed up the pins, having just witnessed her attempting to make the final fitting of a gown Clare had ordered. "If you ask me, the most remarkable thing is why they bother. There's nothing particularly interesting about me."

"Oh, but there is! You're different."

"Different how?" Molly asked cautiously. Jessica screwed up her nose, looking for a way to explain.

"You're very . . . well, exotic. Maybe it's because you were brought up in France." Madame LaFarge nodded knowingly. "But it can't be that," Jessica went on, "because so was Louise Keroualle."

"She's certainly exotic!" Molly said, picturing King Charles's flamboyant mistress.

"Puante," Madame LaFarge sniffed, making a face.

"I don't think she really stinks," Jessica said charitably, "it's just that scent she wears. You're exotic in a different way. A nice way."

"Well, thank you very much," said Molly, "though I'm not at all sure what you mean."

"That may be part of it. Madame Keroualle is so full of herself, just like Clare." The seamstress rolled her eyes, pinning up a sleeve. "But you don't even seem to realize the effect you have on men."

"Could we please talk about something more interesting?" asked Molly, feeling embarrassed.

"You see?" Jessica smiled fondly. "That's just what I mean. I think that's perfect, Madame LaFarge. Don't you, Mary Catherine?"

"Absolutely," Molly agreed, admiring the sleeve's elegant drape.

"And could you possibly have it ready by Saturday?" Jessica asked the seamstress. "I did want to wear it for the king's treasure hunt."

"*Ça depend,*" Madame LaFarge said darkly.

"On what?"

"On your sister."

"Oh, Madame. You should know by now she doesn't mean those things she says about your work."

"Then why does she say them?" The seamstress pouted.

"I only wish I knew. But believe me, that new dress you made for her is breathtaking; you needn't change a stitch."

"*Vraiment?*" the woman asked dubiously.

"*Vraiment,*" Jessica assured her. Then, as the seamstress beamed and bustled away, she added in a low voice to Molly, "What's the point of changing it when Clare won't be satisfied anyway? Undo these hooks, would you, please?"

Molly did as she was bidden, wondering again, as she had so often in the month since her return to London, how God could have made any two sisters so different from

each other. Clare had put on a terrible scene when she saw
the gown Madame LaFarge had been sewing for her, called
the poor woman frightful names, and threatened not to
pay before she flounced out in a fury. As usual, it was left
to Jessica to soothe the seamstress's ruffled feathers and
apologize. "How do you do it, Jess?" Molly had asked
her the week before, after witnessing another such tantrum
at the milliner's. "How ever do you put up with her?"

"Well, she's my sister," Jessica said. "Besides, I think
she must be dreadfully unhappy, to be such a shrew. I
shouldn't like to be Clare. Would you?" Molly wouldn't,
of course, though it didn't seem fair that Jessica should
have to spend her life apologizing for her sister.

"Speaking of the treasure hunt," Jessica said now, putting on her day gown, "whom are you hoping you'll draw
as your partner?"

"It doesn't much matter whom I hope for, does it? There
aren't any guarantees."

"No, but I'll wager if you asked Uncle George for
someone in particular, he'd arrange it."

"Uncle George," said Molly, examining a bolt of Brussels lace, "has more important matters on his mind than
games. Besides, how could he arrange it? He isn't God,
you know."

"No, he just thinks he is." Molly threw a pincushion
at her, and Jessica ducked. "It was only a jest! I am hoping for Harry Wallingford, which of course means that I
won't get him. With my luck, Clare will, and he'll be so
put off by her he'll never want to even look at a Fairfax
girl again!" Molly laughed, and Jessica eyed her curiously. "Tell the truth, pet. There must be one among your
dozens of swains that you prefer to the others."

"They are all very nice."

"*Nice?*" Jessica squealed. "By the by, did you ever find
out which one sent you those lilies of the valley, with that
peculiar note?"

Blue eyes aglow with moonlight . . . *The fool from* King

Lear, *I suppose, for coming at all.* . . . "No, I never did," Molly said.

"Aren't you mad with curiosity?" Jessica demanded.

"If I am, what good can it do? He'll make himself known, I suppose, in time." She hadn't seen the Earl of Ballenrose since that night in the gardens, wouldn't know what to say to him if she did. Molly wished she knew why he was at odds with her uncle, but couldn't think of whom to ask except the duke himself. And she was oddly reluctant to do that.

"A secret admirer." Jessica sighed. "It is just too romantic, I swear."

Just then Clare marched back into the shop. "Aren't you two done yet? I've had that damned carriage go round the square till I'm dizzy!"

"We're just coming now," her sister told her, snatching up her gloves. "Good day, Madame LaFarge. Thank you kindly!"

"Why in God's name would you thank the old hag? Her designs are absolutely ruinous." Clare led the way out to the street. "Move aside, slut!" she commanded a beggar woman who approached them, thin hand outstretched.

"A ha'penny, in the name o' God," the woman whimpered, "just a ha'penny. It's my babe, she's sickly—"

"You shouldn't ought to have had a child if you can't care for it properly," Clare said cuttingly. Molly looked at the beggar woman and felt a shock of recognition. Those wan, hollow eyes, that matted hair and pasty skin—it might have been any of the neighbor women from Gospel Square. It might have been her, once upon a time. . . .

"Where is your baby?" she asked the woman.

Hope flickered in the empty eyes. "Home wi' my husband. He were workin' down at St. Katherine's docks till a bale fell 'n' crushed his leg; he can't walk now."

"Oh, honestly. What a fairy tale," Clare snapped.

" 'Tis God's troth," the woman cried. "I wouldn't beg unless I hadn't got no choice!"

"Hush," Molly told her, taking her hand, "we believe you."

"Jesu, you touched her!" Clare cried.

"Shut up, Clare!" Molly said with such fury that the girl did. She looked at the beggar woman again. "What's ailing your baby?"

"I don't rightly know. She's gone off her suck, 'n' got all hot 'n' feverish, 'n' she jest cries 'n' cries no matter wot I try."

"How old is she?"

"Six months, thereabouts."

"Is she teething?"

"That's the first thing I thought o'. But I can't feel nothin'. If she was teethin', wouldn't I feel somewhat there?"

"Not necessarily. Not in the beginning, anyway. Is she chewing on things—her hands, her blankets?"

"Aye."

"And drooling?"

"Ooh, my Lord, aye, buckets 'n' buckets of it!" she said, nodding eagerly.

"Most likely it's just the teeth coming in," Molly said soothingly. "You can give her valerian steeped in water; that'll take down the fever. But not too much, mind you— just a pinch to a cup. Soak a rag in that and let her chew on it. And licorice root is good too. Here, get yourself to the herb seller." She gave her a five-shilling piece from her purse. "And mind you keep up your strength, or your milk will suffer. You should eat some marrow bone, that's good for nursing, and take chamomile and lady's mantle broth. Will you do that?"

The woman clutched the coin. "Aye, I will, I swear't."

"If the fever doesn't go down in two days, or if you can't feel the teeth coming through by then, take her with you to the herb seller and see what she says." Molly dug in her purse again. "Here's more money, just in case."

"God bless ye, luv!" The woman grabbed Molly's hand and kissed it.

"'There's no need for that. Good luck to you; now, on your way!'" Molly waved as the woman hurried off, then stepped toward the waiting coach. "Aren't you coming?" she asked, turning back for Jessica and Clare. They were staring at her, mouths open, like two boggled fish.

Jessica found her tongue first. "Valerian? Licorice root? Where in heaven's name did you ever learn such stuff?"

Too late Molly realized how peculiar the encounter must have seemed to them. "One of the nuns at the convent taught me," she said. "Sister . . . Sister May."

"Strange name for a Frenchwoman," Clare observed, her dark eyes narrowed.

"She wasn't French. She was Belgian, I think," Molly told her, even as she thought: There you go, Molly Flowers, violating the first rule of lying—always keep it simple. What do you know about Belgians?

"Well, I never," Jessica said, still in shock.

"No, nor I. Do you make it a habit of throwing your money away like that?" Clare asked.

"I wasn't throwing it away. She was in trouble."

"In trouble? Hah. More likely she's in some tavern treating her scurvy friends to ale and laughing at you for a fool."

"I doubt if she is, but so what?" Molly asked, temper flaring. "What you spend on one gown at Madame La-Farge's would buy her family bread for a year. Is it any wonder that the poor take solace in drink when their lives are so grim?"

"How would you know what their lives are like, St. Mary Catherine?" Clare sneered.

"I've got eyes, haven't I? You'd have to be blind not to see the way the poor live in London—crowded together into ramshackle houses, nowhere to wash clothes or bathe or even have just a moment's peace to oneself, always in fear of plague and disease or, God forbid, another Great Fire, and the cost of everything going up and up . . ." Molly paused for breath and saw that now even the coach-man was staring at her in amazement. "It just doesn't seem fair to me sometimes," she finished lamely, "that some folk have got so much and others nothing at all."

"Their lot can't be so dreadful as that," Jessica said, frowning. "After all, there's the church to look after them, and the charitable groups. I know Father gives ten pounds every Christmas to St. Gilbert's hospice for the needy. Do you think I ought to ask him to give more, Mary Catherine?"

"Oh, for God's sake, Jess." Clare rolled her eyes. "Don't be such a sap. Father could give them everything he's got and it would still be a drop in the bucket, so what is the point? The poor are poor because they're loathsome and lazy, and all the money in the world can't change that." Infuriated, Molly opened her mouth to make a sharp retort, but Jessica saw her expression and hastily intervened:

"They're not all lazy, Clare; some just have hard luck, like that woman. You know, Mary Catherine, you ought to talk to Anthony Strakhan if you are interested in the needy. Father says he gives speeches in Parliament all the time about ways to alleviate their plight."

"Father also says he's a damned bloody nuisance," Clare put in tartly.

"Really. I can't imagine, then, why someone like you would find him so appealing," Molly told her, her voice very cool.

"Perhaps because I'd like to find out why he gives those speeches. What's in it for him?"

"Oh, Clare, you are such a cynic," her sister sighed.

"Not a cynic. A realist," Clare corrected her. "I've found it to be true that we take a greater interest in those causes that affect us personally. Who knows? Perhaps the Strakhan family really was impoverished before the king revived the Ballenrose title and made Anthony earl."

"They cannot have been *too* poor," Jessica said, giggling, "or he'd be lazy and loathsome. And you don't find him loathsome, do you, Clare?"

"No," her sister said, and Molly felt the dark heat of

her gaze. "I don't find him loathsome at all. I think it would be wise, Mary Catherine, if you found someone besides Anthony to talk to regarding your concern for the needy."

"And what if I don't?" Molly asked stubbornly.

"Then I might have to turn my attention to the question of why *you're* so interested in the subject. And you might not like that." Clare gave her gloved hand to the coachman so that he could help her into the waiting carriage. "Shall we go?"

"Uncle George," Molly said that night at supper, "Clare Fairfax suspects."

They were alone together in the cavernous dining hall of Buckingham House: he looked at her along the great length of the table. "Suspects what, my dear?"

"That I'm not . . . from a convent in France."

The Duke of Buckingham sliced asparagus spears. "Have you let slip anything that might make her doubt you?"

"No . . ."

He smiled at her. "You don't sound entirely certain."

"Well . . . I don't think I did." She explained to him what had happened on the street outside Madame La-Farge's. "Was I wrong to help the woman, Uncle George, to give her the money?"

He didn't answer for a moment, while he sniffed the champagne sauce bathing the asparagus and then tasted it appreciatively. "Of course you weren't wrong," he said at last. "A bit naive, perhaps. There are charities that look after the poor, you know."

"That's what Jessica said. But I knew plenty of folk back on Gospel Square who were in dire straits, and no charities ever came round to help them."

"They should have sought out help. I never have understood why the poor stand so on pride."

"Perhaps because it's the only thing they have enough of," Molly said wryly.

"Mm. There's too much wine in this sauce again, don't you think?"

"I haven't tried it." Molly did. "It tastes fine to me. Anyway, there was just something about the way Clare looked at me . . ." She frowned, pushing asparagus about her plate. "I don't think she likes me much, Uncle George."

"Little wonder, my dear. Your reappearance meant the end to her hopes of a sizable inheritance. Had I not found you, she, as my first cousin's eldest child, would have been my heir."

"Oh!" Molly pondered that. "I had no idea."

"I wouldn't fret about your cousin Clare," the duke went on calmly. "Perhaps I'll have a chat with her, though."

Molly knew she shouldn't say what she said next, but curiosity got the better of her, and she couldn't resist. "She has got a crush on the Earl of Ballenrose, you know."

"Ballenrose and Clare?" He lifted an eyebrow. "There's an intriguing pair."

Molly tasted disappointment. She'd expected more of a reaction, perhaps even a clue as to why her uncle and the earl were estranged. She pressed on, gingerly:

"I wish you wouldn't mention that I told you. She has the notion that you wouldn't approve—that you dislike him."

"So I do. But a match with Clare Fairfax is something I would only wish on an enemy."

Molly giggled. "You are terrible, Uncle George. But why do you dislike him?"

"Actually, it is more that he dislikes me. He bears a grudge against me for something that happened years and years ago."

"Really?" Molly asked with careful casualness. "What was that?"

"He thinks I jilted his sister."

"Jilted his sister?" Of all things, she had not expected

that. "Good heavens, that hardly seems worth carrying a grudge for!"

"I couldn't agree with you more. Are you finished with your asparagus?" Molly nodded, and he rang for the butler to bring in the veal.

"Well, did you jilt her?"

Her uncle waited until Thompkins had left the room again. "I dislike discussing personal matters in front of the servants, Mary Catherine; you know that."

"Sorry," she mumbled, kicking herself for violating that rule. She was surprised when he went on to answer:

"So far as I was concerned, there was never any question of marriage between us. But she was very young, and very silly, and she took the politeness I showed her as something more. It was one of those unfortunate situations that ofttimes arise when a girl comes to court without proper training. I hope you won't be so foolish as to mistake gallantry for love with your bevy of swains, the way . . ." He paused, laughed. "Do you know, I can't think of her name now, that's how long ago it all was. Well, the way that she did."

Molly assured him she wouldn't, even as her heartbeat quickened. If the source of antagonism between Anthony Strakhan and her uncle were so trivial as that, it surely wasn't insurmountable, given patience and time. "You wouldn't really object, then, to a match between him and Clare? Or him and Jessica, for that matter?"

"Oh, but I would," he said with unexpected vehemence. "Don't get the wrong idea. Our original quarrel may have been petty, but Ballenrose has blown it all out of proportion over the years. He thwarts me at every opportunity, does his damnedest to undermine my standing with the king—why, just the other day Lord Phipps asked his signature on a bill we proposed that would lower the inheritance taxes, and Ballenrose refused him simply because my name was on it too! He's a vicious, unprincipled scoundrel who has carried on his private vendetta against me for years, and I can't for the life of me understand how

any sensible girl could be fooled by his so-called charms."
He stabbed the roast of veal, then looked up again. "Don't
tell me Jessica shares her sister's infatuation. I always
thought more of her than that."

"No," Molly said faintly. "No, she has set her cap for
Lord Wallingford, I think."

"Harry Wallingford, eh?" The duke nodded approval.
"There's a sensible chap—fine family, good prospects,
solid head on his shoulders. Just the sort of fellow I hope
you'll settle down with someday. Of course, you'll want
to aim a bit higher than a viscount." He sliced the roast,
his good humor restored. "I'll have to see what I can do
about throwing the two of them together. And while we're
on the subject, Mary Catherine, what about you? Any of
your adoring admirers that you've singled out yet?"

"Not really," she said. "But I'm not in any hurry."

"Hah! Enjoying playing queen bee, are you?"

"I suppose I am."

"Quite so," said the duke, and winked, passing her a
generous portion of veal.

9

"QUIET, EVERYONE!" SAID King Charles the Second of England, clapping his hands together. "We would like silence, please!" The din of chatter in the receiving room of St. James's Palace subsided to a low buzz. Clare Fairfax, standing in the midst of a cluster of the more disreputable courtiers, let out a loud laugh, and the king frowned in her direction. "If we might have your attention, Lady Clare, we are ready to begin."

"Forgive me, your majesty." Clare dropped him a curtsy, affording all around her a glance into the bodice of her gown, which even by court standards was shockingly low. On the other side of the room, Jessica nibbled her lip.

"I do wish she'd try to be a little more discreet," she whispered to Molly. "Some of those men she's with have dreadful reputations."

"You're not your sister's keeper," Molly whispered back. "No one thinks that her behavior reflects on you."

"That isn't why I care, Mary Catherine. I just don't want to see her hurt."

Molly smiled at her. "I wish I had a sister like you."

"And I wish I had one like *you*," Jessica said feelingly. "Well, here we go!" The king had beckoned to two footmen bearing porcelain jars. "Cross your fingers for me.

I'd cross mine for you if you'd tell me whom you want for your partner. Or perhaps you don't believe in luck."

Molly ran her hands over her deep blue taffeta gown, felt the sapphires hanging at her throat and ears, saw Uncle George smile at her across the heads of the crowd. "I believe in luck, Jessica. More than you'll ever know." Her friend looked at her questioningly, hearing the conviction in her voice. But just then the king put his hand into one of the jars, drawing out the first name. "Lady Deborah Estin," he announced, grinning with anticipation, "and . . ." From the other jar he pulled another slip of paper. "Lord Montgomery!" Those present applauded as the couple made their way toward the dais, where the king presented them with a rolled-up scroll containing the first clue.

"Poor Debs," Jessica whispered as Lord Montgomery claimed his escort. "He must be sixty if he's a day."

"At least he has plenty of experience at treasure-hunting," Molly said wryly. "I won't have the least idea what to do."

"You just figure out the place that's meant in the riddle, go there, and get the next scroll. Clare is very clever at it," Jessica said, then added, "Speak of the devil," as the king announced her sister's name.

"And Lord Buckingham!" Charles went on.

"Well! That certainly proves the teams aren't fixed," Jessica noted, laughing at Clare's badly concealed disappointment. Molly, watching Uncle George offer Clare his arm, wasn't so sure, remembering his plan to "have a little chat" with her. They took their scroll from the king, then left the chamber to claim one of the dozens of coaches lined up outside.

"Lady Camilla Atterby," King Charles read from another slip. "And Lord Kenton." A hum of comment ran through the room.

"Oh, dear," Jessica murmured.

"What is it?" Molly asked.

"They were betrothed to each other last year, but she broke off the engagement."

"Really! What would I do without you, Jess, to give me the gossip?" Camilla Atterby was pleading with the king to have her partner changed. "But if I do it for you," Charles told her crossly, much annoyed at the interruption, "I should have to do it for everyone who asks, and the game would be ruined!"

"But—"

"What's the matter, Camilla, dear?" Lord Kenton asked, grinning. "Afraid that riding alone in a carriage with me might prove too much to resist?"

"Certainly not!" she snapped.

"Well, then, shall we?" He held out his arm. She hesitated, looking to the king for mercy, but he was unmoving. Giving Lord Kenton a look that spoke daggers, she flounced toward the doors.

"Let's get on with it," Charles muttered, "and no more damned protests; one plays by the rules or else one doesn't play. Lady Jessica Fairfax!"

"Please, God," Jessica breathed. Molly went to squeeze her friend's hand and found she'd crossed *all* her fingers. "And Lord Weatherfield!"

"Oh, Jess. I'm so sorry—"

Jessica shook Molly's sympathy off with a shrug. "At least he is young! And anyway, he's a good friend of Wallingford's; I shall bend his poor ear all night asking questions about him!" She headed for the dais, smiling so graciously at gangly Lord Weatherfield that he never could have guessed he wasn't the partner she'd been wishing for. Molly hoped she would prove so good an actress when her own turn came.

The king went on calling out pairs of names—"Lady Margaret Maddox and Lord Spenser! Lady Joan Bennett and Lord Ossory!" Molly felt a twinge of regret at seeing the handsome Irish lord who'd sent her a poem with his flowers go away with someone else; she wouldn't have minded being matched with him for the evening. The crowd was thinning out considerably; of those left, only Malcolm Rhys and Robert Westcott, Viscount Sutherton, were really what one would call eligible bachelors. On the other hand, Molly thought, as Sutherton was matched with Caroline Monteiff, an older fellow like Lord Montgomery wouldn't be so bad; they could discuss something interesting, like the French alliance, and she wouldn't have to listen to a lot of drivel about how lovely she was. Not to mention she'd be less likely to have to ward off improprieties; she didn't relish the notion of spending hours alone in a coach with, say, Alan Lennox, whom Jessica had told her was nicknamed the Squid—

· "Lady Mary Catherine Villiers!" announced the king, pausing to smile at her before he drew a paper from the other jar. "And Lord Ballenrose!"

"Lord Ballen—" In the midst of smiling back at the king, Molly stopped dead. Why, she hadn't even seen him there! But here he was, striding toward the dais, turning to look at her. It was odd, she thought, meeting his gaze, but each time she saw him, he seemed to grow more handsome. She'd not noticed before that his hair was so splendidly thick and curling, or the line of his mouth so fine and strong. He wasn't good-looking in the way Uncle George was, but he had a presence, a quiet intensity that made him stand out in a crowd.

Good Lord, Uncle George! Halfway to the dais, Molly hesitated. He would have a fit if she went on the treasure hunt with Anthony Strakhan; it was just the other night he'd called the man a vicious scoundrel. But she didn't dare annoy Charles by asking to have her partner changed.

One of the Countess of Shrewsbury's adages popped into her head: *In an untenable situation, a lady always faints.* The floor *would* be marble, Molly thought, starting into a swoon. Just as she bent her knees, Ballenrose caught her eye again. He knows what I am doing, she realized, and the shock of having him read her thoughts brought her upright again.

"Lady Mary Catherine! Is something wrong?" King

Charles asked anxiously, having seen her near-stumble. She shook her head, tongue-tied, still staring at the Earl of Ballenrose.

"If the Lady Mary Catherine is unwell . . ." he began stiffly. Molly's cheeks flushed with shame. She had no quarrel with him; was she really required to perpetuate her uncle's, and embarrass Ballenrose in front of the king?

"I'm quite all right," she said quickly, making her decision. She could always plead a headache once they got to the coach, spare him any public humiliation. Hadn't he tried to spare her that once, back in prison, when he argued for her dignity against Dr. Collett? "It's these insufferable shoes, if you must know." She raised her skirts a fraction to show the new Italian slippers she wore. "Human toes were never meant to conform to such a shape; now I know why the Roman Empire collapsed."

King Charles laughed. "Perhaps the legions really did march on their stomachs!"

Ballenrose held out his arm. "Permit me to lend my support to the cause."

Charles gave them the scroll with their clue. "Best of luck!" He was already reaching into the jar for another name. Molly slipped her hand through Ballenrose's arm and let him lead her out to the corridor.

He stopped beneath one of the sconces lining the wall. "There is nothing more annoying than ill-fitting shoes, is there? I have the same problem all the time, as my feet are so big." Molly glanced down and saw that they were. So were his hands, big and broad, the long fingers capped with nails bitten down to the quick. "Not that I meant to imply that *your* feet . . . Oh, Christ."

Molly smiled. The sight of those ragged nails had touched her inside; Lady Agnes had had a dreadful time curing her of the same habit. "That's all right. It wasn't really my feet bothering me anyway."

"No. I know." Looking into his kind, priestly eyes, Molly was glad she'd confessed. "Perhaps it would be best all around if I just saw you home."

"Yes. I think it would be."

They went out to the drive. The footman handed Molly into a coach. "Buckingham House," Ballenrose told the driver, then climbed in, taking the seat across from her. They heard the driver whistle to his team, and then they started away.

He's really being very decent, Molly decided, and then told him so. "My quarrel's not with you," he said, mirroring her earlier thought so exactly that she felt a little chill ripple along her spine. "I'm only sorry to have spoiled your evening for you. Rather rotten luck, wasn't it, our being stuck together? Not that I mean . . . Oh, Christ, have I managed to offend you again?"

"Not at all. I don't believe I've had the chance to thank you yet for those flowers you sent me. They were very lovely."

"I shouldn't have sent them," he said, sounding glum. "But they were just coming up around the springhouse at home, and when I saw them I just . . . I don't know. They made me think of you. I hope I didn't get you in trouble."

"Oh, no. I just told everyone I didn't know who had sent them. My cousin Jessica was all abuzz about my secret admirer."

"She's a charming girl, Jessica Fairfax. Really very nice. Hard to believe, isn't it, that—" He stopped.

"That she and Clare are sisters? I know; I've thought the same thing myself a hundred times. Why not say it?"

"Having already insulted your feet and your company, I thought it might be wise to leave the subject of your family alone."

"I only wish we could," Molly told him truthfully. He was so easy to be with, to talk to now that they'd got started, like a comfortable old friend. For a change she didn't feel she had to sparkle with wit, throw out clever allusions to politics or art or literature. "I am sorry for what my uncle did to your sister."

He looked at her in the dim light of the coach lamps, and his eyes were so filled with sadness that she bit her tongue. But then he said, "Do you know, he's never even said that himself—never even said he was sorry." And she was glad she'd spoken up as she did.

"He has been so very kind to me," she said thoughtfully, "it is hard to believe he would ever be unkind to another. At least, not purposely." The Earl of Ballenrose said nothing to that, and they rode for a time in silence along the esplanade that ran beside the Thames. Molly could see the white sails of the great ships at St. Katherine's docks in the distance, pricked out by moonlight like the wings of sea gulls against the dark sky. When Ballenrose spoke again, she gave a little start, so peaceful had the interlude been.

"I often wonder," he began, "what a man like your uncle would have become had he been born a peasant. That is, how much of his personality has been shaped by the fact that he has always had power and money, and how much was bred in the bone."

Molly blinked. "Why, Uncle George could never have been born a peasant! He is too intelligent—"

"Rubbish," Ballenrose interrupted. "The aristocracy hasn't got any monopoly on brains. Look at Shakespeare, for God's sake, or Geoffrey Chaucer. Or Luther, or Cromwell—"

"Surely you are not an admirer of Cromwell!" Molly protested, remembering that Jessica had told her the earl had fought against the Roundheads.

"No more than I'm an admirer of your uncle. But that doesn't keep me from recognizing their shrewd intelligence—or their dangerousness."

"Uncle George is hardly dangerous," Molly scoffed.

"Like the height of Ben More, that depends on where one stands. Oh, the problem isn't just your uncle, though he's certainly a prime example of the warped class structure in this country, which makes a man's worth dependent on who his father might have been."

"Now, just a moment!" said Molly. "You're a member of the aristocracy."

"So I am—and ofttimes to my rue."

"I don't understand," she told him crossly. "If you're against Cromwell and against the aristocracy, what are you *for?*"

"I'm not sure," he admitted "Something that hasn't evolved yet. Something altogether new."

Molly was intrigued. None of the young men she knew at court talked like this to her; they spoke of frivolous things: fashion, dances, plays. Ballenrose sounded more like one of her old neighbors bellied up to the bar at the Dog and Feathers, griping about class structure and the bloody aristocracy. But, "If you are so concerned about the peasants," she asked, "why don't you give them all your money?"

He grinned. "Do you know, I figured out once what would happen if I did. It came out to tuppence a person for everyone in England. About enough for a week's worth of bread."

"A week's worth of bread is something."

"Aye, but not enough. Give a man a fish, and you have fed him his dinner. But teach him to fish, and you have fed him for life. I think it's more important to hold on to my money, try to use it to bring about change in the laws that keep the poor oppressed."

"Rather an uphill battle," Molly observed, thinking of the judge who'd sentenced her to the Fleet.

"Most battles worth fighting are." The carriage rolled to a stop; Molly glanced from the window and saw that they'd arrived at Buckingham House. "Well," said the Earl of Ballenrose, "I must add boring you to the list of my offenses tonight."

"You haven't bored me at all," she told him as the footman unlatched the door. "On the contrary, I've never known the ride from court to pass so quickly."

He laughed. "You have exquisite manners, Lady Mary Catherine Villiers."

"I mean it," she insisted. "I hope that we will talk again someday."

"So do I." The footman was waiting to help her down from the coach. Ballenrose bent over her hand, kissed her glove. "Good night, milady."

How, Molly wondered, might his mouth taste kissing hers? "Good night, milord." Their eyes locked for a moment, and she saw, she *knew* with absolute certainty, that he was wondering the same. The realization took her breath away; when the coachman handed her down to the drive, she had to stand there and try to recover herself. As she did, the front doors opened and the butler, Thompkins, came out, grinning broadly.

"Lady Mary Catherine! Congratulations," he declared, hurrying toward her. "Ye're the first one here!"

"I'm what?"

"There ye are." He gave her a small scroll tied with a ribbon. "Go on, be on yer way now, while ye've got a good head start."

"My lands, the treasure hunt; I'd forgotten all about it. Do you mean to tell me the first clue . . ." Molly turned back to the coach. "Let's see that scroll the king gave us." Ballenrose had already unwrapped it; he was laughing as he handed it over. Molly held it up to the coach lamp and read the verse inscribed there:

> The second clue waits to be thine
> Where dwells the wild, unruly swine.

"Unruly swine?" she echoed blankly.

Ballenrose nodded, scarcely able to speak for laughing. "Aye," he gasped at last, "that's it—the bucking ham!"

"Oh, dear Lord." Molly laughed with the earl, who doubled over and came perilously close to falling out of the carriage.

"D'ye mean to say ye didn't even read the clue?" Thompkins asked incredulously. Molly shook her head. "Well, I'd call that a right bit of luck!"

"Or a sign from heaven," Ballenrose said. "Do your feet still ache, Lady Mary Catherine?"

"No, only my sides. No one else has gotten it yet, Thompkins?"

"Didn't I say ye're the first?"

Molly looked at her partner. "It does seem a shame to quit now, doesn't it?"

"Aye, who knows what we might accomplish if we actually look at the clues?"

"Let's just have a peek at this next one." Molly opened the scroll; Ballenrose leaned from the coach, reading over her shoulder:

> The third clue's clasped by wings divine
> Where Over made his wife a shrine.

"Well, that's that," said Molly, "I can't make head nor tail of this one. Who on earth is Over?"

"Donne," said Ballenrose.

"Aye, quite so. Well, at least we had a brave beginning."

"No, no, John Donne, the poet," the earl explained, laughing again. "Have you never read his poems to his wife?" Molly shook her head. "They're remarkable works. 'She is all states, and all princes, I,' " he quoted. " 'Nothing else is.' Those are my favorite two lines in all of literature, I think."

"I've never heard of him."

"It's not the sort of stuff they teach in French convents, I would imagine," he remarked, grinning.

"Is it . . . salacious?"

" 'Full nakedness! All joys are due to thee,/ As souls unbodied, bodies unclothed must be,/ To taste whole joys.' "

"He wrote that to his *wife?*" Molly asked, blushing.

"He most certainly did."

"And did he build her a shrine?"

"Only in words. He was dean of St. Paul's; I'll bet the clue leads there."

"A man of God who wrote lewd poems to his wife."
Molly shook her head, laughing in disbelief.

"She bore him twelve children."

"Will wonders never cease?"

"Are ye goin' or stayin', Lady Mary Catherine?"
Thompkins asked in puzzlement.

Molly and the Earl of Ballenrose looked at each other.
Moonlight silvered the cobblestone drive, threw gilt at her
hair. He leaned from the carriage door, holding out his
hand, his priest's eyes bright with challenge. Molly caught
hold of his wrist, and he swung her up onto the seat beside
him; the footman bundled her skirts in after her and
slammed shut the door.

"To St. Paul's," he told the driver, and they rumbled
off into the night. He had not let go of her hand; through
the glove she wore, Molly felt his fingers tighten, entwin-
ing with hers. She was acutely aware of him suddenly; he
alerted all her senses. She could feel the leather of his boot
where his calf touched her skirts, see the sparse black
hairs on the back of his hand, smell his scent, the clean
scent of germander.

"We . . . we really shouldn't, you know," she said nervously. "Go on with the game, I mean. Uncle George
would skin me alive if he knew."

"That would be a pity," Ballenrose said, "for you've
such lovely skin." Molly exhaled her tight-held breath. So
long as he dealt her compliments like that, like any ordi-
nary courtier trying to flatter her, she could hold her own.
"I should like to see you naked in moonlight," he went
on, and she heard her own gasp, felt her heart stand still
at this leap beyond the limits of propriety. "With your hair
unbound . . ." He let go her hand, but only to find the
silver fillet that held her braids and pull it free. "I think I
will propose a law," he said, his voice low as he pulled
out the plaits with his fingers, "that prohibits you from
putting up your hair."

Molly fought for control, fought against the tide of wild
longing his touch, his words threatened to unleash. God's

blood, she scarcely knew him, had exchanged no more than a few dozen words with him in her life. Why should he evoke in her these feelings no other man ever had?

"Do you believe in fate?" he asked, and she stared at him, awed once more by the way he seemed to read her thoughts. He did not wait for her to answer, but went on in that same dreamy tone: "I never did, I had no reason to. Not until that night I saw you standing in the palace gardens, with your hair falling around you like a cloak of fire. . . . I saw you and I knew, was absolutely certain, that I had seen you before. If it wasn't in this life, well, then, it had to be in another. Perhaps we were Antony and Cleopatra once, or Héloise and Abélard. Or just some nameless, unsung couple—a shepherd and his wife, or an old crofter and his missus whiling out their days, sitting before the hearth with their dog and beer. But the sensation was so strong, so utterly convincing. Surely you felt it."

Molly didn't know what to say. He was quite right, of course; he had seen her in another life, as Molly Flowers, inmate of the Fleet. But that was a secret he of all men must never know. For God's sake, Molly, she told herself, he is your uncle's sworn enemy! Why should that seem so unimportant now, with his hands tangled in her hair?

He was waiting, watching her; the coach was a cocoon of quiet surrounded by the rattle of the wheels and the clop of the horses' hooves. Molly found in that moment that she did believe in fate; what else could account for her sudden conviction that whatever she said next would be as important as anything else she ever said for as long as she lived? She opened her mouth to deny it all—fate, feelings, foreboding—and instead heard herself say, "Aye. I felt it too."

The carriage stopped. "St. Paul's Cathedral," the footman said, throwing open the door. Molly's hands flew to her disheveled hair to braid it up again.

"Don't," the Earl of Ballenrose said, pulling them away. She left it loose; he followed her from the coach and gave her his arm, and together they entered through the arched bronze doors.

Candles flickered on the distant altar. Out of the shadows of the pillar-lined nave, a figure hurried toward them: a small man in vestments, with long tapering hands. "Here so soon?" he asked, sounding surprised.

"I understand," the earl said dryly, "time is of the essence."

"So it is, so it is. If the dean finds out about this, my goose is cooked." The priest smiled at Molly, then glanced into the darkness behind them. "Where are your witnesses?"

"What witnesses?" asked Molly.

The priest wrung his long hands. "Oh, dear me, I thought I'd made it quite clear; there can't be a wedding without witnesses."

"We haven't come for a wedding," Ballenrose said, just as a young man burst through the doors behind them.

"Father Drayton?" he cried.

"Oh, dear me," the priest said again. "This must be the bridegroom. But then who are you?" He blinked at Molly and the earl.

"We're on the king's treasure hunt," Ballenrose told him.

"Dear God, is that tonight? I could have sworn it wasn't till the twenty-first."

"This *is* the twenty-first," said Molly.

"You *are* Father Drayton, aren't you?" the young man asked anxiously.

"Oh, yes. That I am. I'm dreadfully sorry," the priest told the earl, "but you see, this fellow has a secret wedding planned—"

"It won't *be* a secret, will it," the bridegroom said crossly, "if you go telling perfect strangers about it?"

"No, quite so," said the priest. "It's just that you two had a look about you . . ."

"Well, we just came for the clue," Molly explained.

"The clue. The clue. Where in blazes did I put those scrolls?" The priest looked about him helplessly.

"What's this about a treasure hunt?" the bridegroom demanded.

"From the court," said Molly. "There are clues hidden all over London, and one leads here."

"Good God, do you mean to tell me there'll be more of you traipsing in?" The poor man looked aghast. "Father Drayton, I thought I explained in my letter! If Miranda's father catches wind of what we're up to—"

"Yes, yes. Family difficulties, you know," the priest told the earl, whose broad shoulders were quaking with suppressed laughter. Carriage wheels rumbled outside. "That will be the bride, I suppose. Or maybe not."

"I've got to hide," said the groom, ducking under a pew. "Here, what are these?" He came up with a load of beribboned scrolls in each hand.

"There they are!" Father Drayton cried triumphantly. "And here *you* are . . ." He presented óne to Molly just as a girl about her age came running into the church.

"Edward?" she called.

"Miranda!" The groom popped up again.

"Best of luck to you both," the earl said politely, grabbing Molly's free hand. "Good-bye!"

Somehow they managed to contain themselves until they got outside. Then they erupted in laughter, laughed until tears streamed down their cheeks, and Molly had to sit on the steps. "Did you ever?" she gasped.

" 'Edward!' " he mimicked.

" 'Miranda!' " Molly wiped her eyes with her glove. Their laughter subsided, then bubbled up once more. "I wonder who they are."

"Perhaps you'd like to stay for the wedding?"

Another carriage rolled up Ludgate Hill. "Witnesses!" Molly and Ballenrose cried in unison, diving for their coach and scrambling in. "Let's go!" the earl shouted.

"Where?" the driver demanded.

"I don't know," Ballenrose admitted. "Hold on."

Molly untied the scroll, and they huddled over it together, still breathless with laughter. "Jesu, what an extraordinary night!"

"Extraordinary," Molly agreed. "Let's see where this clue leads." She looked down at the page, reading aloud:

"Hasten and find the third clue as you go
Where no ships sail, but there's a sea of woe."

All her good humor vanished; she felt the palms of her hands turn clammy inside her gloves. She did not help him with the answer.

" 'Where no ships sail,' " Ballenrose murmured. " 'A sea of woe'? 'Hasten' . . . hasty. Swift? 'Ships'—wait. *Fleet*. 'Fleet' as in 'hasty,' 'fleet' as in 'ships.' Good God." He looked up from the paper. "It's the prison. The Fleet."

10

"I DON'T SEE why you say that," Molly said after a pause.

"It's a *double entendre,* just like 'unruly swine,' " Ballenrose pointed out.

"It can't be. It must be something else," she told him, willing desperately for it to be so.

She saw him smile sadly. "I know how you feel. Hard to believe, isn't it, that even King Charles would build his sport upon the unfortunate creatures imprisoned there." Then the line of his fine mouth hardened. "More than likely your uncle put him up to this, to throw it in my teeth that the inquiry board has had so little success."

"My uncle had nothing to do with it!" Molly said hotly.

"How can you be so sure?"

Of course Molly could not tell him that Uncle George never would hurt her by sending her back to the place where she'd spent those months of miserable captivity for the sake of a game. And especially not if he'd known there was any chance she'd be the partner of Ballenrose or anyone else who'd been on the board and might put two and two together, seeing her at the jail.

The earl was waiting for her answer. "Because he's not that sort of man," she said with a spark of temper. "You are wrong about him. He is not the monster that you make him out to be."

Ballenrose said nothing for a long moment. Molly felt

as though each second of silence added stones to a wall sprung up between them, made it higher and higher. If he doesn't speak soon, she thought, I shall not be able to see him any longer over its edge. . . .

"My opinion of your uncle," he said at last, "has nothing to do with my opinion of you, Lady Mary Catherine." The stone wall came tumbling down, crumbled into dust. Molly had the distinct impression that that simple sentence of reconciliation had cost him a great deal. She wanted to offer him something in return.

"I wish," she said wistfully, "that you could come to know him and admire him as I do."

"Shall I tell you what I do admire?" She nodded. "Someone who puts loyalty to the family above all things." He raised his hand, and gently, like soft wind ruffling foxglove flowers, he touched her cheek.

"M'lord? Where to, m'lord?" called the driver.

"I'll take you home," Ballenrose said, pulling back his hand.

"Wait!" Molly did not want the night to end yet. "On to the Fleet," she told the driver, and when the earl looked at her questioningly, she smiled. "I say we win the prize, and then use the money to hire a solicitor to help some of the women at the prison win their freedom. That way King Charles's game will have done them good."

"What a brilliant idea! But what makes you say a solicitor? If they're already in prison, I should think what they need are the sorts of things the charities provide them—meals and blankets and clothes."

Molly shook her head, holding to the armrest as the coach careened around a bend. "Most of that sort of relief never even reaches the prisoners—it's likely taken by the guards and sold, or doled out in return for favors. But a solicitor who makes regular inquiries about a prisoner's case keeps him or her alive, I think. What those poor men and women fear most is that they'll be forgotten. That there isn't anyone who cares whether they live or die." She'd been remembering how much Tom Peabody's nightly visits to her window had meant to her, speaking as much to herself as to Ballenrose. Not until she saw him staring at her did she realize how peculiar her air of certainty must sound. "At least," she added in a hasty attempt to cover her tracks, "that's what my uncle believes."

"A very sensible approach," he said thoughtfully. "Perhaps I have misjudged him." Molly's heart gave a leap of gladness—before she remembered that the idea hadn't come from her uncle at all. Well, what did it matter, really? Ballenrose *had* misjudged Uncle George, and whatever worked to rectify that was cause to rejoice. "It's rather unusual to find a girl of your age and station who gives a hang about anything other than parties and fashion," he said, still eyeing her curiously.

Molly felt his arm encircle her shoulders, steadying her as the coach rattled around another corner. Her head was light again, blood pounding at her temples; his long fingers moved across her shoulder, brushed her breast. Even through the layers of fabric of her cloak and gown, Molly could feel her flesh tightening to his touch. His hand lingered, stroked again, more forcefully, and he bent his head to put his mouth to hers just as the coach came again to a stop.

"Fleet Prison," the driver announced.

Ballenrose laughed, his lips just brushing hers. "His majesty has mapped the course out carefully. There is just enough pause between clues so as to preserve a lady's virtue," he said ruefully.

Molly didn't answer. Beyond his head she'd glimpsed the tall iron gate of the prison, and at the sight, all the exquisite fluttering sensations he'd aroused in her had abruptly fled. A thick welt of numbed despair rose up and engulfed her; she'd forgotten just how much she dreaded this place.

He'd sensed the change in her as she sagged against him. "Lady Mary Catherine?"

"Oh, God, get me away from here . . ." Images of the past were all she could see: abusive guards, prisoners huddled in dark corners, the smell of soiled straw, sour gruel, Warden Fell's nasty, brutish eyes. Somewhere a dog was barking; she saw Hugh Stalker staring down at her as though he'd eat her alive. . . .

A man was running toward them from the gate. "On the king's game, are ye?" he called, and when the driver said aye, he thrust a scroll at Ballenrose through the window. "First ones by, ye is." The earl was occupied with Molly; disappointed in his hopes for a tip, the man muttered a curse and spat at one of the wheels.

"Hey! Who in hell d'ye think ye are?" cried the footman, taking umbrage. "This is his majesty's carriage!"

"Is it? Well, give this to his majesty," said the gateman, with an obscene gesture.

"By Christ, I'll teach ye to respect yer betters!" the footman announced, leaping down to the drive.

"Ye 'n' who else?" The gateman sneered.

"How 'bout him 'n' me?" the driver suggested, just as the earl, his arm supporting Molly, tossed a coin toward the gateman.

"Get back on the damned coach," he told the footman, "and get us out of here."

"We was just waitin' for ye to say where," the driver grumbled.

"Anywhere, I don't care. Down by the river, where there's some air." Pulling out his handkerchief, he pressed it to Molly's forehead. "Damn Charles anyway; doesn't he know this part of the city's filled with evil vapors? It's no place for ladies." Molly felt like laughing at that; the neighborhood was certainly no worse than Gospel Square. Her faint-headedness had cured itself, anyway, the moment that the Fleet was no longer in sight.

"I'm sorry," she apologized. "I don't know what came over me. I've always hated women who go faint; they seem so silly and weak."

"Really? I always thought it was part of feminine education that you all learn along with showing peeks of stocking and plying a fan." Molly laughed, infinitely relieved that he showed no sign of connecting her with the prison. "All things considered, though," he added, "I suppose I really ought to see you home."

"I suppose," Molly said reluctantly. The night had been so strange, disjointed and magical. Who knew, given the rift between him and her uncle, when, if ever, she might be alone with him again?

Through her glove she felt the pressure of his hand as it wrapped around hers. "I'll console myself," he said softly, "by imagining what that kiss might have been like had it not been interrupted."

"You have the benefit of experience in that, milord Ballenrose," said Molly, her voice equally soft, "for, having never been kissed before, I can imagine no such thing."

"Never kissed before?" Plainly he didn't believe her. "Come, come, Lady Mary Catherine. I've seen the suitors flock around you."

"But you haven't seen them kiss me," she said tartly. "I was taught that if you let a man kiss you, it should mean something."

"Ah. Those wise French nuns." Molly wondered what he might think if she told him it hadn't been nuns at all, but a flower woman living in a hovel not a mile away. "What, pray tell, did it mean, then, that you paid me the honor of being the first?"

That you make me feel things no one else ever has, Molly longed to tell him. That I do not want this night to end. . . . But the Countess of Shrewsbury's lesson sang in her head: "A lady never seems overeager, either at table or in love." "That I think we should at least look at the next clue," was all she said.

He laughed, untying the scroll. "Very well. Let's see what it says." He rapped for the coach to stop, and together they leaned over the parchment in the light of the lamp, reading the verse written there:

The fourth clue's hid close by the turning water,
Where all who enter leave a little shorter.

"They are getting harder," Ballenrose observed.

"That isn't hard," Molly scoffed. "It's the Traitor's Gate at the Tower of London. Don't you know the old rhyme about Anne Boleyn coming out of the Tower shorter by a head?" But of course he wouldn't; it was a jingle she'd sung on the streets as a girl, while she skipped rope with her friends.

"Are you sure?"

"Quite sure."

"Do you want to go on?"

"Yes," Molly said, "I do."

He smiled, and his hand curled around hers again. "To the Tower," he told the driver, and they were on their way.

This time they didn't say much. Molly was busy wondering if she'd been too forward, and then, as the wheels turned round and he scarcely spoke, much less made a move to kiss her again, if perhaps she hadn't been forward enough. That kiss *had* been splendid, she thought longingly as he made some remark about the weather while they came through St. James's Park. Or at least, she'd thought so; perhaps he hadn't. Perhaps she hadn't done what she was supposed to. Lady Agnes' lessons had never gone so far as kissing. Had she kept her lips parted or closed? She couldn't even remember, it had all gone by so fast.

"Don't you agree, Lady Mary Catherine?"

"I beg your pardon?" Molly asked blankly.

"I said, don't you think it looks like rain?"

"Oh. I don't know; perhaps it does." God, Molly, what a twit you sound, she thought, furious with herself. Is it any surprise he doesn't want to kiss you? Stop daydreaming and pay attention to what he says!

"You're probably wondering," said the earl, "why I haven't tried to kiss you again."

"I wasn't doing any such thing!" Molly burst out, and knew that he knew she lied.

"I only mention it because I feared you might think I didn't enjoy it. When the truth is that I enjoyed it all too much.'' Her green gaze slanted toward him. "You see, milady, I've been thinking too. And as I see it, I can spend the rest of this evening doing one of two things.'' He turned to look through the window, while Molly waited breathlessly.

"I could take advantage of your youth and inexperience to seduce you,'' he said then, so bluntly that she yanked her hand away from his. "I won't say I'm not tempted. And I've little doubt I'd succeed. For a first kiss, that showed considerable promise. You're a beautiful girl, Mary Catherine, on the verge of becoming an even more beautiful woman.'' He turned back to her then, smoothed her loose hair away from her face. "To the depths of my soul, I envy the man who will bring out the woman in you.''

"But it won't be you,'' Molly whispered.

He shook his head. "I'll take the second choice: fight like the devil to pretend that first kiss never happened, and play the fond older brother squiring you on a game.''

"Why?'' Molly cried. "What about all those things you said, about fate and knowing me in another lifetime?''

"The judicious explanation for me to give you would be to say that I lied,'' he noted ruefully. "But I didn't. God help me, they were all true. I'm thirty-three years old, Mary Catherine Villiers, and I swear I've never in my life wanted anyone the way I want you.''

This conversation had progressed far past the boundaries Lady Agnes had detailed for Molly; she was on her own, and she felt hurt and confused. "I don't understand. Then why . . .''

"We're Romeo and Juliet all over again, don't you see? Star-crossed lovers from two feuding houses—''

"If you mean because of your sister, that was years and years ago!''

"Aye, but it lives inside me, eats away at me every day. The cards are stacked against us; it's some vicious trick that God has played on us, our being thrust together this way. There's no way it could end happily. So I think it better that it end right here.''

Molly sat, hands folded in her lap, all the magical promise of the evening dissolving into dust around her, and heard herself say in a voice uncannily like Lady Agnes's, ''You're quite right, of course. It's the only way.''

''And you do understand it's not because I don't find you . . . attractive.''

''Lord Ballenrose, I'm not quite the child you have made me out to be,'' Molly told him, and even managed a laugh, just as the driver announced:

''Here we are!''

Outside the window the pale spires of the Tower rose into the sky like some fairy-tale castle. The footman opened the coach door and drew down the steps. Ballenrose descended and turned to help Molly, put his hands on her waist and swung her into the air. Just as he set her on the ground, a spattering of raindrops fell, dusting her face and hair. He brushed them away with his fingertips; she saw that his priest's eyes were solemn beneath the lowering clouds.

''The tide's high,'' he said. ''I'll need to take a boat to the Traitor's Gate. Why don't you wait here?''

''That's all right. I'll come too,'' she said, not quite ready to relinquish the night. He hesitated as though he was going to argue, then shrugged and beckoned to a boatman. If nothing else, thought Molly, he will have to put his arms around me again when he helps me in. . . .

But he left that to the boatman, a gruff, burly fellow who knew nothing about the bloody king's game and plainly didn't want to; he just settled the price with the earl, got Molly seated in the bow, and poled out from shore. The Thames was running fast, swollen by spring rains; Molly held tight to the seat rings. She never had liked boats, didn't care for the way they were apt to shift or spin about without any warning. Ballenrose looked perfectly at ease with the rising wind ruffling his black hair. He would have made a good sailor, Molly thought with regret; once upon a time, I might have met him at the docks fetching tulips from Holland. He'd have whistled and winked, and then he might have wedded me, with no talk of fate or feuds or what wasn't meant to be. It was the first time since she'd ridden away with her uncle from the Fleet more than a year before that she'd wished for her old life back again.

"Hallo!" cried a red-suited guard at the gate, swinging a beckoning lantern. "On the king's game, are ye?"

"Aye," the earl called back.

"Good show! Ye're the first ones here!" And he held up a scroll. "Come 'n' get it!"

"Wot the devil does he think I'm tryin' to do, then?" the boatman grumbled, fighting the pull of the tide to reach the narrow stone landing. "Give us a hand here; put out yer hook!" The guard obliged, setting down the lantern and scroll and thrusting his own long iron-tipped pole out over the water. It caught, not the barge, but the back of Molly's cloak; she felt a tug and gasped:

"Jesu!"

Then she went flying over the side.

The water was so cold it shocked her dumb and still; she didn't flail, just floated with her hair and skirts spread out around her, billowing like sails—until they soaked up water and began to drag her down. Spinning in slow circles, she saw the guard, his broad face moon-pale with fear, and then the burly boatman shouting curses. The Earl of Ballenrose stood in the skiff, tearing off his cloak and shoes. He dived in after her, cutting through the roiling water cleanly, parting the waves in long, swift strokes. Molly bobbed around again and saw the guard—he was screaming now—and the boatman, and the trees on the shore, and, far above her, one ivory pinnacle of the Tower soaring upward. As the waves closed around her head, she saw nothing at all.

Under the water everything was calm and slow; no one was shouting. Molly went on spinning downward, a steady stream of bubbles floating past her head. Isn't it odd, she thought, that Uncle George believed I'd drowned all those years ago, and now I shall? Even odder was that it was taking such a damnably long time. Perhaps I ought to put up more of a fight, she thought guiltily, and made a stab at moving her arms and legs. But the drag of her clothes made that impossible. It was good plush velvet, Madame LaFarge, that you used in this cape, Molly thought, and giggled: Uncle George got his money's worth from—

Oh! Something had lunged at her out of the darkness, wrapped itself around her, clinging barnacle-tight. I can't breathe, Molly thought, constricted by its grasp, and then giggled again, realizing that she couldn't anyway. She pictured a giant squid she'd seen once for sale at the fishmonger's stall, the rows of little round cups on its long tentacles, and began to shiver. Or it might be an eel . . .

But it was Ballenrose, she saw as he heaved her up above water. "Hold on," he told her tersely. Lungs aching, she gasped in air; that was as much as she could do. Seeing her start to sink again, he caught the edges of her cloak in his hands, tore it from her, sent it spinning toward the sea. His priest's eyes were desperate now; he flung his arm across her chest, pulling her close against him, and began to claw his way toward shore.

"Damn him—damn him—damn him," he was grunting with each ragged stroke. Molly's heart was pounding so hard that every part of her hurt—teeth, eyelids, even her hair. "Damn him—damn him," Ballenrose went on cursing, and each curse brought them that much closer to the riverbank. She felt a shudder as his feet touched bottom, and another as, standing at last, he lifted her in his arms and carried her from the water, then collapsed beside her on the rain-soaked grass.

"Oh, God," he said. "Are you living? Are you breathing?" Molly nodded, coughing out river water, lying on her side. "Then I am going back to kill that bloody guard." He pushed himself to his elbows.

"Don't," she said, pulling him back. "Don't go. I'm so glad . . . you can swim."

He laughed then, falling against her, his head at her crooked arm. "So am I."

Beyond his shoulders the lights of the Tower seemed a million miles away. "Look how far we've come," Molly marveled.

"Aye, look how far," he echoed. She could feel his breath against her skin, just where the bodice of her gown dipped between her breasts.

"You saved my life."

On the riverbank, in the darkness, rain falling around them, he put his hand to her face. She laid her small hand against his, trembling with cold and the aftermath of fear and a longing so violent and deep it made the Thames seem a placid millstream. "Even Romeo learned," he whispered, "that you can't defy the stars." His mouth touched hers, gently, gently, and then, all caution abandoned, he fell on her, kissed her as though he would drown in her and die wrapped in her arms.

"Christ," she heard him murmur as he held her close. "So soft, so sweet . . ." His mouth tasted of rainwater and crushed green grass. "Oh, my heart, my love . . ." His body pressed tight to hers; through her soaked clothes Molly could feel the crush of his thighs and a hardness between them as he moved atop her, as he kissed her eyes and throat and hair.

He touched his tongue to her lips, pushed between them, and their mouths merged in a delicious mix of warmth and wetness and hunger. Molly shivered and sighed, returning the pleasure to him with her tongue, and heard him groan, his breath coming faster. His hand found her breast, pushed beneath the layers of sodden satin and linen to cup its weight, and she gasped in startled ecstasy at the way that simple movement turned her blood to fire. Then he slid downward, following his hand with his mouth, lips closing on the taut bud of her nipple, pulling and teasing until she had to push him away, panting, maddened by the pain of desire.

"No more," she begged.

"Much more," he promised, hands hot at her bodice, tongue tickling her ear.

"No," Molly pleaded, more to the passion surging through her than to him.

"Yes, Mary Catherine. Yes." He pulled her gown from her shoulders, buried his face against her pale wet skin. She felt him claw at her skirts, fighting through the layers of her petticoats until he found her stockings, sliding his hand upward until he touched the soft whiteness of her thigh. "Oh," he groaned, pulling her toward him, holding her so that his manhood pressed against her, so that she felt the pulse of his blood through the coarse linen of his breeches. "Oh, God, I never meant for this to happen. God, I can't help myself . . ."

"I know," she whispered, stroking his cheek, kissing his mouth. "It's all right. I know." He fumbled for the buckle of his belt, lost it, found it again, all the time returning her kiss; they were wrapped in a tangle of wet skirts and petticoats and her long wild hair. He struggled to his knees, arched over her, his mouth at her breast. Then he tore at her skirts, raised them to her waist. She put her hands on his shoulders, searched the darkness for his face, for his penitent priest's eyes.

"My name is Anthony," he murmured, pulling at her drawers. "I want to hear you say it." She did, and shuddered with anticipation as he lowered himself onto her, as she felt his weight and the pressure of his long, hard thighs on hers.

"There they are!"

Lanterns, round glaring yellow eyes, bobbed on the water. "Mary Catherine!" Her uncle's voice, echoed by Clare.

"Jesu help me," Molly whispered, going rigid with shock. The Earl of Ballenrose yanked her skirts over her legs just as the searchers' barge scraped shore.

"Mary Catherine!" the duke called again, leaping onto the bank. The glare of the lanterns caught Ballenrose as he stumbled to his feet, belt still hanging unclasped. Molly saw her uncle's eyes, saw the hatred snap down like shutters. Then he drew his sword. "By Christ, you bloody bastard, I'll run you through."

"Uncle George, no!" The realization that he meant to carry out the threat propelled Molly up from the riverbank.

"Shouldn't you cover yourself, cousin dear?" Clare Fairfax suggested, and there was hatred in her gaze too.

Molly clutched her bodice together, took a step toward her uncle. "You don't understand. It isn't the way it looks, honestly it—"

"Don't!" Buckingham ordered in a voice that stopped her dead. "Don't you *dare* to make excuses for him!"

"Uncle George, he saved my life!"

"For what? So he could steal your chastity?"

"He didn't have to steal it, from the looks of things," said Clare. "She was giving it away."

"You shut up," Buckingham told her furiously, then turned the sword point on Ballenrose. "As for you, if you've any last prayers, you had best say them now."

"I'm afraid I can't let ye kill him." For the first time Molly noticed the men ranged behind her uncle: guards from the Tower, in the king's livery. It was one of them who'd spoken, with genuine regret. "Bein' as he's unarmed 'n' all—I'm sorry, m'lord, but it wouldn't be fair."

"Then give him your sword!" the duke snapped. "Go on, you heard me; give him your bloody damned sword and I'll fight him!"

"I can't do that neither. That'd be a duel, and his majesty's prohibited duels."

Buckingham whirled on him. "Is there any law," he demanded, icily polite, "to prevent me from tearing his throat out with my bare hands?"

"None but the law o' common sense," another of the guards said, sizing both men up. "He's got fifteen years on ye, 'n' I'd say about three stone."

"For heaven's sake, Uncle George." Clare was tapping

her toe. "You can't mean to engage the man in a common brawl!"

"You get back on that barge." Buckingham shoved her toward the river, then grabbed Molly's arm and sent her flying after her cousin. "You too. Take the carriage and go home; I'll deal with you later."

Molly turned back to him, wide-eyed, pleading. "Please, Uncle George. Believe me, nothing happened."

"Just do as I tell you, girl!"

Molly took a last look at Ballenrose, standing unmoving, like stone; he still hadn't spoken. Their eyes met. "The stars," she heard him say hoarsely, one palm turned to the sky—a gesture of resigned compliance. Then Clare pulled her onto the barge, and they slipped away on the silent black river in the chill drab rain.

11

"NOTHING HAPPENED?" Clare Fairfax laughed, a small, nasty laugh. "You're lying there half-naked with him sprawled all over you and you've got the nerve to tell Uncle George nothing happened? I've misjudged you, Mary Catherine. Butter wouldn't melt in your mouth, would it, you sly little whore?"

"Shut up. Just shut up!" Molly lashed out at her, seized with fear as she stared over the rail of the barge. What was happening there in the darkness behind them?

"I don't believe Uncle George found you in a nunnery at all," the black-haired girl said coolly. "I'll bet he found you in a brothel."

"Shut up or I'll claw your eyes out."

"You don't frighten me. I hope he sends you back where you came from—for good."

For a moment Molly panicked. He wouldn't send her back to the Fleet, would he? Maybe he would; he'd been angrier than any human being she had ever seen. But he couldn't do that now, not to his own flesh and blood.

"Still, in a way, I'm grateful to you," Clare went on. "I must admit I didn't realize how deep our dear uncle's rancor for Lord Ballenrose ran. I wonder why."

"Uncle George told me all about it. He jilted the earl's sister years ago."

"Did he really? Then that explains it."

"Explains what?" Molly asked after a pause.

"Why Anthony Strakhan was seducing you. To pay Uncle George back."

Molly turned from the railing. "That's a lie," she said passionately.

"Don't be such a goose, coz. It's as plain as day."

"That shows what you know! He's in love with me; he has been since he first saw me in the king's gardens. It was he sent me those lilies of the valley—" Too late Molly stopped, realizing what she'd given away.

"You don't say," Clare purred, her voice like silk. "I'm sure Uncle George will be most interested to find out how long you've been carrying on these little assignations behind his back."

"You wouldn't dare tell him."

"Wouldn't I?" The barge slowed, drew up to the Tower landing. Clare moved to step off to shore. Molly caught her hand.

"Please, Clare. I beg you. Don't tell him."

Her cousin's black eyes glittered. "You would have to make it worth my while."

"How?"

Clare's hand snaked out, touched the sapphires at Molly's throat. "You might start with those."

Molly shrank from her. "Why? You couldn't wear them at court; Uncle George would recognize them."

"No, but I can sell them. I've always found it wise to tuck a little something away for a rainy day." For an instant Molly saw hatred stamped on Clare's exquisite face again. "They would have been mine anyway, you know, if you'd just stayed dead."

"Take them and welcome." Molly unclasped the necklace and dropped it into Clare's palm. "And you'll hold your tongue?"

"I'll think about it." Clare signaled one of the two coaches. "Buckingham House," she told the driver as the footman handed Molly in. "You'd best hurry lest milady catch cold."

"Aren't you going home too?" Molly asked.

"What, and miss being at court when word of your little adventure gets out?" She tossed her black curls. "Not on your life. Good night, dear Mary Catherine. And . . . sweet dreams." The carriage set off, leaving her standing there with Molly's jewels in her hand.

Molly huddled in a ball, hands dug into her eyes to keep from shaking. She'd tried to put on a brave front for Clare, but she was cold and tired and scared to death. What she'd let Ballenrose do was wretched and shameful. Uncle George would be well within his rights to disown her completely for the disgrace she'd brought on herself, on him.

And yet: *It was very nearly worth it.* She thought of those heady moments she'd spent locked in Ballenrose's embrace, lost in his wild kisses, their two hearts beating out one mad impassioned rhythm. . . .

Nearly, but not quite. Brought back to earth by the memory of her uncle's fury, she waited while the carriage bore her homeward to her doom.

The duke returned to Buckingham House a few hours later. Molly had bathed and changed into her nightdress; Parker was combing out her hair for her when they heard his horse's hoofbeats on the drive. Running to her bedchamber window, Molly saw him dismount and toss the reins to the stableboy who hurried to meet him. Then he paused, standing alone in the cobblestone yard, unheeding of the rain. Oh, Molly, girl, she thought, biting her lip as she watched, how could you hurt him so, betray him so, after all that he has done for you?

"D'ye think he'll beat ye?" Parker whispered, looking over her shoulder; Molly had confided the basic details of the evening to her maid.

"*Beat* me? Of course not; Uncle George would never do such a thing!"

The maid shrugged, going back to the dressing table for her comb. "He used t' beat Lady Katherine, ye know. Beat her regular, he did."

"For God's sake, Parker, don't tell such vicious lies!"

"It ain't—" The maid stopped, seeing her mistress's pale, anxious face. "Anyway, that's wot the other girls tell me."

"I'm shocked you'd put any credence in that sort of vile gossip. Has he ever put his hand to you?"

"Nay," Parked admitted.

"Well, then." Molly's heart beat faster as she saw her uncle leave the yard and vanish under the eaves. She waited anxiously until a knock sounded at the bedchamber door, then grabbed a robe and wrapped herself in it. "You'd better leave us," she told Parker, and then said, "Come in."

"M'lord." The maid curtsied as the duke entered. "Shall I bring some tobacco? Some brandy?"

"Nothing," he told her. With a last glance at Molly, she slipped out the door.

Molly stood staring at him, fists clenched on the ties of her robe. He looked awful: haggard, soaked to the bone, his fine wavy hair plastered tight to his skull. This is the man beneath the image of the perfect courtier, she realized, seeing for the first time the crow's-feet at the corners of his eyes, the ashen pallor of his skin, a bit of gray that sprouted just above his left temple. This is what you've brought him to. . . .

"Sit down, Mary Catherine."

How tired he sounded, how . . . old. "Parker was right; I must get you some brandy or you'll catch your death." She started for the bellpull.

"I don't want any brandy. I *do* want you to sit down," he said in that same weary voice. Molly sat, on the very edge of her small dressing chair. He sank onto a chaise across from her, his back to the fire. He pulled out his kerchief, started to use it to dry his face, then winced, wringing rainwater from it instead. "No doubt you are wondering what's happened to your friend Ballenrose."

Taken aback, Molly stammered, "I wasn't . . . he isn't . . ."

"The answer is, I neither know nor care. After I told him what I thought of his using a naive girl like you to revenge himself on me, I left him there on the riverbank—alive, to my regret."

To revenge himself—that was what Clare had said too. Molly shivered. Her uncle sighed. "And yet I see that what happened tonight is my fault."

"*Your* fault?" she echoed in astonishment.'

"Aye. I pushed you too hard, Mary Catherine, brought you here to court before you were ready. I should have realized that a single year wasn't enough time to school you in all you needed to know. But I was so proud of you, of your progress . . . I came within a hairbreadth tonight of seeing all our hard work laid to waste."

"I'm sorry. Truly I am," Molly said miserably.

"Dear child, don't you know what the result would have been had that scoundrel had his way with you?" the duke asked earnestly. "He'd have boasted of it all over court; your reputation would be ruined! No decent man would ever wed you; you'd become one of those pathetic creatures passed from man to man as mistress until you grew too old and bitter to amuse anymore. And what if he'd got you with child, what then? That would make another innocent life wasted by your carelessness. Whatever could have possessed you to put yourself into that man's company after all my warnings to you?"

"I don't know," she admitted.

"I confess I'm quite shaken when I think how narrowly you escaped complete disaster this evening."

"He did save my life," Molly whispered.

"So he did," the duke said sternly. "And that's the sole reason I didn't run him through, law or no law. But tell me, if my butler, Thompkins, pushed you out of the path of a runaway wagon, would you then give yourself to him?"

"Of course not!"

He nodded. "Quite so. Therefore I must conclude you find the Earl of Ballenrose attractive. Do you?"

Molly looked down at her toes. "He said . . . such lovely things to me."

"Let me guess," the duke said dryly. "He suggested, perhaps, that you and he had been lovers in another lifetime? That the fate which drew you together could not be defied?" She stared at him, aghast; it was as though he'd overheard them in their carriage. He smiled, his brilliant smile, tinged with rue. "I see I've hit it. A quite conventional ploy, really, though I suppose the first time a girl hears it, it's bound to be flattering. I may even have used it myself when I was young; I can't recall. I think it might have been included in a pamphlet we lads used to pass around, entitled. 'Ten Sure Means of Seduction.' "

"He wasn't going to seduce me," Molly argued in a last stab at defending what she'd done. "He told me so himself!"

"Before or after he unbuttoned his breeches?" asked the duke, and Molly blushed. "Forgive me, child, for being so frank. But would you honestly expect him to announce his intentions when they were so dastardly? I told you that the man had a *vendetta* against me. He saw his chance for revenge tonight and promptly took it. I just thank God that we arrived in time to thwart him." He paused delicately. "We *did* arrive in time—didn't we?"

"Yes," Molly whispered.

"You're quite sure?"

"Yes." Christ, what a fool she'd been.

Her uncle sighed again, this time in relief. "Then there's no real harm done. Mary Catherine, my dear, I only hope you've learned a lesson from all this. It pains me to say it, but my sex simply isn't to be trusted with a young woman's virtue. When it comes right down to it, no one but you can serve as guardian of your precious chastity. Do you understand that?" Molly nodded, and he smiled. "You'll be glad, you know, when you can present yourself to your husband someday as pure and unblemished as a new-sprung rose. It's the greatest gift that you can ever give him, next to his sons." For a moment his face clouded over, and Molly's heart went out to him, seeing the regret in his dark eyes. She went and threw her arms around his neck, laid her head on his chest.

"Uncle George, I'm so sorry," she sobbed, giving vent to her tears. "I'm so sorry I disgraced you; I swear I won't do it again, not ever in a million years—"

"There, there, child. I know. It's all over now." He stroked her hair, planted a kiss on the nape of her neck. "Don't cry. I should think we have all had enough water for one night." Molly laughed shakily, clinging to him. He was so very good to her.

Gently he pried her arms away, tilted her face to him. "Now, then. I think it would be best if you went home to Cliveden for a time—a month, perhaps six weeks—while all of this dies down. Agnes will be glad for the company; you can bring her the gossip and tell her I'm behaving myself. I don't think Ballenrose will dare open his mouth about tonight, not after I spared his life; like all scoundrels, he's a coward at heart. Why else would a man run around in this day and age without a sword? That leaves only your cousin Clare. I hope to God she has the sense to keep all this to herself—though I must say concern for the family honor doesn't seem her strong suit. I took advantage of the coincidence of our being partners tonight to have a talk with her about her behavior."

"I thought perhaps you'd arranged for her to be your partner," Molly told him.

"How would I do that? You watched the king draw out the names himself. And I'd not doom myself to an entire evening in the company of that vixen for a five-minute chat. Anyway, it may comfort you a bit to know you're not the only one of my kin in the doghouse. That girl needs a tight rein." He frowned. "I shall have to speak to her mother."

"Poor Uncle George," Molly said, "mopping up the family messes. You can be sure I won't give you any more cause for concern."

"I hope not, Mary Catherine. I truly do." He patted

her cheek, got to his feet. "I'll have the carriage ready for the trip to Cliveden first thing in the morning; you can leave as soon as you're packed."

"Thank you, Uncle George," Molly said hesitantly, "for being . . . so wonderful about everything."

He'd gone to the door; now he paused on the threshold, looking back. "It nearly killed me," he said in a strange, strangled voice, "to see you like that with him, of all men. I swear to God it did. If you ever do betray my trust again, don't let it be with Ballenrose; I don't think I could bear it. I've come to love you, Mary Catherine, more than you can know."

"Oh, Uncle George." There were tears in her eyes. "I do love you too."

"Prove it to me, my dear, with your actions. Good night, now. And we'll never speak of this evening's events again." He closed the door with a sharp click of finality.

Molly nearly called him back to make a clean breast of everything—tell him about meeting Ballenrose in the king's gardens, and the flowers he'd sent her, and about giving her sapphires to Clare. Then she stopped herself. What would be the point now? It was all over and done; she wouldn't be seeing the earl anymore except in passing, in public. All that romantic claptrap he'd fed her was lies, just as Uncle George said, as even Clare had recognized. He really had been using her as a pawn in his game of revenge. Well, she would not be so stupid again.

She rang the bell—two short pulls—to send for Parker so they could begin her packing. She was anxious to get back to Cliveden, put the past behind her, and prepare to start anew. This time she'd make her uncle proud of her. This time she'd find a young man for her swain whom Uncle George would welcome into the family, marry him and have his children, lots of children. Uncle George would like that. He would give her away at the wedding; Madame LaFarge would make her a glorious gown . . .

"M'lady?" Parker had come in wearing a most peculiar expression.

"It's all right, Parker," Molly assured her, "everything's all right. Uncle George has forgiven me, God bless him, and my penance is to be a month at Cliveden. We'll be leaving in the morning, so we must get . . . What's this?"

The maid was holding out a small package wrapped in brown paper and string. "Someone left it for ye at the stables just now," she hissed, " 'n' gave it to one o' the boys to give to me to give ye in secret. Gave the boy ten shillings, too," she added, impressed. "Half for him, half for me."

"In secret? I just can't imagine . . ." Molly untied the string, unwrapped the paper, felt a queer little flutter in her heart as she looked down at the small kid-bound book in her hands. Even before she opened it to see the title page, she knew what would be printed there:

The Poems of John Donne.

12

"*BALLENROSE,*" LADY AGNES said, looking up from the letter Uncle George had sent home to Cliveden along with Molly. Her tone was the sort one imagined she might use to point out a dead rat to the servants. "I must say, Mary Catherine, you surprise me. What in God's name could possess you to take up with that man?"

What indeed? A fortnight later, Molly lay in her bed in the heat of a close July night, the sheets tangled beneath her, trying not to remember the way his arms had felt circling round her, or the stark need in his voice when he'd whispered, "My name is Anthony . . . I want to hear you say it." Or the exquisite excitement that had raced through her blood when he lowered his head to put his mouth to her breast. . . .

Dammit all, why couldn't she forget him? Lady Agnes had been even more blunt than Uncle George in her assessment of the earl's motives. "You silly chit," she'd fumed, "couldn't you see that seducing you would put the cap to all his schemes to ruin your uncle? And I suppose you thought he found you irresistible." Molly knew she'd blushed. "All I can say," the countess had continued, "is that your uncle's a good deal more forgiving than I am. If you were my daughter I'd have packed you straight off to a convent for the rest of your days!"

A convent was pretty much what Cliveden seemed like

after her taste of life at court. Molly had heard enough gossip about others during her brief stay there to imagine what was being said about her own sudden departure. The letter she'd had from Jessica—"Everyone is so awfully sorry you've been taken ill; get well, and hurry back!"— hadn't allayed her fears at all. Her cousin was too kind to pass along the truth anyway. Had Uncle George got Clare to hold her tongue? Was Ballenrose boasting? That thought chilled her despite the heat. Something he'd said to her in the carriage kept coming back to haunt her:

"Shall I tell you what I do admire? Someone who puts loyalty to the family above all things." Was he just being loyal to his sister when he'd made love to her? That was certainly the consensus of those who knew him better than she.

And yet he'd sent her the book.

Her hand groped beneath her pile of pillows, found it, curled round its leather cover, taking comfort in its substance. What a frightful risk he'd taken in getting it to her; what if Parker or the stableboy had gone to her uncle with it? Surely the book proved that Uncle George and Lady Agnes and Clare were wrong, that he hadn't just been using her for some devious end.

She ought to have sent it back to him, she knew, or else burned it. After all, she'd promised her uncle that she wouldn't see Ballenrose again, and she had every intention of living up to her word. And yet she kept the slim volume hidden amongst the bedclothes, unwilling to part with its tangible evidence of that evening of passion. It was no different, she told herself, from saving the bouquet or fan one carried at one's first ball. Someday, when she was safely married to Lord Darby or Lord Prescott or Lord Montfort, she'd find this tucked away in a drawer and smile at the memory of her first love, how young and naive she'd once been.

And yet the book *was* different from a fan or flowers, because it wasn't a dead thing, because it didn't just speak to the past:

To enter in these bonds is to be free,
Then where my hand is set my seal shall be.

Each time she opened the book, with every page, she felt anew the trembling excitement that had seized her when she lay in Ballenrose's arms, when he'd set his hands where no man had ever touched her before and made some part of her forever his, irrevocably.

Oh, God, she really ought to burn it, she thought, slamming the book shut as a warmth owing nothing to the sultry night air swept through her. No good could come from living over and over again her memories of that night.

Crawling out from the clammy web of the bedclothes, she went to the window, praying for a breath of breeze. There was a ring of pale fire circling the full-blown moon, and three stars cupped in its corona—a promise of rain to come, Aunt May had always said. Rain . . . falling against her skin, covering his, soaking their soaked hair, turning them warm and slippery as quicksilver as they clung together—

Damn! She closed the shutters with a bang. Must every blessed thing put her in memory of that man? She went back to her bed, resolutely shunned Done, and picked up a volume of dry-as-dust Virgil instead.

The Roman poet produced the desired effect; a single page of his paean to farming had Molly drowsing. She heard a smattering of raindrops on the shutters, wished sleepily that she had left them open to catch the wind, but was too tired to rise. . . .

More raindrops fell. Or was it hail? she wondered, listening to the sharp clatter. Hail in this heat . . . that certainly was odd. And the wind had picked up too; she could hear it whistling, could almost imagine that it sang out her name—

Jesu! She sat up with a start as something sounding the size of a meteor crashed against the window. And it wasn't the wind whispering, ''Mary Catherine!''; it was someone, a man, from somewhere outside. In disbelief she ran to open the shutters, looked down over the drive, and saw, just as she knew she would, the Earl of Ballenrose standing there, in a black cape and hat, searching the ground around him for another stone.

"Are you out of your *mind?*" was all that she could think to hiss at him from two stories above. "My uncle—"

"Is safely in London, at a meeting of the Royal Society. I would have come here sooner, but he's set some men to watching me, spying on me. It took me this long to evade them. You sleep like the dead; I thought I'd have to conjure Gabriel and his trumpet to wake you."

Molly stared at him. He had his thumbs caught in his belt loops, still wasn't wearing a sword, was *grinning*, for God's sake, like a boy who'd played a clever trick on his schoolmaster. "You're mad," she said, "you must be."

"Didn't I tell you I was your poor fool?" he agreed amiably. "But it does go to prove what I told you about our fates, your coming to close the shutters just as I was riding up here. Otherwise I wouldn't have had any notion which window was yours."

"Where is your horse?" Molly asked. He pointed behind him, across the lawn to the tall surrounding wall. "How did you get in?"

" 'With love's light wings did I o'erperch these walls,' " he started to quote from *Romeo and Juliet*, " 'for stony limits cannot—' "

"For the love of Jesu, be serious!"

He picked up a rope and tackle from the grass beside him. "Military training. I always knew someday it would come in handy." Then he swung the tackle halfway toward her, playing out the rope. "Shall I demonstrate?"

"No!"

"Ah, then you're coming down."

"Don't you realize you could get killed for being here?" Molly asked, desperate to make him see reason.

"It would be worth it. My life's not worth a fig without you anyway." Though the words were jocular enough,

Molly heard the conviction behind them, knew he meant what he said. The thought that he would risk his life for her made her solemn and scared.

"Please, Anthony, you've got to go. I couldn't bear it if anyone were to—"

"God, I love the way you say my name. I love your voice, the way you talk, with every word like singing. Do you know what it always makes me think of? Have you ever been to Smithfield Market? But of course you haven't. There are women there who cry out the names of the wares they're selling just like songs: 'Fresh hot buns!' they call, and 'Lovely live chickens!' They—"

"Anthony, get out of here!" Molly closed the shutters with a click, counted to a hundred, opened them again. He hadn't moved.

"I'll go," he said more quietly, "if you tell me you don't want to see me—tell me so I believe it." Molly didn't, couldn't speak. He smiled in the moonlight, recoiling the rope. "I am coming up."

"No!" Molly cried, heart loud as a drum in her chest. "No, wait. I'll come down. Go around the house to the gardens so you won't stick out so. Wait for me there."

She'd just explain to him, she promised herself as she slipped downstairs through the dark, silent house, that she couldn't see him ever. She'd say she didn't care for him, that she was in love with someone else. Aye, that was it, that was what she'd do.

But when she came through the garden doors and saw him waiting for her, that idea went straight out of her head. How had she ever thought him plain? He was the handsomest man in the world, and his priest's eyes, his beautiful wise eyes, were filled with love for her.

"Look at you," he said, his voice rich and low. "You look . . . like an angel. Too beautiful for this earth." He held out his arms and she stepped into them, into the silken bonds of his embrace. For a moment he just held her, his face against the smooth gold weight of her hair. Then he tilted back her head and kissed her, put his mouth to hers and drank in the taste of her like a man with a thirst that could never be quenched.

"You smell of roses," he told her, pulling away at last, catching her up in his arms and whirling her in circles. "The whole world smells of roses." And it did; there were roses all around them, bushes laden, drooping with the weight of full-blown damasks and Provences and musks and the small sweet dog rose. "Marry me," he said.

Molly laughed. "You truly are crazy. You're the craziest man I ever met in my life, madder than poor Tom Peabody."

"Madder than who?"

"Nobody. Nothing," she said, biting her tongue. "Someone I knew a long time ago."

"Marry me," he said again. "I mean it."

"What a splendid idea. Uncle George can give me away."

"I don't give a hang about your bloody uncle. We don't need him. He can't stop us. Come away with me now, just like that; we could be married tonight—" He claimed her mouth again in a kiss that sent flames racing through her. Molly pushed him away.

"Stop. Don't say such things. You have no idea of all that Uncle George has done for me . . ."

"You're right." He stood apart from her, angry now. "I don't know what he's done for you. All I see is what he's doing to you—keeping you locked away from the man who loves you more than anyone else ever could."

"He hasn't got me locked away!"

"He might as well! I tell you, he's got men standing watch over me, following me everywhere I go."

"I don't believe he'd do that."

Moonlight glinted in his eyes; they were no longer priestly. "Are you calling me a liar?"

"Of course I'm not, but you could be mistaken!"

He looked at her silently, coldly.

"Oh, Anthony." Molly took a step toward him, put her

hand on his chest. "Please try to understand. Uncle George loves me too. In his heart he wants what's best for me. I know that I can bring him around if you'll just give me time."

"I haven't got any time," he said in anguish. "I can't stand for us to be apart; I lie in bed at night and I burn for you." He pulled her against him, and Molly shivered, feeling through the thin linen of her nightdress the way his muscles were taut with need.

"I'm sorry," she said helplessly, "there's nothing I can do."

"How can you tell me that," he whispered hoarsely, "when you know there is?"

"Anthony—no."

"Mary Catherine." He had backed her up against the trunk of a hawthorn tree, was reaching for the ties to her night-dress. "Oh, Christ, Mary Catherine. I want you so . . ." The laces slid through his eager fingers; baring her breasts, he bent his head and kissed them hungrily. Molly trembled, dizzied by his nearness, the heat, the press of his flesh against hers, and the thick scent of roses that hung in the air. She felt the soft garden earth beneath her bare feet, heard the catch of his breath as he slid his hands down her back to her buttocks, hiked up her skirts and found she wore no stockings. "Oh," he groaned, moving against her, sending waves of pleasure through her body.

"Anthony—"

"God, if you knew what you do to me!"

Molly was very much afraid she did; she was on the verge of giving in to him. He pulled her down on the grass beside him, pulled handfuls of roses from the nearest bush and tore the petals loose to drift around them like snow. Then he cupped her breasts in his hands and covered them with kisses, crushed the sweet rose petals against her skin with his mouth and tongue.

"I love you," he whispered. "Let me show you—" He brushed her cheek with his mouth. "Don't you know I'd sooner die than hurt you?"

"But you are a dead man," Molly cried, "if my uncle finds you here!"

"I don't care," he said passionately. "I don't care about anyone or anything but you. Oh, Mary Catherine . . . " His hands were at her breasts again, stroking their tips to hardness, two perfect pink rosebuds; her legs were pinned beneath his, her skirts hiked to her thighs.

"I love you," Molly sobbed, a host of wayward emotions at war in her soul—love, longing, joy, and terror.

He paused in his sweet assault, smiled against her breast, raised his head, and kissed her tenderly. "Then let them come and take me—but I'll have you first." His hand slipped under her skirts, found the string of her drawers, and loosed them. Molly didn't move, didn't breathe as he reached down to part her thighs. She felt the touch of his fingers, gentle as the petals of roses sliding against her, and then a rush of fire as they found the sweet bud hidden there.

"Oh," she whispered, drawing in her breath, skin tightening, tingling. He touched her again; the fire leapt and flared. "Oh, dear God in heaven." He drew back and she arched to follow, afraid now that he would stop. "Don't . . . don't go." She reached for him, felt him shudder against her as her hand closed around his manhood, thick as a sapling, hard and flush with life. He was breathing fast, panting for her; their hearts were pounding together; they moved as one as he lowered himself onto her, as the roses poured their attar out into the night . . .

"If there is anyone in this garden who does not wish to be seen by my husband," came a voice from the house, "I'd suggest he leave now, as the duke has just come riding up the drive."

"Jesu!" Molly gasped, the fire dying inside her.

Ballenrose groaned, banging his fist and head against the ground. "Who the devil is that?"

"The duchess—Lady Katherine. You have got to go—"

"No, dammit all! How can I leave you now?"

"His grace the duke is dismounting," that voice from the doorway warned.

"Anthony, for God's sake!"

"I don't care; let him find me."

"He will murder us both," Molly said desperately.

"Damn, damn, damn!" He sat back quickly and buckled his trousers.

"You will have to excuse me now," Lady Katherine said in her dull, flat voice. "His grace the duke is just come inside."

"Go!" Molly hissed, pushing him away, fumbling for her bodice laces. "Go, get out, run!"

"I'll be back," he vowed. "I'll come back for you always—"

"Mary Catherine!" Molly heard her uncle calling from within the house.

"Not if you're dead, you won't," she told Ballenrose, grabbing his rope and tackle and pushing them at him. He hesitated, long enough to bend and kiss her.

"Someday," he whispered, "we will look back at this and laugh, and tell our children's children."

"Mary Catherine, where are you?"

"Will you go?" Molly hissed, squirming out of his embrace, running her hands through her disheveled hair before she answered the duke: "I'm out here, Uncle George!"

"I love you," Ballenrose said, then ducked low and ran for the cover of the hawthorn trees. Molly heard the clang of his tackling hook against the garden wall just as her uncle appeared in the doorway.

"Mary Catherine? What in heaven's name are you doing out here at this hour of the night?"

"Uncle George!" She ran toward him along the path. "I couldn't sleep for the heat; isn't it dreadful? I came out to get a breath of air."

"Barefoot? In your nightdress?" he demanded, frowning. "What if the servants saw you?"

Molly slipped her arm through his, leading him into the

house. "It was naughty, I know, but I just couldn't bear to put on more clothes, I was so sticky and hot."

He paused by a wall sconce. "You look a bit feverish. I do hope you're not ill." He laid his hand on her forehead. Molly willed her racing pulse to slow, held her breath lest he hear her panting. "They say there's plague in Walford," he said worriedly.

"Well, I won't catch it. I had the plague already, when I was four."

"Did you? How extraordinary. Dr. Collett was speaking to the Royal Society on that very subject this evening. What had you for supper?"

Molly struggled to remember in light of everything that had happened since then. "Capon," she announced, a trifle too triumphantly. "There was plenty to spare, shall I fetch you some?"

"No need, I'll ring for it. You had better hie yourself to bed."

"Very well, I won't let the cook catch me in my nightdress," she teased to hide her nervousness, and gave his cheek a kiss. "But what brings you home so unexpectedly?"

He met her gaze, looking a bit abashed. "You will laugh at me—"

"I? Never."

He hesitated, then said, "I have had some men keeping an eye on Ballenrose, just to make certain he doesn't try his tricks on you again. He gave them the slip tonight, and I feared he might have come here."

"You've had men *spying* on him?" Molly made a silent apology to Ballenrose for doubting what he'd said. "Surely you are carrying this all a bit too far, Uncle George."

"I'm not," he said with sudden vehemence. "There are things about that man that you don't know."

"What things?"

He started to say more, then stopped. "You would not understand."

"Try me," she pleaded. "Trust me."

The Duke of Buckingham sighed. "I do trust you, pet. I simply don't trust him."

Molly felt a quick, hard stab of doubt, like a capon bone caught in her craw. "Uncle George, if there is something you know that you haven't told me, some reason to question his intentions—"

"Question his intentions?" Her uncle laughed bitterly. "There was never any question of his intentions, Mary Catherine. He meant to ruin you, seduce you the same way . . ."

"The same way what?" she asked when he didn't go on, and heard her voice go higher, quaver. "The same way what, Uncle George?"

He had that haggard look about him again. "The same way any such villain would seek to ruin an innocent young girl like you," he said, but she sensed he was prevaricating. "He needs no more reason than the utter blackness of his soul." Molly shivered. He was holding back; there *was* something more. Christ Jesu, what could it be?

"Uncle George—"

"Go to bed, Mary Catherine," he said heavily, wearily. "It is late, and we leave early tomorrow."

"Leave?" she echoed.

"Aye. That's the other reason I've come home—to tell you that you may return to court. I fear I was too harsh with you before, in the heat of the moment. The fault lay with that bastard Ballenrose, not with you. Forgive me my impetuousness. Your exile's done."

Molly felt at that moment like the worst Judas since the Garden of Gethsemane. "Oh, Uncle George—"

"Get on with you, now; I'm hungry for my capon." He smiled, his dazzling, enchanting smile, leaving Molly to start for the stairs with a heart turned heavier than lead.

"Damn," she whispered into the dark silence of the great hall, "why must everything be such a bloody muddle?"

"He got safe away," hissed a voice right at her elbow which made her startle with fear.

"Lady Katherine!"

"I watched from the window. Don't fret, girl. He made it over the wall." Molly felt the duchess's hand crab at her wrist, give it a little pat.

"How . . . how did you know he was there?" she whispered tentatively.

"I don't sleep well, you know. Sometimes I walk about at night. I heard him call your name."

"Do you know who he is?"

The duchess laughed in the darkness. "Aye, girl. He's your lover!"

"Hush!" Molly moved toward the staircase. "I mean his name."

"Oh, aye, I know that too. 'Tis poor Magdalene's brother."

"Magdalene?" Molly whispered.

"Aye, Magdalene Strakhan, that George was to marry before me."

Molly heard her heart pounding in her ears, wondered if the other woman could hear it as well. "You knew her, then."

"Knew her? We were as close as sisters until George worked his devilment between us. It was the money, you see. Always the damned money."

"What money?" Molly asked.

"She had it first," the duchess said simply, "but then I had more after my father died. No one expected that. He was so young, you see. They thought he'd have a son."

"I don't understand."

"He—wanted—my—money," she said very distinctly. "He threw her over so that he could marry me. Well, she got the best part in the end, didn't she? I hear her laughing at me sometimes, laughing from her grave."

"From the grave . . ." Despite the stifling heat, Molly felt fingers of ice tapping up her spine. "She's dead, then?" The duchess was wandering away in the darkness, climbing up the staircase. Molly hurried after her. "Did you say she is dead?"

"I didn't know," the duchess crooned, her voice taking on the singsong of madness. "I didn't know. How could I? We were like sisters, Magdalene and I; I thought she told me everything—"

"What didn't you know? What didn't she tell you?"

The woman turned around so suddenly that Molly nearly tripped. "Be wary with your lover, with your fine handsome lover," she hissed. "They're all alike, men; they're all devils; I would see them all hanged."

"What didn't she tell you?" Molly asked again, fiercely.

"Magdalene? Why, that George had got her with child."

"No," Molly said, catching hold of the banister as her knees went soft. "No, he hadn't. He couldn't—"

"I helped you tonight," the Duchess of Buckingham went on, "because I feel sorry for you. You're just like me, just like Magdalene, just like that doomed cow Agnes. We are all taken in by him. But mind you watch your young man! Oh, they're all devils, I tell you; I would see them all hanged—"

"Oh, God," Molly whispered with a sudden bizarre, bone-chilling intimation of what was to come.

"—Hanged just like poor sweet Magdalene. Did I tell you that we were like sisters?" the duchess asked. "Right up until she hanged herself on my wedding day."

13

THERE WERE SOME things, Aunt May used to tell Molly, that a soul was better off not knowing. Why Mamie Struthers had got but one leg, for instance, or how sausage was made. Or how the rich lived; that was another. Whenever Molly would ask as a child, the old woman would shake her head and say, "Now, why would ye want t' know that, pet? 'Twould only drive ye daft t' know the waste 'n' foolishness that goes on amongst them folk." The truth about Magdalene Strakhan's death, Molly had concluded, was one more instance of something she'd have been better off not knowing.

She'd confronted Uncle George, of course. Not that same night, not with Ballenrose's kisses still sweet in her mouth, the memory of his hands still hot on her belly and breasts, but straight off the next morning. Coming downstairs to find him at breakfast with Lady Agnes, she'd piqued the countess by asking her to grant them a private talk. Uncle George, thank God, had noticed her distrait pallor and sent his lover away with his usual gracious tact. Then, "Something has upset you terribly, I can see," he told Molly, patting the chair beside him, pouring her tea. "You must come and tell me what it is."

She repeated what the duchess had told her, then cried, "Is it true?"

He was silent for a moment, studying the plate of veal

and eggs that lay before him. "Well," he said finally. "Poor Mary Catherine. So you have discovered our unhappy secret at last."

"So it *is* true," Molly breathed. "Oh, Uncle George, why didn't you tell me before?" But she already knew: for the same reason he hadn't told her until he had to that he and Lady Agnes were lovers. Because it put him in a bad light; because he was only human, after all.

"It isn't all true," he said quickly, bristling like a boar. "What Katherine told you about the money, about why I changed my mind and didn't marry Magdalene, that's a lie. That's Katherine's own guilt and bitterness coming out—as usual, at my expense."

"You said you couldn't even remember her name," Molly recalled plaintively. "How could you say that?"

"I didn't want you asking any more questions. It's a part of my past, a pitiful, tragic part that I have tried hard to put behind me. Surely you can understand why it is painful to me. But I'll swear one thing to you, Mary Catherine, on my very life. I never knew that Magdalene was with child. She never told me." His denial had the unmistakable ring of truth. He held Molly's gaze, then looked down at the table, stirring sugar into his tea. When he spoke again, it was more quietly.

"No doubt you are shocked that I had relations with her before we were married, after the lectures I have given you on the value of chastity." He was wrong about that; she wasn't shocked, for her own experience had taught Molly how exceedingly fine the line was drawn between honor and disgrace. "But it is precisely because of the tragedy of Magdalene that I feel so strongly about the matter," he went on earnestly. "I have witnessed firsthand the disaster that can result from such premature dalliances."

"Dalliances?" That did shock Molly. "How can you dismiss it as a dalliance when that poor girl killed herself because of you?"

"Hold on!" With a spark of temper, he held up his

hand. "I will accept full responsibility for having seduced Magdalene—though, by the by, I wasn't the first lamb to that shearing, if you take my meaning. I'll accept the responsibility for having jilted her too, though as I say, she never even hinted to me that she was in a family way. I absolutely *will not,* however, foot the blame for her suicide. That was the act of an unbalanced mind, and it can only be laid at Magdalene's own door."

"An unbalanced mind," Molly repeated slowly.

"Aye! Why the devil do you think I broke off our betrothal?" he demanded with impatience. "Because the girl was mad!"

"What made you think so?" she asked tentatively.

Her uncle frowned. "It isn't easy to explain. But I felt there was something . . . well, uncivilized about the way she cared for me. It just wasn't proper. She didn't understand the *limits;* she was always talking about her love knowing no bounds."

"Are there limits to true love, real love?" she asked her uncle. "Shouldn't love be boundless?"

"We are talking about real life, Mary Catherine," he told her briskly, "not about fairy tales. All that metaphysical blather about two souls melding and fusing into one is nothing but claptrap."

"Still," Molly said rather wistfully, "surely you found it flattering to be loved so intently."

"Flattering?" He laughed. "I found it a bloody bother, if you'll pardon my French. She was like a puppy, following me everywhere I'd go, never giving me a moment's peace. I tell you, she hounded me! No one who knew the circumstances blamed me for calling off our engagement. It was plain as day that Magdalene was deranged—as the manner of her death surely proved."

Of course he was right; she had to have been insane. People didn't really kill themselves for love, except in books and plays. Good Lord, if they did—if every pair of young lovers whose families disapproved behaved like Romeo and Juliet—the world would be knee-deep in corpses.

"And that is why I reacted as I did that night when I found you and Ballenrose together," her uncle went on, his manner grave again. "Knowing that he blames me for his sister's death, I've no doubt that his hatred for me runs as deep and strong as did Magdalene's love. Some ancestor of theirs was actually beheaded for refusing to adhere to Henry the Eighth's Oath of Supremacy. It is not a family known for doing things by halves. They simply cannot seem to keep their passions in check." Sitting there at the breakfast table, in bright slanting sunlight, Molly had shivered, remembering the careless words she'd called to Ballenrose the night before: *You're mad,* she'd said, *you must be. . . .*

"You think, then, that he only made love to me for reasons of revenge," she said, flushing.

"My dear girl, I am convinced of it. Can't you see how the symmetry of such a vengeance would appeal to his warped brain? The only reprisal more fitting would be the seduction of my duchess—which, by the by, he has already tried."

"No!" Molly stared. "He didn't!"

"Oh, yes he did! But I don't suppose Katherine mentioned that when she was airing the family linen. Poor Kate." He sighed. "She and Magdalene were so close. The suicide was a dreadful shock to her, too, coming as it did on the very day of our wedding. Sometimes I think our marriage was doomed to unhappiness even then—I have the Ballenrose family to thank for that too."

Molly had chewed on her lip. "I wish that you had told me all this long ago, Uncle George."

"Blame a fond uncle's vanity for that. I wanted so desperately for you to think well of me, Mary Catherine. And I hoped that the mistakes of my youth would never come to light." He shrugged. "Well, now they have. But sooner or later, it makes no difference. After all, you've had no contact with Ballenrose since leaving court . . ." His fine dark eyes had narrowed. "Have you?"

"No . . ." But even to Molly's ears her denial sounded unconvincing.

"You're sure? No correspondence, nothing?"

"He sent me a book," she admitted reluctantly, hoping that half-truth would serve.

"The devil he did! What book?"

"The Poems of John Donne."

"I might have guessed," he said grimly. "Donne was Magdalene's favorite. Oh, that man's madness is an ugly thing! Perhaps 'tis just as well all this came out before you came back to court. They do say forewarned is forearmed."

There had been roses in a vase on the table; their scent made Molly suddenly nauseous. "So they do," she agreed, stumbling up from her chair. "Excuse me, Uncle, please."

That was three months ago. The summer passed, and most of autumn. Molly hadn't spoken one word to the Earl of Ballenrose in all that time. The first day she cut him dead, she felt as though she were severing a part of her body. He had stared at her in disbelief, stared with those grave priest's eyes, then evidently concluded that she meant to throw her uncle off their track. But she went on snubbing him, had Parker send back his barrage of letters unopened, along with the hillside's worth of lilies of the valley that continued to arrive anonymously. When that didn't work, when he still contrived to see and speak to her, she tore the pages out of John Donne's book, burned them, and sent the ashes to him inside the leather cover.

After that, the letters stopped, but still, in public places, at the palace or theater, she would glimpse him standing apart from the crowd of her eager suitors and know he was watching her always, a tall grim figure dressed in black. His silent vigil unnerved her, but it also provided indisputable proof of what her uncle had told her: the man *was* mad.

The summer had been chilly and damp, and much of the court removed to the country, but Uncle George stayed at Buckingham House, reasoning that they were far enough away from the parts of the city ravaged by poxes and fever to be safe. The strain of breaking with Ballenrose took its toll on Molly, though; in August, for the first time since the bout of plague she'd suffered at four, she'd taken ill. The duke immediately placed her under Dr. Collett's care. He postulated that the problem was some infection left in her lungs from her time in prison, and treated her with leeches and poultices and a syrup of his own devising that smelled like rotted mutton and tasted worse. Still, the regimen worked: though she continued to have occasional bouts of dizziness and chills, she lost her sickly pallor and, by the end of October, regained her appetite, though at the doctor's insistence she remained at home.

She was impressed with him. From listening to his conversations with her uncle when he came to dinner, she'd always thought him rather a dilettante, even, as Aunt May would have said, "a trifle touched." He had the craziest theories about the human body—that fever was a good thing, for instance, signaling that the patient was trying to fight off some dangerous influence from without, or that cholera was caused by some sort of invisible pest that multiplied in the waters of the Thames when the weather turned hot. It was with some surprise, then, that she found him so good a physician, attentive and curious, asking dozens of questions about how she felt, what she'd eaten, how this or that suggestion had helped, and jotting down everything she said in a little notebook. If only he could have gotten to Aunt May before she died, Molly sometimes thought, he likely would have cured her blindness and helped her live another fifty years.

"M'lady?" Parker stuck her capped, curly head through the drawing-room doors. "Lady Jessica's without in her carriage, 'n' wantin' t' know is ye well enough t' go round t' the dressmaker's with her."

Molly set aside the volume of Shakespeare's sonnets she'd been reading. "Oh, how I'd love to go. Ask her to wait, Parker, won't you, while I ask Uncle George?"

He was in the library working on his correspondence, and wanted to know what Dr. Collett had said about such outings. "As soon as I felt up to it," Molly told him, lying only a little bit. "And I do, honestly I do."

"Well . . ." He hesitated, quill in hand. "I suppose it's all right, then. But mind you wear a wrap, and stay in the carriage; don't go into Madame LaFarge's. Half the women she outfits have been ill."

"Yes, Uncle George," Molly said dutifully.

"And don't stay out too long. I should never forgive myself if you suffered a relapse."

"I promise I won't!" She blew him a kiss, grabbed her cloak from Parker, and hurried outside before he changed his mind.

"Hurrah! You're free!" Jessica called from the carriage.

"Not for long," Molly told her as she climbed in. "And you had better not kiss me; Dr. Collett says I may still be breathing contagions, whatever they are."

"What does that old quack know?" Jessica demanded, and kissed her anyway. "He will lose all his clientele if he keeps you at home much longer. The court bachelors are all in a dither."

"Oh, are they?"

"Absolutely pining away," her cousin confirmed cheerfully. "And you must be dying of ennui, poor thing."

"I've done plenty of reading," Molly said wryly. "Thank God you came by!" Through the carriage window she drank in the gorgeous October blue sky, the oak trees in their red-and-gold autumn coats, the barges on the Thames . . . "Hold on," she said, "this isn't the way to Madame LaFarge's."

"No. I thought you might like to ride along the esplanade a bit first, since you've been cooped up so long."

Something in her voice struck Molly as false; when she turned back to her, Jessica smiled a little too brightly. "Jessica Fairfax," Molly said suspiciously, "what is going on?"

"Oh, dear. I never have been very good at hiding secrets." But she seemed rather relieved to have been found out. "The truth is, I've arranged a tryst."

"You've *what?*" Molly asked, nearly tumbling off the seat.

"With Anthony Strakhan," her cousin admitted, then added quickly. "Just hear me out, Mary Catherine! He's been completely distraught ever since you took ill—badgering me with questions, begging me to give you these." She reached into her skirts and drew out a fat packet of letters. "I didn't dare forward them to the house, for fear Uncle George might be reading your correspondence."

Molly didn't touch the letters, instead folded her hands in her lap. "Uncle George wouldn't do that."

"Knowing how he feels about the Earl of Ballenrose, I think he just might. Anthony told me what happened on the night of the treasure hunt."

Molly's hands curled into fists. "I might have known he'd boast of that."

"He wasn't boasting," Jessica said. "He was just trying to explain why he couldn't ask to see you openly. I never thought I'd say such a thing about a rich, handsome fellow like that, but I feel sorry for him. He is simply mad about you."

No, he is simply mad, period, Molly nearly told her, but held her tongue. "I am sure you meant well, Jess," she said instead, "but I won't accept those letters. And I'm certainly not going to meet the Earl of Ballenrose. Not today, and not ever. So you may as well just turn this carriage round again."

"I think that you are making a mistake," her cousin said earnestly, leaning toward her. "God knows I'm no expert in such things, but if you ask me, a love like the one Anthony harbors for you cannot come too often in one lifetime."

"I'm afraid it's all a good deal more complicated than that."

"Why? Because of Uncle George? Mary Catherine, did

it ever occur to you that our uncle may not have your best interests in mind?''

Molly's eyes narrowed. ''What do you mean by that?''

''Don't be cross with me,'' Jessica said quickly. ''But Anthony is quite sure that Uncle George would do anything to keep the two of you apart. He even suggested that Uncle George may have given you something that would make you ill—''

''Poisoned me, do you mean?'' Molly laughed in disbelief. ''Honestly, how can you listen to such stuff and nonsense?''

Jessica nibbled her lip. ''I agree it doesn't sound too likely, put like that, but the way Anthony said it . . . I don't know. He just has a way of sounding so *convincing.*''

Molly hardly needed to be told that. ''The truth is, Jess, that I feel sorry for Ballenrose too. 'Tis clear as day the man is daft. I know some things about him that you don't.'' Briefly she explained about Magdalene's death. ''And that is why Ballenrose has been so persistent in courting me, you see,'' she concluded. ''He wants to revenge himself on Uncle George by ruining me.''

''Dear God.'' Her cousin had gone pale. ''I'd no idea! Anthony never mentioned—''

''No, nor to me either.'' Molly hesitated. ''You said before that you couldn't hold a secret. Did you mean that?''

''Well . . . if it is something truly important, I can.''

''I'll tell you something, then, if you promise never to repeat it to another living soul. Promise?'' Jessica nodded. ''He came to see me at Cliveden,'' Molly said, voice dropping to a whisper. ''At night. He threw stones at my window until I agreed to come down to the gardens. And when I got there . . . well, he very nearly accomplished what he'd set out to do.''

''You mean . . .'' Jessica's eyes were blue saucers.

Molly nodded. ''We were that close to . . . to . . . when

my Aunt Kate called out that Uncle George had come home.''

"Mary Catherine, how *could* you?" Jessica squealed, and in the same breath, "What was it like?"

"I can scarcely recall, it all happened so fast." She clenched her eyes shut. "I remember the roses. It was July, and all the roses were blooming. He crushed the petals into my hair and my—" She stopped, her hand at her breast. Then her eyes opened wide. "I swear to God, Jess, if you ever tell your sister—"

"I never would. It all sounds so romantic," she said wistfully. "Are you sure he isn't really in love with you? After all, it seems a frightful lot of trouble to go to in revenge for something that happened such a long time ago."

"No one would sooner believe that than I," Molly said, equally wistful. "But I'm afraid there's no question. Why, he told me himself once that he admires loyalty to one's family above all things. Uncle George says it's a family trait with the Strakhans, like red hair, or our birthmarks. They aren't able to control their passions the way normal folk do."

"He surely had me fooled," Jessica said. "What birthmarks?"

"Why, the ones down here." Molly patted her behind. "Haven't you got one?"

Jessica shook her head. "But I am only one-eighth a Villiers. What does it look like?"

"A bird, sort of. That is how Uncle George first—" Molly stopped. That was one secret she didn't dare share.

"First what?"

"Nothing. Where did you set up this tryst with Ballenrose, anyway?"

"On the esplanade, just past the Queen's Stair." Jessica glanced out the window. "Oh, dear God, we're here. And there he is!"

Molly leaned across her cousin to look out, and drew in her breath. He was standing close by the water, in clothes black as a mourning widower's weeds, but when he caught sight of her through the window his eyes seemed to kindle with the fire of hope. All the world's a stage, she reminded herself, and he's a damned fine player. No doubt he's only rejoicing because he thinks I've fallen into his trap again.

"Keep going!" Jessica called to the driver, jangling the bell. "Keep going, don't stop!" Molly tugged the window shutter to close it, but it stuck, so that she was still looking at the Earl of Ballenrose as they went by. The hope died on his face; she saw anger, hard as bone, born there instead as he realized he'd been made out a fool.

Good, Molly thought. Finally he shows his true colors. On impulse she seized the bundle of letters from her cousin and flung it out the window at him. The ribbon that had bound them came loose, and they fluttered into the air like a covey of ringdoves scattered by a poacher's gun. That ought to teach him, she decided, and then was surprised, looking back, to see he made no move to gather them up, just stood staring after the coach, motionless as Lot's wife. The sight made her shiver uncontrollably.

"Good Lord, now you've caught a chill," Jessica fussed, settling a shawl around Molly's shoulders. "I'd best get you home straightaway, or Uncle George will have my head."

"You were a damned bloody fool, Jessica, to believe Ballenrose's lies," Molly said suddenly, her voice unaccustomedly sharp. Her cousin raised wounded eyes to her; guiltily, Molly relented. "But then, so was I. I haven't got a chill. Let's go round, shall we, and see Madame La-Farge. Maybe some new gowns are what we both need."

14

Not until she and Jessica reached Madame LaFarge's did Molly remember her promise to her uncle not to enter the establishment. "Drat," she muttered as the carriage pulled up. "I gave Uncle George my word that I'd stay in the coach; he says half of Madame's clientele has been sick this autumn."

"I've been coming here every week," Jessica pointed out, "and I'm fit as a fiddle. Come on; what he doesn't know won't hurt him."

"No, you go ahead. Take your time. I'll just sit and watch the world go by."

"Well, if you're sure—I only need a sleeve fitting; I'll be but a minute." The footman helped Jessica down just as the door to Madame LaFarge's opened. "Oh my," Jessica whispered as a red-haired woman clad in an outlandish froth of bright red taffeta and black lace emerged.. "If Madame concocted that, I shall have to find a new dressmaker!" But once outside, the woman turned to shake her fist at Madame's assistant and cried in the hard round vowels of lower-class London:

"Ye can keep yer bleedin' gowns, then; I wouldn't be seen dead in 'em anyway!" Then she snapped up a black lace parasol and tottered down the street on her high-heeled shoes, still grumbling: "Bunch o' right ruddy snobs, that's all they is. Ain't I a freeborn Englishwoman?

But my money ain't good enough for 'em, the bloody little frogs!''

Jessica giggled, looking back at Molly and rolling her eyes as the woman passed her. " 'N' ye can go to hell too!'' the woman snapped, giving her a jab in the skirts with her parasol tip.

"Well, I never! No, never mind," Jessica told the footman as he started after her attacker. "No harm done." She gave a little wave to Molly and vanished inside.

But the footman was still bristling at this insult to his mistress. "Ye'd best watch yer step around yer betters," he shouted after the woman. She whirled in a swirl of red skirts, lowered the parasol, and cursed him soundly.

Molly froze, suddenly recognizing that voice, the woman's flashing dark eyes: it was Charity Campbell of Gospel Square.

She's come up in the world, Molly thought with a little pang of jealousy—before she realized how absurd such envy was, when she herself was sitting in a handsome carriage, dressed in tasteful silk and pearls. Evidently Charity had chosen the more usual route out of poverty, lying flat on her back. Well, Molly couldn't blame her for that. What had happened to her baby, she wondered, the one Dr. Collett had delivered? What were Charity's sisters up to? Was anyone living in her old room above the butcher shop? Whatever happened to Andrew Stiles?

She drew a deep breath, suddenly overrun by a wave of nostalgia for old days, old friends, even old enemies. Life had been hard, but in some ways it had been easier too—at least, less complicated. In her mind's eye she could see them all as they'd been once upon a time: herself, the Campbell girls, Billy Buttons, Aunt May. . . .

"Here, open up, please; I'm going for a walk," she told the footman, rapping on the carriage door.

"I'll come with ye, milady."

"No, there's no need. I'd rather go alone." Far down the street Molly could still see a bobbing black parasol and the flash of red skirts.

"But—"

"I'll be right back! Stay here; don't come after me!" she said emphatically. Then she gathered up her own skirts and hurried after Charity at as fast a clip as she dared.

Fortunately, her quarry was inclined to dawdle. From a distance, Molly watched her buy some grapes from a cart, pause by a sweet-shop window, stop once or twice to tug at her uncomfortable shoes. As Charity neared Clerkenwell Road, Molly almost caught up to her, but then the woman approached one of the city watchmen and engaged him in a heated conversation, complaining of her treatment at Madame LaFarge's. Molly hung back, pretending to examine some baskets that a weaver was selling, until the watchman disengaged himself, all the while agreeing that the foreigners in London all ought to be sent back where they came from, and went on his way.

"Charity?" Molly called, coming out of the shadow of the weaver's stall. "Charity Campbell?"

The woman turned to her impatiently. "Aye. Who're ye?"

Molly took a quick glance around to make sure no one who knew Mary Catherine Villiers was in sight. "It's Molly, Charity. Molly Flowers, that used to live upstairs."

"Molly Flowers?" Charity paled. "Ye can't be! She died in the Fleet; old Tom Peabody said so!" She peered at Molly more closely. "Though ye does look as like her as two peas in a pod."

"I didn't die. I had a bit of luck instead, and got out early."

"A bit o' luck? I'll say ye did. Them pearls—is they real?"

"These? Oh, no," Molly lied, fingering the necklace at her throat.

"Hmph, I didn't think so. Still, 'tis plain ye're doin' well. I'd never have recognized ye. Ye sounds different too."

"I've been ill," Molly told her, clearing her throat.

Charity stood back a few steps. "Good God, girl. Not the plague!"

"Oh, no, nothing like that."

"It's been bad, ye know, in Smithfield this summer. Plenty o' folks died. Prissy Wingate 'n' her little boy—d'ye remember her? Oh, 'n' the parson at St. Etheldreda's, 'n' Bart Connor's boy Ian."

"I'm right sorry t' hear it," Molly said, bending her speech back into the rhythms of Gospel Square. "How're yer mother 'n' father?"

"Well enough, I reckon. I don't get home too much these days. Been livin' up in Bethnal Green, I have."

"Have ye really? Andrew must be doin' well, then." Charity looked at her blankly. "Andrew Stiles, I mean. Didn't ye 'n' he—"

"Andrew Stiles!" Charity laughed. "Christ, I'd forgot all about him! Got kicked out o' the city watch, ye know, for takin' bribes 'n' brawlin'."

"No, I hadn't heard." Well, there's a bit of justice, Molly mused.

"Aye, 'n' then got stabbed t' death' whilst he was drunk. I've got a new sweetheart now, a real gentleman. In trade, he is—wines 'n' tobacco. Keeps me right nice, he does. The pity is, he's married. Still, he's a far sight better than old Andrew Stiles! Speakin' o' the Fleet—ye're lucky to have got out o' there alive, aren't ye?"

"What d'ye mean?"

"Oy, ye know the rumors. They say there's a guard in there named Walker or Blocker or somethin' that kidnaps the prisoners 'n' sells 'em to a witch."

"Stalker," Molly murmured.

"Aye, Stalker, that's it. Tom Peabody swore up 'n' down that was wot happened to ye."

"Poor Tom," said Molly, remembering how he'd run away from the gate. "But, Charity, how's yer daughter?"

"My wot?" Charity blinked.

"I'd heard ye had a little girl."

"Born dead," the woman said succinctly, " 'n' I can't say I'm sorry."

Now Molly blinked. "Are ye sure? I thought that Dr. Collett—"

"Oy, that's right," Charity interrupted, "that doctor fellow was a friend o' yers, weren't he? 'Twas a right stroke o' luck he showed up that night to take yer Aunt May away; I was havin' a terrible time of it. But he took care o' everythin', he did—even took the babe away to bury it for me." She gave a little shudder. "Well, like I say, I ain't sorry. If it'd lived, I never would o' met my Dick; I'd still be stuck in Gospel Square changin' nappies, like them sisters o' mine."

How odd, thought Molly. She was absolutely certain Dr. Collett had told her both mother and child were doing fine.

"Oops!" Charity said, waving at an approaching cabriolet, "there's Dick now; I've got t' be off. Say, ye wouldn't happen t' know a decent dressmaker, would ye?" She eyed Molly's gown. "Nah, I don't reckon ye do. That's nice enough, mind ye, but so awfully plain. Hallo, Dick!" She stood on tiptoe to give the beefy man who climbed down from the coach a kiss. "This here's an old friend, Dick—Miss Molly Flowers. Sort of a ghost from my past, eh, Molly?"

"Pleased t' meet ye," Dick said shortly. "Come on, Charity, I'm late."

"Hold on to yer breeches. Always rushin' me about, this one is," Charity told Molly. "Well, lovely chattin' with ye, I'm sure. If ye're ever up in Bethnal Green—"

"Dammit, Charity, come on!" Dick bundled her into the coach, then whistled to the driver. "Let's go!"

Charity hung from the window, waving back at Molly as they sped away. "Give my best regards t' Aunt May!"

It took a moment for her words to sink in. "But Aunt May's dead," Molly said aloud. "She must know that." Or had she just forgotten? "Charity, wait!" she called. But the coach was out of earshot already, dodging a donkey cart as it rumbled onto Clerkenwell Road. Molly stood in the street in the bright autumn sunshine and stared after her old neighbor with a growing sense of disquiet. Aunt May alive, and the baby dead—the complete opposite of what Dr. Collett had said.

Of course, Charity was hardly what one would call reliable, she reminded herself. She'd scarcely remembered Andrew Stiles when Molly mentioned him, and it was he who had got her with child. Besides, Dr. Collett would have no reason to lie.

Still, the disquiet lay like a stone in her belly. There hadn't been any doubt in Charity's voice; she'd sounded quite offhand.

"Mary Catherine! Mary Catherine!" Molly jumped back as Jessica's carriage rolled up beside her, with her cousin calling her name. "What in the world are you doing standing in the middle of the road?" Jessica demanded. "Are you taken sick again?"

"No," Molly said slowly. "Well . . . yes. Do you know Dr. John Collett's house on High Holborn?" she asked the coachman. He nodded. "Will you please take me there?"

"If you're not well, Mary Catherine," Jessica said worriedly, "hadn't you better go home and have Uncle send for the doctor?"

Molly shook her head. "I don't want Uncle George to know."

"But—"

"If you won't take me, I'll hire a coach." She turned in the street, searching for a livery.

"Don't be silly," Jessica said hastily. "Of course I'll take you. I only hope this isn't my fault—that seeing Ballenrose again isn't what's upset you."

It wasn't, of course; Charity Campbell's careless words of farewell had made Molly forget all about him. She heard them again in her mind against the clatter of the carriage wheels as they set out for High Holborn:

Give my best regards t' Aunt May!

* * *

"There's a perfectly simple explanation," Dr. Collett said, taking off his spectacles and rubbing his pale eyes as he sat behind his big oak desk, "which I'll be happy to get to—just as soon as you explain two things to me: what you were doing out-of-doors in direct contradiction to my orders, and what could have possessed you to speak to this apparition from your past. Your uncle will be most disappointed in you—*most* disappointed."

Molly beat down an urge to beg him not to tell on her. Here in his study, surrounded by huge dark books and instruments and seals and diplomas, he seemed a good deal more intimidating than at the dinner table. "I imagine a good many people tell you things in the course of your practice that they wish kept confidential, Dr. Collett. I am relying on your discretion. That is why I came to see you here."

"And induced me to cancel two appointments because you told my man it was an emergency."

"So far as I'm concerned, it is. I don't understand why she should have thought my Aunt May was alive—or why you told me her baby was well when it was born dead."

Dr. Collett sighed and rubbed his eyes again. "There's a good deal more to the practice of medicine than simply healing bodies, Mary Catherine. There is also what we physicians call the patient's mental state. It is my opinion, though I haven't proved it through experimentation yet, that the cause of many physical illnesses can be laid at the door of a patient's mental well-being—or, more precisely, lack of well-being. I believe that is why diseases such as cholera and smallpox take a far greater toll on the inhabitants of the poorer quarters of the city than on the well-to-do."

"Fascinating," Molly said, tight-lipped. "What's that got to do with Aunt May?"

"I don't think you're aware, my dear girl, of just how precarious the state of your health was when your uncle found you. This most recent illness of yours is proof enough of that. Even after a year and a half, contamination remains in your chest, ready to flare up again at the slightest instigation.''

"The point, please, Dr. Collett."

"The point," he said sharply, "is that when you came out of the Fleet, you were very close to death."

"Balderdash," Molly scoffed. "I felt fine."

"You *thought* you felt fine," the doctor corrected her, "because the decline in your health had been so very gradual as to be imperceptible to you. It was perfectly plain, however, to my trained eye."

"I still don't see what all this has got to do with Aunt May," Molly said grudgingly.

"I am endeavoring to explain. Once your uncle ascertained your true identity, you became my patient. I committed myself to devoting all my training and skills to preserving your life, knowing that had your uncle found you after all those years only to lose you to some noxious prison fever, it would prove a tragedy from which he might never recover. He has already overcome enough tragedies in his lifetime for any one man."

He meant Uncle George's father's murder, Molly supposed, and her own mother's death—not to mention the duchess's madness. "That's certainly true," she agreed.

"*Your* well-being became my primary concern," he emphasized again, "and, indirectly, your uncle's. He's an extraordinary man, Mary Catherine; I wonder do you realize that? He has made it his goal to preserve a way of life in this nation that any number of rabble-rousing iconoclasts would prefer to see break down. Though constantly beset by enemies, he devotes himself to maintaining the standards of morals and decorum that have made England great. Sometimes I greatly fear he is the last of his kind—that this kingdom will never see his like again."

"I know he is indeed remarkable," Molly said slowly. She had never really considered Uncle George in this light.

Dr. Collett nodded approval. "Then I know you'll understand the choice I made when I went to Gospel Square that night."

"What choice?" she asked.

The doctor pulled his spectacles on over his ears again; they made his pale eyes seem watery and huge. "Your Aunt May *was* alive when I got there—"

"What?" Molly cried, jumping up from her seat.

"—but only just barely." He motioned her down again; Molly ignored it. "She was severely undernourished— really, she was starved."

"Oh, God." Molly bit down on her hand.

"And so far as I could tell, none of her senses were functioning. That is, she couldn't hear, or see, or speak."

"I don't understand," Molly whispered. "How could Billy have let her get in such a state? And what about the Campbells? Didn't they feed her?"

"I'm sure they tried," Dr. Collett said soothingly, "but in my opinion your Aunt May had lost her will to live. And in such cases, there is really very little to be done. So I made my decision. I arranged for your aunt to be taken to a hospital where I knew she'd be well cared for, to live out what little remained of her life in peace."

Molly stared at him in shock. "Who do you think you are?" she asked when she could speak. "You had no right to do that! You should have brought her to me! I was the one she relied on; I could have made her eat, made her well again—"

"Mary Catherine, no one could have saved her. Believe me. And the strain of trying to, of seeing her that way, would very likely have killed you as well."

"That wasn't for you to decide!"

"On the contrary, I was the only one equipped to make a dispassionate decision. Look at yourself, look at how agitated you are even now, after all this time."

"Of course I am agitated! She was my family, the only family I had—"

"But she wasn't, was she?" he interrupted her. "She was no kin to you; she was just an old woman—"

"Who'd taken me in when no one else would! Who saved my life—"

"Who had lived out her days," he went on calmly, "and was ready to die. Do you honestly think she would have wanted you to put your own health at risk for her sake?"

"What she might have wanted hasn't got a thing to do with it!" Molly choked back tears. "How could you be so beastly as to take her off to die amongst a bunch of strangers?"

"Mary Catherine, she wasn't sentient. She wouldn't have known you from . . . from the bedpost, even if I had brought her to you."

"She would have. She would have known me." Molly refused the handkerchief he offered, looking at him accusingly. "Did Uncle George know about this?"

"No," he said after the merest pause. "I wanted to spare him as well as you."

"You were afraid to tell him, that's more like it. You knew that he'd be furious, just like me. I'll tell you one thing, Dr. Collett," Molly said vehemently. "I shall never forgive you for this, not so long as I live."

"I made what I considered to be the right decision at the time," he told her stolidly, "and I would make it again under the same circumstances."

Molly wiped her eyes on her sleeve. "What about the baby?"

"What about what baby?" he asked, blinking those pale eyes.

"Charity's baby! Why did you lie to me, say it was doing well?"

"For the same reason, of course. I didn't want to upset you."

"Well, you *have* upset me now." Molly looked at him with distaste. "I've a mind to tell Uncle George about this."

Dr. Collett picked up his quill pen, weighed it between his hands. "I shouldn't if I were you—not unless you want him to learn about your discussion with Mistress Campbell today."

She arched her brows. "Are you threatening me?"

" 'Threatening' is an ugly word, Mary Catherine. Let's just say I am offering a quid pro quo."

"Call it what you like, it's still blackmail—"

A knock sounded at the study door. "Yes, Jules?"

"Warden Fell is here for his appointment, sir," his manservant announced.

Molly saw the doctor's colorless eyes slant toward her beneath the spectacle frames as she drew in her breath. "Do you mean to tell me you treat that . . . that monster?" she demanded, appalled.

"He has gout. I am in the business of healing men's bodies, not of judging their souls."

Molly drew her shawl tight around her shoulders. "I can tell you one thing that's certain, Dr. Collett. You have treated me for the last time." She started toward the door.

"I should be curious to know how you intend to explain that to your uncle," he called after her.

"I'll worry about that," she told him, then turned back. "What hospital was it?"

"I beg your pardon?"

"What hospital was it that you took Aunt May to?"

He considered her impassively. "Why would you want to know that?"

"I'd like to make a donation to it, in her name."

"St. Thomas's," he said briefly. "I believe."

"You *believe?*"

'I refer patients to St. Thomas's, St. Bartholomew's, and Bridewell," he told her with a touch of impatience. "I cannot be certain which I would have chosen on the spur of the moment more than eighteen months ago."

"But you were notified of her death. There must be some record—" Molly stared at him with growing horror. "You *were* notified of her death, weren't you? She hasn't been languishing in some hospital for all this time?"

"Certainly not; that would be quite impossible, given her condition. I'm sure I have a record somewhere."

"I should like to see it."

"Very well." He got up from his desk, took off his waistcoat, and tied on an apron.

"I should like to see it *now*," Molly insisted.

"I have a patient waiting. Excuse me, please." He tried to brush past her, and she caught his arm.

"I said now."

"Take your hand off me," he told her in a tone quite different from any she had ever heard him use before. Behind the thick glass of the spectacles his eyes were marble-cold, ice-pale. Molly let drop his arm, suddenly reminded of Hugh Stalker, of all people.

"I want to see that record," she said stubbornly.

"And so you shall. I'll send it to you just as soon as I've a chance to find it. Now I'd suggest you return home and rest, Mary Catherine. It's quite clear your meeting with this Mistress Campbell has made you overwrought."

"I meant what I said before. I'll not have you as my physician any longer."

"As milady wishes," said Dr. Collett, his voice once more impassive, but with his strange pale eyes still glittering and cold.

15

"BY THE BY, this came for you last night, while you were at the king's ball," the Duke of Buckingham said, laying a folded letter on the coffee tray and motioning for Thompkins to take it to Molly at the other end of the breakfast table. "Dr. Collett's man brought it by."

"Well, it's about time!" Molly muttered, seizing it eagerly and breaking the wafer seal. Three weeks had passed since her visit to the doctor's study, and she'd sent two notes reminding him of his promise to locate Aunt May's record for her.

"What is it?" her uncle asked, then dabbed his mouth with a napkin. "Dammit, Thompkins, you've filled my cup too full again."

"Forgive me, m'lord. Tea, m'lady?"

"Please. It's nothing, really," Molly said, scanning the letter quickly and then folding it up again. "Just a note about a charity I'd asked him to look into."

"Really. Which one is that?"

"St. Bartholomew's hospital. I though I might establish a bed there in memory of Aunt May—if it's all right with you, that is."

"Certainly," said the duke. "I'm delighted to see you taking an interest in charitable work. But why St. Bart's?"

"No reason in particular," she said quickly, "except that it is closest to Smithfield. And I cannot help thinking of my old friends and neighbors, especially now that winter has come. I feel quite guilty at times that I should have so much, and they so little.''

''Perhaps you would like me to open the west wing of the house to them,'' her uncle said dryly.

''Don't be droll. I know that everyone can't be rich, but I do wish the poor could be more comfortable. It's quite dreadful being cold or hungry.''

''I learned that lesson very well indeed during the wars, my dear; you needn't tell me. There were weeks on end in Scotland that we ate nothing but brown bread and salmon and bad wine.'' Molly was tempted to tell him that diet would have seemed quite ample during a winter in Smithfield, but didn't. There were some things Uncle George just couldn't understand. ''In fact, just thinking of it makes me quite ravenous,'' he went on. ''Thompkins, bring the grapes back in, please.''

''Very good, m'lord.''

When the butler had gone, Uncle George leaned forward. ''You do realize that there may be questions if you endow this bed in Aunt May's name.''

Molly nibbled her lip. ''I hadn't thought of that.''

''Perhaps you should consider making the endowment anonymous. Anyway, didn't our Lord say one should keep one's good works to oneself?'' The duke paused to choose a bunch of grapes from the bowl Thompkins brought him, bit one off, and swallowed.

''I suppose you're right.''

''I'm sure John would be happy to arrange it all for you.''

''No.'' Molly fingered the folds in the letter she still held. ''No, I'd prefer to see to it myself.''

The duke shrugged. ''Well, then, I'll draft a proposal for you, to the board of directors.''

Date of death: April 6, 1670, the letter said. *Place: St. Bartholomew's Hospital, City of London. Cause: Debilitated old age.* There it all was, set out in black and white, just as she'd asked for. Why, then, did she still feel such unease?

"Actually, I'd like to do it in person," she said hesitantly.

Her uncle looked up from his grapes. "Go there, do you mean? I hardly think that's wise. You're barely up from the sickbed yourself. Speaking of which, it's been some time, hasn't it, since John was by to see you? We must send for him. See to it, Thompkins."

"No!" Molly cried. "I don't want to see him."

"My dear girl, you may feel in the peak of health now, but you've been gravely ill. Dr. Collett should examine you for any signs of a relapse."

"Not him. I'll see another doctor if you like, but not him."

The duke's fine dark eyes narrowed. "Leave us, Thompkins," he ordered brusquely. "Close the doors." When they were alone, he turned to Molly again. "Has Dr. Collett made advances to you?"

"Advances?"

"Has he tried to take advantage of you in some way?"

"Heavens, no. It's nothing like that."

"Well, what is it, then?"

"It's nothing specific, really." Molly said faintly. "I just don't like him."

"He's very good, you know," he told her with some reproach. "The very best there is. He'll likely be named president of the Royal Society at the next election."

"They can have him, and welcome."

"I must confess, Mary Catherine, I don't understand."

"There's naught to understand. I don't like him, that's all. He gives me the shivers."

"He what?" the duke asked, arching a brow.

"He makes me nervous," she amended.

He looked at her for a moment. Then, "Perhaps he serves as a reminder to you of unpleasant things," he suggested gently. "Your time in prison. Aunt May's death."

"Yes. I'm sure that's it," Molly said gratefully.

"Well. In that case, another physician certainly is in order. I'll make some inquiries, find out who else is good."

"Thank you, Uncle George." He pushed back his chair as she rose. "About St. Bartholomew's—"

"Yes?"

"Surely it couldn't do any harm for me just to stop in briefly, to have a look at the place. I wouldn't tour the wards."

"I suppose not. Are you going there now?" Molly nodded. "You'll want to take a nosegay, to fight the stench." Leafing through the remainder of his correspondence, he made a face. "Good God, another letter from Agnes; that's the fifth one this week. If you should run into any doctors there, do ask if they've a cure for love."

Molly laughed and went to kiss his cheek. "You know you'd feel completely bereft if she didn't write to you."

"The devil I would." Absently the duke reached for his grapes, found he'd eaten them all, and jangled the bell at his elbow. "Thompkins! Bring back that bowl."

It was nearly noon before Molly arrived at the hospital. The moment she stepped through the doors she regretted not having taken Uncle George's advice about the nosegay; the long hallway smelled worse than the slaughtering stalls at Smithfield, with a faint undercurrent of boiled cabbage. Poor Aunt May, Molly thought, biting her lip as she gave her name to the porter and asked to speak to the administrator.

The administrator was a tall brown man named Nivens—brown hair, brown eyes, brown waistcoat and breeches. Even his office was brown, paneled in some shiny indeterminate wood. He seemed distracted, even defensive, until Molly explained the reason for her visit. Then his brown eyes lost their wariness; he rang for tea and settled back in his chair.

"There's a pleasant switch, Mistress Villiers. I had you pegged for one of those zealots come to scold me about intolerable conditions and such. If more of them would put their money where their mouths are, this place wouldn't be such a sty. Sugar? Cream? You say an endowed bed— were you thinking of any particular ward?''

"I'm not sure . . .''

"Surgery's far and away the most fashionable endowment,'' he noted, passing her crumpets, "I suppose because the work done there is so dramatic.''

"I was thinking, actually, of something to help elderly patients,'' she told him. "Suppose an old woman without any family was brought here to die. Where would she be put?''

"Just in General Ward, most likely. Mistress Villiers, I can't help thinking you have someone in particular in mind. Don't tell me your uncle the duke is about to turn some antique family retainer out into the streets.''

"Please, Mr. Nivens, don't be absurd.''

"Regrettably, it's not so absurd as one might think. Just last year we had a case—the Earl of Ormely's butler. Poor fellow must have been near eighty years old, and his master turned him out without so much as a pension. Came here with palsy, finally.'' He took a bite of crumpet. "Funny thing. He was ever so proper, right up to the end. Said 'Pardon me' to one of the sisters one morning, then died.''

Molly coughed on a mouthful of tea. "You sound as though it were a joke,'' she said reproachfully.

"My dear Mistress Villiers, at any given time this hospital contains three hundred patients, of whom perhaps one-fifth can be expected to live. Our potter's field''—he gestured beyond the window to a green hill behind the hospital—"is full to bursting. I'm not a callous man, but if I didn't retain some sense of perspective, I'd have thrown this work over a long time ago.''

"One-fifth!'' Molly swallowed. "I had no idea.''

"Quite so. Folk rarely resort to hospital, you see, until they've exhausted every other alternative, because we have a reputation as a charnel house. Consequently they are usually too far gone to live despite our care—which reinforces our unfortunate reputation. If we could only treat some of these patients *before* the point of no return—" He stopped, shrugged. "But I don't want to bore you, and run the risk you'll take your money elsewhere."

"You aren't boring me at all." Molly smiled; she liked this blunt-spoken man. She had the sense, too, that he could be trusted. "Mr. Nivens, may I ask you something in confidence?"

"Certainly. It wouldn't happen to concern an old woman without any family who was brought here to die, would it?" He laughed, seeing her color rise. "Ah hah. I had an inkling your interest in St. Bart's was more than general."

"It wasn't anything like the Earl of Ormely's butler," Molly said quickly. "I'd been told, you see, that she was already dead. I've only just learned she was brought here. If I'd known, I never in the world . . . I just want to know . . . whether she was in pain. What it was like for her at the end."

"That, I'm afraid, is one of God's great mysteries," Nivens said, then shook his head. "Forgive me, Mistress Villiers; perhaps this work has made me too flippant. I don't know what I can do. Perhaps if you tell me the patient's name . . . ?"

"I've got this notice of her death." Molly handed him the letter. He read it over, then raised his brown eyes to hers.

"John Collett, eh? Rather odd for him to be treating an indigent patient."

"I'm relying on your confidence, Mr. Nivens." Molly cocked her head. "You sound as though you don't like him."

"I shall rely on your confidence too, Mistress Villiers. I don't."

"Yet I'm told he's a very fine physician."

"Oh, that he is. But to me he seems to lack . . . What shall I call it? The human touch."

"Do you know, that's just how I feel about him," Molly told him.

"Well." He folded up the letter, passed it back to her, and turned to a cabinet behind him. "Let me see what else we might have in our records." He riffled through a sheaf of papers, paused, looked again. "Odd. We don't seem to have any mention of a May Willoughby. I must have sent the file on to Dr. Collett." He frowned, turning back. "Or perhaps he just came and took it; he's a bit high-handed. Anyway, the death notice is in order. I don't know what more I can tell you, unless . . . Perhaps you should speak to Sister Dodgett."

"Who is she?"

"Chief nurse of the General Ward. She might remember the woman."

"With all the patients she treats? After all this time?" Molly asked dubiously.

"Sister Dodgett," Nivens said with satisfaction, "has got the human touch in spades. And there's no harm in trying. Have some more tea, why don't you. I'll fetch her."

Sister Dodgett was white where Mr. Nivens was brown, from her head to the hem of her apron, but Molly saw right away what the administrator had meant about her human touch; she'd never met anyone who so embodied competence and kindness. The woman was most distraught when Aunt May's name rang no bell. "That's odd," she kept saying, "I most always remembers 'em when they's old 'n' alone, on account o' they're the ones I gives a bit o' extra attention to. Besides, Willoughby was the name o' my cousin Selma's first husband; ye'd think I'd recall her just by that."

"Perhaps you weren't on duty while she was here," Molly suggested.

"Oh, no, mum. If she was here fer three days, like that there record says, I'd o' seen her. I been here dawn to dusk, six days a week, for the past twenty years."

"Good Lord!" Molly marveled.

"And you can take my word," Nivens put in, grinning at his chief nurse, "she doesn't do it for the pay."

Sister Dodgett blushed above her neat white collar. "Well, I always think, don't I, when I see the poor souls wot come here, with a bit o' bad luck 'n' hard times, it could just as well be me."

"I'll tell you what," said Molly. "It doesn't even matter that you don't remember her. Just knowing that she would have been in your care puts my mind at ease."

"Well." The nurse smiled shyly. "I'm sure that's very kind o' ye t' say. We does wot we can, don't we, Mr. Nivens?"

"That we do, Dodgett. That we do."

"I'd like very much to make your hard work easier," Molly said impulsively, then looked at Nivens. "Suppose that I endow three beds."

"Three! A veritable windfall, Dodgett, wouldn't you say?"

"In General Ward? Oh, mum . . ." The nurse blinked at a sudden loud commotion outside the office. "Good God, don't tell me we've a loony-tick loose again!"

Just then the office door burst open. Molly turned in her chair, staring in astonishment at the Earl of Ballenrose, his hair and clothes disheveled, his face very pale. "Michael," he said to Nivens, taking no notice of anyone else, "you've got to help me. Please."

16

"ANTHONY!" Nivens got up from his chair. "What's happened? What's the matter?"

Anthony Strakhan was panting for breath. "Note came," he gasped out. "Little boy . . . here. Wagon. Hit him—"

Nivens reached into a drawer of his desk, took out a bottle, and thrust it at him. "You've got to calm down, Anthony; I can't understand you. Have a swallow of this."

Ballenrose took a long draft and promptly choked. "Christ!" he sputtered, holding the bottle at arm's length, staring at it. "What's that supposed to be?"

"Brandy," Nivens told him. "The best I can afford on what you hospital directors pay me."

"Then you've earned a raise. I was saying—I got a note at home that my gatekeeper's son had been hit by a wagon. The note said that he'd been taken here—"

"A wagon accident?" Nivens and Sister Dodgett exchanged puzzled glances. "When?"

"Just now, this morning. The poor man lost his wife and daughters to cholera three years ago, Michael; the boy's all he has left. If anything should happen to him—"

Nivens was shaking his head. "I heard nothing about an accident victim this morning. Dodgett, did you?"

"No, sir. But I'll gladly run back t' the ward 'n' check—"

"Do that, please. I'll ask in surgery. You sit down, Anthony; what the devil did you do, run all the way from your house? If you don't like my brandy, have a cup of tea."

"Thanks, Michael." Ballenrose collapsed into a chair, reaching for the teapot, and for the first time noticed there was someone else in the room. "I beg your pardon! I didn't mean to interrupt—"

Molly had turned away from him in a panic; now, slowly, she turned back. The teapot lid rattled as he set it down, nearly missing the tray. "Mary Catherine," he said hoarsely. "What are you doing here?"

God, he'd looked like that on the esplanade the last time she saw him, black hair wild with wind, his white shirt open at the throat . . . "Nothing," Molly said quickly. "That is, I was just leaving." She stood up, skirts in her hands, and blundered toward the door. Her shoe caught on an uneven floorboard, and she stumbled. His long arm came out to steady her, hand closing over her wrist. She drew in breath as he touched her, looking down at him. The light she had seen in his eyes at first had disappeared; his jaw was tight now as he released her.

"Nonsense, I'll go," he said. "I shouldn't have burst in on you that way."

"But you can't go. They won't know where to find you when they find the boy," Molly pointed out.

"I'll wait outside."

"No, really, I will."

They were both on their feet, at an impasse, when Michael Nivens came back in. "I don't know what to tell you, Anthony," he said, his brow wrinkled. "There hasn't been any such victim admitted here today; Dodgett and I are sure. Are you certain the note said St. Bart's?"

"Of course I'm sure," Ballenrose growled.

"Well, all I can think is that someone's playing a particularly ugly trick on your poor gatekeeper," Nivens said.

"On Prescott? Why the devil would somebody do that?"

"Or on you. Have you disgruntled any husba—" The door opened again behind him. "Good God, it's like a carnival in here today. What is it now?"

"A Mr. Prescott, sir, to see the earl," the porter told him.

"Prescott!" Ballenrose waved him in. "Any news?"

"Aye, sir, though I scarce know how t' tell ye," said his gatekeeper, standing in the doorway. " 'Tis Jackie—"

"Have you found him? Is he safe?"

"Aye, m'lord," said Prescott, looking abashed. "Safe 'n' sound 'n' at home in the cottage all this time."

"What?" Anthony Strakhan demanded.

"Well, m'lord, I never even thought t' look there once that note arrived. I can't for the life o' me think who'd pull such a stunt, though."

"No, nor I." Ballenrose, scratching his chin, caught Nivens' bemused glance. "In answer to your earlier question, Michael, no. I haven't disgruntled any husbands lately. On the contrary, I've been chaste as a monk. Sworn off the fairer sex altogether, in fact."

Nivens snorted. "I'm sure. Well, all's well that ends well, isn't it? So long as you are here, you ought to speak to Mistress Villiers. She's just told me she is planning to endow three beds in our General Ward. That ought to gladden your heart." He turned to Molly. "Anthony takes a special interest in St. Bart's, you know."

"No," she said faintly. "I didn't."

"I hope that news won't dampen Mistress Villiers' sudden enthusiasm for good works," the earl drawled.

"You needn't sound as though you're the only one in London who cares about the less fortunate," Molly snapped.

Michael Nivens looked from one to the other, nonplussed. "I see you are acquainted," he said at last. "Anyone for tea?"

"How did you find out I'd be here?" Molly asked Ballenrose suspiciously.

"How did I *what?*"

"You really ought to be ashamed," she went on, gesturing to Prescott, "using him that way. But then, you never worry about hurting those you use, do you?"

Light dawned in Ballenrose's blue eyes. "You think I concocted that story about his son just to get to see you? Oh, you flatter yourself, Mistress Villiers."

"Here, now, the master wouldn't do nothin' like that!" Prescott said stoutly from the doorway.

"Don't waste your breath, Prescott," Ballenrose told him. "Mistress Villiers is willing to believe any calumny, I've found, if it's to do with me."

"Calumny, sir?"

"Lies, Prescott, lies."

"You're a fine one to talk about lies," Molly cried, green eyes flashing.

Nivens ambled toward the doorway, beyond which a small crowd of curious patients and nurses had gathered. "Go along home, Prescott, why don't you," he suggested, "and see to that boy of yours? The tea must be cold by now; I'll fetch another pot." He went out, closing the door behind him. Molly moved toward it swiftly, but Ballenrose moved faster, blocking her path.

Her green gaze narrowed. "Get out of my way."

"Where in the world did you learn your manners, Mistress Villiers, in Smithfield Market? Not until you apologize for that ridiculous accusation."

His jest stung far too close to home. "The devil I will. Move or I'll scream my head off."

"Go right ahead. This place is used to screaming. When it comes to that, who's to say you didn't send that note yourself?"

Molly forgot about screaming and gaped. "Why in God's name would I?"

"How should I know? Why did you ride out to the esplanade that day only to snub me? Why did you make love to me one night and cut me dead the next? I suppose because it gives you pleasure to play such games."

"It was because I found out the truth about you!"

"What truth? From whom?"

"From Uncle George. He told me—" She stopped; he was laughing.

"You couldn't pull truth from George Villiers with a hammer and tongs."

"What about you?" Molly cried angrily. "All that fine high-blown talk of yours about honor and love, and all the time you were only out to ruin me, using me to get back at Uncle George because of your sister!"

The room grew suddenly quiet. "He told you that?" Anthony Strakhan said then, softly. "Well, damn his black soul to hell." His anger seethed over. "Aye, and you with him for having believed it!"

"Who wouldn't?" Molly retorted. "It is perfectly—"

"No!" He brought his hand up close to her face; she flinched, fearing he'd strike her, but he just stabbed the air. "Not someone who loved me the way I loved you. Not the woman I thought you were." He stepped aside abruptly. "Go on, I've nothing more to say to you."

She reached the door, felt the comfort of the latch in her hand, and only then turned back. "Anthony." He didn't look at her, just stood with his head lowered. She pressed on, feeling she owed him this, something. "Anthony, I'm sorry about Magdalene, truly I am, and so is Uncle George. But you mustn't let the past control your life this way. Uncle George says—"

"Uncle George says!" he cried out, fists at his temples. "Did Uncle George say why he didn't wed her?"

Molly dropped her gaze. "I think you know why."

His head jerked up. "What did he tell you?"

"Because . . . because of her madness."

"Her madness." She heard him laughing, looked up, saw that he was near crying. "Oh, Christ, *her* madness!"

"He said some people thought it was for Aunt Kate's money," Molly said nervously, "but—"

"God, no," he interrupted. "It wouldn't be for money.

Never for anything so sane or simple as money, not Buckingham. Anyway, he's got plenty of that."

"He's got plenty of *everything,*" Molly said after a pause.

"Ah, that's where you're wrong," the Earl of Ballenrose said. "He hasn't got enough *power.* Not anyone on earth—not King Charles, not Louis of France, not the Sultan of Islam—has got the sort of power he craves. Only God and the devil might—and I'd not bet on that."

"I don't know why you say such hateful things about him," Molly said, near tears herself, "unless it is because, just as Uncle George says, you're mad too, just like your sister!"

He closed the space between them in a single stride and pinned her back against the door, his hand circling her throat. "My sister," he said, his face inches from hers, his eyes alive with blue fire. "Let me tell you about my sister, Mary Catherine. She was the purest, brightest soul I ever knew—a white rose, a star. A lily flower. Everyone . . ." He breathed. "Everyone said so. That was why he had to have her, can't you see? *Because* she was so good. Because he had to prove he could."

Molly brought her hand up to pry his away. "But suicide is a sin," she whispered. "She killed herself. She isn't blameless."

"Was it suicide when Christ went to Gethsemane, knowing he'd be taken there?" he countered.

"What has that to do with it?"

"That was why she killed herself. A sacrifice," he told her. Molly shuddered. "She sacrificed herself to keep from bringing the offspring of his evil into this world."

"May God forgive you for saying that!"

"May he damn your uncle to eternal fire for giving me cause." He loosed his hand. "It brings me no joy to tell you these things, Mary Catherine, knowing that they hurt you—just as it's brought me precious little to have fallen in love with you."

"How can you speak of loving me," Molly demanded, astonished, "and tell such vile tales about my uncle?"

"How could I love you and *not* tell you?" He raised his hand again, though only to stroke her hair, to lay his fingers along the line of her cheek. "Precious little joy," he repeated, "and yet, what there was, was worth it. My love for you is a flame that will burn in me until the day I die."

Molly looked into his eyes—priest's eyes, weary and sad with the weight of confession. "Uncle George says your family knows no bounds to its passions."

The Earl of Ballenrose smiled. "Ah. I take it back; there's one thing your uncle says that's true."

"He also says . . ." She hesitated, then went on. "He says there have to be limits, or what would happen to the world?"

"What indeed?" He moved away from her at last. "There's the difference, I suppose, between the Duke of Buckingham's vision for the world and mine."

Molly groped for the latch again. "How long," he asked at her back, "are you going to listen to what your uncle says instead of to your heart?"

"They're the same," she told him.

"I'll believe that when you walk out that door."

Molly raised the latch, held it, heard the blood surging in her veins, coursing round her bones, pulsing in her head . . . "Oh, God," she cried, turning back. "Oh, God, I don't know what to do!"

His arms were open. She swayed, sagged, leaned toward him. He gathered her into his embrace.

"I'm afraid," Molly whispered.

"I've been afraid since that first night when I saw you in the king's gardens."

"Of what?"

"Of you. Of what you do to me."

They held each other silently for a moment. His embrace was strong and sure and warm—and Molly melted to it, clung to him as all her doubts dissolved. "Oh, love," he groaned, his body pressed to hers. "My dear, dear heart. If I ever find who played that trick on Prescott, I'll put him up for knighthood."

"It was fate," Molly whispered, returning his hot, sweet kiss. "Our stars, just as you said; it had to be." His tongue teased her lips apart and slipped between them; his hand cupped her breast through the cloth of her cloak, and she sighed and shivered, every fiber of her flesh aching for him. "Anthony—"

"Nothing must ever part us again," he murmured, pulling open the cloak, kissing her throat, the soft white mounds of her breasts.

Out in the hallway someone called: "Milord?"

"Michael," Anthony murmured, returning her kiss. "He's discreet enough not to come in."

"I don't care if he does," she said defiantly. "I don't care who does."

"Milord," Michael Nivens called again, "wait! I wouldn't go in there—"

The door flew open with such force that the wood paneling rattled. Beyond Anthony's shoulder Molly saw her uncle, in his dark blue riding cape and gloves. His dark eyes bored into Ballenrose's, and his fine mouth twisted. Then he yanked off his glove and threw it down at the earl's feet.

"Dawn tomorrow at Rawnleigh, on the embankment." He spat the words out with cold, crisp precision.

"With pleasure," Anthony shot back.

"The choice of weapons is yours, I believe. Sword or pistol?"

"Pistol," Anthony replied. "Your second?"

"Dr. John Collett. High Holborn Street. Yours?"

Anthony glanced beyond his foe to where Nivens stood, aghast, in the doorway. "Will you stand for me, Michael?"

"It's against the law!"

"Will you?"

"You could both be beheaded!"

"Only the winner takes that risk," the Duke of Buckingham drawled. "What's the matter, Ballenrose, can't find a nobleman to second you? Forced to rely on a pathetic civil servant instead?"

Nivens straightened his shoulders. "I'd be honored, Anthony," he said.

Molly, to whom the refinements of a formal challenge had been the stuff of fiction, at last grasped what was to take place. "Uncle George, no! You can't!" she cried, stumbling toward him.

"On the contrary." He caught her arm, yanked her to his side as he started away. "I must and I will."

"Anthony." She turned back, green eyes pleading. "For the love of God—"

"He's right." The hatred in his voice made her shiver. "It's the only way."

"I won't let you! I'll go and tell the king," she threatened, struggling to pull herself free. Her uncle's hands clamped around her wrists, dragging her across the hospital floor.

"You won't be telling anyone anything," he promised grimly. "You'll be locked in your room until I've shot that bastard dead."

17

"I'll do anything for you, Parker," Molly bargained through the unbudging thickness of her bedchamber door. "I'll give you money . . . give you all my jewels . . ."

"A lot o' good they'd do me dead," the maid replied implacably. " 'N' that's wot I'd be, too, if I let ye out; his grace made that plain."

"But you could run away with it all! He'd never find you."

"Oy, he'd find me, all right, never ye fear. He found ye, didn't he, then, after all those years?"

Molly leaned against the wall, cursing her captivity. "Let me talk to Thompkins. Please."

"Sorry, m'lady. He's abed—which is right where ye might as well be."

Molly pounded on the door in terror and frustration. "Damn you, Parker, don't you understand? Someone, one or the other of them, is going to die! How can I let that happen?"

"Ye'd best resign yerself, m'lady. The duke's fought ten duels at least in the years I been with him, 'n' he ain't lost one yet."

"Sweet Jesu in heaven." Molly crumpled in a heap on the floor, her fists aching.

"Wot's all this racket, then?"

Molly pushed herself to her knees, hearing the

housekeeper's voice. "Mrs. Johnstone, thank God! You've got to help me put a stop to this madness. Unlock the door, please!"

"Faith, child, there's no use in tryin'. No sense in blamin' yerself, neither; this here duel's been brewin' for a long time, since long before ye came here."

Molly punched the door again, wishing it were the woman's broad, complacent face. Who'd ever heard of such incorruptible servants? Nothing she'd offered could sway them. "There'll be little sense in your having obeyed my uncle once he's dead!"

The housekeeper laughed. "I ain't concerned about the master. I only hope the Earl o' Ballenrose has made his peace with God."

Though Molly couldn't bear the thought of either Uncle George or Anthony dying, the household's shared conviction that Ballenrose hadn't a chance made her frantic with fear. Against her will, her gaze was drawn again to the uncurtained windows across the room, beyond which stretched the eastern sky. Was the horizon less deep a shade of black? Were those clouds above the River Thames, or the first tentative fingers of the morning light? The night had been a thousand lifetimes long, and yet she knew that when dawn came the darkness would seem to have passed in the winking of an eye.

"Go to sleep, child," Mrs. Johnstone advised, and Molly heard her heavy footsteps retreating toward the servants' wing.

"Parker?" she called. "Are you there?"

"I ain't goin' no place," the maid replied.

"Parker, I'm hungry. Famished."

"It ain't gonna kill ye to wait until mornin'."

"Some wine, then," Molly begged her. "I would sleep, but I can't. Please, Parker, bring some wine. My poor head just keeps spinning and spinning—"

"Save yer breath," said the maid. "Yer uncle don't hire help on the basis o' their bein' fools."

Molly sagged down to the floor again, not knowing what

else to try. From the garden below the windows, a song-bird cried. Molly cried too, thinking of Juliet's words to Romeo after their one night together. She would not even have the memory of one such night with Anthony for solace when he was dead.

She crawled to the closest window, dragged herself up to the sill. Oh, God, for wings! she thought, staring down into the gardens three long stories below. A flutter of white a dozen yards to her left caught her eye: the linens set to dry the night in the laundry yards. She'd heard her uncle give the orders himself to see that plenty of bedding was boiled and washed in case he had a need for bandages.

Wind raised the sheets and cracked them with a sound sharp as a pistol shot. She shuddered, turned away, and then looked back, eyeing their faint white forms stretched across the sturdy drying racks and anchored with pins. Their fastenings withstood this swirling wind. Might they not hold her? At least they'd break her fall to the earth below.

The balcony outside her window, meant for decoration rather than use, was a scant half-foot wide. It ended a yard or more short of that below the next window—a spare bedchamber, unoccupied—which in turn led after a space to one more balcony, much larger, outside the wide French windows of the music room. The laundry racks were ranged beneath that, six feet or so from the wall.

It could be done.

She stripped off her dress, with its billowing skirts and tight bodice, and put on a double layer of the warm wool surplices she wore beneath her other clothes in winter. They fell only to her knees, but despite the winter chill, she left her legs and feet bare. Then she unlatched her window with stealthy care, pausing to see if Parker raised an alarm. All remained quiet, so she stepped gingerly over the windowsill to the balcony, wincing as her toes touched rough stone. Two years ago she'd been able to walk through the streets of Smithfield barefoot. These months of easy living had made her soft.

By turning sideways and hugging the house, she was able to scuttle, crablike, along the length of the first balcony. When she reached the end, she climbed, on tiptoe, atop the low edge. Careful not to look down, she dug her nails into the mortar spaces of the wall, found fingerholds of a sort, and then stretched one foot as far as she could to her right, wiggling it up and down in hopes of hitting the next balcony.

She didn't. Puzzled, she glanced over and saw she was a good six inches short. "Damn," she muttered, swinging her leg back, adjusting her hands further over, and then trying again. This time her toe just scraped the distant ledge. Increasingly frantic with each passing minute, she pulled herself back and made one more awkward lunge. Her foot landed solidly at last, and she scrambled hand over hand onto the second balcony.

The third was easier to reach; there was a stone boss ornamenting the wall on which she could perch halfway. She breathed a sigh of relief, but nearly lost her nerve completely when she turned about and looked into the yard below. Good God, it was a long way down! And though she knew the sheets were more than six feet square, from this height they suddenly seemed exceedingly small.

"They're both good men, Lord," she whispered. "I know you can't want either of them to die." She gazed down again. "Or me either, I hope." Then she climbed up onto the edge of the balcony, fought the urge to close her eyes, and jumped.

The square of white linen rushed toward her with dizzying speed. She was falling headfirst, she realized, and flailed frantically, trying to twist about. There wasn't time. She hit the top sheet square on her nose; the linen gave, rack straining for one breath-stopping instant, and then held, bouncing her up into the air. When she landed again, it was on her shoulder, with far less velocity. She nearly shouted in triumph, then gasped as the rack collapsed, tumbling her to the ground.

It seemed to her to make a deafening racket. Flat on

her back, she stared up at the house, holding her breath
for someone to sound a general alarm. When no one did,
she crawled out of the tangled wood and linen, skirted the
house, crossed the yards to the garden gate, ducked
through, and began to run.

The road was too rough for her bare feet, so she kept
to the ditch beside it, where water and matted marsh grass
made a frigid cushion of sorts. The night was still dark,
but more birds had started to twitter in the leafless trees.
What had Uncle George meant exactly by dawn, she wondered? The duel couldn't take place until there was at least
enough light to see.

Parker had said her uncle went to dine at Dr. Collett's
and planned to spend the night there. He'd taken his long-
handled dueling pistols with him—those deadly guns with
which he'd never lost a fight. How had Anthony spent the
night? Perhaps escaping to France, she hoped, but without
conviction. Mrs. Johnstone was right; this duel had been
brewing for a long time, and Molly couldn't see either
man giving up the chance to finish off his enemy. How
could it be that two peers of the realm in what was supposed to be the most advanced nation on earth couldn't
find some more civilized way of settling their differences?
Even back in Smithfield two such aggrieved parties would
just have beaten each other bloody on Gospel Square and
have done.

She slowed her pace a bit as she felt the road beside her
curve toward the river. Fog was rising off the water, swirling up in windblown funnels, and in its ghostly smoke
she feared she might run right past Rawnleigh. Between
the damned birds and the blood pounding in her head, she
could hear nothing more. Suddenly she tripped, sprawling
facedown in the chilly ditch water as her calves banged
against some obstacle—the monastery's ruined outer wall.

She pushed herself up, head cocked, listening. More
chattering birds, running water—was that the neigh of a
horse, or just the rush of wind? She started running again,
across an open field toward the dense shadows of trees

that loomed close by the riverbank. A branch snapped beneath her foot, and she gasped in fright at the sharp crack it made.

The sky was still gloomy, but she could see it growing lighter, could smell dawn on the drenched grass and feel it warm the frost-tinged air. Ahead of her, beyond the trees, a buffet of wind caught the fog and lifted it like a curtain, revealing a taut tableau of figures there: the duelists, back to back, and their two seconds. "Seventeen," Dr. Collett's voice boomed out across the meadow, and the protagonists took another measured step. "Eighteen."

"Uncle George!" Molly cried, running toward them. He never turned, never flinched.

"Nineteen," called Dr. Collett.

"For the love of God—"

"Twenty!"

The duelists whirled to face each other, pistols cocked and drawn.

"Anthony, no!"

A single shot shattered the morning air. The birds fell silent, then exploded in a frenzy of wings. The Earl of Ballenrose turned toward Molly, thin wisps of smoke rising out of his pistol. But Molly wasn't watching him. All she could see was Uncle George, who'd stood so straight and tall, crumpling to his knees.

"No!" she screamed to the bleak morning sky. "No, no, no, no!"

"Mary Catherine," Anthony called, starting toward her. But Michael Nivens caught his arm, pulling him back:

"Not now, man!"

Dr. Collett had run to the duke as he fell, and held him, half-sitting, half-sprawled across the dew-soaked grass. Molly flew to her uncle, crying as she saw the bright red blood that soaked his white shirt, dead center in his chest. "Oh, Jesu," she sobbed, kneeling at his side, watching his life seep away. "Sweet Jesu in heaven—"

"M'lord!" came a shout from the road—one of the duke's men, running toward them out of the trees. "Soldiers comin'—the king's soldiers are comin'!'' He stopped, seeing his master lying in the grass, and then let loose a moan. ''Oy, rue the day; all's lost!''

''Quit your wailing,'' the doctor snapped at him, '' and help me get him into the carriage!''

'He shouldn't be moved—should he?'' Molly asked, shivering with cold and despair.

''If the king's men find there's been a duel, they'll take him straight to prison, and I'll have no chance to save him.''

''Save him?'' Molly echoed in disbelief. *''Can* you save him?''

''God alone knows, but I'd bloody well like the chance! Get his legs,'' the doctor directed the frightened servant. ''Mary Catherine, find his pistol. Hurry! Move!'' With the servant's help, he hauled the duke's limp body off the ground and toward the waiting coach.

Anthony called out her name again, but she ignored him, searching the ground for the pistol, then running after the doctor. ''Mary Catherine, for God's sake!'' Anthony shouted. ''You've got to listen to me!''

Nivens yanked him toward their own coach. ''Didn't you hear? Are you mad? The king's men are coming.''

''I don't care; let them come. Mary Catherine—''

''Well, I care, dammit! Collett's right; we'll all go to prison. Now come on!''

''Easy,'' Dr. Collett warned as the driver threw open the coach door to admit the duke. ''Mary Catherine, take his head in your hands; keep it above his heart. And one, two, three, up!'' The three men lifted the duke onto the seat, while Molly cradled his head to her bosom. His eyes were closed, his face ashen in the thin gray light.

''Oh, Uncle George, I'm so sorry!'' she sobbed.

''No time for that, girl,'' the doctor said sharply, then turned to the driver. ''Get us to Buckingham House as fast as you can. Your master's life depends on you!''

''I'll go like the wind, sir!'' he promised, slamming shut the door.

So much blood, Molly thought. How could there be so much blood in a man? Dr. Collett clamped a folded cloth across the duke's chest and wrapped his cloak around him. Anthony had broken free of Nivens' grasp; as the coach started off, he appeared in the window. "Mary Catherine—"

"You get away!" she screamed, trying to jam the shutter closed. "I never, ever want to see you again!"

He had his hand thrust through to block the shutter, was running along beside the carriage. "I have got to tell you—"

"Leave off, you murdering villain!" Dr. Collett shouted, jabbing the earl's arm with a surgical knife. Still more blood, Molly thought, dazed.

The coach picked up speed. "I didn't mean . . ." Anthony panted, still running, but that was all Molly heard, for her uncle's lips had moved, whispering her name:

"Mary Catherine?"

"I'm here, Uncle George." She leaned over him, choking back tears. Dr. Collett had got the shutter closed at last; Anthony's shouts died away.

"Mary Catherine?" His eyes opened, but could not seem to focus.

"I'm here. Right here," she sobbed, clinging to his hand.

"I . . . love you, Mary Catherine."

"Oh, dear God, I love you too!"

"Don't talk, George," the doctor warned. "Save your strength."

The duke licked his lips. "Got to. Got to ask her . . ."

"Ask me what?" Molly urged.

"Don't encourage him," Dr. Collett said angrily.

"Shut up!" Molly cried, lashing out at him. "You had the chance to end this lunacy before it began; where in God's name were you then?" He fell back, staring at her. Defiantly she leaned over the duke again. "What do you have to ask me, Uncle George?"

He was failing fast; all the blood on his breeches and

shirt seemed to have drained from his face. Again his mouth moved, murmuring something unintelligible. "What?" Molly asked desperately. He tried once more, forming the words with excruciating care:

"Promise me . . ."

"Anything!"

"That you won't . . . won't . . ."

"Oh, God, see him again? Speak to him? How could I? I never will, I swear it!"

He drew in air, blood rattling in his throat. "Worth . . . it, then," he breathed.

Worth . . . it. "Worth what, Uncle George?" Molly whispered, though she feared she already knew.

"Worth dying . . . to keep you away from him," he said with sudden, startling clarity and satisfaction. Then his head fell to one side, his eyes rolling back.

"Now you've done it," Dr. Collett said.

Molly didn't stop sobbing for a long, long time.

IV

18

IT WAS TUESDAY, Molly realized as she opened her eyes, and that meant two things: salmon, which she hated, for supper, and a letter from London. The prospect of the latter propelled her out of bed and down the stairs in record time. Lady Agnes was just finishing her breakfast in the dining hall. "Did it come yet?" Molly asked eagerly.

The countess looked up, blue eyes frosty. "You might at least observe the common decencies, Mary Catherine."

"I beg your pardon," Molly murmured, blushing. She couldn't blame the woman for hating her, not after what she'd done. "Good morning, Lady Agnes. I hope the day finds you well."

"Passing well. Yourself?"

"Quite well, thank you." The countess nodded at a chair, and Molly slipped into it.

"No bad dreams?" Lady Agnes probed, ringing for the maid.

"No, milady."

"Good," said the countess, though her tone was not sympathetic. "I certainly hope we've put *that* behind us. Being cooped up here with *two* lunatics was more than anyone should have to bear." Molly didn't take offense; for months on end she'd awakened night after night screaming with horrible dreams. "Tell Turner what you'll have," Lady Agnes instructed as the maid arrived.

"Ah . . ." Molly tried to think. She could see the letter lying right beside the countess's plate, knew the woman was deliberately provoking her by stalling, and still she couldn't complain. "Oatmeal, Turner, please. And stewed fruit, if there is any."

"Peaches, m'lady, or pears?"

"Pears," Molly answered impatiently.

"Toast, m'lady?"

"No, thank you."

"Muffins, then?" the maid inquired. "Cook's made some lovely muffins."

Had even the servants been instructed in this maddening conspiracy of delay? But of course not; they didn't know. "Just the oatmeal and fruit, Turner, thank you."

"Very good, m'lady."

The maid left them. Molly looked pleadingly at the countess, who shook her auburn head, lips pursed tight. "*After* you've breakfasted."

"But—"

"You know perfectly well, Mary Catherine, we can't run the risk of having Turner or anyone else overhear."

"Let me read it to myself, then. Please."

The countess sniffed through her elegant nose. "I scarcely think you've earned that right." And Molly, because she had no standing to complain, sat with her hands folded in her lap and waited for her oatmeal to come.

When it did, Lady Agnes sent Turner back to the kitchens for coffee. That was a good sign, Molly thought hopefully. At least the countess wasn't going to leave the table and make her wait till suppertime again, as more than once she had. "Mary Catherine." That sharp voice skewered her reverie. "You are bolting your food."

"I beg your pardon." Molly set down her spoon, counted silently to three, and took another bite.

The countess rang for Turner again. "I believe I will have one of those muffins, Turner. Mary Catherine?"

"No, thank you," Molly said, teeth grating.

The muffin came.

"And some sweet butter," ordered the countess.

Turner brought sweet butter.

"I've changed my mind," said the countess. "I'll have raspberry jam."

"Now, see here," said Molly, long since finished her oatmeal. "I know you blame me, Lady Agnes, for all that has happened. But I hardly think that gives you cause to . . . to torment me every single Tuesday with these childish games!"

"You're a fine one to talk about games," the countess snapped, "after the one you led my poor dear George on!"

"It wasn't a game! And I never, *ever* imagined it would end in a du—"

"Raspberry jam, m'lady," Turner announced, coming in.

The countess glared at Molly. "Leave us, Turner," she commanded, and when the maid had gone, let loose her wrath. "You know better than to mention that word! You *know* what it could mean! Aren't you satisfied already with the damage you've done, you foolish, willful girl?"

Molly drew a deep breath. "I have to live every single day with the consequences of my folly," she said steadily. "I don't need you to remind me. Now, in God's name, won't you tell me what that letter says?"

Agnes contemplated her for a moment, then shoved the sheet of paper toward her. Molly unfolded and scanned it as quickly as she could; Dr. Collett's handwriting was atrocious. "Patient was able to ride for half an hour on Friday without pain," she read. "On Sunday, patient was present at his majesty's reception for the French ambassadors and engaged in dancing in blatant contradiction to my orders . . ."

"Dancing!" Molly looked up, eyes glowing. 'This is wonderful news!"

"What, that George is ignoring Dr. Collett's instructions? I hardly think so!"

"Of course I don't mean that; it's very naughty of him.

But still, riding and dancing!'' Molly felt a bit like dancing herself.

"It's just like George,'' Lady Agnes fretted, "to try to do too much too soon. Why, he is lucky just to be alive.''

He was more than lucky, Molly knew; it was a miracle he'd survived the bullet Dr. Collett dug from his chest. A miracle for which she'd prayed as never before.

"You'll notice, too,'' the countess went on, "that letter doesn't say a thing about George coming to visit.''

Molly actually felt a stab of sympathy for the woman. "I miss him terribly too. But you know that he doesn't dare leave the city so long as Parliament is in session. As Dr. Collett said, no one must ever suspect that he was one of the men involved in that . . . er, incident. Uncle George must do his best to carry on as if he never were wounded.''

"At least we can count on that snake Ballenrose to keep quiet too, since his majesty decreed death for the participants—should they ever be found.''

"I've told you before—never mention that man's name in my presence,'' Molly said quietly, but with steel in her voice.

"Hmph,'' the countess sniffed. "If you'd listened to your uncle and me in the first place, none of this would have happened.''

"Do you think I don't know that? Do you honestly believe I don't tell myself that a hundred times a day?''

"Well, that's your punishment,'' Lady Agnes said smugly. "That and being exiled here to Cliveden. Mind you, had it been up to me—''

"Punishment for what?'' asked the Duchess of Buckingham, wandering in in her nightclothes.

Lady Agnes snatched the letter from Molly and hid it in her bodice, then left the room without a word. "Don't tell me, then,'' the duchess said idly. "Sooner or later I will find out anyway. I always do.'' She sat down in the countess's place and began to pick at the remains of her rival's muffin. Then she rang the bell for Turner. "Butter, please.'' Her blue gaze met Molly's. "It's been a long time since he visited her, hasn't it? Got a new one, has he? One not quite so long in the tooth?''

"He's been busy with the Parliament,'' Molly explained, torn between staying and going. Life at Cliveden had grown tedious after nearly three months, and when the duchess was lucid, she did provide company.

"Ah, busy with Parliament,'' Lady Katherine said, mimicking Molly's grave tone. Then she snickered. "That's what he used to tell me. Busy sailing the great ship of state, he'd say, when all the time he was dallying with some nasty strumpet like Agnes Shrewsbur—''

"Excuse me, please.'' There wasn't any sense in staying, Molly knew, if she was just going to say vile things about her husband and Lady Agnes.

"Don't go,'' the duchess said suddenly, plaintively. "I won't talk about that. I'll talk about anything you choose. How's that young man of yours—Magdalene's brother?''

Molly sighed. What one told Lady Katherine just flowed in one ear and out the other. "I've asked you before not to mention him.''

"Threw you over, did he?'' The duchess nodded knowingly. "Didn't I tell you men are all swine? You no sooner give yourself to one and he's gone. Take my advice and keep your legs crossed. It's the only way.'' Molly pushed back her chair. "I'm sorry!'' Lady Katherine cried. "Please stay! We'll talk of literature if you like. What are you reading?'' She caught Molly's hand. "Or of gardening. There are crocuses up out back; do you want to go see?''

Molly disengaged the woman's bony fingers. "Later, perhaps,'' she said, and escaped from the dining hall.

But in truth, there wasn't any escape at Cliveden. She missed her uncle wretchedly. She missed her cousin Jessica, and the gay life at court—good God, she almost missed Clare. She lived in constant fear that next Tuesday's letter would bring news of some setback in the healing process—infection, gangrene, a fever in the blood—or, worse, word that King Charles had somehow discovered the identities of the two duelists his soldiers had so nearly come upon at Rawnleigh that day.

But even worse—because it was a fear she could share with no one—was her terror that the wound in her heart which opened anew each time the Earl of Ballenrose was mentioned would never heal over, that despite his villainy and betrayal, she was doomed to feel that scar till Judgment Day.

Two Tuesdays later, there was no letter at breakfast. Molly and Lady Agnes ate a grim, anxious meal, allies for once in their apprehension, speaking only to offer each other hollow-sounding reasons to explain the delay. "Perhaps the weather," Molly ventured, though the day was fair enough.

The countess nodded, made a stab at swallowing some bread. "Or perhaps George finally feels up to writing himself, rather than having Dr. Collett do it for him, and it is taking longer than usual. After all, John mentioned last week he'd regained a little strength in his right hand."

"That must be it," Molly murmured. "Or perhaps . . ."

"Yes?"

"Well, there could be some hubbub at court."

"Yes, that could be."

"Or Dr. Collett could have some emergency with another patient."

"That's certainly possible," the countess agreed. Neither mentioned the other, darker possibility that loomed in their minds.

No word had come by noon, nor by two. Molly gave up all pretense of occupying herself and loitered by the front doors; the countess retired to her rooms with a headache. When a carriage rumbled up the drive, however, she appeared at Molly's side with astonishing quickness.

The footman leapt down from his box, unlatched the door, pulled out the steps. Then the door swung open, to reveal an exceedingly surly Clare Fairfax. "You can be damned sure I intend to tell the duke about this horrible trip!'' she snapped at the driver as she climbed down. Jessica followed close behind her sister, chiding gently:

''The roads are always full of ruts in spring, Clare; you can't blame the driver. And what possessed you to try embroidery in a moving carriage, anyway? You are bad enough at it sitting stone still.''

''I thought I might as well get used to it; there'll be precious little else to do in this godforsaken—'' She stopped, suddenly taking notice of Lady Agnes standing in the doorway, looking utterly aghast.

''My heavens,'' said the countess. ''What are you two doing here?''

''Don't worry,'' Clare told her, ''we aren't any happier to see you than you are to see us.''

''Speak for yourself,'' Jessica said cheerily. ''How do you do, Lady Agnes? You're looking well. Mary Catherine!'' She ran and embraced Molly, kissing her cheeks. ''I've missed you so!''

''What a wonderful surprise!'' Molly returned the hug. ''But what *are* you doing here?''

''Exiled,'' Jessica burbled.

''Dear God,'' the countess said, paling. ''Both of you?''

''Just Clare,'' Jessica clarified. ''I'm just along for company—and to see Mary Catherine, you poor dear. How have you been? We've been so worried about you ever since your relapse—''

''Relapse, my foot,'' Clare said with a sniff. ''The only thing to be said for being sent out here in the middle of nowhere is we *may* find out the real story behind your sudden disappearance from court, Mary Catherine. There have been the *most* intriguing rumors—''

''Just one moment,'' Lady Agnes interrupted in her steel-cutter's voice. ''Who sent you here?''

''Uncle George, of course,'' Jessica told her.

Molly and the countess exchanged glances. ''Is Uncle George . . . well?'' Molly asked tentatively.

''How odd you should ask that,'' Clare drawled. ''There

have been strange rumors buzzing around about him too. Some say he's got the French pox.''

''For God's sake, Clare!'' Her sister looked at Lady Agnes apologetically. ''He's fine, really he is. He saw us off this morning. Oh, and there's a letter.'' She fished for it in her cloak. ''Explaining Clare's grand *faux pas*, I guess.''

''What exactly,'' the countess asked Clare, ''did you do?''

''I was caught in what one might call compromising circumstances—''

The countess rolled her eyes.

''With the Duke of York—''

Molly gasped.

''By the Duchess of York,'' Clare finished.

''Dear God,'' Lady Agnes breathed. ''The king's own brother? I honestly don't know what's becoming of the younger generation. Why, in my day—''

''In your day, you'd likely have arranged his wife's murder,'' Clare said coolly. ''I hardly think you're the one to lecture on morality.''

''Clare, that's enough!'' Jessica said sharply. ''I apologize, Lady Agnes, for my sister's bad manners.''

''I don't see why you should,'' Clare retorted. ''It was Uncle George's suggestion that I take up with the duke in the first place. And I think it shows exceedingly bad manners on *his* part to banish me here just because I got caught.''

''Oh, Clare,'' Molly stared at her. ''How dare you tell such wicked, wicked lies?''

Her cousin's narrow black eyes, so much like Buckingham's, glittered. ''Wake up and look about you, Mary Catherine, dear. It's a wicked world out there; why should I be any different? You're a part of it too, don't think you're not. And Uncle George is the great puppeteer, pulling all the strings. Why—''

''Clare,'' Lady Agnes broke in, ''I'd like to speak to you in private, inside.'' She grabbed the girl's arm and yanked her through the doors. Molly and Jessica looked at one another, then giggled nervously.

"Two of a kind," Jessica said with a sigh. "Poor Clare. She's really done it this time. I've never seen Uncle George more wroth." She patted Molly's hand. "But it's a blessing in disguise, I suppose, since I get to see you! How are you?'

"Bored," Molly admitted. "It has been a long winter, with only Lady Agnes and Aunt Kate for company."

"Aunt Kate." Jessica frowned. "I haven't seen her since I was a girl. They say she is mad."

"She is," Molly admitted. "And yet there are times when she seems perfectly sane. It isn't likely you'll see much of her. She does most of her wandering at night."

"Like a ghost," Jessica said, and shivered. "I don't know how you stand it. I don't even like the looks of this place; I rather think it would drive anyone mad."

"That's just because it's so big." Molly slipped an arm through hers. "You'll get used to it. Now, tell me all the news."

"Let's walk on the lawn," Jessica proposed. "I've been cooped up in that coach for hours; I'm not ready to go inside." The afternoon air was chilly, but Jessica seemed edgy, so Molly acquiesced.

"Well, everyone sends his love," Jessica began as they crossed the lawn. "Alex Randall, Robert Iswell, Lord Cunningham, Lord Ossory—they all instructed me to say that they're bereft without you. Oh, Lord Ossory made me promise to add that the sun hasn't shone a single day since you left London. They say they write but you don't answer."

"I mean to," Molly said faintly. "But . . ."

"There *have* been rumors about you, you know. The day you left, the king's soldiers got wind of a duel taking place along the river near Buckingham House. You wouldn't happen to know anything about that, would you?"

"Don't ask me questions, Jess. That way I won't have to lie."

"Mary Catherine." Jessica's round face was earnest. "You know you can trust me with anything, don't you?"

"Not with this. It . . . it isn't just me. There are others involved."

"It doesn't matter. I can guess." Jessica plucked a stalk of wild oats and chewed on it thoughtfully. "Anthony Strakhan disappeared too, you know. Not that same day, but soon after. Posted as a special envoy to the Netherlands, I heard."

Molly could feel the layers of scars across her wounded heart peeling back like onion skin. "Don't speak of him, Jess. Please. Not now or ever."

"Well." Jessica turned and headed toward the house. "At least no one was hurt; you must be grateful for that. And Uncle George seems in marvelous spirits, or at least he did until Clare got herself in this mess. Oh, and you should have seen his St. Nicholas' Day gift to the king— a brace of Irish wolfhounds. They led the pack on that afternoon's hunt, only poor Charles couldn't control them properly, and they got the fox between them and would have ripped it to shreds if Uncle George hadn't managed to pull them off. But Charles likes them anyway. He's named them Atlas and Samson. They truly are giants, more like horses than dogs, only as Louise Keroualle says, horses don't drool so much. And speaking of the fair Louise, she's in a bit of a panic. The king's actress mistress, that Nell Gwyn, is said to be with child again. And did you hear about the argument between Rochford and Ossory? It's been the talk of the town."

That's more like it, Molly thought as Jessica's cheery recitative flowed on unabated. Let me drown in a torrent of gossip. Tell me all about the intimate lives of strangers; fill me full of tittle-tattle that concerns nodding acquaintances. But of him, that other half of myself, speak not one single word. . . .

". . . And then Rochford said, 'Well, Lord Ossory is

Irish, so what would he know?' Then Ossory picked up his wine and flung it right at Rochford! And . . .''

Molly looked at her cousin, tears in her eyes. ''Oh, Jess. Thank God you're here.''

19

SPRING CAME IN earnest toward the end of March, with snowdrops and narcissus and the quaint speckled bells of guinea-hen flowers. Flocks of geese veered across the clear skies, heading northward to Yorkshire and Scotland, and the linden and hawthorn trees took on a faint sheen of green. It was well that the weather turned, for within the walls of Cliveden the weeks had taken their toll: Lady Agnes and Clare weren't speaking, and the duchess, always agitated as the dual anniversary of her wedding and Magdalene Strakhan's death approached, was wreaking havoc on everyone's nerves. Molly and Jessica took to exploring the countryside whenever it was warm enough, and sometimes when it wasn't, just to escape the tension that hung thick in the air.

Sometimes Clare came with them, but more often than not she stayed behind, writing pleading letters to the duke asking him to let her come back to court or hanging about Lady Katherine, asking questions about the old days. "Probably trying to turn up something she can use as leverage against Uncle George," Jessica told Molly with a sigh as the two of them set out one morning with a basket of food and flask of wine for their dinner. "Clare's not really the sort to cultivate the sick for their own benefit."

"What sort is it that I'm not?"

They turned at the gate to see Clare hurrying after them.

"The sort to stick by a plan," Jessica told her. "I thought you weren't coming."

"I wasn't, but the old spook's really round the bend this morning. Can't get her to talk about anything except that mess on her wedding day with Ballenrose's sister, the stupid cow. Uncle George certainly has a way of picking women, doesn't he? First Miss Suicide Strakhan, then Weird Kate, and now that fat bitch Agnes."

"And you're the very soul of sensitivity, aren't you?" Her sister cast a quick glance at Molly. "Agnes isn't fat."

"She's getting damned close to it. That's what happens to those buxom types when they reach thirty." Clare's dark gaze raked Molly's bodice. "You'll want to watch yourself, cousin dear."

"At least she's got something to watch," Jessica retorted.

Clare ignored her. "What did Cook pack for dinner—chicken again? I'm so bloody sick of chicken; you'd think so long as Uncle George has stuck us here, he'd see we're decently fed."

Molly looked beneath the napkins. "Veal."

"Oh, Christ, that's worse."

"You *could* turn around," Molly pointed out.

"What's the sense?" Clare scanned the sparkling landscape. "God, what a bloody pit. And not a single gentleman. I'd settle for a strapping shepherd at this point."

"They're plowing the south meadow," Molly said helpfully, pointing. "Lots of sweating field hands."

Clare sniffed in disgust, eyed their surroundings, gaze fixing on a stand of trees atop a far hillside. "What's up there?"

"Oaks," Molly said.

"I see that. What else? It looks like some sort of building."

"I don't know." Now that she looked, Molly could see the shadowy outline of a wall.

"Well, let's go find out," Clare proposed.

Her sister hesitated. "It's an awfully long way."

"I beg your pardon; I didn't realize there was anything to hurry back for."

"Let's go up there," said Molly. "It will be an adventure."

Clare rolled her eyes. "How absolutely pathetic."

Her sister gripped the basket. "Shut up, Clare."

Jessica was first to recognize the nature of the ruined structure as they climbed the hillside. "It's a chapel."

"Hmph!" Clare threw herself down in the weeds. "All this way for a bloody chapel? Knowing Uncle George, I'd been hoping for a secret dungeon, at least."

"There's one of them in the house," Jessica said with a giggle.

"Really? How do you know?"

"Aunt Kate told me."

"Then it's likely not true, or he'd have stuck her there long ago."

Molly hadn't said anything. As they reached the ruins, a bank of clouds had obscured the sun, and a long V of geese had passed above them, honking and squawking. The sudden pallor of gray, the birds, the broken stone walls, had transported her back to that awful dawn on the bank of the Thames; she'd been running on bare feet through the fog . . .

"It's rather charming, don't you think?" Jessica pulled a trail of briars back from the crumbling foundation. "And just look at that view! One would have felt quite close to God here."

"And quite removed from him at the house," Clare pointed out, rolling over and looking back at Cliveden across the forests and fields.

"Don't you ever see the beauty in things?" her sister asked with a sigh.

Molly shook off the memory and joined Clare in the grass, turning her back on the ruins. "We may as well eat."

Jessica settled down so she could see the chapel. "Well, I think it's romantic."

"You think everything's romantic," Clare told her. "You're a simpleton." She opened up the basket and shuddered. "Cold veal on bread, pickled eggs, and apples. Thank God there's wine."

Molly uncorked the flask; she felt in need of a swallow, of food, of talk—anything to break the spell. "It does seem odd they'd build a chapel here. I must remember to ask Uncle George about it."

"What makes you think he'll know anything?" Clare asked. "Wait, I take that back—he does think he's God."

Jessica frowned at her, chewing. "I can't understand the way you speak of him after all he's done for us."

"Such as what? Sending us here to rot for the rest of our lives?"

"You can't blame him for something that's your own fault," her sister said sternly. "And if he hadn't offered to augment our dowries, we'd be poor as church mice."

"That's the least he could do, don't you think, after yanking my inheritance out from under my feet by turning up dear cousin Mary Catherine after all those years?"

"You know, Clare," Jessica said angrily, "that's your problem. You only think of yourself; you never even consider—" She broke off so abruptly that Molly glanced up from her egg.

"What's the matter?"

Jessica blinked, shook her head. "Nothing. A bone."

"In veal?" Clare wagged her own head. "That cook is worse than I thought. Well, go on. You were in the midst of showing me the error of my ways."

"I . . ." Jessica set down her half-eaten food. "I'm not very hungry. I think I'll go for a walk."

"We just *finished* a walk," Clare noted, eyeing her strangely.

"Aye, but I have to—you know." She scrambled up from the grass, holding the front of her skirts, and dashed away.

Molly and Clare watched her run toward the ruined

chapel. "See if you can find the baptismal font to use!" Clare called after her, then took a long draft of wine. "I'm afraid this solitary life is beginning to go to my dear sister's head."

"It was a good deal more solitary before you two got here," Molly told her in a rare burst of magnanimity toward the dark-haired girl.

"Well, if you think I'm content to spend the best years of my life stuck playing nursemaid and companion to you, you're mistaken."

"Ouch," said Molly.

"Oh, did I hurt your feelings, cousin dear?"

Molly shook her head, hiking up her skirts. "No. I sat on a burr."

"What's that?" asked Clare, pointing.

"This?" Molly twisted to see her right thigh. "My Buckingham birthmark."

"Your what?"

"My family birthmark. You know. Uncle George has got it too."

"Has he really." Molly glanced at her, startled by the satisfied purr of her tone. Clare tossed her half-eaten dinner aside and stood up. "I'm going back to the house. I've got a letter to write. Jess!" she shouted toward the chapel. "What the devil are you doing?"

"Coming!" Jessica's voice floated toward them from the trees.

"Well, you'd better come quick; we're ready to go," Clare called.

Jessica appeared a moment later, cheeks flushed, an odd light in her blue eyes. "I don't see what the rush is," she grumbled. "It was your idea to come all the way up here."

"What were you doing all that time?" Molly asked.

"Just exploring."

"Did you turn up anything interesting?"

"Not a thing," Jessica said, repacking the basket. "Come on. Let's go home."

* * *

"Whist! Mary Catherine!"

Molly was roused from sound sleep by an urgent whisper close to her bedside. She sat up, fumbling for a candle and flint, and felt a hand on her hand.

"No. No light," said the voice, and she knew it then as Jessica's.

"Jess, what's wrong? Are you ill?"

"Hush! Keep your voice down." Molly heard the bed creak as the girl climbed up beside her. She pushed back her hair, feeling tired and cross.

"You startled me half to death, Jess; you might at least tell me why!"

"You've got to keep quiet; nobody must overhear! Do you understand?" Jessica hissed.

Molly nodded, taken aback by her urgency.

"Anthony is here."

"Here?" Molly shoved back against the headboard, covers clutched to her chest. "Jesu! Where?"

"Not here in the house," Jessica said impatiently. "Up on the hill today. That's why I got up from my dinner."

"You saw him? You spoke to him? Oh, Jess, you shouldn't have!"

"Why not?"

"He isn't to be trusted." A horrible thought crossed Molly's mind. "Did he try to seduce you?"

"Me? Of course he didn't. He only wanted to talk about you."

"What about me?" she asked suspiciously.

"He asked me—he begged me—to arrange a meeting with you."

Molly sat up straight. "Well, he can stay on that hill until he's as old as that chapel before I'll do that."

"But, Mary Catherine—"

"I told you before, I don't want that man mentioned in my presence. So you may as well go back to your bed."

"If I had a man as much in love with me as he is with you—"

Molly clapped her hands over her ears. "Leave me be!

Get out!'' After a moment, when she didn't hear anything, she took her hands away. Her cousin's pleading voice came out of the darkness:

"Won't you at least tell me why?"

"I can't."

Jessica pressed: "It's something to do with Uncle George, isn't it? Something about that du—"

"Don't say that word!" Molly hissed. "Do you want to get Uncle George sent to jail?"

"Uncle George be damned. Mary Catherine, Anthony loves you!"

"Then why did he shoot Uncle George?" Molly cried, caution forgotten. "Why did he go ahead and shoot when I begged him not to?"

Simultaneously, Jessica clamped her hand over Molly's mouth and gasped. They sat in silence, listening, but the house was still. Then Jessica pulled her hand away. "He shot Uncle George?"

"Right in the chest," Molly whispered miserably. "I tried to stop them from dueling, and I almost did, only Uncle George wouldn't turn around when I shouted! And then Anthony wouldn't listen either. He raised up his gun and just . . . and he just . . . Oh, God, Jess, the blood! There was so much blood!"

Jessica wrapped her in her arms and let her sob out the terrible secret. "I thought he was dead, and it was all my fault!" Molly confessed. "And then the soldiers were coming, and we had to put him in the coach—it was horrible, Jess! He was so pale, and just covered with blood, and he made me promise never to speak to Ballenrose again—not that I'd ever want to. I'd asked him to stop, you see! How could he love me and do such an awful thing?"

"I don't understand." Jessica held her by the shoulders. "This was in November?"

"Aye—November twenty-fourth. I will never forget that—"

"And Uncle George was wounded?"

"He was nearly dead!"

"And that same day, you were sent here to Cliveden."

"Aye," Molly whispered. "Because I was . . . I couldn't stop crying and screaming, and Dr. Collett was afraid that if the soldiers came to the house, I'd give it all away."

"Queen Catherine's birthday was the twenty-fifth."

Molly stopped sobbing, struck by the irrelevance of this pronouncement. "Who the devil cares?"

"Uncle George was there at court. I know he was; I saw him."

"Of course he was," Molly said impatiently. "He had to keep up the pretense that nothing had happened, lest the king realize he had been involved in the duel. Oh, God, the poor man. It must have been dreadfully painful for him even to dress."

"He danced," Jessica said flatly.

"Oh, no, Jess. You're mistaken. He couldn't possibly—"

"I know he did. He danced with me. He danced with Clare, and the queen—he danced with every woman there."

"He *couldn't* have," Molly said again.

"And I am telling you he did! What's more, it was but a fortnight later he wrestled those monstrous Irish wolfhounds away from the fox at the St. Nicholas' Day hunt. No one who'd been shot in the chest could have done such a thing."

Molly blinked, feeling dazed. "But I've been getting letters from Dr. Collett reporting on his progress. They said he didn't ride until a few weeks ago. That he still couldn't write—"

"It's all lies," Jessica told her, "every bit of it! Why, I've had letters from him myself, and there's nothing wrong with his hand. He's been riding, and dancing, and paying court to the ladies. If he was ever shot at all, I'll . . . I'll eat my bonnet!"

Molly felt as though a great void had opened up beneath

her feet, as though the earth had tilted on its axis. "But . . . why? Why would he want to lie to me? To play such a despicable trick?"

"Oh, Mary Catherine, don't you see? To keep you away from Anthony!"

Molly couldn't stand being still; she got up from the bed. "No. No! Uncle George wouldn't do that to me. He wouldn't hurt me that way."

"He would and he has," Jessica hissed. "It was all a giant hoax—"

"No!"

"To make sure you and Ballenrose were finished once and for all," her cousin went on inexorably.

"But I saw the wound, Jess! I saw it with my own eyes!"

"You saw blood, that's what you saw. Pig's blood, I'd wager, pricked out of a bladder with a pin, just as actors do onstage."

Molly was breathless, speechless. Was it possible that Uncle George would go to such lengths to keep her from the arms of his avowed enemy? Could his hatred for the Earl of Ballenrose really run that deep? "I cannot believe it," she said finally. "I *will not* believe it. Not after all that Uncle George has done for me."

"Believe what you like," Jess said briskly, "but it's perfectly clear. He saw a chance to poison your mind against Anthony forever, and he took it." Her tone softened. "I'm sure that in his own misguided way he thought it was for your own good."

"Anthony fired that shot," Molly said. "Uncle George *was* wounded." But even she could hear the hollow note of uncertainty that lay beneath her words.

"Don't you think you at least owe Anthony the benefit of the doubt?" her cousin argued. "Shouldn't you just hear what he has to say? After all, if Uncle George did lie to you . . ."

Then Anthony didn't betray me, Molly realized, heart quickening. Then he held his fire, and his love for me holds true. . . .

"Where is he?" she asked, wanting and yet not wanting the answer.

"In the rose garden." Molly could hear the smile in Jessica's voice. "He said he'd be there every night from now to eternity, waiting for you."

20

❧

THE GREAT ARCHING branches of the roses were bare in the thin silver light of a crescent moon as Molly slipped outside. A chill wind from the north sent old dried leaves scuttling along the paths; she steeled herself against the unquiet rustle and walked into the shadows, waiting for Anthony to make himself known. She did not wait long.

"Thank God. You've come." His voice came out of the darkness. Molly stopped; she had not anticipated how her heart would leap up at the sound. He did not move toward her, but she could see him now, his black cloak against the black trees, and his face, paler but still indistinct.

"Only to ask you . . . to tell you to leave me in peace." Her mouth felt burned, dry as the dead leaves.

"Mary Catherine, I never shot him."

"Don't bother lying. I saw you do—"

"I fired at the sky. I heard you cry out to me and yanked my hand up and fired into the air. As God is my witness, that shot came nowhere near him."

"Guns misfire," Molly said stolidly.

"Mine didn't." He breathed out, in. "Sweet Jesu, do you honestly think I would kill him right before your eyes?"

"What difference would that make? You were dying to kill him."

"I'm not a man of violence; I saw enough of it at war,"

he said steadily. "I've never fought a duel before in my life—I don't even wear a sword. I didn't challenge him. He challenged me."

She turned away from him, took a few steps toward the skeletal roses. "It is all so absurd, anyway. Two grown men, peers of the realm, going at each other like Roman gladiators—"

"Not so absurd as that cheap trick of your uncle's," he told her angrily, "feigning that he'd been hit."

"What makes you think he was feigning?" she asked, whirling on him.

"I told you—I never shot him. And shall I tell you something else? Didn't you find it strange that when you stumbled on us and called out to him, he never stopped, never turned? It was as though he was waiting for you, expecting you to be there."

"That shows how little you know! He had me locked in my room, for your information, with the servants for guards. I had to climb out a window and jump; I might have broken my neck if it weren't for—" She stopped. For the laundry. The linens that her uncle had made a point of ordering hung out that night. . . . She shook her head, shook the suspicion away. And yet it was odd that he had just kept walking, counting off the paces, the morning of the duel.

"At Queen Catherine's birthday ball, he danced thirty-six dances, including six galliards," he went on doggedly. "I had him watched. I had them counted."

"He was being stoic."

"Come now, Mary Catherine, Zeno himself couldn't be that stoic—not when the day before he'd leaked ten gallons of blood!" He gave a small, short laugh. "The damnedest thing is, I find myself admiring the bastard for having the audacity to try to pull it off. It goes to show how much he loves you. And that means he can't be all bad."

She looked at him with a glimmer of hope. "If he could hear you say that—"

"Don't press your luck; he never will. I cannot forgive or forget what he did to Magdalene."

Molly's gaze dropped to the stone paving once more. "Then why did you come here?"

"Because I can't forget you either. I've tried these past months; I've tried everything. But it's just no use. You've gotten inside me, under my skin; you're like a burr I rub up against first thing in the morning and last thing at night—"

"How very flattering."

"I'm beyond flattery. I'm beyond reason. I can't live without you; it's as simple as that. Sometimes I've found myself wishing your uncle had killed me in that absurd duel."

"Oh, Anthony. You mustn't say that."

"It is God's truth."

Molly's hands wrapped tight in the folds of her gown. "That isn't fair. You aren't being fair! You want me to feel sorry for you—"

"No," he said quietly. "No. I want you to love me. If you do, then nothing else, not your uncle or my sister or what's happened in the past, can matter. If you don't, you cannot make my life and my happiness your responsibility. So—do you love me?" Molly stared at the ground. He laughed and tipped her chin up to him. "You won't find the answer there." Her gaze glanced off his, went beyond him to the stars. His voice pulled her back. "Or there." Trapped, she looked into his eyes, priest's eyes, wise and ageless and the color of the vast blue sky.

"I do," she said at last.

Even in the darkness she could see the curve of his smile. "Well. That's settled. Now, come here."

His arms were as strong and warm as she remembered. Molly rested her head against his black cloak, surrendering to his embrace, and began to cry. He smoothed her hair with his hand. "What's wrong?"

"Oh, Anthony. What are we going to do?"

"First off, I thought we'd be married. That's the usual next step in these circum—"

"But we can't. We couldn't!"

"Why not?"

She laughed at his naiveté. "Uncle George will stop us!"

"Even George Villiers can't stop what he doesn't know. And once we are married, what can he do?"

"Kill you," Molly said glumly.

"Most girls would at least mention being cut off from an inheritance worth a few hundred thousand." He kissed her nose. "That's what I like about you."

"I don't give a hoot about his money," she said honestly. "Once you've been . . ."

He waited. "Once you've been what?"

Molly felt a small twinge of apprehension. Should she tell him about her former life, about Gospel Square and the Fleet? But it didn't matter now; he himself had said nothing mattered about the past. ". . . been the niece of a duke, I was going to say, I don't suppose being the wife of an earl is too much of a step down."

"Minx." He tweaked the nose he'd just kissed.

"But how will we go about it?" she asked with mounting excitement.

"Do you remember Father Drayton, from St. Paul's Cathedral? I've sent for him in London. He'll be here tomorrow night to wed us. And Michael Nivens will be there too, as my witness. Your cousin Jessica said she'd do the honor for you."

"My, my, my. Awfully sure of yourself, aren't you, Anthony Strakhan?"

"Not so sure as all that," he admitted, grinning. "I didn't signal my man to leave until you came through the doors. But I did think that once I got you out here I'd manage to convince you. If charm and reason failed . . ." He let his hand trail over her breast. "There was always this."

Molly leaned her head back, reveling in his touch. "Oh,

how I have missed you." She pressed against him, kissing his throat, her arms about his neck. "Why must we wait until tomorrow? We could go to London tonight—"

He groaned, but shook his head. "I want this all done by the book—a proper pastor, witnesses who are above corruption. There must be no irregularity your uncle can use to have the marriage annulled. And until tomorrow evening, you and Jessica must do nothing to arouse suspicion."

"Don't worry." Molly smiled. "I've pretended not to be in love with you for so long that I'm a master at acting."

"Maybe so, but your cousin Clare is a master at causing trouble. Watch out for her," he warned. "She and your uncle are two of a kind."

"You really shouldn't speak that way of your future relatives," Molly teased, and then grew solemn. "Uncle George will come around to the idea of our marriage, don't you think, in time?"

It was a moment before he answered. "I wish I could say yes and mean it, Mary Catherine. But I honestly don't know. If he doesn't—if he cuts you off, refuses to receive us—can you live with that?"

"I suppose I will have to." But the prospect saddened her immensely. Surely, she thought, surely Uncle George will accept my decision someday. He certainly loves me. She shook off her sadness and kissed him again. "You haven't told me where my wedding will be."

"Up there on the hill, I thought. It's the closest place to Cliveden that is hallowed ground. And no one should look askance if you and Jessica take another evening stroll up there."

"What if Clare wants to come with us?"

"Jessica says she won't, now she knows there's just an old church there. Something about witches shunning consecrated places—"

"Very amusing." She pinched him. "What if it rains?"

"Good Lord, I can't plan for every contingency! We

will just have to trust that it won't. Then, as soon as the ceremony is finished, we'll spend the night at Ballenrose Hall, leave an announcement for the papers, and then sail for France. We can send a message to your uncle from there; we'll be man and wife, and far beyond his reach.''

"Man and wife." The prospect made Molly shiver in anticipation. "I remember the first time I ever saw your house; Uncle George and I rode by in the carriage from . . . I thought it the grandest place I'd ever seen," she covered quickly.

"That must have been before you saw Cliveden," he said with wry humor.

Molly looked back at the huge dark mansion. "Cliveden is very grand too. But as Jess says, there is something about it . . . It is not a very happy house."

"Nor has mine been, not for many years." She knew he was thinking of Magdalene. "But all that is about to change."

"Oh, Anthony." Safe in the circle of his arms, she sighed her bliss. "Will it really work, do you think?"

"If there's any power in love, it will. And I think there must be, don't you, if we have come all this way in spite of everything?"

"Our fate," she said, and saw the night sky spread out above them. "Our stars, just as you said."

His arms had tightened around her. His mouth touched her forehead, grazed her cheek, found her lips, parted and waiting. Molly could hear his heartbeat, or was it her own? It didn't matter; come the morrow, they'd be joined together, two as one. Until the end of time. . . .

Her love for him swelled up inside her like a rain-soaked seed, ready to burst with fullness and life. "I don't know how I'll wait until tomorrow," she whispered.

He groaned, one hand at her breast, the other pulling her tight against him, molding her body to his. "Oh, my love, if you knew how I ache for you . . ." he murmured, even as he drew her down on the grass. She pushed back his cloak, ran her hands down his chest to his belt and then lower still. He shuddered at her touch; she heard the sharp intake of his breath.

"Oh, Mary Catherine." He kissed her, twisting so that he lay atop her, his manhood against her thighs. "Oh, my dear heart." He fumbled for her bodice buttons, mouth still pressed to hers, the urgent rhythm of his breath matching hers. Molly could not feel the hard earth, the night chill; all she knew was the quickening pleasure he aroused in her, her growing want, her fierce need.

"Yes," she whispered as he bared her breasts to the sky, buried his head against their moonlit softness. Her flesh came alive to his caresses, her nipples hardening beneath his urgent kisses, the wanton play of his tongue. "Oh, yes, my love." He pulled her gown from her shoulders, kissed her there, at her throat, at her ear, firing her blood. She arched up against him, heard his breathless groan as she stroked his manhood, smooth and hard and throbbing for release. "Now, Anthony. Please . . ."

He pushed her tangled skirts aside, ran his hand along her legs, moving higher and higher, parting her knees. She moaned and writhed as he reached her thighs, as his long fingers slid beneath the hem of her drawers and touched her there. . . . She cried out, straining against him, wild with desire. He knelt above her, blocking out the sky, drawing in his breath . . .

"No." The word was whispered, torn from him by sheer will. "I won't. I can't."

Panting, disbelieving, Molly pushed herself up on her elbows. "Please don't tease me, Anthony!"

He laughed raggedly. "God help me, it's no game. But . . . we've waited this long, my love. Surely we can wait one night longer."

"But we have waited *too* long!"

He sat back on his heels, a sheen of sweat showing the effort his restraint cost him. "You deserve better than this for your first time . . ." He pulled the edges of her bodice together, seeing her shivering. "Besides, you'll catch the ague; it's bloody cold out here."

But Molly wasn't shivering from the night air. "That's not the real reason." She bit her lip; it was bruised with his kisses. "I want the truth, if you please."

"The truth." He sighed. "My dear love. If something were to happen between now and tomorrow—"

"What?" she broke in, frightened by his grave tone. "What could happen?"

"Who knows?" He kissed her upturned chin. "But if something *were* to happen—not that there's the ghost of a chance it will—and we couldn't be married . . ." The words were jocular enough, but his voice was shaking. "I could not bear for you to think I'd only meant to seduce you—that I never meant the wedding to take place."

"Oh, Anthony—"

"Hush." He buttoned up her bodice, gentle as a mother with her child. "That's the way I want it, and that's how it will be. So into the house with you, before I repent." He stood, scooping her up, and kissed her once more, tenderly, before he set her down. "I'll wait for you on the hill. Tomorrow at dusk."

"It will seem a million years till then," she said plaintively.

"We'll soon have forever." He steered her toward the house with a soft pat on her bottom. "Go on. And remember, be careful. Act nonchalant."

"Oh, I'm sure I'll have no trouble at that. It is only to be the most important day of my life." She trailed away from him, turned back. "What shall I wear? I don't know what to wear!"

"So long as you leave your hair loose, I don't care."

She darted back to him for one more kiss, her tongue seeking his, teasing as she savored its sweet warmth. "It's not too late to change your mind," she whispered.

Laughing, he pushed her away. "Go to bed!"

"I am going," she said indignantly, and then ran back to him. "I don't want to go!"

"And I don't want to let you." He held her tightly, his cheek against her hair. "I can feel your heart beating."

"I can feel yours." She pressed her hand to his chest, feeling the strong, steady pulse of his heart. "It says: I love you, I love you."

He shook his head, pulling away. "It says: Good night, good night."

"Oh, you. This time I really am going." She made it all the way to the walk before stopping to look back.

"Sleep well, my love," he called.

"And you too, love. Good night!" She ran toward the house, paused, laughed. "A thousand times good night!"

"At dusk tomorrow," he reminded her. "Here." He threw something to her, and she caught it: a rose, browned by the winter's frost but still holding hidden in its petals a faint scent of the coming promise of summer and sunlight. "My heart. Mind you guard it well till then."

21

"WHAT ARE YOU doing?"

At the sound of Clare's voice, Molly froze, then shot a warning glance at Jessica. There wasn't any need, for without the slightest pause, Jessica turned to her sister and said calmly, "Trying on dresses; what does it look like? And have you ever heard of the custom of knocking before entering a room?"

"Aunt Kate doesn't, why should I?" Clare draped herself in a chair, surveying Molly as she stood before the looking glass. "That one makes you look fat."

"Oh, honestly, Clare, as if she ever could." Jessica gave Molly's shoulder a small surreptitious pat, and she let out her breath, willing her taut muscles to unwind. Don't look guilty, she reminded herself, or do anything suspicious.

"You do look rather peculiar," Clare noted, cocking her head, "and it isn't the dress. Are you coming down with something?"

"Probably," said Jessica. "Why don't you stay around and catch it?"

Molly forced herself to meet Clare's sharp, dark gaze in the mirror. "I didn't sleep well. My monthlies."

"Ah. The blight of every young lady's existence. Mother used to make us drink henbane tea, Jess, do you remember?"

"How could I forget? The stench still makes me nauseous. As for you, sister dear, you look like the cat that swallowed the bird."

"That's probably because I have a secret."

"Have you really? What secret?"

"All things will reveal themselves in time," Clare said enigmatically, and considered the dresses strewn across the bed. "What brought on this burst of fashionable energy, pray tell?"

If Jessica could make idle chitchat, Molly thought, so could she. "Uncle George is bound to want us back at court sooner or later. I thought it wise to be ready."

"Wise indeed. Especially since it's likely to be sooner, not later."

Jessica looked at her. "What have you been up to?"

"Just doing my best to move our redemption forward, sister dear." She let her jeweled slipper fall off her heel and dangle from her toes, swinging it back and forth.

Molly's nerves, already ragged, frayed still more beneath Clare's smug scrutiny. "Let's do this later, Jess."

"Don't be daft; we're almost finished. Try this one on." She drew another gown from the pile.

"Oh, really, Jess." Clare sniffed. "No one is wearing sleeves like that this year."

"Why do you think we're trying them on, goose? To see what needs updating."

"You should burn the whole lot and get Uncle George to buy you new ones." Clare sat up slightly. "Except that blue one. That's rather nice."

"This?" Molly held it up. "This is as old as the hills. I wore it the first time I was presented at court." The night she met Anthony in the king's gardens. . . .

"The night we first met you," Jessica said. "Lord, it does seem a lifetime ago."

"It's got a sort of ageless elegance to it," Clare said appraisingly. "And the color doesn't make you look all washed-out, the way those others do. I'm so glad I haven't got your pale skin and hair."

"You'd kill for her coloring, you cat, and you know it."
Jessica looked at Molly, bemused. "Well? Do you want
to try on Clare's choice?"

Molly knew why she was smiling; there was something
perverse in having Clare select her wedding gown. "Why
not?" She shrugged. Jessica winked and began to undo
Molly's buttons.

"Why don't you get a maid to do that?" Clare asked,
helping herself to a cup of wine.

"Because we felt like being alone," her sister told her.

The hint was wasted on Clare. "Do you know what that
dress needs?" she asked idly, sipping wine.

"Let me guess. A lower bodice," Molly said dryly.

"Well, it could use that. But actually, I was thinking of
sapphires. What a pity you haven't still got the ones Uncle
George gave you." She smiled brazenly, licking a drop of
wine from her upper lip.

"Oh, I remember those; they were magnificent! What
happened to them?" Jessica asked.

"You misplaced them, didn't you, Mary Catherine?"

"I certainly did," Molly said with distaste, then sighed
as someone knocked on the door. "Come in!"

"I wondered where everyone was," Lady Agnes said
as she entered. Her gaze took in the pile of gowns on the
bed. "Ah. Getting ready to return to court, are we?" She
sounded glum, almost wistful. "You look lovely, Mary
Catherine. I always did like that gown."

"You helped me choose it," Molly said, embroidering
the truth a bit because she felt sorry for the countess.
Uncle George had been neglecting her shamefully of late.
"What would you wear with this?"

"Sapphires," Clare said again.

"Oh, no, that would be rather much, I think," the
countess demurred. "I'd leave the throat bare. You have
such a splendid *poitrine*, Mary Catherine—and such lovely
pale skin."

"You're very kind," Molly murmured, to which Clare
gave a derisive snort.

"Not at all. The only thing I might add . . ." Lady Agnes held up a finger. "Wait here."

"Stupid cow," Clare muttered as the countess left the room. "I'd never let myself be shuffled off into oblivion just because my lover had a new mistress."

"Uncle George has a new mistress?" Molly echoed, surprised.

"If he hasn't already, I'm sure he will soon. After all, what does she have to offer anymore?"

"The young." The voice from the doorway made them all jump. "Always so sure of themselves."

"Hello, Aunt Kate," Jessica said pleasantly.

The wraithlike duchess ignored her, floating toward Clare. "I'll wager you think you'll be the one to keep him, don't you?"

Clare looked her aunt in the eye. "Lunatic," she said. The duchess laughed shrilly.

"Here we are!" Lady Agnes announced, sailing in. "Oh, dear, what's *she* doing here?"

"Watching," Lady Katherine said softly. "As I watch everything."

Molly looked at her, alarmed. The duchess smiled and winked.

"Lady Agnes," Jessica said quickly—her first show of nerves—"what have you got there?"

"This? It's a girdle I thought would go well with that gown." She crossed to Molly and fastened it around her waist. It was made of little silver scallop shells joined with carved beads of lapis lazuli. "There! That's perfect," she declared.

"Something borrowed," the duchess murmured, *"and* something blue."

"She isn't getting married, you crazy old woman," Clare said with disdain. Molly held her breath, meeting her aunt's eyes in the mirror in silent beseeching.

"And it's well she's not. They're all pigs, men. Aren't they, Agnes? The rest of you are so young. You'll learn, though, to your rue." Her eyes met Molly's again. "Of course, if you find a good one, you'd be wise to keep him.''

Molly's hands shook as she unfastened the girdle. ''This is beautiful, Lady Agnes. But who knows when I'll be wearing this dress again?''

''Keep it until you do,'' the countess urged her. ''I never have cared for silver anyway.''

''Not to mention,'' Clare said nastily, ''that it wouldn't fit around your waist.''

''Clare!'' Jessica hissed.

''Lady Katherine. Lady Agnes.'' The butler bowed from the doorway, letter tray in hand. ''A message from his grace in London.''

''Well, let's have it,'' the countess said imperiously, holding out her hand.

''It isn't for ye, m'lady.''

Lady Katherine's long-dead eyes came alive. ''For me?'' she cried, her voice almost girlish.

''Nay, mum. 'Tis for Lady Clare.''

Looking not one whit surprised, Clare took the letter from him.

''I don't understand,'' Lady Agnes said peevishly. ''All this time without a letter from George, and now he writes to you? Why?''

Clare shrugged, breaking the seal with one long fingernail.

''Well, what does it say?''

''Wonderful news,'' Clare drawled, ''for some of us. We're to go back to London.''

''We who?'' Jessica demanded.

''You and I. And Mary Catherine.''

Molly and Jessica exchanged startled glances. ''Wh-when?'' Molly stammered.

''First thing in the morning.''

''*Tomorrow* morning?''

Clare considered her curiously. ''I must say, you hardly sound delighted.''

Steady, Molly warned herself. "Of course I am. But there's so much to do before then to get ready . . ."

"At least you've made a start." Clare nodded toward the gowns on the bed. "I'd best do the same. Coming, Jess?"

"In a moment." Jessica pressed Molly's cold hand. "I hope you won't be so busy packing, Mary Catherine, that we have to postpone our outing."

"What outing?" asked Clare.

"Mary Catherine promised to walk up to that ruined chapel with me once more. I want to make a sketch of it to show Lord Wallingford. He has an interest in antiquities." Molly held her breath. Did the story they'd agreed on sound contrived?

But Clare only laughed. "And you've an interest in Lord Wallingford. Honestly, Jess, when are you going to learn? The way to a man's heart isn't through sketches."

"You flirt your way," Jessica said calmly, "and I'll flirt mine. Do you want to come?"

"Not on your life," Clare said, and Molly dared breathe again. "You'd better go soon if you're going, though. It will be dark in an hour or two. And what about supper?"

"We'll take it with us," Molly said.

"On your last night here?" Lady Agnes asked rather forlornly. "I must say, I think you're being very selfish." She trailed toward the door. Clare followed, making a face at her back.

"I've a mind to go up to that chapel too," Lady Katherine said out of the blue. Molly and Jessica stared at her, appalled. She smiled. "But I won't. I'd only slow you down. And youth always is in such a rush." She came and kissed Molly's cheek. "Just in case for some reason I should miss you in the morning, God be with you." She went out, closing the door—the first time Molly had ever seen her bother.

Molly collapsed on the bed.

Jessica fell down beside her, whispering, "She knows!"

"Aye, she knows."

"But how?"

"She must have seen Anthony and me in the garden." Molly sat up, clutching her stomach. "Oh, God, I feel sick."

"That is only nerves—and little wonder, with the lot of them trampling in and out like that! Why on earth do you suppose Uncle George has summoned us back?"

"I can't imagine."

"Well, I can—my sister's up to something." Jessica nibbled her lip. "Will it change your plans?"

"I don't know." Molly could not stop trembling. Jessica sat up too, and reached for her hands.

"It is perfectly normal for a bride-to-be to have butterflies," she teased gently, "though in your case I imagine they're the size of elephants. You love Anthony, don't you?" Molly nodded. "And you know he loves you. So everything will be all right in the end. You'll see."

"But—"

"No buts. Get up, now, you're mussing your skirts." She pulled her off the bed. "And put on your cloak—there's a good girl. I'll go to the kitchens and fetch the wedding supper. White wine or red?"

"I—"

"Never mind, you won't be drinking it, will you? You'll be on your way home as the Countess of Ballenrose, won't you?"

"I—"

"Mary Catherine." Jessica paused at the door. "You haven't got any doubts, have you? *Real* doubts, I mean. Because, if you have . . ."

Molly closed her eyes tightly, conjuring Anthony's face. Then she shook her head.

"Well, thank God for that," Jessica said briskly. "I'll meet you at the front doors in two minutes. Make that three—I've got to get my sketching pad." She blew Molly a kiss and left her alone.

Molly turned back to the mirror, the cloak clutched close around her shoulders. Her hair was still bound up in plaits;

remembering Anthony's request, she pulled them out and combed through the long cascade of pale gold. Then she stood and stared at her reflection. "Well, Molly Flowers," she whispered, "you have come a long way, haven't you, from Gospel Square?" The Countess of Ballenrose, that was what she'd be in less than an hour. Anthony's wife. Odd. Right up to last night, she'd always imagined that when she married, Uncle George would be there.

She owed him everything, and now she was about to betray him. Would he ever forgive her? He'd be frantic with worry when he learned that she had disappeared. She would have to write to him right away. But how could she ever put down on paper words that would make him understand what she'd done? The prospect filled her with dread on what ought to have been the happiest day of her life.

What could she do that would make things right?

The idea dawned on her slowly as she gazed into the mirror, and with it came a rich sense of peace. "Yes," she said aloud, and the sound quickened her will. It was the right, the only thing to do. Anthony might not like it, but he would just have to understand.

Ready at last, she fastened her cloak and hurried down the stairs.

22

THE LATE-DAY SUN hung low in the west, tipping the fields with fire as Molly and Jessica crossed them. "This is surely the longest walk any bride ever took to the altar," Jessica jested rather breathlessly, her skirts hiked up in one hand.

"But the most beautiful too." In the long, slanting rays of light, Molly searched the top of the hillside that lay before them. "Can you see anyone?"

"No—and if Anthony has got any sense, he'll be disguised as a tree. After all, this is enemy territory."

Molly laughed for sheer joy, the sun on her face, the spring wind caught in her hair. "Not for long it isn't. There they are!"

The last few hundred yards seemed to last forever. She could see Michael Nivens standing beside Anthony; both men looked tense and edgy. But as she and Jessica gained the crest of the hill and Anthony came to meet her, the lines of worry disappeared from his face.

"My love." His kiss was warm as the sunshine. "You're here."

"Did you doubt me?"

"Not for a moment."

"Hah," said Michael Nivens. "He's had me up here since noon keeping an eye on the house. Lady Mary Catherine." He bowed over Molly's hand.

"Just Mary Catherine, please. Thank you so much for

coming! This is my cousin Lady Jessica Fairfax. Jessica, Mr. Michael Nivens.''

Jessica gave him a wide, dimpled smile. "Have you ever been in a wedding before, Mr. Nivens?''

"Never.''

"Neither have I. Isn't it wonderful?''

"It will be if the priest gets here,'' Anthony grumbled.

"Where is Father Drayton?'' Molly asked anxiously.

"As it turns out,'' Michael said, "he's from Buckinghamshire. His parents live just a few miles from here, and he stopped to see them. He should be—'' Hoofbeats pounded on the plain below them. Anthony whirled around, muscles going taut, then relaxed as he recognized the priest. "Here now,'' Michael finished, and grinned at Jessica. "Is the bride as jumpy as the groom?''

"Worse,'' she said fondly.

"I imagine that's what true love is like.''

Jessica shrugged prettily. "I'm afraid I wouldn't know.''

"Really? A beautiful young lady like you unacquainted with true love? You should remedy that.''

"Michael,'' Anthony said with a sigh, "must you flirt even at my wedding? Father Drayton!'' The horseman below raised his head as Anthony called and waved. "Up here!''

The priest rode up to them, blinking his owl's eyes. "Ah, so you are! Charming spot for a wedding.'' Anthony held his horse while he dismounted, then shook his hand.

"It's good of you to come, Father.''

"Always glad to serve,'' he said mildly, pulling a prayer book from his saddlebag.

"Mary Catherine, you remember Father Drayton?'' Anthony asked.

"Of course. How are you, Father?''

"Well, my mother said I look thin. But she always says that.'' He smiled at Jessica. "You're the other witness, I take it?''

"Jessica Fairfax.'' She curtsied. "Tell me, Father, are you often called on for this sort of thing?''

"Secret weddings, do you mean? More often than you'd think. Why, just the other day—''

"I don't mean to be rude," Anthony said apologetically, "but do you suppose we might have the ceremony first, and the niceties after? I can't help worrying that something will go wrong."

"Certainly," the priest said without blinking. "Is there an altar?"

Anthony led him to it. "And you're sure the marriage is legal and binding if we have it here?"

"Makes no difference whatsoever,"Father Drayton said brightly. "You could have it in a barn. Long version or short?"

"Short," Molly and Anthony said in unison.

"Marital harmony." The priest beamed. "That's what I like to see. Shall we begin?"

"Anthony," Molly said, "there is just one thing—''

"Can it wait until after we're married?"

He sounded rather desperate. She nodded. "Of course it can."

She could never remember very much afterward about the ceremony that followed—the words were a blur, and it was over so quickly. But she never would forget Anthony's eyes as he turned to kiss her at the end; they were dark blue, fathomless as the eastern sky, and brimming over with love. "Done," he whispered as their mouths sealed the promises they had made. "Done!" And then he caught her up in his arms and whirled her in a circle there amidst the ruins. Jessica cried. Michael Nivens kissed the bride, said, "Oh, hell," and then kissed Anthony too, making Molly laugh. "I expect a healthy contribution to St. Bart's for this," he told Anthony, who grinned.

"That's done too. And here." He pulled a heavy purse from his cloak, giving it to Father Drayton. "Though it's little enough to show our thanks."

"The children of the parish will appreciate it." He produced a quill and ink from his saddlebag, along with a document in Latin. "If you'll just sign here . . . there, that makes it official. This will be on record at St. Paul's, if you should ever need it."

"I'd be grateful, Father Drayton," said Molly, "if you wouldn't mention the marriage to anyone until . . . well, until you hear from Anthony or me."

"Very well, if you like."

Anthony had his arm around Molly; now he pulled back, looking down at her. "What's this? I thought we had agreed to make an announcement—"

"Yes, love, I know. But . . . this is what I wanted to ask you before. I've given it a great deal of thought, and I want to tell Uncle George about this myself."

"Fine," he agreed instantly, to her relief. "We can go to Buckingham House in a few days—"

"I want to tell him *alone*, Anthony. I have to. And I'd like to do it tomorrow. We're all supposed to go back to London tomorrow anyway," she rushed on nervously, "Clare and Jessica and I. So I thought I'd just spend the night here at Cliveden, and—"

"Our *wedding* night?" he said incredulously.

"It is only one night more to wait. Anthony, don't you see? I know Uncle George. When he hears I am missing, he'll be frantic with worry."

"Jessica can tell him—"

"That isn't fair to Jess—or to Uncle George either. He deserves to hear the news from me. And I just know he will take it ever so much better if he isn't already upset because I am missing."

"If you are having second thoughts . . ." he began ominously, a vein pulsing at his temple.

"I am *not* having second thoughts! I married you, didn't I? It is already a *fait accompli.*"

Father Drayton cleared his throat. "Pardon me. Not exactly."

"*What?*" Anthony demanded, whirling on the priest. "By God, if this has all been some sort of trick—"

"My dear fellow," Father Drayton said hastily, "I only

meant, the marriage isn't a *fait accompli* until you've spent the night together as man and wife. Or rather, until . . .'' His voice trailed away.

"Oh," Molly said. "I hadn't thought of that . . . I mean, of course I had thought of it. I just hadn't realized . . .'' Blushing, she looked at the priest. "That's a legal requirement?''

"Absolutely.''

"If you've some objection, Mary Catherine . . .'' Anthony was sounding more and more angry.

"Oh, Anthony, for heaven's sake. Of course I haven't. I was only hoping I could break it to Uncle George under the best possible circumstances.''

"If you're so bloody worried about your Uncle George—''

"Please, Anthony! Don't take that tone with me.''

"If you'll permit me . . .'' Father Drayton stepped in. "Perhaps I can provide a solution. As Michael may have mentioned, my parents live not far from here. It's certainly not a luxurious house, but it is a respectable one. And I'm sure they'd be delighted to offer you the spare room.''

Molly and Anthony exchanged uncertain glances. "That's very kind of you,'' Anthony said humbly, "but—''

"But after all, they're strangers,'' Molly whispered, holding tight to his hand.

"And we wouldn't want to impose,'' Anthony finished haltingly.

"They're both quite deaf,'' Father Drayton added.

Michael burst out laughing. *"Really,* Father!'' Jessica said.

Anthony was laughing too. "Well, Father, in that case . . .'' Molly's blush was beet-red.

"Mind you,'' the priest warned, "it really is a very plain sort of place.''

"But there is a bed.'' Anthony's good humor was restored.

"Oh, aye. And with a feather mattress at that. Dad raises chickens.''

Anthony's arm encircled Molly's waist again. "I always have wanted to honeymoon on a chicken farm, love. Haven't you?"

"Are you sure you don't mind?" she asked anxiously.

"Absolutely sure. And I promise to have you back here so early tomorrow that no one will notice you were gone."

"You had better get started, then," Michael said, embracing the newlyweds.

"Don't worry about anything," Jessica told Molly. "I'll see you in the morning. Oh—here!" She handed over the basket she'd brought. "Your wedding supper. You will need it after all. I hope it's all right—"

"Jess, why are you crying?" Molly demanded.

"Because I'm so happy. It is so romantic!"

"It's so dark," Michael said, tugging Jessica away from Molly's arms; the sun had long since sunk in the west. "Come on. I'll see you down the hill."

Molly gave her cousin one more kiss. "I don't know how to thank you, Jess, for everything. If it weren't for you—"

"Just promise me you'll tell me all about tonight!" Jessica hissed in her ear. "Good-bye, Anthony!"

"Good-bye, Jessica! Thanks, Michael!"

"Good-bye! Good luck!" The two waved at Anthony and Molly, then started down the hill toward Cliveden, Jessica chattering away.

Father Drayton blinked like an owl in the faint evening light. "Well, shall we go?" he said.

Night had fallen by the time they reached the elder Draytons' home. The squat little cottage sat by the side of the road, drooping beneath the weight of its high thatched roof. But candlelight glowed in the windows, and the front path led from the gate to the door through a tangle of daffodils and bluebells. "Oh," Molly breathed as Anthony helped her down from his horse. "When I was small I used to dream about living in a house like this!"

He laughed. "I suppose it would seem like heaven compared to a drafty old convent."

"Good Lord," Father Drayton said at their side, "don't let Dad hear you mention a convent! He thinks papists are worse than a fox in the chicken house." He rapped loudly at the door. "Dad! Mum!" he called, and knocked again even harder. "Dad! Mum! It's Tim!" Molly was just wondering whether they would have to break the door down when it opened.

"All right, Timmy!" the old man on the threshold bellowed. "There isn't any need to shout!"

"Hullo, Dad!" Father Drayton roared. "Where's Mum?"

"Right here, dearie." A small white-haired woman pushed past the old man to kiss the priest's cheek. "Back again so soon?"

"Mum, I've a favor to ask you."

"Going over to Askew, ye say?"

"No, no! A favor to ask you—a boon!"

"That's what I said—so soon!"

Her son got right up to her ear. "I say, a favor to ask you!"

"Oh! Oh, go on, then. Ask away."

Father Drayton gestured to Molly and Anthony. "These are friends of mine—Mr. and Mrs. Jones!"

"Well, how d'ye do?" Mrs. Drayton asked, smiling and bobbing her head. Her husband shook Anthony's hand, while the priest spoke in a murmur:

"It's no use telling them who you really are; they'd only make a fuss—assuming I could get the message across. They've just been married tonight, Mum!" he added loudly.

"Tonight?" Mr. Drayton echoed, roaring. "Well, congratulations!" He winked at Anthony. "Or condolences, eh, as the case may be!"

"Oh, hush up, Ethan!" his wife shouted, elbowing his ribs. She beamed at Molly. "I'm so happy for ye, my dear!"

"Thank you," Molly said, then remembered to shout it: "Thank you very much!"

"They need a place to stay the night," Father Drayton explained, enunciating carefully.

"Well, of course! They must have the spare room, isn't that right, Ethan?"

"They could have the spare room!" Mr. Drayton bellowed.

"Just what I was thinking," his son noted, smiling. "It's been very good training, as you can see, for being heard from the pulpit in St. Paul's," he added to Molly. "That would be splendid!" he roared in his mother's ear.

"Of course it's been tended!" she shouted back indignantly. "Just because ye've moved away t' the big city don't mean we've let the place to t' the dogs!"

"Quite so," Father Drayton said. "Well, then, I'll leave you to it."

"Come in, dearie!" his mother told Molly, pulling her inside.

"I do hope we aren't putting you out!"

"Shout? No, no, you do have to shout for Ethan, here, but not for me; my ears are still young."

"Good luck," Father Drayton murmured with a wink. "I'll be off now. Good night, Mum, Dad!"

Inside the cottage, a huge fire was roaring in the hearth, and two big yellow dogs stretched across the floor before it. "I'll get ye some supper, shall I?" Mrs. Drayton shouted.

Molly held up her basket. "Someone packed us one! May we share it with you?"

"Oh, no, thank ye, dearie! We've eaten already; we're stuffed to the gills."

Mr. Drayton bustled over to a table by the fireplace, eyes gleaming. "Game of draughts?" he roared at Anthony in invitation.

"It's the man's wedding night," his wife bellowed, rolling her eyes. "He don't want to play draughts wi' ye!"

"Well, there's no harm in askin'!"

"Old fool," Mrs. Drayton muttered, and beckoned to Anthony and Molly as she picked up a candle. "Come along; I'll show ye to yer room!"

It was off the main cottage, with stone walls and a dirt floor strewn with straw. "Not very fancy," their hostess roared, "but the mattress is good; I plucked it out myself." She lit the fire that was laid, and tossed in a handful of bark. "Applewood. It'll take the must off. Here's yer linens, then, 'n' a pitcher 'n' bowl. Anythin' else ye need?"

Molly shook her head. "It's so very kind of you to take us in—"

"Fah, don't mention it, dearie! Any friend o' Timmy's—"

"Anyone for ale?" Mr. Drayton bellowed, thrusting his head in. "It's my own special brew!"

"I could use a drink," Anthony admitted.

"Hah! Come along, then!"

"Just bring them in a pitcher, Ethan," his wife shouted, "and let's leave them to their peace!"

When the ale had arrived and their hostess was gone, closing the door behind her with a cheery, ear-splitting, "Good night!", Molly looked at Anthony and giggled. "Well, you must admit, it makes for a night we'll always remember."

"What?" he asked, cupping his ear. Then he smiled. "I knew I would remember it anyway."

They looked at each other. Then Molly moved across the room. "Drink your ale, and I'll make up the bed."

"I'll help." He came and stood behind her, his hands on her waist.

"Not from there you won't." She slipped out of his grasp, walking around the bed and shaking out the sheet so it settled over the feather mattress. "Have you never made up a bed before?"

"Only once. When Magdalene and I accidentally set

my bed on fire and tried to cover it up. I remember we got caught, so I must not have done a very good job.''

''You must fold the corners under. No, Anthony!'' She laughed as he stuffed the sheet under the mattress. ''Like so.''

''Ah. Those finicky French nuns. What difference does it make?''

''Do you want it to come loose and tangle all around your ankles?''

''It is going to come loose anyway, believe me.'' Molly felt herself blushing, and turned to reach for a blanket. ''Love? Is something wrong?''

She shook her head, fussing with the bedclothes. ''No . . .''

He leaned across the mattress, stilling her busy hands. ''I think there is.''

''I just feel . . . I don't know.''

He squeezed her hands, then released them. ''Would you like something to eat?'' She nodded gratefully. ''Good. I'm starved.''

They sat on the bed with the basket between them. Molly could manage no more than a few nibbles of bread and cheese and some of the red wine Jessica had packed, but Anthony finished most of a joint of ham and all of the ale. The food and wine calmed her enough that she could laugh at the silly jests Anthony was making to put her at ease.

''Won't you try some of this? It's quite good.'' He offered her a slice of ham on his knife.

Molly shook her head, then giggled. ''Lady Agnes—the Countess of Shrewsbury—would be proud of me. She always thought I had a most unladylike appetite.''

''There is nothing unladylike about you,'' he scoffed. ''It's plain to see you were born to royalty, at least. I'm astonished you've settled for a lowly earl like me.''

Molly ran her fingers over the worn, nubbly blanket beneath them. ''Do you ever think what your life might be like if you weren't an earl?''

"Of course I do, every time I ride through the city. What is it John Bradford said? 'There but for the grace of God go I.' " He smiled at her. "Why do you ask?"

She sighed. How to explain to him the strange sense she had at times, was having now, that her life wasn't real? That everything she'd experienced in the past two years was only a dream, and that at any moment she'd awaken to find herself back at the Fleet, curled on the stone floor next to Meg Calloway?

"I don't know," she said at last. "I think perhaps I feel guilty for being so happy."

He didn't laugh, as she'd thought he might; instead he stroked her cheek with his hand. "My dear love. What a marriage this will be! We'll work together for good, be the conscience of the king, make Charles and those fat, complacent peers of his see that everyone in England deserves to be happy, and warm, and fed—and they'll listen to us, I know they will, because unlike Michael and Father Drayton and so many others who are trying to change this nation, we're of their class. If you and I have consciences despite our impeccably blue blood, then so must they."

"Even Uncle George."

"Even Uncle George," he acknowledged, grinning.

"Oh, Anthony. I'm so glad you didn't give up on me."

"How could I have," he asked, his voice low and husky, "when I love you more than life itself?"

Molly's shyness fell away; she leaned across the bed and twined her arms around his neck. "I love you too. More than I can ever say," she whispered, and kissed him.

He returned her kiss, gently at first and then, when she didn't pull away, with a passion that left her breathless and sent his ale cup tumbling to the floor with a fearful clatter. They both froze, but no sound came from the rest of the cottage. "The dogs must be deaf as well," he said, and laughed. "Come, wife. Let's to bed."

While he cleared away the remains of their supper,

Molly took off her shoes and started to roll down her stockings. "Wait. Let me do that," he protested.

"But what shall I do?"

"Sit and be beautiful." He knelt on the floor at her feet and drew the stockings off with infinite care.

"At that pace, we will be the whole night with undressing," she teased.

"I promised to go slowly this time, and so I will." But as he reached back for her bodice hooks, his hands brushed her breasts, and his breathing quickened. "Or at least, I'll try."

"Clare chose this gown—though of course, she didn't know why I was going to wear it." Molly leaned her head back as he fought with the intricate fastenings. "Do you know, I hadn't thought of it before, but it was rather like a bridal dressing. Everyone came into my rooms for one reason or another and stood there while I put on my clothes."

"Pity they're not here to get you out again," he grunted, prying at the clasp on her girdle.

She pushed his hands away and released the clasp with a single snap. "Aunt Kate even made a jest about that old rhyme—you know, 'Something old, something new, something borrowed, something blue.' I think she must have been watching us in the garden last night."

"Well, it doesn't matter now." He leaned back on his haunches, nonplussed. "Kindly show me how these bloody skirts undo."

"For someone who managed to strip me nearly bare in the dark yesterday, you are having a great deal of trouble."

"I perform best in the heat of battle—always have." Molly laughed, standing up and pulling her arms from the sleeves, and the gown fell away. "Oh, my," he murmured, staring up at her.

"Jessica chose this," she told him of her thin silk chemise. "Do you like it, then?"

"I like what it promises." He reached for its laces, but she danced from his grasp.

"I don't think we should begin this marriage with such a show of inequality," she said gravely.

"Meaning what?"

"Meaning, take off *your* clothes."

He did so, with alacrity, taking off everything. As he stepped from his breeches, his manhood already upright and hard, her green eyes widened. With trembling hands, she unlaced her chemise and drawers and let them slide to the floor. She stood before him, naked, haloed in candle-light and firelight, her hair a long sheath of pure pale gold.

They gazed at each other for a timeless moment, then he caught her up in his arms and carried her to the bed.

As he laid her down and stretched out beside her, the whole great length of his body pressed against hers, flesh to flesh, nothing between them, Molly felt a rush of profound, exquisite peace. Every night of our lives we will share this sweet communion, she thought, and I would be content with nothing more. . . . But then he turned to her and kissed her, and the contentment was replaced by the sharp gnawing of desire. She returned the kiss, her hands on his shoulders, pulling him closer than close, wanting to gather him into her forever. Her lips parted to his; her legs parted too, wrapping around him. He drew back, groaning, then leaned over her and put his mouth to her breast. The pleasure overwhelmed her; she began to move her hips against his to the rhythm of his tongue.

Her hand slid down to reach his manhood and he shuddered as she stroked its taut, swollen head. His chest was heaving, and a sheen of sweat covered his shoulders.

He leaned over, kissing her breasts, then her belly. Then he moved lower still, his lips brushing her thighs as he stroked them with his hands, his mouth soft against her soft white skin. He kissed the V of golden curls between her legs, pressing her back against the bed, his tongue trailing fire along her inner thigh, reaching higher . . .

Molly gasped and her body went taut as he found the

bud of her desire and kissed it, fondled it with his tongue. Her hands clawed at his shoulders, nails digging into his skin with each tantalizing caress that brought a pleasure so intense it burned. "No more," she begged, "please. Please, stop."

He looked up at her and smiled, and she returned his smile, wide-eyed. "It is *wonderful,* isn't it? Wonderful and terrible too."

"Just wait," he promised. "There's more."

He knelt above her and kissed her mouth with a tenderness that turned bruising as his manhood pushed against her thighs and slid back and forth between them in a quickening pace. Gradually, he thrust inside her, moving deeper and deeper until he filled her completely. He paused there, head lowered, panting. "Did I hurt you?"

"No," Molly breathed, and suddenly he was moving again, rearing up and plunging down onto her, into her. She gasped as the pleasure took hold once more, flowing through her like a river of fire. The flames coiled and leapt and danced with his rhythm, and she arched up to meet him, pulled him down to her, had to bite her lip to keep from crying out his name. He was groaning, breathing hard, thrusting farther and faster, and she was moving with him; they were one wild, straining thing, reaching for the sky. And then the bed, the room, the cottage, the world, all fell away as they went soaring upward, racing into the heavens on a plume of sheer white-hot brilliance. They arced and crested and peaked together in a shuddering, dazzling burst of impossible ecstasy, then fell back to earth like twin falling stars, still trailing shards of light.

"Oh," Molly whispered in awe, and heard him laugh against her breast, his breath still ragged.

"Oh," he agreed, holding her so close, his hands caught in her hair.

"Why didn't you *tell* me?" she asked.

"Would you have believed me?"

She pushed him up so she could see his face, her lips parted, green eyes ablaze with newfound knowledge. "Again," she said. "Again!"

23

IT WAS NEITHER the lark nor the nightingale that woke Anthony, but a fat red rooster, standing atop a knoll just outside the cottage and crowing his boasts to the dawn. "Hush, you old braggart!" he whispered, and rapped on the window. The bird's beady gaze darted toward him; then, chest puffed, tailfeathers preening, he hopped down from his perch and went in search of something to peck.

Anthony leaned back and, in the frail light of first morning, looked down at the girl still sleeping beside him. No, no longer a girl. She'd become a woman last night, and they, husband and wife. Even in sleep, she was the most beautiful creature he had ever seen. He lifted a thick strand of her hair and let it fall through his fingers—like yellow silk it was, or like fine spun gold. She lay facing him, curled on her side, and the sight of her breasts, pale as veined marble, heavy and round and tipped with areolae of deep rose, made his flesh tighten despite his exhaustion. He longed to wake her and take her again, but didn't, knowing that to do so would only hasten the moment when they must part.

Her blue gown still lay in a heap on the straw-covered floor. There would not be many mornings like this, he knew: the stillness, the country peace, the smell of tilled earth and green hay on the air. No servants, no business more urgent than breakfast . . .

He thought of the first time he saw her, drenched in moonlight in the kings' garden, coming toward him down the path in that same blue gown, with her hair falling straight to her knees. He'd been late, that was why he'd come to the palace that way—oddly enough, it had been a letter from the Duke of Buckingham that had detained him. He'd heard her voice, sweet as warm rain, on the spring wind, and then he saw her. That moment had been burned like a brand on his brain, had haunted him every night for the past two years. He remembered, too, the despair that had filled him when he learned who she was—heir to his arch-rival, niece of the man whose life he'd sworn, in the heat of a twelve-year-old's bewildered fury, he would have someday in exchange for Magdalene's.

Their entire courtship from that start to this finish had been the stuff of drama, with more turns and folds, false starts and premature endings, than any audience would ever have put up with. But through it all, one thing had never swerved or faltered: his love for her, conceived in an instant in that moonlit garden, whole and complete and all-consuming.

" 'She is all states, and all princes, I,' " he whispered into the silence, gazing down at her as she slept. " 'Nothing else is . . .' "

She stirred. He held his breath, his hand against her cheek, wishing her back into the soft cocoon of slumber, not yet ready to share her with the hurly-burly world that awaited them beyond the cottage walls. Earl and countess, lord and lady of Ballenrose, courtier and dame-in-waiting, someday, God willing, father and mother—all these roles would demand their time and leave so little for them as lovers, mere lovers. *Sleep on,* he willed her, *don't waken . . .*

But her eyes opened wide. "Anthony?"

"Who else, wife?" He kissed her. Her mouth was soft and warm with the salt tang of sleep.

"It's lovely sharing a bed, isn't it?" she asked dreamily when he finally released her.

"You're lovely," he told her. "How do you feel?"

"Wonderful." She stretched beneath the blankets. "Weary and wonderful and impossibly happy." She looked toward the window. "It's dawn, isn't it?"

"You haven't heard the cock yet, have you?" he countered, not exactly lying.

"What wakened you, then?"

"An overabundance of love." She smiled and pulled him down to her just as the rooster let loose another crow from his hill in the yard. "Nightingale," he murmured, his mouth at her breast. "A very loud nightingale."

"Aye—with a red comb and wattles." But she sighed with his caresses, nipples tightening, hips moving against his, so that he dared hope for a moment she'd forgotten her plan of the evening before. Then she slipped out of his arms and up from the bed. "Forgive me, love. I have to go."

He groaned, newly aroused, manhood hardened. "I thought perhaps you'd changed your mind."

"I can't. I owe this to Uncle George, Anthony. Please, please understand."

Uncle George, her damned Uncle George. Suddenly, irrationally, he hated even the way she said that name, so comfortable and loving. By God, Strakhan, he thought, biting his lip to take the edge from his desire, you're jealous, that's what it is. Jealous of the place he holds in her heart and always will.

She looked at him gravely, and kissed him. "We will have the rest of our lives together, you know."

"Aye." He heard himself sounding like a petulant child and had to laugh. Looking relieved, she turned to retrieve her dress. He sighed, eyeing her from the back, the smooth long line of her shoulders sweeping to her slim waist, her firm round buttocks and slender thighs—"What the devil— what's that?"

"What?" She twisted, saw him pointing. "This? My Buckingham birthmark. Uncle George has got it too. He says it's handed down in the family, generation after . . . Anthony, what's wrong?''

He hated himself for it, but he'd shuddered. He had not expected his children, their children, to carry a Buckingham brand. The mark of Cain.

She stood before him unmoving, the gown bundled up to her chest. ''I never thought to mention it,'' she said stiffly. ''I never thought that it could matter.''

''It doesn't.'' *But it did.*

''No,'' he said aloud. No. I won't let it matter. Dammit, no! He couldn't blame her for the mark any more than for her blood; it would be as futile as loving her for having yellow hair. He got up from the bed and took her into his arms. ''Get dressed,'' he said gently, and kissed her forehead. ''I'll take you back to Cliveden. And you can go to London and tell Uncle George . . . You can thank him,'' he corrected himself, ''for having found you for me.''

When the time came to let her go, though—when they stood in the thin morning light on the hill overlooking Cliveden, good-byes whispered, last kisses taken and given—he hesitated, unnerved by some unexplainable foreboding. ''Don't go,'' he said, holding her close.

''Anthony.'' She laughed, pulling away. ''I swear, you are making me nervous. I'll be in London by this afternoon. It shouldn't take more than half an hour to break the news to Uncle George, and then I'll come straight to Ballenrose Hall. I'll be there in time for tea.''

''I hate tea.''

''Coffee, then. Or sherry.'' She made a wry face. ''I may need a drink. Now, kiss me good-bye, once and for all.''

Once and for all . . .

He did, reluctantly. ''Ta, then, as they say at market,'' she told him gaily, waving as she turned from him.

''Mary Catherine—''

She turned back, sighing. ''Yes, love?''

"Your uncle would never . . . he wouldn't hurt you, would he?"

Her shock was genuine, unmistakable. "Do you mean strike me?" He nodded. "Oh, Anthony, no! If only you knew how much he loves me . . . all he has done for me . . ." Her voice trailed away; shadows crossed her lovely face. "But I'll tell you, shall I, as soon as I come back. Once I do, you'll understand. Only now I must run, or someone will miss me at the house and raise a fuss. Trust me, love. This is the best, the only way. And prithee, don't look so glum! You will give marriage a bad name."

He forced a dutiful smile. "I love you."

"I love you, too—and I *do* like tea, so see that you lay some in. India tea, if you please." She was halfway down the hill. "And biscuits! Raisin-nut biscuits!"

"I'll fill the house with them," he called after her. "Good-bye!"

She waved again, blue skirts and yellow hair wild with wind, and without stopping, bent to crop a wildflower and tuck it into the basket she held. "Wife," he whispered, watching her go with a catch in his heart, fighting off the urge to gallop after her and sweep her away.

24

THE CARRIAGE BUMPED onto Marlborough Street and sent a flock of pigeons wheeling into the sky. Molly sneaked a peek at Clare from beneath lowered lashes and bit down on her cheek, finding her cousin eyeing her curiously. Clearly she suspected that something was up, but what it was, she'd never guess in a thousand years.

"Almost home," Jessica announced, and giggled.

"What, pray tell, is so amusing about that?" demanded Clare.

"Not a thing," her sister said demurely. That started Molly giggling, and she in turn touched Jessica off again. Clare looked from one to the other of them in disgust.

"I'd like to know what's going on."

"Mm, so should I," Jessica agreed. "Being away from court so long does make one eager for gossip."

"I meant, going on right here."

"Oh, Lord." Molly held up the shift she'd been sewing since they left Cliveden. "Look at this. I've put the sleeve in upside down!" She and Jessica collapsed with laughter.

"Oh," Jessica gasped when she could speak, "I pity the poor soul that gets you for his wife!"

"Well, save your pity," Molly told her. "I'm sure I'll manage to content him somehow."

"Are you really?"

"Yes, I am, really."

"I am much relieved to hear that," Jessica said gravely, then burst out laughing once more.

"If I didn't know better, I'd think you both were drunk," Clare snapped.

"Not I," Jessica protested, "though Mary Catherine may have been tippling. Mary Catherine, have you been tippling?"

"Do I look the sort of girl who tipples?"

"As a matter of fact, you do!"

"Idiots," Clare said sourly as they started giggling.

"We're sorry, Clare," Molly apologized. "It is just that we're so happy to be back in London—"

"Aye, to be home," Jessica chimed in.

"—to take our rightful places at the head of society."

"Or wherever else," Jessica said significantly, "our rightful places turn out to be."

"Well, you're both daft, if you ask me. And I don't think it's right for you to be keeping secrets, since it's thanks to me you *are* back in London."

"Speaking of that," Jessica said curiously, "how exactly did you manage it?"

"That's none of your business."

Molly laughed. "Now, why do you suppose anyone would keep a secret from you?"

"There are secrets, and then there are secrets," Clare said archly. "Frankly, I doubt that any secret you two might have could even be worth knowing."

"You're absolutely right, Clare," her sister said. "So why don't you give up on worming it out of us?"

"I wasn't worming."

"Yes, you were." The carriage stopped in front of the Fairfax house. "Well, well! We're here. Why don't you run inside and say hello to Mother and Father, Clare?"

"I'm in no rush. I'll wait for you."

Deprived of privacy, as they had been all day, Molly and Jessica kissed. "Good luck," Jessica said. "Are you sure you don't want me to come with you now? I'd be glad to see Uncle George."

"Thanks, but no. I'd like the chance to see him alone. There's so much to tell him."

"Such as what?" Clare demanded. "That his wife's still crazy and his mistress is fat?"

"Charming Clare. I'll leave that news for you to pass along to him," Molly said shortly. "Jess . . ."

"Yes?"

"I'd appreciate it if you wouldn't pass along any gossip until I see you again."

"Word of honor," Jessica promised, crossing her heart. "My mouth is sealed."

"Gossip about what?" Clare wanted to know. The footman opened the door just then.

"M'ladies. The baggage is unloaded."

"I'll be by soon," Molly told Jessica.

"You'd better!" She stepped down from the carriage. "Good-bye!"

"I'll get it out of her anyway," Clare vowed as the footman helped her down.

Molly leaned back against the seat. Now that the moment for confession was nearly here, she felt, not the panic she'd expected, but an odd sense of calm. What was done was done, after all, and what could Uncle George say? He'd likely rant and rail a bit, but soon the storm would be over, and he'd come to accept the marriage. Eventually he might even grow fond of Anthony. They were not so different from each other, really, her two stubborn, strong-willed men. And then there would be children. That would bring Uncle George round as nothing else could; she'd seen it happen that way time after time back on Gospel Square. Mothers- and fathers-in-law who swore up and down that they hated their children's spouses melted like ice at spring thaw once the grandchildren came. . . .

"M'lady?"

Molly blinked; lost in her hopeful thoughts, she hadn't noticed the carriage stopping or the footman opening the door.

"You needn't unpack my bags, Barnes," she said, and saw him blink in turn. "Not just yet."

Thompkins, stout-chested as ever, greeted her at the doors with a bow and a smile. "Good t' have ye back with us, Mistress Mary Catherine."

"It's lovely to be back, Thompkins. Is my uncle in?"

"Aye, m'lady. In his study, with Dr. Collett."

She'd hoped to find him alone. "Would you ask him if I might speak with him privately, Thompkins, in the drawing room? It's . . . it's quite important."

"Of course, m'lady. Would ye be wanting tea?"

"No, thank you, Thompkins," she said, and slipped into the drawing room.

The draperies were pulled against the afternoon sunlight. Full-blown white roses nodded in a vase on the mantelpiece—five pounds' worth of flowers, at least, brought from Spain at this time of year, she noted out of habit. It was in this same room that she'd first gotten flowers from Anthony—lilies of the valley—on the morning after they'd met.

"Mary Catherine." Her uncle's voice, so magical, full of music and laughter. She turned from the mantel and saw his dazzling smile. "Welcome home, my dear girl. It was only cutting off my nose to spite my own face, sending you away for so long. I've missed you terribly."

He was still the most handsome man she'd ever seen, Molly thought fondly—more regal than the king. Very nearly like a god.

He stopped as he came toward her, seeing her staring. "Have I egg on my waistcoat?"

She smiled back at him. "If you must know, I was thinking how handsome you are."

He laughed and kissed her cheek. "And here I feared you wanted to see me in private to scold me for having left you imprisoned at Cliveden so long."

"As prisons go, 'tis a fine one."

"Spoken with authority." He went to the sideboard and poured himself a sherry. "How is Agnes?"

"Quite well." She paused, reconsidered. "I think perhaps she is lonely."

He nodded. "A gentle reprimand, and deserved. I've been remiss in not visiting her."

"I didn't mean it as a reprimand."

"Nonetheless . . ." He sprawled elegantly in a chair. "And your aunt?"

"The same as ever."

"Well, thanks be she's no worse."

Molly perched on the arm of the chair across from his. "How is your chest?"

"My chest?" he echoed blankly.

"Where you were shot."

"Oh! Ah, of course." He raised his right arm, wincing. "Better, though it still pains me quite a bit when—"

"Uncle George," she broke in, hating to see him lying—he really was dreadful at it; how had she ever been fooled?—"that bullet never hit you, did it?"

He stared at her for a moment. Then, "What's this?" he blustered. "Never hit me? Of course it hit me; you saw the wound yourself!"

"I saw the blood," she corrected him. "I couldn't see the wound, because there never was one. You were only pretending that you'd been hit."

He took a gulp of sherry. "You've been spending too much time with your poor Aunt Kate, my dear girl, and it's made you giddy. Why, John Collett is right in my study; he'll tell you—"

"I've no doubt Dr. Collett will say anything you ask him to," Molly interrupted wryly, "but the fact remains that Jessica saw you dancing at the queen's birthday ball the day after you were supposedly hit in the chest with a bullet."

"Oh, damn. Dammit all," he muttered, "I'd forgot all about that when I sent them to Cliveden. Damn!"

"Then you admit it?"

"Not much sense in denying it, is there?" he demanded crossly.

"Shame on you, Uncle George," she said gravely. "You had Lady Agnes and me frightened to death all last winter."

"I'm sorry," he mumbled, then added with a touch of belligerence, "But I'd do it again, if it would keep you away from that man!"

"There won't be any need to do it again," Molly said quietly.

"Hmph! I hope this means you're finished with the Earl of Ballenrose once and for all!"

"Not exactly, Uncle George. I've married him."

He had the sherry glass halfway to his mouth; she saw his hand tighten around it till the knuckles went white. But the expression on his face never changed as he set the glass down again and rang the bell at his side. "Thompkins," he said when the butler appeared, "bring Dr. Collett in."

Good Lord, Molly thought, chewing her lip, have I brought on an attack of apoplexy? But he didn't look pale, or ill; he looked . . .

Dr. Collett hurried through the door. "What is it, George?"

Smug, Molly realized suddenly. He looks smug.

The Duke of Buckingham held out his hand. "John. You owe me five hundred pounds."

Dr. Collett froze. "The devil!" he burst out.

The duke laughed, roundly and gaily. "Pay up, my good man!"

"You're jesting." The doctor turned to Molly, gaping. "It can't be true. You're married to Ballenrose?" She nodded dumbly, too stunned herself for words.

"And the marriage was consummated, I trust," the duke said, his voice brisk. "So, Saint Anthony has stuck his arrow in the quiver, and we can all drop this bloody charade."

"Uncle George!" Molly was startled into speech by his vulgarity.

"Will a bank draft do?" Dr. Collett asked, reaching into his vest.

"I suppose so, though I'd prefer gold. It has a nicer feel when one collects a bet."

Molly looked from one man to the other in disbelief. "You had a wager on whether I would marry Anthony?"

"Aye," said Dr. Collett, taking the quill and ink that Thompkins produced. "To my rue."

"And you bet that I *would?*" she asked her uncle.

"Certainly. Champagne, Thompkins, please. The best we've got."

"Very good, m'lord."

Molly sank into her chair, feeling weak at the knees. "I don't understand. You did everything you could to keep us apart—"

"On the contrary. Everything I did was carefully designed to bring you together. Admit it, John—I'm a master of human nature."

"Obviously," the doctor said grudgingly, handing over the draft he had written. "Five hundred pounds."

"It's not the money, John, you know," said the duke, pocketing the paper.

"Oh, quite."

"And here's the champagne! That's all, Thompkins; I'll pour."

"Very good, sir." The butler bowed and backed out, closing the drawing-room doors. The cork popped with a sound like a gunshot. "Quite appropriate, eh?" the duke asked, grinning as the pale gold wine overflowed. "Here's for you, John, and me . . . and I suppose a glass for you as well, Molly Flowers. I feel magnanimous in my victory."

The sound of her old name brought Molly out of her stupor. "What do you mean, everything you did?" she asked cautiously. "I know about pretending you'd been shot, but what else?"

"Everything!" the duke cried, enjoying himself immensely. "From your first meeting in the king's gardens by moonlight, to your being partners in the treasure hunt—that was a night of genius! I wrote the clues myself, you know. First to bring you here—dutiful niece that you were, I knew you'd insist he take you straight home. Then to the Fleet; I had to be sure he wouldn't remember you, seeing you there. And I arranged to have the guard pluck you from the boat at the Tower; what a stroke that was! What else, John? Ah, yes, Ballenrose evading the men I set to watch him so that he could visit you at Cliveden, sending Clare and Jessica there to make sure you'd discover I was shamming my wound—all! I did it all!''

"The note that brought Anthony to St. Bart's," Molly said slowly.

"Moi," he admitted with glee.

"And the laundry put out so that I could climb from my window—"

"Mais oui."

"Having you be ill for so long last summer was *my* idea," Dr. Collett said rather proudly. "Absence makes the heart grow fonder, and all that. Though I wish now I hadn't helped. But I honestly believed, George, that you hadn't a chance."

"You made me ill?" Molly asked incredulously.

"It was the perfect opportunity to test a theory. I exposed you to plague."

"Good God!"

"Well, you told George you'd already had it, so I was fairly sure you wouldn't die."

"Fairly sure? What if I had?"

"That would have been a terrible pity," said the duke, sipping champagne, "after all I had invested in you."

"I should say so!" Molly laughed. "I should be angry, I know, but I am just too relieved. To go to so much trouble . . . and all this time I thought you hated Anthony!"

The triumphant smile disappeared from her uncle's face. "Oh, I do hate him," he said quietly. "I hate the very air he breathes." As Molly's green eyes went wide, he nodded to Dr. Collett. "John. Take this down, please. An announcement to be placed in the *London Mercury,* the

two *Courants,* the *Intelligence,* and the *Orange Gazette.*
There's paper in the drawer there.'' Dr. Collett found it,
and dipped his pen. The duke brought his hands together
in front of his nose, tapping his fingertips.

'' 'To whom it may concern,' '' he began:

'' 'Be it hereby known that George Villiers, Duke of
Buckingham,' etc., etc.—the usual titles—'refuses to acknowledge any debts or forfeitures incurred after'—what
the devil's the date, John?''

''March twenty-fourth,'' Dr. Collett told him, busily
writing.

''March twenty-fourth. What a delicious coincidence,
eh, Mary Catherine? The very day on which you were
born a mere two years ago. 'After March twenty-fourth
Anno Domini one thousand, six hundred and seventy-
one—' ''

''Write it out, or numerals?'' Dr. Collett inquired.

''Oh, write it out, by all means; it will look so much
better. Where was I? Oh. 'By the person lately purporting
to be his niece, Mary Catherine Villiers—' ''

''Purporting?'' Molly echoed blankly.

The duke ignored her, going on: '' '—as it has come to
his attention that said person is a rank impostor and is in
truth one Mary Catherine Willoughby, also known as
Molly Flowers, a common criminal escaped from the Fleet
Prison.' Paragraph.''

Molly's champagne glass fell through her hand to the
floor.

''Too fast for you, John?'' the duke inquired.

'' 'A criminal,' '' Dr. Collett repeated, '' 'escaped
from the Fleet—' ''

''A *common* criminal,'' the duke corrected him.

''Right, *common* criminal.'' The doctor scribbled away,
tongue between his teeth. ''Paragraph.''

''Yes, paragraph. Let's see. 'His grace sincerely regrets
having been'—what's the word I want, John?''

''Ah, 'hoodwinked'? 'Tricked'?''

''No, no; I don't want to look a twit.'' He thought,

sipping. " 'Deceived' will do nicely. '. . . having been deceived by said person, as well as any confusion'—no, strike that; make it 'inconvenience.' '. . . any inconvenience that may have resulted from his unfortunate mistake.' "

" 'Unfortunate mistake,' " Dr. Collett murmured, and looked up, pen poised. "Yes?"

"That's quite enough, I think. Copies to each periodical, and then I'll sign them."

Molly licked her dry lip. "You can't do that."

Her uncle looked at her. "Why not?"

"Because it's not true!"

"Oh, but my dear girl, it is. John, see if for an extra few pounds they'll place it directly under the wedding announcement." He smiled beatifically, dark eyes shining. "That will make a fine gift to Ballenrose, I think."

Molly felt a strange heightening of her senses; she could see the small hairs growing out of Dr. Collett's nostrils, could hear her uncle's short, sibilant breaths, could even smell the roses on the mantel as they rotted, stems turning soft and putrid and brown. "Uncle George, please! I knew you'd be angry, but this . . . this is madness!"

"How can I be angry," he said patiently, "when everything has fallen out exactly as I planned it? And don't call me Uncle George anymore. In truth, I found that the most distasteful aspect of this entire drama—being addressed as 'Uncle' by the likes of you."

Molly fought for control, fought not to dissolve into hysteria. In the faint light, with her skin and eyes and ears tingling, the two men looked so different suddenly. Dr. Collett's thin nose quivered like a weasel's, and the Duke of Buckingham's was curved and sharp like the beak of a hawk. "I am your niece," she said heavily. "Your flesh and blood. You cannot disown me—"

"But I never have owned you. You disappoint me, Mary Catherine. One of the reasons I chose you for this task in the first place was that you were not wont to be dense. You are not my niece."

"I am!" she cried. "What about my mother? You showed me her portrait—"

"Painted up to resemble you by a cheap Chelsea artist. Likewise the miniature you are wearing about your neck."

Molly put her hand to the locket, shuddering. "You are lying! You made me remember her!"

"I merely conjured up the sort of images any impressionable young girl might hold about her unknown mother. In fact, I managed to track your real mother down. She was a waterfront harlot by the name of Nell Scutley. Stabbed to death in a brawl on St. Katherine's docks nineteen years ago come April."

"I don't believe you!" Molly swallowed hard. "How could you have found that out?"

He smiled indulgently. "Surely by now you've discovered what doors money and power can open. The identity of your father, alas, is lost in the sands of time. But considering what is known about your mother, that's probably just as well."

Molly gripped her silk skirts. It wasn't possible. He was lying, he had to be. Paying her back for her marriage. "What about the birthmark?" she demanded in triumph. "We share the Buckingham birthmark; you can't deny that!"

The duke stood up, turned his back to her, and dropped his breeches. His thighs shone pale and unblemished as cold white stone. "Put on by Dr. Collett with pen and ink—and a fine job you did of it, too, John." He yanked his clothes up and faced them.

"Years of practice in medical sketching," Dr. Collett said modestly.

A pit had opened up beneath Molly's feet, a yawning black hole that grew wider and wider, stretching to engulf her. She pushed herself from her chair, backing away from them. "Why?" she whispered. "In God's name, why?"

"To ruin Anthony Strakhan, of course," the duke said briskly. "Once the king and court discover that he's married to a common street criminal, the daughter of a whore, he'll be ruined. No one will receive him. He'll be a laughingstock, *persona non grata*. And I shall be free of his meddlesome influence upon silly, sotted King Charles once and for all.'' His eyes glowed. ''Free to see that this country is ruled the way that I see fit. By me, by way of the king.''

''Oh!'' Molly clutched her chest; she could not seem to catch her breath. ''Oh, you are mad, both of you!''

''Some would have it there is madness in genius,'' Dr. Collett acknowledged, ''but I—''

''Who do you think you are?'' Molly screamed at the duke. ''Do you think you are God, trifling with lives this way?''

''Do you know what I really like about my little drama, John?'' he asked fondly. ''Strakhan is too bloody damned noble to put her away. His own honor will doom him.'' He waved an indifferent hand in Molly's direction. ''Go on, then. Go to your husband. Give him my heartfelt congratulations on his nuptials. Oh . . . and thanks to you, my dear Mary Catherine, for playing your part so exceedingly well.''

Had she had a knife in her hand, Molly would have killed him. Her gaze darted about the room, searching for a weapon. There had to be something . . .

''Ah, ah, my dear.'' The duke wagged a finger. ''That would only make matters worse. Would you have your precious Anthony wedded to a murderess as well?''

Her eyes flew back to him. ''Bastard,'' she spat. ''You lying, filthy bastard . . .''

''Have you ever noticed, John, how unimaginative the lower classes are with their epithets? It really is true; one can take the girl out of Smithfield, but you cannot take Smithfield out of the girl.''

''I'll place an announcement of my own,'' Molly threatened in a burst of inspiration born of hate. ''I'll explain just what happened, how you came and got me out of prison . . .''

Buckingham was cleaning beneath his pared nails with

the edge of a calling card. "Who do you think will believe you? It will be the word of a cheap London hussy against mine—not to mention that of the future director of the Royal Society." Dr. Collett grinned, returning his nod.

"Warden Fell, at the prison—he'd back my story!"

"Warden Fell will do whatever I tell him," Dr. Collett said complacently.

"Besides," the duke chimed in, "the fact remains that you're married to Anthony Strakhan. For better or for worse." He tittered. "This scandal is going to give new meaning to those words."

Molly could think of nothing else to say; her mind was blank with horror. Desperate, still hoping what he'd said was a lie, she fell on her knees at his feet. "Please, Uncle George," she begged, "please, that's enough. Tell me this is a jest."

The man she'd worshiped and adored looked down at her, and there was no mistaking the revulsion on his handsome face. "Get out, you pathetic baggage. Go to your husband. Nothing can save you now." Then he jangled the bell at his elbow. "Thompkins, show her out. See her into the carriage; she is going to Ballenrose Hall. And then come back and clean these boots; she's put her hands on them."

"Very good, m'lord."

"I'll get started on those copies, shall I?" Dr. Collett asked as the butler hauled Molly up from the floor.

"There's no rush, John; let's savor our victory. Thompkins!"

"Aye, m'lord?" The butler paused with Molly halfway to the door.

"Another bottle of this champagne, too."

"Very good, m'lord."

The sun was still shining as Molly staggered out of Buckingham House, and that surprised her: her world had turned black. Two gardeners looked on curiously as Thompkins handed her to Barnes, the footman. "Ballenrose Hall,'' the butler directed. ''Unload her and her trunks at the gate, then come straight back here.''

Inside the coach, Molly sagged against the seat like a rag doll. She was far beyond tears; Buckingham's cruelty left her numb. She had never imagined there could be such evil in a man. Suddenly Anthony's voice, speaking of his sister, rang in her head: *She killed herself,* he'd said, *to keep from bringing that devil's spawn into this world.* . . . Oh, Magdalene, she thought, God have mercy on you, for you were right, and I was wrong.

The duke was right too, for nothing could save her. She, who only yesterday had been the light of Anthony's life, was about to become the instrument of destruction for his hopes and dreams. Molly had seen enough of the casual cruelty of Charles's court to know what the reaction to this marriage would be. Anthony would become a pariah, ridiculed and shunned. She could hear the buzzing now; and the loudest buzz of all would come from Clare.

The coach was stifling, suffocating. She drew back the window and saw they'd reached the esplanade along the Thames. The water stretched beneath the clear spring sky like an unwound bolt of blue satin, seamless and smooth. She felt it beckoning to her in her despair. *The end,* that wide expanse of water promised. *The end to your pain.* . . .

Drowning, they said, was not a bad way to die—though how they knew, she wasn't certain. Anthony would mourn her, of course, but wouldn't he also, secretly, be relieved? Not here, though. Not along the esplanade, where the footman or driver might stop her. When they reached the city, when she could slip away into the crowds, she would make her move. She would wait. It was only fitting.

Ashes to ashes. Dust to dust. In the seclusion of the jolting carriage, she took the locket from her throat, took off her pigskin gloves. Neatly, methodically, she removed her traveling cloak and folded it on the seat beside her. Next came her gown, her stockings, her shoes.

When she'd stripped down to her underskirts and chemise, she felt calm, reassured. Like Magdalene, what she was doing was right, was inevitable. The roofs of the city drew nearer. She pushed back the slat behind the driver's seat. "Take the road by St. Katherine's docks, please."

That was where Aunt May had found her, where her mother—no duchess's daughter, no French *comte*'s wife, but a London streetwalker—had died so many years ago. "Ashes to ashes," she whispered, fingers wrapped tight in the linen of her petticoats. It was where she'd die too.

She ought to have known, really, she thought with a vague, sad smile. When you came right down to it, it had all been much too good to be true.

25

THE INDIA TEA —the third pot the cook had brewed up—
was cold, and the raisin-nut biscuits, four kinds, from four
different shops, two dozen of each, were hardening at the
edges. Anthony nibbled at the corner of one. A plain sort
of cake, really, for a countess. But he'd passed by the
French pastries robed in marzipan, the high, delicate me-
ringues, and brought her what she asked for. He put the
biscuit down; it tasted dry.

"I could cover 'em, sir, with a wet towel."

"What's that?"

"I could cover 'em up," said the maid, hovering in the
doorway. "It'd keep 'em fresher."

"Oh."

She flitted closer, a little wary. "Shall I, then?"

"There's no need, Bess. My guest will soon be here."

He'd held off telling the servants that they had a new
mistress; he wanted Mary Catherine to see their surprise.
And they would be surprised too. Nay, astonished. His
valet, Cray, had a long-standing bet with the butler,
Atkin, that their master never would marry, or so the
housekeeper had told him. He wondered what the amount
was. It would be a nice gesture to Cray if he made it good.

"Bess?"

"Aye, sir?" She was at his side in an instant. Anthony
knew why she was edgy. She'd been with the house all her

life, and her mother before her, and was able to read his moods expertly. Now she couldn't, didn't know what kept him in the drawing room with the tea tray set for two.

"What's the time?" he asked, hiding a secretive smile.

"Half-past five, sir."

Half-past five. Even taking into consideration the fact that there had been three women leaving Cliveden, one being the vain, difficult Clare Fairfax, they should have gotten on the road by eleven—noon at the absolute latest. The duke's horses were the finest, his carriages swift and sound. She must've been at Buckingham House for an hour. Surely that was time enough to give George Villiers the news. He hoped she wasn't pleading with him, trying to effect a reconciliation, for he knew that was hopeless, even if she wasn't willing to admit as much.

He pondered the possibility of an accident for a moment, then rejected it. No. Lady Fate wouldn't play such a trick, not after showing time and again that she was on their side. The story of their courtship was enough to convince any doubter of the efficacy of the stars. Look at the evidence! That first chance meeting in the king's garden, their being paired on that magical night of the treasure hunt, the mysterious note about his gatekeeper's son that had brought him to St. Bart's while she was there . . . And most remarkable of all, not even that old fox Villiers, with his multitude of lies and hoaxes, had been able to prevent the stars' decree.

Marriage. He smiled again, and from the corner of his eye saw Bess frown in perplexity. Well, she'd have her curiosity satisfied soon enough. He noticed a smudge on the teapot and rubbed it absently with his thumb. This old house wanted cheering, as it had ever since Magdalene's death. Mary Catherine would provide that; he'd seen her light up whole rooms just by entering them, like the sun.

Marriage—and children. To think there had been a time when he was content to let his family tree wither and die, to leave no legacy of sons and daughters behind him. Now . . . now he could almost see it flourishing before his eyes, reaching toward the skies, toward infinity. He laughed aloud with pleasure, with the warmth of his memories of the night before, and heard Bess give a faint gasp that only made him laugh more. "Sir?" she asked timidly in the face of his mirth. "Sir, is aught amiss?"

Things had come to a pretty pass in this house, he reflected, when the master could not laugh without frightening the servants! "Nay, lass," he told the maid kindly, gently. "On the contrary. This topsy-turvy world has at long last come upright again."

By a quarter to seven, he was no longer laughing. Bess, on the other hand, was sanguine; this was the brooding, distracted lord she remembered. Without even asking his permission, she'd removed the tea tray, with its untouched pot and the dozens of cakes gone stale. Now she lingered by the doorway, an experienced sailor preparing to ride out the storm.

"What's the time, Bess?" Anthony asked, and then bit his tongue, realizing it had been not two minutes since his last inquiry.

"Quarter to seven, m'lord," she told him again, without the slightest irritation. "Can I fetch ye the brandy?"

Her third offer. He shook his head, then added on an impulse, "You are good to me, Bess."

"Well, that'd be because ye're good t' me in turn, sir. There's no better lord t' serve in all o' England than the Earl o' Ballenrose; everyone knows that's true."

"Is that so," he said distractedly.

"Oh, aye, sir! Why, last month when the post for underchambers maid opened, there was a queue a mile long to fill it."

"Underchambers maid—that would be Janet Bell, wouldn't it? A tiny little chit. Red hair and freckles."

"There, now, that's just wot I mean." Bess nodded approval. "How many lords could say they knows their staffs so well? Most masters don't give a hang who's in service to 'em—'n' if ye asks me, that's why the service they gets is so bad. Me own cousin was in service t' the Duke o' Buckingham himself," Bess chattered, " 'n' the poor man got flogged within an inch o' his life. 'N' wot for? Why, for nothin' at all. His grace just took it into his head! On a whim, as they say." She blinked; Anthony had bolted up from his chair. "Why—wot is it, sir?"

He should have gone with her. Dammit, he knew he should have gone with her and had let her talk him out of it despite his qualms. He couldn't blame her; she had a blind spot when it came to her uncle. But he had known better . . .

"Have the black saddled for me right away, Bess."

"Aye, sir." She bobbed and retreated. "I'll fetch yer cloak; 'tis raining."

"I don't need a cloak."

She brought it to him anyway, and found him loading the silver-handled pistols he'd carried as a boy in the Civil Wars—and, so far as she knew, only one time since, on a cold November morning four months past. "Sir?" she said tentatively, questioningly.

"Don't worry, Bess." He flashed her a smile, not bright and not joyful, but genuine. "Just a precaution."

It was a lie. If Buckingham had touched her, he was dead.

26

ANTHONY REMEMBERED BUCKINGHAM'S butler vaguely from the night of the treasure hunt. "Thompkins, isn't it?" he demanded as the portly man stood blocking the threshold. "I'd see your master."

There was a twist to the butler's mouth that he hadn't remembered. "His grace is not at home," he said with undisguised insolence, just as the duke's voice roared from within:

"Thompkins! More champagne!"

Champagne . . . Anthony pushed past the butler and his squawking protests, found the drawing-room doors, thrust them open. The duke lounged in a chair with a visitor, a long-nosed man with pale eyes. Anthony recalled him from the inquiry board at the Fleet, and didn't like what he recalled: John Collett, physician and member of the Royal Society. Neither man looked up as he came in. "Well, pop it open, Thompkins," the duke said impatiently. "What the devil are you waiting for?"

"Where is she?" Anthony asked, his voice barely controlled.

The duke turned to him then, his sharp dark eyes taking a moment to focus, and Anthony realized that for the first time in the two score years he'd been acquainted with him, Buckingham was drunk. "Well! Look who's here!" he cried, sloshing wine over the rim of the glass he lifted.

"Come for a toast to your nuptials? We've just finished this bottle—actually, we've finished quite a few—but there's another on the way. Sit down, sit down! John, you remember his lordship?"

Collett was giggling into his glass. "Shertainly," he said. "And howsh your charming wife?"

Anthony pushed back his cloak, felt the cold silver of the pistol hilts against his palms. "Damn you, where is she?"

Buckingham sat up a little straighter; Anthony could see the muscles in his fine cheekbones tighten. It was an involuntary movement, one that in his condition he could not have feigned. "Isn't she . . . with you?"

"She was here?"

The duke nodded, blinking.

"She never came home," Anthony growled.

Now the duke was sitting very straight indeed. John Collett hiccuped, put his hand over his mouth. "Oh, dear . . ."

"By Christ, if you've hurt her . . ." Anthony began.

"Hurt her? Of course I didn't hurt her." Buckingham had stopped slurring his words, seemed to be shrugging off his inebriation with the force of sheer will. As he spoke, Anthony saw something else he'd never seen in all the years of their acquaintance: deep down in those fine jet eyes, the slightest glimmer of fear. "I packed her off . . . What's the time?"

"Near eight," Dr. Collett informed him, and he, too, sounded considerably more sober.

"A good three hours ago, John, wouldn't you say? Thompkins!"

"Aye, m'lord?" The butler was at Anthony's elbow.

"The carriage to Ballenrose Hall—who drove it?"

"Barnes and Perkins, m'lord."

"Are they returned yet?"

"I don't know, m'lord."

"Damn you, go and see!"

Anthony's own gaze narrowed. Something was amiss

here, gravely amiss—something he could not fathom. "You were celebrating my nuptials, you say?" he asked Collett, instinctively honing in on the weaker opponent.

"Aye. Well, that is, we—" Collett stopped, looking to the duke.

"I always say let bygones be bygones," Buckingham said suavely, his sangfroid restored. "Mary Catherine's happiness has always been my ultimate concern, and—"

Anthony moved like the wind, had the gun at his head. "You despicable dog, you lie."

"I assure you," the duke continued, without the slightest quiver, "Mary Catherine's whereabouts at the moment are of every bit as much concern to me as to you. Well, Thompkins?"

The butler stood, pale, in the doorway. "They've not returned, m'lord."

"Ah. I'd say we have a veritable mystery on our hands."

Collett had been writing, Anthony saw; a single sheet of parchment lay beneath his abandoned champagne glass. "What's that?" he demanded, gesturing with the pistol.

"This?" Collett snatched it up, once more glancing at his host. "It's . . . it's . . ."

"An announcement of the marriage, of course," the duke said. "You don't mind if I place it? There are a few details I didn't get from Mary Catherine, though, in all the excitement, so we might as well begin again." He took the parchment from the doctor and pitched it onto the fire. "Perhaps you could provide them. The names of the witnesses, for example, and of the clergyman? And exactly where and when did this wedding take place?"

Anthony felt a prickling sixth sense that danger lurked ahead or behind him, unseen. And he was certain of this: anything the duke asked for was safer withheld. "No," he stated flatly.

"Oh, come, come, my dear man. Why such hostility?"

"Milord Ballenrose," Collett said nervously, "don't you think you might put that pistol away? I've seen the careless use of guns result in far too many accidents in my day.''

''I don't intend to be careless,'' Anthony told him. ''Neither do I intend to leave here without Mary Catherine.''

''I don't blame you for your concern,'' Buckingham said, ''but your wife isn't here. Let me hazard a guess—that her cousin Jessica stood up for her. Perhaps she's gone there?''

Anthony wavered. What could be the harm in confirming Jessica's role in the wedding? Perhaps Mary Catherine had stopped there to visit—

He saw the duke's black eyes gleam at his moment's hesitation, and his defenses rose again. ''She'd have had no reason to go to Jessica's,'' he said carefully, just as a commotion sounded from the front hall.

''Must be Barnes 'n' Perkins returned, m'lord,'' said Thompkins.

He withdrew to the hall and dragged the two men in. One look at their terrified faces and Anthony instantly credited Bess's tale of her cousin; these were servants in fear for their lives. Their fear was contagious; it coiled tight around his own bowels.

''Well, Perkins?'' the duke said. ''What's happened?''

''M'lord.'' The man was blubbering, thick-lipped in his misery. ''M'lord, there wasn't nothin' we could do, I swear it. We got to the city, 'n' . . . 'n' . . .'' He broke down completely, buried his face in his hands.

''Barnes!'' Buckingham commanded. ''Where is she?''

''She . . . she . . . she . . .''

''Christ Jesu, what a pair of fools! Shall I beat it out of you?'' The duke stood, towering over them.

''But it weren't our fault!'' the hapless footman wailed.

''Perkins,'' Anthony said softly, gently. ''You got to the city. And . . . ?''

Perkins raised his head, saw the gun still cocked at his master's head. The peculiar sight must have given him courage; he rubbed his eyes with the backs of his hands.

"There was a fight," he said hoarsely, "some 'prentices shoutin' back 'n' forth wi' each other—"

"And they hurt Lady Mary Catherine?" Anthony asked somewhat incredulously. There hadn't been apprentice riots in London for some thirty years.

"Nay, nay, m'lord. But we had to stop the coach, ye see, as they was blockin' the street. 'N' when we did—"

"Aye?" Anthony prompted again.

Perkins swallowed. "She opened up the coach door, m'lord, 'n' ran out."

"She ran out of the coach?" Buckingham echoed in astonishment.

Barnes and the footman exchanged glances. "There's more," Barnes mumbled, wringing his hands. "She were naked—stripped down to her underthings."

"She left her clothes in the coach," his unfortunate mate confirmed. "Right down t' her shoes."

Anthony was so completely astonished, he let go of the gun. It fell to the floor beside a spilled wineglass. The duke made a lunge for the pistol, bringing Anthony to his senses. "Don't bother," he said shortly, kicking the weapon away and producing its match. "I've got another."

"I trust you went after her, Barnes?" Dr. Collett demanded.

"O' course we did! But the streets was still blocked, 'n' a crowd out to watch the 'prentices fight—"

"She moved like the devil himself was bitin' at her heels," Perkins said softly.

"*Where* did she move?" asked the duke. "Where was she going?"

"T' the docks, sir," said Barnes. "St. Katherine's docks. She had asked me to drive her that way."

"St. Katherine's docks . . ." The matter grew still more baffling to Anthony. "In her underclothes, you say?" The driver nodded. "Well, what the bloody hell would she be doing there?"

"We searched high 'n' low for her," said the disconsolate driver, "for nigh on three hours, 'n' found not a trace."

The Duke of Buckingham stood up, ignoring Anthony's pistol. "I don't like this. I don't like it at all."

"You don't like it?" Anthony felt like laughing. "By Christ, it's your fault, you bloody bastard! What did you say to her? What went on here?"

"I surely said nothing that would cause her to take off her clothes and run half-naked onto the wharves!" the duke snapped back. Anthony looked at him; their eyes met, locked. "What could I possibly have said to make her do such a thing?" Buckingham demanded, voice hard and challenging. "Have you any suggestions?"

Involuntarily Anthony shook his head; it was spinning. The man had him there, damn his black soul. Whatever scene had been played out in this room, why wouldn't she have come home to him? Oh, Mary Catherine, he thought, the fear moving higher, toward his heart. Where are you? What have you done? Oh, my love . . .

"Well, then." The duke took charge, crisp and efficient. "To hell with the whys; the thing to do is find her. Get every man you can, Thompkins; Strakhan, I assume you'll do the same. And we'll call out the city watch, and the Tower guard; I'm sure his majesty won't mind. John."

"Aye, George?" Collett asked.

"Those copies I asked you to make—you know the ones I mean?" The doctor nodded, with a veiled glance at Anthony. "Hold off on them. They must wait. Everything must wait until Mary Catherine is found." He turned to Thompkins again. "Make sure all the men clearly understand how vital this is—for whom they are searching. The Earl of Ballenrose's wife—and my niece."

While the duke was busy giving orders, Anthony stared down at the floor. He hadn't missed the look exchanged by Buckingham and Collett. He thought of the paper the duke had so hastily destroyed, saw that discarded wineglass lying at his feet . . .

"No," he said suddenly.

"No?" The duke eyed him blankly. "No what? What do you mean, no?"

Mary Catherine, forgive me. . . . "She isn't my wife," Anthony told him, and licked his lips. "I never married her."

The duke stood stone still, his natural pallor heightening. The skin across his temples was stretched very thin. "That's a lie. She wedded you. She told me so. John's my witness."

Anthony fought back a grim smile. So his guess had been right; it was the wedding, something about the wedding. He felt like Peter at Pilate's gate, hearing the cock crow after he'd denied the Lord. *But it can't be helped, love,* he argued silently. *He wants it, and I won't give it to him because he wants it. Because I know him. It's as simple as that.*

"You're mistaken," he told the duke.

"My God, man," Dr. Collett blurted, "do you mean to desert her now, in her hour of need?"

That hurt—but it would have hurt more if Anthony hadn't seen the swift, approving glance Buckingham gave his friend. *This fox is getting old,* he thought, *or he is truly rattled; it isn't like him to give himself away.* The realization strengthened his resolve. " 'Tis true we plan to marry," he told the doctor, "for we love each other. But Mary Catherine still hopes to reconcile her uncle to the idea. If she told you we'd been married, I can only assume she was testing the waters, to see what the reaction might be."

"You lie," the duke rasped. "That wedding took place."

Anthony shrugged his shoulders. "Prove that it did." He could rely on Michael's discretion to the ends of the earth, he knew, and on Father Drayton's. As for Jessica, he wasn't so sure. There was the tie of family binding her to Buckingham. And it was true that before the duke found Mary Catherine in France, the Fairfax sisters had been his heirs.

"We're wasting time," he said, picking up his pistol, moving toward the door. "What matters is to find her, just as you said."

"Oh, we'll find her, all right," Buckingham agreed, snapping his fingers for his cloak and hat to be brought. "And I will prove that you wedded her."

Anthony's blue eyes met the duke's haughty, hateful black ones. "We'll deal with that when she's found."

Four hundred men—servants, soldiers, watch guards— searched St. Katherine's docks all that night and through the next morning. They searched the ships on the wharves, the taverns, the houses. They scoured the streets and the bridges. They found not a trace.

The hunt expanded. Every merchant Mary Catherine ever patronized, every friend she'd ever visited, even the king's palaces were examined. Rewards were posted, huge ones. They were not claimed.

Near nightfall on the third day, Anthony stood on the docks and watched as they dragged the river. With every swing of the weighted nets, his heart threatened to burst in his chest.

"Sometimes they never does find 'em," a little old fellow who'd come to watch the excitement confided, standing at his side. "Sometimes, if the tides is right, they sweeps straight out to sea. 'N' them wot drowns themselves—suicides, as they calls 'em—why, if they weights themselves down proper-like, with stones in their pockets, they just lies there on the bottom with the fish peckin' at their—"

"Shut your bloody mouth," Anthony said, with something in his tone that made the voluble onlooker edge away. Water splashed his clenched hands as the giant net was hauled up again. Salt water. Tears. The last time he'd cried this way had been when they told him about Magdalene. *Not Mary Catherine too, God,* he prayed. *Please, God, not her too. . . .*

On the fifth day they stopped dragging the river. King

Charles apologetically reappropriated his soldiers; they were needed elsewhere. The city watch quit too, bored despite the promised rewards. False leads still trickled in, were tracked down, led nowhere. Only the gossip in the coffeehouses and drawing rooms went on. "Have you heard?" new arrivals to London were asked in hushed voices. "The Duke of Buckingham's niece, Mary Catherine? That pretty girl with the pale gold hair? She's vanished into thin air."

V

"You're lovely," he told her. "How do you feel?"

"Wonderful." She stretched beneath the blankets.

He got up from the bench. "Don't say anything, then —— thought too. We have a long time yet.

27

❧

ON A BRIGHT June day at the height of summer, the broad
plain at Smithfield had more the air of a fair than a market.
Acrobats and jugglers moved between the stalls, plying
their skills in hopes of earning a few farthings, dogged by
crowds of children who could not pay but yearned to
watch. In the ebb and flow of the usual market din, a
snatch of tambour or fiddle music would rise up now and
again like a bright-colored flag. Girls tied their hair back
in ribbons and came to be ogled by the gangs of boys who
commandeered every patch of shade. Old ladies toddled
about, baskets over their arms, remarking on the weather
as though this were the last fine day they might live to see.
Even the city watchmen, scorned as venal buffoons by
those they guarded, took on a certain aura of dignity as
they rode through like medieval knights at a joust, the sun
glinting on their lances and their tall hats of black and
gold.

"Go, Katrine!" Piers Van Eyck said in his heavy Dutch
accent, throwing open his arms to embrace the bright pan-
oply beyond the dim sorting shed. "Go! Enjoy, ja? Take
the afternoon. See the yugglers."

"The jugglers," the girl he'd caught looking through
the doorway corrected him.

"Ja, ja, the yugglers. You are too pale; you look like a
ghost. Get out! Maybe find a young man, heh?" He

laughed, belly jiggling, and tugged a hank of the short dark hair that showed beneath her white cap.

"Not today," she demurred, moving away from the doorway. "There's too much to do. Maybe tomorrow."

"To do? What is to do?"

"The herbs that came in need unboxing. And I haven't stripped the thorns from the roses. On a day like this, you could sell lots of roses."

"Ja? You think?"

She nodded, taking her seat on the low wooden bench, picking up her shears. "Once the 'prentices out there stop teasing the girls, they'll want to woo them."

Piers scratched his chin. "To sell more roses, this would be good. You make me a sign, ja? Three roses a shilling."

"I've told you before, there's no sense in signs. They can't read."

"I like signs," the Dutchman said stubbornly. "When I hire you, it is because you say you can make them. Where is the sense in having the most smart sorting girl in the market if I don't use what you know?"

" 'Smartest,' " she said absently, "not 'most smart.' All right. I'll make you a sign. But no one out there has got a shilling to spend on flowers. Make it one rose for twopence."

"I won't make as much money."

She held up the rose she was stripping, showed him how its stem bent. "If you don't sell these soon, you'll end up drying them for sachet."

Piers pulled out his pipe. "Why do you all the time tell me how to run my business?"

"That's what you hired me for. Don't you dare light that pipe in here."

"Und why not?"

"Because no one wants to buy roses that smell like tobacco."

"Bah." But he put the pipe back in its pouch, then stood and watched as, in three quick movements, she stripped the thorns from another rose stem. "Do you never hurt yourself on those?"

She shook her head. "Not anymore. Not for a long, long time. There." She laid the last rose aside. "I'll make the sign now if you bring me the ink and brush."

"Bah! Who works for whom?" But he brought them to her anyway, and hovered over her shoulder as she lettered the words on the side of an empty crate. Then she stuck the roses in a pitcher of water, put them in the crate, and thrust it at him. "Here. I've done all I can. Now, you sell them."

His broad, ruddy face brightened. "I have idea, Katrine! You take the box und walk around the market to sell them!"

"It's a good idea, Piers," she admitted, making him beam, "but I can't do it."

"Katrine, why?"

"Because I can't."

"Take the afternoon off," he said again.

"Maybe tomorrow."

"Tomorrow. Always tomorrow! But tomorrow never comes, does it, Katrine?"

"Maybe it will tomorrow."

"Bah." He left the shed, box in hand; she heard his booming voice through the doorway: "Roses!" he called. "Twopence for one rose! Come buy my roses and make love with them!" A crowd of 'prentices hooted at the Dutchman's offer; she started to the doorway to correct his English, then didn't. It was a novel approach, but who could tell? It might work.

As his voice faded, she reached beneath the bench for the discarded copy of the *Orange Gazette* she'd found in the gutter that morning outside the shed. June 18, 1672— that would be four days past. Uncrinkling the front page with nervous fingers, she saw the notice posted in the lower-right-hand corner, bordered in heavy black: "Missing," it began. She knew the words by heart, having read them dozens of times in one abandoned newspaper or an-

other: five hundred pounds' reward for information leading to the whereabouts of Lady Mary Catherine Villiers,
niece of his grace, the honorable George Villiers, Duke
of Buckingham. And then the description: slim, medium
height, green eyes, long gold hair.

"Katrine?"

Piers stuck his head back into the shed, and she stuffed
the newspaper back under the bench. "Aye?"

He'd seen her, she knew, and still he didn't raise his
blond eyebrows. That was why she liked Piers. "Why,"
he asked, "do the boys laugh at me?"

"Have you sold any roses?"

"Six," he said, thick chest thrust out proudly.

"Let the boys laugh."

He grinned and went out again.

She pulled the box of herbs over to the bench and began
to separate them into small string-tied bundles. Lady's
mantle, rue, deadnettle, amaranth, melissa—their pungent
scents, comfortingly familiar, clung to her fingers and
spread through the shed. When she came upon the moon-
wort, she shook dirt from its thick roots and set them
aside; with walnut juice and childing daisies they made
the dark dye that, applied to her close-shorn locks,
thwarted the last part of the notice's description. Green
eyes could not be seen in the dim sorting shed, nor in the
hours between sunset and dawn. As for slimness, well,
time was taking care of that. Safe, she thought, and whispered it aloud: "Safe." And someday, one day, that notice
in the papers would disappear.

Rosemary, betony, vervain, the deadly monkshood. She
held this last in her hand, considered the handsome blue
flowers, the ferny gray leaves. *Safe.* Yet if worse came to
worst, there were in this shed a dozen different means to
bring the play to an end. The thought was comforting.

Sea lavender. Mouseweed. Lilies of the valley. Her deft
fingers fumbled as she found these, smelled the rich heady
scent of the wax-white flowers. Good for apoplexy and
dumb palsy, she told herself, taking refuge in a dull list of

the plant's virtues. An aid to gout. Cures inflammations of the eyes. Comforts the heart. Restores the memory . . .

Oh, God, as though hers needed restoring!

She bundled the stems up quickly, looking away. She would tell Piers to sell them cheap: two bunches a farthing. She wanted them gone by the end of the day.

"Kate?"

She looked up and saw Rachel, the girl who worked the stall out front: she was kind and plain and rather stupid. "Are ye cryin', Kate?" she asked now.

She shook her head, wiped her face with her apron. "No. It's the oils in the herbs; they make my eyes sting."

"Oh."

"What do you need?"

"There's a lady askin' for somethin' against the mornin' sickness. Wot'll I give her?"

"Here." She reached into her apron pocket, pulled out a little cloth bag, and shook half its contents into Rachel's hand. "Fennel, dillweed, and chamomile. Have her take it steeped in wine, if she can afford that. Or she can just chew the leaves."

Rachel had a layman's awe of such things, was reluctant to hold the herbs in her hand. "Can I use this?" she asked, reaching beneath the bench for the crumpled newspaper.

"Aye, go ahead."

"How much should I charge her?"

Her own queasiness rose up as though in sympathy. "Nothing."

Rather stupid except when it came to money, Rachel frowned. "Nothin? Why should I give it to her for nothin'?"

"Because it will work, and she'll keep coming back. Just do as I say."

Rachel shrugged, turned around at the doorway. "D'ye know Mr. Van Eyck is out there marchin' about like a fool with a whole crowd o' 'prentices followin' after him?"

"Mr. Van Eyck is out there selling roses, Rachel. Now please get back to the stall."

When the girl had gone, she took a pinch of leaves from the bag and chewed them up slowly, bending over with her head between her knees, waiting for the wave of nausea to subside. This one was bad, probably because she'd neglected to eat her dinner again. She'd forgotten how working with herbs and flowers all day could dull the appetite, make one long for fresh air. But that would have to wait until the sun went down.

She put her hands to her breasts, ran them over her belly. Only the barest swelling there, and that just in the past fortnight or so. The morning sickness was new too, come on since the start of her third month. Neither sign offered an answer to the question she'd pondered time and again: how had she known? How, as the cold dark water of the Thames closed over her head, had she realized with sudden, startling certainty that she was carrying Anthony's child?

One last trick of that cruel prankster God, she supposed, swallowing bile as she straightened up on the bench. Or penultimate trick, rather; last place was surely reserved for the fact that she'd been fished from the flood by Piers Jakob Van Eyck, who couldn't read English and could barely speak it, and was thus the one man on St. Katherine's docks that day likely to remain ignorant of the prize he'd found.

She'd like to believe that a gentler God had sent Piers to her—jolly, good-natured Piers, such a hopeless dreamer that he'd been shipped off by his exasperated parents in Rotterdam to England with a hundred pounds and their blessing, there to seek his fortune or at least to stop squandering theirs. Piers, who'd pulled her out of the river, sputtering and huffing, and then greeted her with a beguiling grin and the sole full sentence he knew in his new country's language: "I drink to the health of King Charles!"

She'd never know if it was the barrier of language or merely his nature that kept Piers from asking questions when she chopped off her hair and colored it brown, or refused to leave the shed in daylight. So far he seemed satisfied with the bargain they'd struck, to be partners of sorts in their flower stall. He'd put up the capital, and used his Dutch to bargain with the Amsterdam shippers for the best prices. She told him what to charge for his wares, told Rachel what to prescribe for this or that ailment, did the sorting and bundling, and stayed out of sight. She also taught Piers English, and hoped that by the time he could read it that notice would have long since disappeared.

What would have happened, she wondered idly, if Piers hadn't been wandering the docks back in March, fresh off the ship and looking for an alehouse where he could try out his toast to the king? If she'd drowned, if her body had washed up onshore, would Buckingham have gone ahead with his public disavowal of her? Probably. Because surely then Anthony would have acknowledged her as his wife.

At first it tore her apart that he didn't, that the newspapers and posted signs spoke only of Mary Catherine Villiers, the Duke of Buckingham's niece. Only gradually did she come to realize that her husband must have smelled a fish, that dear Uncle George must have tipped his hand.

Knowing her erstwhile uncle's resources and determination, Molly had thought it wisest to return to Smithfield with a new name. She was careful, too, never to go near the corner where her former neighbors from Gospel Square had their stalls, not even at night.

It was a lonely life that Molly led. Only the promise of the child kept her from the lure of the river—that and visiting the potter's field by St. Bart's, where the hospital buried its indigent patients. Aunt May's bones would be there somewhere, unmarked beneath the turf that never quite healed over before it was turned up again. If there was one thing London had in abundance, Molly thought grimly, tying stalks of catmint and heal-all together, it was impoverished dead.

"He's done it," Michael Nivens said shortly as Bess showed him into the study where her master sat slumped at his desk.

Anthony straightened his shoulders, looked into his friend's angry eyes. "Christ, Michael. I'm so sorry—"

"Don't be. You've got nothing to be sorry for. If you want to know the truth, I'm surprised I kept the post this long." He paced across the room. "I'll tell you one thing, though. This nation's in a sad state when one man's whim's as good as bloody law."

"I should have done more to stop him," Anthony said hollowly.

"You did what you could, Tony. I'm not blaming you. God knows you've enough on your mind. But guess who's been named administrator in my place?" Anthony didn't. "Dr. John Collett, that's who! And St. Bart's was doing so well! Well . . . we were doing better. Honestly, it makes me want to cry."

Anthony reached for his quill. "I'll make a note to speak to his majesty—"

"Oh, what's the point? It's over and done." Michael threw himself down in a chair. "Though if I'm to lose my job over this, I'd at least like to know why. Why, Tony? Why does that bastard want to know so badly if that wedding took place?"

"I've done nothing but try to answer that question for the past three months." Anthony put down the quill and picked up a decanter instead. "Brandy?"

Michael shook his head. "That doesn't help, you know."

"Oh, you'd be surprised," Anthony told him, and refilled his own glass. His hand trembled slightly. Michael reached over and covered it with his.

"Let her go," he said quietly, gently. "She's dead. God help me, if I thought there was a chance, any chance, that she wasn't, I'd be the first to say so. But this . . . this serves no purpose. Let her go, mourn her and be done. You've got to move on."

"She isn't dead."

"How can you be sure?"

"If she were, I'd know it. I'd feel it."

Michael Nivens sighed, with more than a touch of exasperation. "You've got to face the facts! You've got to pull yourself up by the bootstraps—"

"I am sorry you have lost your job, Michael," Anthony interrupted with a small, wry smile. "But I know what I know."

Michael started to say something more, then stopped and shrugged. "All right. Have it your way. What about the convent in France that she was brought up in, have you found that?"

"Not yet. It would help if Buckingham would tell me where it is, of course. As it is, the going's rather slow."

"It's rather odd that he won't, don't you think?"

It was Anthony's turn to shrug. "He did write to me and say he'd had the place checked. She isn't there."

Michael picked up a crystal paperweight from the desk, weighed it in his hand. "And you're sure this isn't his doing. That he hasn't hidden her away somewhere."

"I'm sure. You should have seen how rattled he was that day when I burst in on him and John Collett."

"George Villiers rattled, eh? That's something I and any number of other folk would pay money to see." He replaced the paperweight atop the stack of reports—all negative—from the men Anthony had hired to search for his wife. "How was he rattled, Tony? I mean, did you get some sense of what had upset him?"

Anthony closed his eyes, leaned back in his chair, trying to remember the details of that scene in Buckingham's drawing room. He'd been half-crazed himself with fear for Mary Catherine; brandy and time had blurred the edges of the picture as well. "Do you recall Dr. Hodges at Oxford," he asked finally, "who taught us astronomy, and the day he lectured on how to determine the distance from the earth to the sun?"

Michael nodded. "He wrote out that whole enormous series of mathematical equations that wound up proving the sun was precisely two miles away!"

"Well, that's rather how George Villiers looked. As though he'd made some miscalculation. As though some equation hadn't worked out the way that he planned."

"He surely thinks she's still alive," Michael noted. "He's raised the reward he's offering to five hundred pounds."

"I know. I saw the papers today."

They sat for a moment in silence. Then Michael went to pick up the paperweight again. Anthony forestalled him, moving it out of reach. "Just say what's on your mind."

"Well. If she should still be alive, have you thought how she must feel knowing that you haven't acknowledged her as your wife?"

"Only a hundred times each day," Anthony said morosely. "But she left me, Michael. She ran out of that carriage."

"And you hadn't quarreled? The wedding night was . . ." He paused.

Anthony took a long swallow of brandy. "It was everything either of us could have wanted," he said steadily.

"I only meant . . . sometimes young girls do get frightened."

The way she looked stepping out of her clothes, coming toward him. The way she called his name at the consummation, turned to him afterward, green eyes shining, and whispered, *Again* . . .

He sent the memories reeling with another draft of brandy. "She wasn't afraid of me."

Michael shook his head, nonplussed. "I don't know what more to say."

Anthony stood up and went to the window, opening the shutters, looking out over the wide, sprawling city. "It's the wedding, Michael. It's something about the wedding. That's why you've lost your post—because you wouldn't admit to Buckingham that you took part in it. And when I burst in on him and Collett that day, he said they were toasting my nuptials. Why would he do that?"

"Drowning his sorrows, perhaps?"

"Only he wasn't sorry. He looked like the fox that got into the henhouse, Michael—sleek and smug and contented. And after he sought to thwart our courtship every step of the way—Christ, it just doesn't make sense."

"Well, maybe he just decided what was done was done, and that he'd better make the best of it."

Anthony snorted. "What, George Villiers?"

"I admit it doesn't sound likely. But the only alternative is that he wanted you married."

"I know." Anthony turned back from the window, his face gaunt and drawn. "Sometimes I wonder . . ."

"What?"

"That note to my footman about his boy, the one that brought me to St. Bart's. Could he have sent it? After all, he knew Mary Catherine was there."

"Brought the two of you together so that he could show up to challenge you, you mean? I wouldn't put it past him. But that would only have been so that he could feign being shot, turn Mary Catherine against you once and for all."

"Aye . . ."

Michael stood up too. "I have got to be going. But there's something else I suppose you should know. He offered me a hospital of my own today. A new one, built wherever I should like it, with myself as chief of the directors."

Anthony looked at him, stricken. "Oh, Christ."

"I'll say this for him, he knows how to latch on to what a man holds most dear," Michael said cheerfully. "And all it would cost me was a signed admission that I'd been present at the marriage of Anthony Strakhan and Mary Catherine Villiers. So I daresay you're right. It's proof of the wedding he wants. Is Father Drayton incorruptible?"

"He hasn't come forward so far. Of course, if Buckingham posts a notice offering the archbishopric of Canterbury to whoever performed the wedding, who's to say? There's one thing, though. When I last spoke to him, he told me he couldn't remove our wedding certificate from the records at St. Paul's. So if Buckingham should decide to make a search of the records of every church in England—''

"That would take forever!"

"He swore to me he'd find proof, Michael. And God knows he's tried."

"What about Father Drayton's parents, that you spent the night with?"

"He told them our name was Jones, so as not to overwhelm them. So at least we're safe there."

"That leaves Lady Jessica."

"Yes." The two men exchanged glances. "Of course, he can't be certain she was even there."

"Have you seen her? Spoken to her?"

Anthony shook his head. "I don't dare try, lest he become suspicious. I heard she's gone back to Cliveden."

"Poor girl," Michael said softly. "I wonder how she is holding up. What do you suppose her Uncle George would offer her as a bribe?"

"I don't know." Anthony downed the last of the brandy, then looked his friend in the eye. "But after Mary Catherine, she comes next in my prayers every day."

28

"YOU ARE MAKING a great deal of trouble for everyone, you know," declared the Countess of Shrewsbury, "not least of all yourself. I would have expected such willful behavior from Mary Catherine or your sister, Clare. But never from you!"

Jessica Fairfax calmly went on with her sewing. "I am not being willful, Lady Agnes. I simply don't know what Uncle George is talking about."

"He is talking about your cousin's wedding!"

"What wedding?"

"Why don't you tell me? You were there."

Jessica contemplated her embroidery. "Do you think this bird would look better in blue or in green, Lady Agnes?"

"Do you want to be stuck here at Cliveden for the rest of your life sewing birds?" the countess demanded. "Because so long as you keep defying your uncle, you will be."

"I find Cliveden very restful—or would, if you didn't keep badgering me about some imaginary wedding. Isn't there any news of interest in Uncle George's letter?"

Lady Agnes's shrewd blue eyes narrowed. "As a matter of fact, there is. I believe you know Lord Wallingford?"

Jessica nodded, beating back a little pang of apprehension. "Aye."

"Well, he is paying court to Lord Kenton's daughter. Gossip says they'll be betrothed before the summer is out."

"Really? I wish them every happiness."

"If I'm not mistaken, you had set your cap for Lord Wallingford once upon a time."

"And what if I had?"

"Why, you little fool, if you were to admit to your uncle your part in that wedding, you could go back to London and do something about Lord Wallingford's new infatuation."

"If Lord Wallingford prefers Alice Kenton to me," Jessica said with a faint smile, "then he's not the man I thought him. And anyway, as I've told you time and again, how can I admit to something I know nothing about?"

"Your obstinacy," said Lady Agnes, lowering a finger at her, "does you no credit. You wouldn't catch me giving up the man of my dreams for the sake of someone who'd brought such ignominy on my family."

"I suppose, Lady Agnes, that is just one of the many differences between you and me."

"Fah," said the countess, folding up the letter from the duke and pushing back her chair. "Three months of this nonsense is all I can stand. Let your uncle talk some sense into you; I've done all I can."

"Uncle George is coming here?" Jessica asked, heartbeat quickening.

"Aye. He'll arrive on the morrow. And I may as well warn you: it isn't likely he'll be as patient as I've tried to be. So if I were you, young lady, I'd give some serious thought to what I intend to do when he gets here." Gathering up her skirts with a silken swish, she stormed out of the room.

When she'd gone, Jessica set down the hoop that hid her clenched fingers and gave vent to a shiver. Despite the brave front she put on, these months of silence had taken their toll. One thing was sure, she thought ruefully: the next time she made someone a promise, she'd give a good deal more consideration to what the consequences might be.

"Damn you, Mary Catherine," she said aloud—not for the first time. But then she bit her tongue. Whatever reason her cousin had for disappearing, it must have been compelling. She'd been too filled with joy the morning after her wedding for Jessica to believe anything else, no matter what Uncle George might say.

That first night when he came to the house to tell her and Clare that Mary Catherine was missing, begging for their help, she very nearly told him what he wanted to know. But some good angel made her ask to see Anthony first, and her uncle's curt refusal had put her on guard. He went on refusing, even brought her to Cliveden to keep Anthony from her, with the excuse that he didn't intend to have two nieces ruined by the Earl of Ballenrose. After that, the reasons he gave for having to know about the wedding only grew more fantastical.

Anthony might have tricked Mary Catherine into marrying him and then murdered her for her inheritance, he told her. Or—and with opposite logic—he feared they hadn't been married, that the priest who had wedded them wasn't really a priest. Then, and this was Jessica's favorite, he postulated that Mary Catherine had returned to France to join the convent where she'd been brought up after her brief taste of marriage. What a dolt he must think me, Jessica mused, staring down at her uneven stitches. What a dolt everyone thinks me. Trying to get me to talk with that absurd lie about Lord Wallingford and Alice Kenton . . . as though Harry would ever take up with the likes of that girl.

Of course, she was somewhat pretty, in a coarse sort of way. Some men liked that—

Stop it, Jessica! she told herself sternly. That is just what they are all trying to do, as you know perfectly well—sow doubts in your mind. You made a promise to Mary Catherine not to tell anyone about the wedding until you saw her again, and it's up to you to keep faith no matter what.

The Duchess of Buckingham, thin as a rail beneath clouds of diaphanous gauze, glided into the room with her pale eyes glowing. "They were there last night in the gardens," she crooned, hovering over her niece. "Young lovers trysting in the darkness. My, they were lovely, all soaked in moonlight!"

But, oh, Mary Catherine, Jessica thought as her aunt rambled on, I do hope you return soon!

The duke arrived at Cliveden at ten, and he'd brought someone with him: Clare, dressed in a new gown of purple velvet, with a necklace of glorious sapphires encircling her dusky throat. "Aren't those Mary Catherine's jewels?" Jessica asked as Clare stepped from the carriage.

"They're mine now," said her sister, smoothing out her skirts and nodding to the countess. "Lady Agnes. I see the summer heat hasn't affected your appetite. You really ought to have that bodice let out."

"Why, you little—" Lady Agnes broke off as the duke turned to her. "George. Thank God you've come."

"Agnes." He kissed her cheek, gaze glancing off her to where Jessica stood waiting. He made no move to embrace her, instead frowned, his dark eyes cold. "I'm most displeased, Jessica. *Most* displeased."

"Yes, Uncle George," she whispered. "I know. But—"

"Your cousin Mary Catherine has been missing three months now. She could have been kidnapped. She could be lying dead in a ditch somewhere, with maggots crawling through her—"

"Oh, George, really," the countess said, blanching.

"But we don't know where she might be, do we," the duke went on, "because you won't talk!"

"I don't know where she is," Jessica said truthfully.

"No, but you hold the key to her disappearance—the proof of that wedding."

"What wedding?" Jessica asked, and flinched as he raised a fist.

"Not here, George," Lady Agnes murmured. "The servants—"

"To hell with the servants." But he grabbed Jessica's arm, pulling her inside and all the way up the stairs to her rooms.

Lady Agnes and Clare came in after them. "Leave us, Agnes," the duke directed.

"I think that I can be of some assis—"

"I said leave us!"

"Very well." She pursed her lips. "Come along, Clare."

"He didn't tell me to go," Clare said coolly, taking a seat at the dressing table and examining her reflection in the silvered glass.

"Well, I'm quite sure he meant to!"

"If I'd meant to, I would have," the duke said evenly. "Now, leave us."

The countess stood for a moment, looking at her lover. Then she left the room without another word, quietly closing the door.

Clare had found her sister's favorite rosewater and was applying it liberally to her wrists and throat. "How are you, Jess?" she asked.

"Well, thank you," Jessica said, her mouth dry. "How are Father and Mother?"

Clare shrugged. "Well enough, I suppose. I haven't seen much of them since I've been staying at Buckingham House."

"Oh. Are you staying there?"

"It's so much more convenient while I help Uncle George with the search."

"Of course. It would be. Is there any news?"

"Oh, there's plenty of news. But no one's found Mary Catherine, if that's what you mean. Have you heard about your Harry and Alice Kenton?"

"Uncle George put it in his letter to Lady Agnes that

they were courting. Though I didn't give it much credence. Knowing Harry, I mean.'' She glanced at her uncle, half-apologetic, half-defiant.

''Well, you'd better. He's given her that pearl ring that was his mother's, the one you always admired.''

''He didn't!'' Jessica blurted in shock.

''Oh, yes he did. Wake up, Jessica dear. It isn't the quiet, faithful girl who wins her man in the end. If you care about Harry, it's high time you came back to London and fought for him.''

''Believe me, there is nothing I'd like better than to return to London.''

''Except to go on defying me,'' the duke put in.

''I don't mean to defy you, Uncle George.''

''Then why don't you admit that you were at that wedding?''

''I can't,'' she said softly, miserably. ''Why won't you let me see Anthony Strakhan? If you only would—''

''Your precious Lord Ballenrose is far too busy to be bothered with you,'' Clare told her sister. ''He's taken up with Anne Cunningham.''

''He wouldn't!'' Jessica cried. ''He adores Mary Catherine; he must be absolutely distraught that she hasn't been found.''

''Well, he certainly has an odd way of showing it,'' Clare drawled. ''He and Mistress Cunningham were at the theater together last week, laughing their heads off at Etheredge's new comedy.''

''He doesn't even like the theater,'' Jessica said in bewilderment. ''Why do you keep on lying to me?''

''Perhaps she's right, Clare,'' the duke said slowly. ''Perhaps it's time we told her the truth, however shocking it may be.''

Clare turned from the looking glass. ''Are you certain that's wise?''

''She's proved her ability to keep a secret these past months,'' the duke noted, ''though her loyalty is sadly misguided. Perhaps a simple, forthright explanation is all that's needed to end this nonsense once and for all."

"Explanation of what?" Jessica said warily.

"Of why we have got to find that conniving liar Mary Catherine," her sister said.

"Clare! How can you speak of your own cousin that way?"

"That's just it, Jess. That's the truth. She isn't our cousin. She isn't any kin to us or to Uncle George at all."

"Oh, really," Jessica said after a moment's pause. "This is reaching new heights of absurdity."

"Absurd it may be," said the duke, "but unfortunately true. The girl you know as Mary Catherine Villiers has pulled a hoax as big as Atlas on me and everyone who knows her. Including you."

"I see," Jessica said. "And who is she really?"

"The daughter of a London streetwalker named Nell Scutley," her uncle said. "And, up until two years ago, a prisoner at the Fleet jail."

Jessica burst out laughing. "Mary Catherine? Honestly, Uncle George!"

"Honestly, my dear Jessica. And believe me, no one is more appalled at the situation than am I."

Jessica glanced at her sister, expecting to see her hiding a smile. But to her surprise, for once Clara looked serious. "Don't tell me you've fallen for this story!"

"It's no story, Jess. And I'm the one who first told Uncle George that Mary Catherine wasn't who she was supposed to be."

"Perhaps it would be best if I began at the beginning," the duke said sheepishly. "You know, Jessica, that I told everyone I'd found Mary Catherine in a convent in France? That was a lie, I'm afraid, though only meant to protect her. The first time I really met her was there in the Fleet. I was serving on a board of inquiry, examining the prisoners for signs of mistreatment. Mary Catherine was one of those prisoners, only then she called herself Molly Willoughby or Molly Flowers. She was serving a one-year term for disturbing the peace. She was frightfully dirty, of course, and quite illiterate. But beneath all that grime, she had a certain *je ne sais quoi*.

"You're too young, Jessica, of course," the duke went on, "to remember when my sister Frances was drowned en route from France. For years afterward, various women came forth claiming to be her. Or else they'd bring me babies, foundlings that they said were her daughter Mary Catherine. None of their stories held up under scrutiny, and in time they stopped trying, just as in time I gave up all hope that Frances or her daughter, the niece I'd never met, might still be alive. I put them out of my mind, right up until that day when I saw Molly Willoughby." He let out a sigh, settling into a chair.

"She looked like Frances," he said then. "I noticed that at once. And there were things about her—her carriage, the way she cocked her head when she laughed— that just called out to me. She seemed . . . familiar; I don't know how else to explain it. I didn't say anything to her or anyone else at the time. But later that same night, Dr. Collett and I returned to the prison to have another look at her.

"I asked her about her parents. She didn't remember her father, she said, but she did have vague recollections of her mother—a tall blond woman, very elegant and gracious. And sometimes, she said, she thought she could remember living in a castle somewhere. In her nightmares, she saw a storm at sea. Oh, God, she was good, Jessica! Mind you, I hadn't said a word to her about Frances. So far as I knew, she was speaking completely extemporaneously. And even though I knew it wasn't likely, I couldn't stop myself from thinking: could this be Frances' daughter? After all those years? It was then, while I was wavering on the very brink of hope, that she showed me the locket."

"The locket?" Jessica echoed.

Her uncle nodded, reaching into his coat and pulling out a pendant and chain. "She said that it was of her mother." He snapped it open to show her the miniature painting inside. "I recognized it at once. It was Frances. A copy of the portrait that hangs here at Cliveden, made just before she left to be married in France."

Jessica stared at the tiny painting. "You can imagine my excitement," the duke continued. "No doubt I should have been more cautious. But the clever chit caught me off-guard. I lost my head, embraced her, claimed her for my niece. I spirited her out of prison that very night, brought her here to Cliveden, where I had Agnes instruct her in everything she needed to know to take her rightful place as my niece and heir."

"And this was how long ago, you said?" Jessica asked dryly.

"Two years last March. Two years before her disappearance, right to the day."

"So, one year before her debut at court," she calculated quickly. "Do you honestly expect me to believe you made a lady out of this felon in just a twelvemonth?"

"There never was any question Mary Catherine had brains," Clare interjected.

"She was an astonishingly quick learner," the Duke of Buckingham said. "And yes. The night on which she was presented to his majesty was one year after she left prison. You saw yourself what a success she was at court. The little vixen pulled the wool over everyone's eyes."

"I see. And just when, pray tell, did you find the wool lifted?"

"Not until very recently. And it was thanks to your sister, Clare."

"Do you remember, Jess," Clare said, primping her black coiffure, "that day when we went up the hill to that abandoned chapel? Well, Mary Catherine was lolling about on the grass, and her skirt got hiked up. I saw a mark on her thigh. A birthmark, shaped like a bird. I asked about it, and she told me it was a family trait, that Uncle George had one too. I knew that wasn't true."

Jessica blushed. "Honestly, Clare. How could you know

such a thing?'' Her sister looked at her coolly, defiantly, then crossed the room to the duke's chair and let her small white hand rest on his shoulder. "Oh, God, no," Jessica whispered as the answer dawned on her. "Oh, Clare."

"You needn't sound so appalled, sister dear," Clare said, her voice rippling with laughter. "I am twenty years old; did you really think me still a virgin?"

"But he's our uncle!"

"First cousin once removed, actually. And who better to initiate me into the pleasures of the boudoir than a member of my own loving family?"

Jessica fought down a wave of nausea. "You disgust me, Clare. Both of you disgust me."

"My relations with your sister," the duke said crisply, "are neither here nor there. What matters is that she immediately wrote to me with this information. Since I was aware that my sister Frances' child had borne no such mark—"

"How?" Jessica demanded.

"When my niece was born, I sent a man to France with a birth gift for her. He saw the child naked, and reported to me that she was quite unblemished. So when I received Clare's letter, I made the inquiries I ought to have made two years ago regarding Mary Catherine's background. It wasn't hard to trace. Once I knew the name of her mother, this harlot, Nell Scutley, I even managed to decipher where she got hold of the locket. One of her mother's nefarious friends had been in service to me at the time of Frances' death, and had the miniature made with the intention of passing her own child off as my niece. That plan was foiled by the child's death. Mary Catherine's mother held on to the locket, no doubt intending to try the same trick with her daughter. But her brutish life ended on St. Katherine's docks before she ever had the chance. With this information in hand, I immediately wrote to your sister ordering you all to return to London, intending to confront Mary Catherine with my knowledge of her fraud."

"Which he no sooner did," Clare finished for him,

"than she promptly disappeared. So you see, Jess, your loyalty to Mary Catherine is completely misguided. She isn't even of our class."

Jessica started to laugh, and couldn't seem to stop once she'd started. "Oh, Lord," she gasped, holding her sides. "What a pair you are, the two of you! What a shameless, brazen pair!"

"What's gotten into you, girl?" the duke demanded.

"That is without a doubt, absolutely, bar none, the greatest heap of poppycock I've ever heard in my life! Mary Catherine a harlot's daughter? Good God!"

"It's the truth, dammit!" Buckingham barked.

Jessica was still laughing. "Lady Agnes taught her all that in a year, eh? Aye, and I'm the Queen of Sheba."

Clare moved toward the door. "I'll go bring the countess. She'll tell her."

"Don't bother, Clare," her sister said, suddenly sober. "I've no doubt that poor woman would swear herself a swine if Uncle George asked her to. But I've no stomach for any more of your lies."

The duke's dark eyes glinted. "You listen to me, young lady. You—"

"No," she broke in. "No, you listen to me. Whatever reason Mary Catherine had for running away, there isn't any question in my mind it was to get away from you. And no number of farfetched tales, no amount of rigmarole is going to get me to help you find her. So you may as well hie yourself back to London, and take my sister with you. Go on, get out. It makes me sick to look at you."

"You prissy little miss," Clare spat. "How dare you judge me?"

"I'll leave that to God," Jessica shot back. "I just want you out of my sight."

The duke hadn't moved during this interchange. Now he stood up slowly, stretching his legs, and reached for the bellpull by Jessica's bed. "It seems I've been far too lenient with you, my dear girl," he said, "but then, I always have had a soft spot for family. That's how Mary

Catherine was able to hoodwink me. I assure you, everything I said about her here today was God's truth. Taking that into account, perhaps you'd care to reconsider helping me?'' Jessica shook her head, lips pursed tight. ''Are you sure? One last chance.''

''Aye, m'lord?'' asked the manservant who'd come in answer to the bell.

The duke looked at Jessica. She met his gaze, head held high, and said nothing. He sighed and reached into his waistcoat, pulling out a key. ''Take Lady Jessica to the dungeon,''he ordered. ''She is to be confined there until such time as she tells you she is ready to talk to me.''

''You can't be serious,'' Jessica said, paling as the servant took her by the arms.

''Oh, I'm deadly serious, my girl,'' Buckingham told her, teeth showing as he smiled. ''When you decide to give in—and you will, believe me—I'll be holding the key.''

29

THE NARTHEX OF St. Paul's Cathedral was robed in black, the darkness unrelieved by even one candle. The grating of the huge bronze door as it opened resounded all through the empty church like some grim tocsin-bell, startling Father Drayton in the pew where he slept. He waited patiently until he heard footsteps on the marble floor beside him, then struck his flint and rose up, round head glowing in the sudden flare of light like a great harvest moon.

"Jesu!" gasped the man who'd been tiptoeing past.

"No, just his humble servant," the priest said, face split by a smile as he touched the flame to a taper. "And yours. May I help you, my son?"

"Ah," the man said. "You scared the wits out of me. I didn't expect anyone to be here."

"The Lord is always in residence."

"Yes, well, I meant anyone mortal."

" 'And the Word was made flesh, and dwelt among us,' " Father Drayton murmured. The man stared at him. The priest laughed quietly. "Forgive me, won't you? My little joke. I'm Father Timothy Drayton. And you are . . . ?"

"The name's Collett," the visitor said reluctantly.

"Not . . . not Dr. Collett, are you? The famous physician?" He nodded. "Well, well, well!" Father Drayton rubbed his long, beautiful hands together. "We are honored indeed! Come to pray for a patient, have you?"

"Not exactly." The priest waited, smiling expectantly. "I wanted to examine your records. Your marriage records, actually."

"Oh. Rather late at night for that sort of thing, isn't it?"

"Rather late for you to be hanging about in St. Paul's, when it comes to that."

"Vandals," Father Drayton said easily.

"I beg your pardon?"

"There's been a rash of vandalism in the city lately; haven't you heard? Somebody has been breaking in and ransacking any number of churches. They've had the same trouble up in Buckinghamshire, or so I've heard from my parents, who live up there. Misguided youths, most likely, or it could be Catholics. But one can't be too careful. Anyway, I'm standing guard."

"I hadn't heard," said Dr. Collett. "But it's shocking. Quite shocking."

"Yes. So you see, under the circumstances, it might be best if you came back tomorrow, in daylight. I'm sure the clerk would be only too happy to help you find what you need."

"I'd like to do that, but I can't. I'm afraid this is an emergency."

Father Drayton blinked, a pale perplexed owl. "Really? Hard to imagine any sort of emergency having to do with dusty old church records."

"Yes, well, it is one of my patients, as it happens. A woman. She's in labor, and it doesn't look as though she'll make it. So I am trying to find out the name of her husband so that I can notify him."

"Dear, dear." Father Drayton crossed himself, lips moving in a prayer, then looked up again. "Shouldn't you be with her?"

"I'm afraid there's nothing to be done."

"And she can't tell you her husband's name herself?"

"She's delirious with fever. Look here, I haven't got all night to stand about and be interrogated. Do you intend to show me your records or not?"

"Of course. Forgive me. Come right this way." He padded into the nave, with the doctor following close behind. The priest's candle sent shadows flickering across the great stone columns and pale marble floor. Halfway to the transept, the sound of quiet sobbing made the doctor pause.

"What the devil's that?"

"Pigeons. Up in the belfry," Father Drayton told him. "Or it could be a ghost. Some folks say St. Paul's is haunted."

"I don't believe in ghosts," Dr. Collett said shortly.

"No, as a man of science I don't suppose you would. The records are being stored down here in the vaults, just until this vandalism business can be cleared up." He ducked to pass beneath a low doorway, turned back to warn, "Mind yourself on the steps."

The narrow winding staircase twisted downward between sheer stone walls, opening some twenty feet below into a small square chamber. As Dr. Collett bent beneath the lintel to enter the room, he laughed. "Cheery little place."

The light of the candle glanced off rows of stone coffins set into the walls; in one corner a skull stared down blankly from a tilted niche. "Some people find it disturbing," Father Drayton said apologetically.

"Not me. I see much worse in my line of work every day."

"Mm. So you would. I've always thought medicine must be a fascinating field. In ancient times a priest like me would have been trained in it, of course. There was something to be said for that, don't you think? Healing for both the soul and the—"

"Do you mind?" Collett asked. "I haven't got all night."

"Of course. That poor woman . . ." Father Drayton

set the candle in the niche by the skull and, with some difficulty, raised the lid on one coffin. "Do you happen to know the year in which she was married?"

"This year."

"And brought to childbed already? Well, better late wedded than never." He pulled a thick leatherbound book from inside the sarcophagus. "Here we are. If you'll just give me her name—"

"I'll do the looking," Collett told him. "It will go faster that way."

"I'd rather you didn't." The doctor yanked the book from his hands. "But if you insist . . . do you know for certain that she was married by someone from here at St. Paul's?"

"That's what she says." Starting at the beginning, Collett leafed through the parchment pages.

"I thought she was delirious."

"Just before she became delirious."

"How resourceful of her," Father Drayton murmured. "Pity she couldn't hold on long enough to give her husband's name too."

Collett glanced up from the book. The priest smiled beatifically, fine long-fingered hands smoothing down his surplice front. "If you've got something else that you ought to be doing . . ." the doctor growled.

"Oh, no. I'm fine right here."

Collett turned four more pages, finger running down the entries listed there. "Have you got another candle on you?" he demanded, squinting in the dim light.

"I'm afraid not."

Collett grunted and turned another page. The priest began to hum softly:

> Praise God from whom all blessings flow,
> Praise him, all creatures here below . . .

"Shut up," Collett said, and added, "Please," quite belatedly.

Father Drayton took the candle from the niche and came to stand behind his shoulder. "This should help. My, my, all the way to March already, are you? We hadn't many weddings in Mar . . . ah! Ah-choo!" The force of his sneeze blew out the candle. In the sudden darkness he reached out his hand and deftly turned two pages ahead.

"Would you light that bloody thing?" Collett snapped.

"Of course. Forgive me." Father Drayton's flint flared and caught. Candlelight filled the chamber again. "Ever so sorry," he said. "It's the dust, you know. There, you see? That's the end of March, and April begun."

The doctor slammed the book closed. "April's too late. It's not here."

"Oh. Well. I'm ever so sorry that we couldn't help."

"So am I."

"If you'd be so kind as to hold on to this . . ." The priest traded him the candle for the book, and replaced the latter in its stone crypt. Then he took the candle back again and led the doctor up the stairs. "If there's anything more I could do . . . "

"There isn't," Collett told him, already halfway to the doors.

"Well, best of luck to you, then!" Father Drayton called after him. "I'll just say a few prayers for your unfortunate patient."

"You do that," said Dr. Collett, and vanished into the night.

When he'd gone, Father Drayton knelt at the altar and delivered a prayer of thanks to the Creator of dust and sneezes. Then, feeling quite chipper for the first time in weeks, he extinguished the candle and went home to bed.

"Piers, Piers, Piers." Molly sighed, trying her best to look stern.

"Ja, Katrine?"

"You can't keep on giving flowers away to every pretty girl who comes by the stall."

"Und why not?" asked the big Dutchman, not in the least abashed.

"Because it isn't good for business."

"There is always big crowd around the stall, ja?"

"Ja," Molly acknowledged, "but they aren't buying. What good is a big crowd if the purses stay shut?"

"In my country," said Piers, "we have a saying. 'A pretty girl makes the heart sing.' So I think, if these girls make me glad, should not I give them something in return?"

Molly was beginning to understand why Piers's parents had shipped him to England. "We have a saying here, too: 'A fool and his money are soon parted,' " she said with a touch of impatience. "If you go on giving flowers away, we won't have any to sell."

"Bah." Piers waved a meaty hand. "What difference can it make, two or three flowers a day?"

"Two dozen," Molly corrected him.

"Nein!"

"Ja. Two dozen anemones today, and nearly three dozen yesterday."

"Two dozen?" Piers blinked blue eyes. "I did not know so many."

"I had Rachel count them."

"You set my own employee to . . . to spy on me?" he asked, looking highly offended.

"*Our* employee," Molly corrected him. "And I hadn't any choice. I had to know where the profits were going."

Piers could look very stubborn at times. "Ja? You talk to me about profits? Und what of the herbs you take when your stomach is sick, heh, und the ones you use to dye your hair?"

Molly blushed; she hadn't realized he'd noticed her morning sickness. "As it happens, I keep track of everything I use," she said, voice brisk to mask her confusion. "Right here in the back of the account book." She showed him the page, with its long list of tallies. "Then I subtract its worth—wholesale, of course—from my half of the split every week. You see, it doesn't cost you a penny.''

Piers looked down at the book, then back at her in admiration. ''You are good honest businesswoman, Katrine. You make me ashamed.''

''Oh, Piers. I don't want to make you ashamed. I just—''

''You just want me to stop giving the flowers away, ja?'' He grinned.

''Ja.'' She smiled back at him. ''Or at least be a little more discriminating when you're eyeing the girls. Save the posies for the real beauties. And you might give them marguerites or pansies instead of anemones. They cost a hell of a lot less.''

''All right, Katrine. I try.''

He sounded so contrite that Molly felt guilty. ''I don't mean to be an old shrew, always nattering at you. It's just that—''

He held up his hand. ''Nein, nein. I understand. It is necessary that one of us knows where the money goes. And you worry, too, for when the child comes.''

Molly felt the blood drain from her face. ''You . . . you know?''

Piers shrugged. ''You could not keep it secret forever.''

She looked down at her loose twill smock. ''No . . . but I'd hoped for a little more time.''

''Well.'' He sat down on the bench beside her. ''I have five sisters—did I ever tell you this? All older than I am. And they have many children. Besides, it explains why you put yourself in the river—although that was a very stupid thing to do.''

Of course, that wasn't why she'd jumped in the river, but Molly didn't correct him. ''Are you . . . shocked?'' she asked, oddly relieved that he knew. It had been a lonely secret to keep.

''Bah, of course I am not shocked. Do you think you are the first girl this ever happens to?''

''No,'' said Molly. ''But it's the first time it's ever happened to *me.*" Piers laughed, and she joined in weakly. It felt good to laugh.

"The man," he said, "he is married?"

She hesitated, then nodded; after all, it was the truth. "How did you guess that?"

He gently touched the dull brown hair that showed beneath her cap. "Only a married man, or else a fool, would cause someone so beautiful such distress."

"You're very kind," Molly whispered, blushing again.

"I only say the truth. Do you want to tell me about him?"

"No," she said quickly.

He didn't look askance, just stretched out his thick brawny legs. "I have given this some thought, Katrine, since I realized you would have this baby. After it comes, when you are well enough, you can bring it here to the shed while you work, ja?"

"That would be wonderful," Molly said gratefully, "if you don't think it will be too much trouble."

"How much trouble can it be? I like babies. Und if Rachel does not, we get rid of her, ja?" Molly laughed again, and he smiled, taking a marguerite daisy from the table in front of them and sliding it toward her. "I am being very dis . . . dis . . ."

"Discriminating."

"Ja. You are very pretty when you laugh."

"Thank you, Piers." She expected him to leave with that, but he didn't, stretched out his legs again instead.

"There is something else I give some thought to."

"Ja?" she asked, teasing.

"This baby of yours. It ought to have a father, a name. These are things I could give to it if we were married. You and I, I mean. We make good partners, ja? I think that we could make good marriage too." He winked. "Besides, it would be one way to stop me giving flowers to the girls."

Tears stung Molly's eyes at the unexpected largess of his offer. "Oh, Piers . . ."

IIe got up from the bench. "Don't say anything now. You give it some thought too. We have a long time yet. Now I say good night. Good night!' He waved cheerfully and left the shed.

Dear, sweet Piers, Molly thought, ready to jump in again and save me. Wasn't that just like him? For a moment she actually considered the notion. Growing up without a father was hard, as she knew full well. And Piers would be good to them both, she was certain of that.

But . . . no. Even if she weren't already married, such a union would be cruelly unfair to Piers. She could never be the sort of wife he deserved, not so long as she was still in love with Anthony.

And she always would be in love with him. After nearly four months, the pain had not lessened; the loneliness that made her heart ache each time she thought of him had not diminished one jot. She was only beginning to realize that this would be her lot for so long as she lived: that smiles would come hard, that her laughter would forever sound strange.

She laid her hands across her barely swollen belly, holding tight to the child that was all she had left of him. Damn the Duke of Buckingham, she thought, and then reconsidered. If not for him, after all, she never would have met Anthony, and then where would she be?

Right here in Smithfield Market selling flowers, most likely. But with her own hair, and without a heart that was broken. One couldn't miss what one had never known.

She took a bundle of marguerites from the table, noted down their worth in the account book, and went to lay them on the potter's field that was Aunt May's grave.

Since the sun set so late now that it was midsummer, and because she still did not dare leave the shed during daylight, it was after ten when Molly reached the graveyard. There had been a burial that day; she could feel the patch of upturned earth give beneath her bare toes as she crossed the field, and when she looked down, she could see in the moonlight the marks of the gravediggers' heels. God grant you rest, poor soul, she thought as she went past. Back on Gospel Square, her old neighbors had dreaded being buried here, without so much as a cross or a headstone to mark their passing.

She laid the daisies she'd brought in the center of the field and then knelt down to pray—not for the souls of the dead, since they were beyond prayer's reach, but for those still living—for Anthony, for Jessica, for Piers, for the child in her womb. She was so lost in thought that she did not notice the shadow coming toward her across the desolate hillside until it was nearly upon her; then she cried out in fright: "Who's there? Get away!"

The shadow resolved from a heap of dank rags into a being, with two arms, legs, a head topped with a tattered fur hat. "Molly Flowers," its voice hissed. "I thought so! It is ye!"

Molly drew her shawl over her face even as she recognized mad Tom Peabody. "Go away," she mumbled again. "I'm not who you say."

"Aye, but ye is," Tom said, moving closer. "I know ye is. Only he's changed ye, the same way he changed me. I tried to warn ye, didn't I? I told ye not to go with him!"

Molly stood up, torn between running and staying. Tom's was a face and a voice from the old days, from home, even if he was daft. No one was likely to pay any more attention to him if he said he'd seen her than she did once upon a time when he talked of his private demons. "Hello, Tom," she said quietly, reluctantly.

"I knew it! I knew it!" he crowed, dancing a little jig across the field. "Ye got away too, just the same as I did!" He came back, leaning toward her, and she caught the smell of him, sweat and must and earth from the new graves, as he lowered his voice conspiratorially: "How did ye manage it?"

"Manage what, Tom?"

"Gettin' away from him!"

"From the prison, do you mean?"

He shook his head impatiently. "Nay, nay; are ye wood? I saw ye get away from the prison! From *him*—from the doctor!"

"Do you mean Dr. Collett?" Molly asked, wondering how in the world poor mad Tom could know the physician.

"He puts 'em here," he said, ignoring her question. "After he's finished with 'em. Oh, not himself, no, but that one wot works for him—the Stalker. 'N' ye can hear the dogs barking o' nights when he walks abroad."

Same old fool, Molly thought, biting back a smile. Still going on about the dogs and the Stalker. "Have you seen anyone from Gospel Square lately, Tom? How is Billy Buttons? Does Bart Connor still have the Dog and Feathers?"

"Aye, aye, the dogs, lass; that's how ye know ye've got to run. And 'tis ye 'n' me has got to be more wary than anyone else, ye know. He'll be out to find us. 'N' he won't let us get away twice." He looked over one shoulder, then the other, scanning the moonlit graveyard. "D'ye hear any dogs, Molly Flowers? I think I hears a dog."

"I don't hear anything, Tom."

He was fumbling with his rag clothes, edging closer and closer, she backed away from him quickly. She'd always thought him harmless enough, but now she wondered if that had been a mistake. What if he tried to force himself on her? What of the baby? He might have a weapon hidden there amongst the rags. "I have got to be going," she said.

He was off an another tangent again, pawing the ground with his bare knobbed toes. "There's dozens 'n' dozens of 'em down here," he said, "dozens 'n' dozens. 'N' we came that close to bein' here too, didn't we, Molly? Gor, it gives me the shivers."

He was giving Molly the shivers. "I really have to be going, Tom. God be with you. Please don't tell anyone that you saw me, all right? Will you promise me that?"

"O' course I won't tell, lass. Mum's the word. But mind ye keep yerself well hid." She looked at him in the moonlight, saw his wretched, ragged face etched with suffering and fear. It was hard to credit what Aunt May had told her about him—that he'd once been as likely a man as one could ever see. "He got yer Aunt May too," he said suddenly, just as though he'd read her thoughts. "Aye, came himself 'n' got her. I seen him do it. I was watchin'."

He meant Dr. Collett, Molly realized. "You went to Gospel Square from the prison, Tom? You saw Dr. Collett taking Aunt May to the hospital?"

"Hospital? Hah! He weren't takin' her to no hospital."

"Oh, for goodness' sake. Of course he was."

"Oh, no he weren't! He was takin' her *there*," he hissed with agitated emphasis, " 'n' from there to here." He waved at the field. "Her 'n' the baby, aye, Charity's baby. I heard it squallin' 'n' wailin' t' heaven, the poor wee thing."

"You couldn't have heard the baby, Tom. The baby was dead."

"Not yet it weren't! Not till he got through with it. Oh, ain't he the devil himself, Molly Flowers, t' do wot he done t' a poor helpless babe?"

Molly stared at him in the moonlight, knowing he was mad but frightened nonetheless by his madness, feeling cold fingers of doubt tapping at her spine. "What are you talking about, Tom?" she asked slowly. "Where would Dr. Collett have taken Aunt May and the baby? What would he do to a baby?"

"Oy, ye'll not catch me sayin' it aloud." He gave her a ludicrous wink. "But we know, don't we, ye 'n' me?"

"Tom—"

Down below in the city, some abandoned hound let out a long, unearthly howl of mourning. Another joined in to make a desolate chorus, then another and another, till the night air rang with their cries. "Run!" Tom hissed, gathering his rags about him. "Run, Molly, run for ycr life!" He ducked low and sprinted off across the graveyard, moving with astonishing quickness considering his age; she saw his fur hat bob as he vanished into a thicket of pricklewood trees.

For a moment she considered going after him, asking him again what he knew of Aunt May and the doctor. The dogs were still clamoring; she remembered the way the thin moonlight pricked out the worn lines of his face. There was something there, she thought, beneath the dither and twaddle, some germ of truth, though it were tiny as a mustard seed. . . .

But then she remembered her aching feet, the swelling in her ankles, and the notion of walking any further than home and to bed was more than she could bear. Things have come to a pretty pass, Molly Flowers, she thought wryly as she set off toward her cot in the shed, when you'll entertain the idea of chasing after a madman like Tom for the sake of his company!

30

"M'LORD?"

Anthony glanced up as Bess poked her capped head into the study. "Aye?" he asked absently.

"I just wondered if ye was finished with yer supper tray."

"With my . . . Ah." He saw the domed plates at his elbow. "Yes, thank you, Bess. I've finished."

"I'll just clear it away, then." The maid bustled in, pausing to lift up one of the covers. "Sir . . ."

"Mm?" Anthony had turned back to the report he was reading, one listing the activities of the Duke of Buckingham in the last fortnight.

"Ye ain't touched this food," Bess said sternly.

"Haven't I?" He reached for the soup she'd uncovered, took a few spoonfuls. "There you are. Delicious. My compliments to Mrs. Dixon."

She looked at him in disgust. "Gor, 'tis stone cold!"

He set the spoon down. "Is this the prelude to another of your lectures, Bess, on how I haven't been taking care of myself—"

"Well, ye ain't been."

"—and how I ought to get out more—"

"Well, so ye should."

"—and are you going to bring up that exceedingly dreary great-uncle of yours who went into a decline and died of the vapors because he wouldn't take an interest in life after his pet parrot got out of its cage?''

"It weren't a parrot; it were a canary. But now that ye mention it—''

"Because if you are, I've just spared you the trouble. If you truly want to be a help, you might send to the cellars for another bottle of brandy.''

"Did I happen to add," Bess asked darkly, "that Great-Uncle's vapors was brought on by drinkin'?''

"No, you didn't. But if you like, I'll raise him a toast with my very next glass." She flounced out. He went back to his reading, looking up when she returned and set the brandy bottle down on his deck with a clunk. "Thank you, Bess.''

"Ye ain't welcome." She picked up the tray. "I could have Cook heat this up for ye; it wouldn't take but a moment.''

"No thank you, Bess. I'm not hungry." He filled his cup with brandy, aware that she stood in the doorway forlornly. "Is there something else?''

"Ye might at least let me tidy up in here a bit, sir; 'tis a frightful jumble. 'N' ye can't think clearly, can ye, when there's such a muddle around ye? At least I know I can't.''

He surveyed the study. She was right; the room was overflowing with books and reports and papers, all overlain with a coating of dust, and cobwebs had begun to grow in the corners. "All right, then. But mind you don't throw anything out. Just stack the papers up neatly.''

"Yes, sir!" said Bess, overjoyed. " 'N' ye can pop down to the dinin' room 'n' have a nice hot supper while I—''

"I'll be staying right here, so mind you don't make too much noise.''

"Hmph," said Bess. "Ta, I'm sure. 'T'won't be no trouble at all just workin' around ye—''

Ta, as they say at market! Mary Catherine's carefree words to him as she waved and set off down the hill to Cliveden. . . .

"Sir? Wot is it, sir, wot's wrong?"

"Nothing." He unclenched his hands from the edge of his desk, unclenched his jaw, opened his eyes, and then reached for the brandy, ignoring her disapproving scowl.

"Ye'll rot yer guts wi' that stuff."

"They're my guts," he said shortly, and turned back to his report on Buckingham. The duke had been at court on Midsummer's Eve, to a meeting of the Royal Society the following night, to Lord Phipps's on Monday for dinner, and afterward to Cliveden. To Cliveden every Monday night, Anthony mused, and back again late Tuesday, as regular as clockwork for the past month. And always with Clare Fairfax. Visiting Jessica, no doubt, to weasel out confirmation of the wedding. But so far she must have held her tongue.

He'd had a note from Father Drayton telling of Dr. Collett's nocturnal visit to St. Paul's, so that was one worry gone. Michael Nivens had sailed for France, to look for the convent Mary Catherine had grown up in and, not incidentally, to remove himself from Buckingham's clutches. So that still left Jessica. Anthony's heart ached for the girl, knowing the pressure she must be under, but there was nothing he could do to help her. At least, with her sister right there, the duke wouldn't dare hurt her. And Anthony suspected that beneath her fluffy sentimentality, Jessica was a good deal tougher than anyone supposed.

At least, he hoped to hell she was.

"Did you say something, Bess?" he asked, realizing that she'd been speaking.

"I said, seein' as ye *used* to take an interest in yer staff, ye might like t' know that new understairs maid Mrs. Johnstone took on—"

"Janet Bell."

"Aye. Well, it turns out she's bearin'."

"That's nice," Anthony murmured.

" 'Tain't nice at all," Bess corrected him, "seein' as she ain't wedded."

"Oh." There was nothing suggestive in the report on

Buckingham; Anthony laid it aside and picked up another, from one of the small army of men he had hired to look for Mary Catherine. Like all the rest, it was brief and to the point: no news. "So who's the scoundrel who had his way with her, Bess?" he asked absently. "Not one of the staff, I hope."

"Oh, no, sir. She says 'twas one o' King Charles's soldiers."

"You must get his name from her. I'll make certain he's held accountable for the child's support."

Bess snorted. " 'Tain't likely he told her his real name. No, more'n likely he were just out to get a bit o' flesh on the cheap."

Anthony winced again, swallowing brandy. His maid was showing a marked propensity tonight for using the same phrases Mary Catherine once had. He could see her standing before him, green eyes flashing with anger: *The bloody hell I will! Ye're just out t' see a bit o' flesh on the cheap.* . . .

What the devil. Mary Catherine never would have said such a thing. And yet for a moment he'd seen her so clearly, mouthing those words . . .

He closed his eyes, trying to summon up the image again so that he might assign it a time, a place, but to no avail. Perhaps she'd said it in jest, mimicking someone, a servant? Even so, he couldn't remember her ever having been so crude.

He blinked; Bess was right. He'd had far too much brandy. "Leave them," he told the maid, who was picking up books from the floor. "If it's not too late, ask Cook to heat me that supper."

"Right away, sir!" she said with delight, hurrying away.

I may as well eat, Anthony thought wearily; all the brandy in the world isn't enough to help me forget. It was worse at night, when despite all his will he saw her as she'd looked in the Draytons' cottage, pale gold hair flowing around her shoulders as she loosened her smock . . .

Her chemise, he meant. She hadn't worn a smock on

their wedding night; it had been a chemise, a silk one with embroidery. His memory was playing tricks, had clad her in a filthy gray smock that she reached up to open with hate and resentment smoldering in her eyes. And her hair hadn't flowed; it had been all a tangle of mats. . . .

"There ye go, sir." Bess set the tray before him, glowing with her triumph. He ate without tasting, wondering idly how the Duke of Buckingham's appetite was these days. Buckingham and Ballenrose. Someone had confused them once, he remembered, called the duke by his name. How furious George Villiers had been. Where had that been? At the Fleet, during the inquiry. The report he'd made for the king sat on the bookshelf gathering dust; like as not Charles had never even read his copy. Another worthy effort come to naught, thanks to Buckingham. . . .

"I've had a bath drawn up for ye, sir," Bess said earnestly as he laid down his fork. "Won't ye go up 'n' take it? 'N' there's nice fresh linens on yer bed—"

"Don't push your luck, Bess."

"No, sir, I wouldn't ever. It's just I can't help thinkin' that wotever it is that's troublin' ye, it wouldn't look half so bleak if ye'd a good night's sleep."

"Bess."

"Aye, sir?"

"Go away."

"Hmph. But ye do feel better, don't ye, sir, for havin' eaten?"

No news. The reports from his spies, useless as the one he'd written on the prison. He'd never see her again. His wife. Mary Catherine. Despair rose up to claim him, a black-winged bird that tore incessantly at his liver, ate his heart every day. . . .

"Aye. I feel better," he lied.

"Please." Jessica reached for the forearm that thrust through the slot in the door with her supper. "Please, tarry a bit. Talk to me."

"Orders, mum," the servant's muffled voice replied.

"Oh, hang your orders! Who's to know if you stay?"

"The countess'd know, mum. She watches t' see when I'm comin' 'n' goin'."

The countess. Jessica nibbled her lip, taking the bowl of stew. "Tell Lady Agnes that I've got to see her. Tell her it's important."

" 'Tain't no use, mum. Wotever ye told her last time she came down here got her all in a huff. There was a dreadful scene when his grace came t' visit."

What Jessica had told her, of course, was that the Duke of Buckingham was having an affair with her sister, Clare. That had been her trump card, held patiently in reserve until she thought she honestly could not endure another night in her prison. The countess laughed it off, said her confinement must be making her crazy. But at least she'd confronted the duke, according to the servant. That was something. The seed of doubt had been sown.

"Just . . . just give her the message, please," she begged now, clinging to the disembodied hand.

"All right, mum, but ye've got to let go now; if I don't get back, I'll be whipped."

Reluctantly she relinquished her hold. "What day is it?" she cried as the hand slipped out of sight.

"Monday, mum!" the retreating voice called. "His grace'll be here t'night. 'N' if ye know wot's good for ye, ye'll tell him wot he wants to know 'n' have an end t' it!" She heard the click of his footsteps on the stairs; then that sound, too, faded, and she was left alone again.

Alone. God, who would ever have thought just being alone was so dreadful? She'd never realized how little time she'd spent alone before. Wherever she'd been, all her life, she'd been surrounded by people: her parents, playmates, courtiers, servants. And always, always, there had been her sister, Clare.

Thinking of Clare only made her more wretched. What could have gone wrong to make her turn out so twisted? Jessica had always known her sister was headstrong and vain, but despite those faults she still loved her, could

never have borne to see her hurt or in pain. And yet each
week Clare came here with her lover—their own uncle, for
God's sake, a man who'd clearly proved himself evil—and
stood by as Jessica's sentence was extended because she
wouldn't turn on a friend.

Yet perhaps she ought to have seen this coming. She
couldn't count the number of times, when they were children, that Clare had pinned the blame on her for her petty
crimes. And when they grew old enough to understand
such things, it always rankled Clare that their mother had
married beneath her station, had given up her chance at
money and power and a lofty title for the sake of love.

Money, power, and station—just what Uncle George
prized. It wasn't really so surprising, then, that they'd been
drawn to each other. They were two of a kind; they shared
the same fine looks, even had the same dazzling smile.
But even more, they both went through life like . . . like
feudal lords, Jessica thought, unaccountable to anyone,
wringing all they could from those they were supposed to
serve. In a perfect world, sooner or later they'd get their
comeuppance. But she was coming to realize that the world
was a very imperfect place.

Her stew had grown cold. She spooned it up from the
bowl in minuscule mouthfuls, prolonging the diversion it
offered, rolling each bit on her tongue. Even so, it was all
too soon finished, leaving her with nothing to do but stare
at the four walls in the light from the tiny barred window
high above her head. Leaving her to wonder just how far
her uncle would go. . . .

At least he was feeding her; at least he didn't mean to
let her starve. That was comfort, though cold as the stew.
And because it was summer, her cell was warm enough—
though exceedingly damp. Long before autumn came,
something would have happened. One of the others might
talk—Father Drayton, or that nice Michael Nivens. Or
Mary Catherine might be found—

Stop it, Jess! she told herself sharply. You mustn't wish
for that; it is playing right into Uncle George's hands. Your

only strength, the sole reason you might outlast him, is that he can't believe you won't break at any minute.

She hugged herself in the shadowy cell. Night was falling. And the nights seemed to last forever.

"I'll do my best, Mary Catherine," she whispered. "I'll hold out as long as I can."

"Good morning, Jessica!"

She woke to her sister's bright trill and, disoriented, sat up smiling. "Clare . . ." Only then did she realize the voice came through the slot in the cell door.

"Here we are, come to see you again, sister dear!" Clare burbled on happily. "It's so nice to be out of the city on a beautiful day such as this. Birds are singing, the sun is shining, and there isn't a cloud in the sky! Ah—but you wouldn't know, would you, Jess?"

She sounded positively gleeful, Jessica thought. The shock sharpened her tongue. "You might have spared yourself the journey."

"Now, now, let's not be disagreeable on such a splendid morning. I told George as we set out last night that I had a feeling today just might be the day when you give up this nonsense."

"What a pity you're wrong. Have you got my breakfast?"

"All in good time." Her dark eyes appeared at the slot. "My God, you do look a sight, Jess. How long have you been wearing that gown now, a month? You must be dying for a bath. And it would be so easy to get yourself one, so very, very easy."

"Go away, Clare," Jessica said, denying how glad she was even for her company.

"Uncle George is very, very vexed with you," her sister went on blithely. "That was a nasty trick you played, telling Lady Agnes on us. Too bad she didn't believe you."

"Is Uncle George here?"

"He'll be here by and by. He had a little task he had to do."

Jessica moved toward the door. This could be her chance; he'd never left Clare alone with her before. "I was thinking last night, Clare, about when we were children."

"Well, you've got plenty of time for thinking."

"I was remembering all the things we used to do together. Like . . . like taking dancing lessons from that silly woman. What was her name?"

"Mistress Moorehead."

"That's right. You called her Mistress Fishhead. And because you were the taller, you would always lead. And we used to play King Arthur too; do you remember that? I'd be Guinevere, and you'd be the Lady of the Lake. We used Father's walking stick for Excalibur—"

"I remember. I put that black spaniel's eye out with it, pretending he was a dragon."

Jessica shuddered. It was true, she had. "But not on purpose."

"No, not on purpose. I showed the cat that nest of baby swans you found on purpose, though. And do you remember when the milkmaid's little boy fell into the millpond and nearly drowned? I pushed him. I did that."

"Jesu, Clare!"

"I wanted to see how long he'd stay afloat. But then Father came by and saved him. I was so angry with him for that." She laughed. "See, Jess? I have fond memories of our childhood too."

The conversation wasn't going at all the way Jessica had hoped. She thought it best to change the subject. "Is there any news at court?"

"I'm glad you reminded me. Lord Wallingford asked about you."

"Really?" Her heartbeat quickened.

"Aye. He asked if you'd be back in London to come to his wedding. He and Alice Kenton have set the date. September twenty-third."

Oh, Harry, Jessica thought sadly.

"I told him I expect you back any day."

"What does he think I am doing?" Jessica asked, a small break in her voice. "What does everyone think I am doing? Don't Mother and Father wonder that they never hear from me?"

"Not at all. I tell them that you're well. They think it's very kind of Uncle George to have you at Cliveden—you know Mother always worries about the miasma in London in summer. And she's delighted at the special interest he has taken in me."

"She'd kill him if she knew the truth."

"Oh, really, Jess, don't be such a baby. Why should she care?"

"Because she loves you. Just the same as I do."

"I'm very touched," Clare drawled. "So long as we are on the subject of familial love, let me remind you that Mary Catherine isn't any relation of ours. Don't you think your love for your kin might be better served by telling Uncle George what he wants to know than by protecting some scheming little stranger?"

"I have already told you what I think of that nonsense about Mary Catherine."

"He's brought papers to show you. Papers that prove—"

"Forged, I'm sure. Don't bother. I won't look at them." There was a gnawing in Jessica's stomach. "What about that breakfast? Or do you intend to starve me into compliance?"

"Jess, Jess, Jess. Of course we don't. There are easier ways."

The gnawing turned to fear. There was something in her sister's voice—that touch of glee again. . . .

"Speaking of our childhood, Jess, do you recall when we used to visit Father's parents in Chester?"

"Of course I do. We went there every summer."

"Every summer up until you turned eight," Clare corrected her. "After that you wouldn't go back. Do you remember why?"

Jessica searched her memory. She had no trouble recalling her grandparents or their house in Chester. It had been in the old part of the city, small and cramped; Clare had hated it there. But she herself had liked it, up until . . . Until what? What had happened? Her mind ran up against a great blankness, like the cell's stone walls.

"We'd gone down into the cellars," Clare's silky voice went on, "even though it was strictly forbidden. You didn't much care for it once we got down there, though. Surely you remember. It was very cold and very dark and very damp."

That's strange, Jessica thought. I ought to remember. I wonder why I don't.

"And somehow," Clare said, "when I came upstairs again, you didn't come with me. Somehow the door locked behind me, and you were stuck down there all—"

"Oh, God," Jessica whispered as the long-buried memory came back to her.

"—night," her sister finished with satisfaction. "So you *do* remember! I thought you would."

She'd huddled at the top of the stairs in the darkness, Jessica recalled, pounding on the door until her hands were bruised, screaming for Clare to come back and get her, not to leave her there. But nobody came. Then, as she paused for breath—Jesu, even now, a dozen years later, she could feel herself shaking—she'd heard noises from the dank room below her: small scurrying noises, and the sound of little noses twitching and sniffing, and then, sidling up the stairs, tiny scrabbling claws—

"Here comes Uncle George now," Clare announced, dark eyes vanishing from the slot. *"And* here's your breakfast." Jessica didn't, couldn't move to take it; the bread and boiled eggs fell to the floor. "Too bad," her sister crooned. "But never fear, Jess. Uncle George has brought some friends to keep you company. And I'm sure they'll help to tidy up the cell."

"No," Jessica said. "No. Clare, for the love of heaven—"

"Mind you don't fall asleep, though, Jess, or they might have a nibble on you! Oh, my, such jolly big ones!"

Jessica watched, dumb with horror, as one sleek, squirming gray-brown body and then another were squeezed through the slot, landing with soft plops and high squeals squarely on her breakfast.

"Uncle George asked me your worst nightmare, Jess. Was I right?"

Oh, God, she was.

Rats.

31

SOMETHING HAD BEEN nagging at the back of Anthony's mind ever since the night Bess had straightened his study. He kept picturing Mary Catherine as she'd looked on their wedding night, shy yet excited, reaching up to unfasten the fine silk chemise she wore. But the image would no sooner form than it began to unravel, transform itself into a vision of a barefoot hoyden, filthy and tangle-haired, clad in a tattered smock. "Out t' see a bit o' flesh on the cheap?" the girl would ask, angry and taunting. Her almond-shaped eyes were green as new grass, just like Mary Catherine's, but the voice was a stranger's, with the broad vowels and harsh rhythms of the very lowest class.

He was thinking of this now as he sat in his study, shutters pulled against the waning of a fine July day. A girl in a smock. Tangled gold hair. Green eyes that stared and then flashed as the Duke of Buckingham ordered her to take off her clothes: *The bloody hell I will! Don't ye think I know wot ye're up to? Ye're all out t' see a bit o' flesh on the cheap!* Buckingham's face as she appealed to him: *They say ye're a good sort, M'lord Ballenrose. . . .* Mistaking one for the other. Dr. Collett gasping. Fat little Lord Phipps drooling into his wine . . .

Anthony moved to the bookcase, searching for the report he had made for King Charles, long useless, unread. His hands shook as he found it, turned the pages.

Meg Calloway. Hannah Crandall. Lizzie Cutler. Nan Wiggins. Molly Flowers, also known as Mary Catherine Willoughby—

Molly Flowers.

The two images in his mind abruptly fused into one. "Sweet holy Jesu," he said, closing his eyes and seeing with unmistakable clarity that her face, small and pale and tormented, was the face of his bride.

As though a veil had been lifted from his eyes, he saw it all, saw the duke's entire daring, dazzling plan laid out in its breathtaking simplicity. He'd created a niece from the girl in the prison, brought her to court, engineered a romance between her and Anthony—for wasn't the sweetest fruit always that which was forbidden? Hadn't his fascination been kindled there in the king's garden when she told him who her uncle was?

If he knew Buckingham, the bastard had probably plotted every step in their courtship, pulling strings like some monstrous puppeteer. A hundred minute coincidences, unremarked at the time, tumbled into place. The note to Anthony's gateman. The duke's sudden appearance on the banks of the Thames during the king's treasure hunt. Jessica and Clare being sent to Cliveden when Mary Catherine was there. While he—oh, but he had been a fool!—he'd laid the blame on the stars. And hadn't she played her part, the vicious girl, as well as any actress? Why, the king's own Nell Gwyn couldn't hold a candle to her.

He slumped over the bookcase, laughing bitterly. "Oh, Christ," he cried, straightening up. "Oh, the beauty of it all! The perfection . . ."

He went back to his desk and scribbled a hasty letter to Michael Nivens in France, in care of the English ambassador. He stopped, considering what he'd written: *My marriage, it turns out, is a fraud, arranged by Buckingham for his own purposes. Mary Catherine isn't his niece at all, and was certainly never in France. You may as well come home.* He'd been mistaken; the duke's plan wasn't perfect. Not without proof that the marriage had taken

place. Christ, no wonder he'd been so desperate for witnesses!

There was still a piece missing from the puzzle. If the
purpose of Buckingham's plan had been to see him married to a girl from the gutter—and it surely was, since the
duke was so anxious to find proof of the wedding—why
had the girl, his willing pawn in the game, disappeared?

And there was something more. He was thinking of her
now as a stranger, hated her for the wiles she'd practiced
on him at the duke's instigation. But the fact remained that
he'd been in love with her, ached for her, was intoxicated
by her. Did her duplicity change that?

Of course it did. He despised her for the way she'd used
him.

And yet. And yet she had disappeared.

Not, he reminded himself, folding and sealing the letter, until the deed was done. That she'd double-crossed
Buckingham in the end made no difference. Not only was
she legally his wife; she'd cost him uncountable hours of
time, not to mention a great deal of money. God help her,
she would pay for her part in the duke's scheme if he had
to hunt her down for the rest of his days.

He'd start at the Fleet. Knowing her past hadn't helped
Buckingham find her, but at least it was a clue, a beginning. And that was more than he'd had before.

By the time Michael returned, he'd have Molly Flowers.
From now on his search for her wouldn't be complicated
by any emotion but hate. And hatred could be a greater
goad even than love. If nothing else, the Duke of Buckingham's charade had taught him that.

Abraham Fell was still sly and cocky, but Anthony
thought he detected a hint of nervousness beneath the
man's swagger as he was admitted to the warden's office
at the Fleet and stated his business: "I've come for information on one of your prisoners—a former prisoner. Mary
Catherine Willoughby."

The warden's small eyes shifted from Anthony's face to

the report he held and then back again. "I never had no prisoner by that name."

Anthony hid a grim smile; the man's transparent lie was all the confirmation he needed that his theory was right. Still he pressed on, partly to see what tidbits he might glean and partly for the sheer pleasure of seeing the bastard squirm. "Come, come, Warden Fell. How can you be so sure? Hundreds of prisoners pass through here each year."

"But I'd remember that one." Fell licked his thin lips. "On account o' . . . on account o' her name. Willoughby. That was my . . . my sister's husband's name."

"I see. Perhaps you can explain, then, how I came to interview a prisoner by that name in the room next door to this one two and a half years ago."

"No, sir."

"I beg your pardon?"

"I . . . I can't explain it. Not unless you would have got the name wrong, of course."

"I'm quite sure of the name. My notes say she'd had a stall at Smithfield Market, had been convicted of disturbing the peace. She had another name she used." He consulted the report. "Molly Flowers."

Warden Fell shook his head. "That don't ring a bell neither. Are ye sure 'twas at the Fleet?"

"Oh, yes. Yours was the first prison the inquiry board investigated, thanks to its particularly appalling reputation. As you know, we never finished our work, as other considerations subsumed King Charles's fervor for prison reform. You wouldn't want to risk that fervor being revived because of a report of a missing prisoner, would you, Warden Fell?"

"There's naught amiss wi' the way I runs this prison," Fell said belligerently. "The prisoners in here is criminals, ye know. No point in coddlin' 'em when they've done wrong. They're in here t' pay."

"Your zest for your work is admirable, Mr. Fell. But it

doesn't explain why I should have notes on a prisoner you tell me never was here.''

"Ye're welcome t' examine the records," the warden told him, leaning back in his chair.

Anthony stood up. "That won't be necessary. I'm sure the Duke of Buckingham ordered you to destroy all her records when he took the girl away from here."

Fell wasn't quite quick enough to conceal his start of surprise; belatedly he converted it into a shrug. "M'lord Ballenrose, I'm offended. Highly offended. Tamperin' with the prison records is against the law, 'n' I'm pledged t' uphold the law, not t' break it."

"Of course you are, Mr. Fell." Anthony briefly considered offering a bribe, then decided against it. Fell had grown rich enough already off the misery of others, and Buckingham had no doubt greased those slick palms well. He'd found out all he expected to. "Should your memory improve, you know where I can be found."

Those beady eyes met his. "It won't be improvin'."

"No, I don't suppose it will. Good day, Warden Fell."

"Good day, m'lord."

Outside the prison, Anthony waited with his horse just out of sight of the gates. He did not have to wait long; not five minutes later, Fell himself appeared atop a thick-legged piebald and set off toward the river. Anthony didn't bother to follow him; he was that sure of the warden's destination. So Buckingham would very shortly learn that Anthony knew who Mary Catherine really was. Good. Perhaps it would give him pause. Anthony doubted it, though. The fact that he'd carried the scheme this far proved the duke didn't rattle easily.

Fell's rump bumped off in the distance. Anthony turned his mount in the opposite direction, toward Smithfield Market. The race had begun in earnest, and he had work to do.

"What is it, Mr. Fell?" the Duke of Buckingham asked, eyeing with distaste the sweaty, shaken man who stood before him. Fell's beady gaze fixed on the black-haired woman in elegant *déshabillé* who sat across from the duke at the breakfast table, picking apart a herring with her hands.

"If we could talk in private, m'lord—"

"His grace has no secrets from me," Clare Fairfix said, daintily licking fish from her fingertips.

"That's a presumptuous statement, my dear," the duke said softly, then looked back at the warden. "Though true in this instance. Speak freely, Mr. Fell."

The warden couldn't keep from staring at the steady rise and fall of Clare's white breasts beneath her nearly transparent nightdress.

"Mr. Fell?" the duke said again.

The warden dragged his eyes away from Clare. "It's about that girl, m'lord. The one ye took away."

The duke sat up slightly. "Have you seen her?"

"Nay, m'lord. But the Earl of Ballenrose was at the prison today askin' questions about her."

"Was he really?" The duke's expression did not change. "What sort of questions?"

"Just . . . was she ever there, did I remember her. That sort o' thing."

"And what did you say?"

"Just wot ye told me t', m'lord. I never heard o' her."

"Well. Good for you. If that's all—"

"It ain't, m'lord. Not quite. Ye know ye said before that if I did wot ye wanted, about the girl, I mean, ye'd put an end to that there board o' inquiry."

"And so I did."

"Aye, m'lord. But Ballenrose, he was makin' threats that if I didn't tell him about the girl, he'd see it was opened up again. I wouldn't want that. And neither would yer friend Dr. Collett, believe ye me."

"I wouldn't worry, Mr. Fell," the duke said suavely. "I think you'll find within a matter of days that the Earl of Ballenrose is in no position to open anything more than a bottle of brandy."

Fell blinked. "M'lord?"

Buckingham traced a small pattern on the tablecloth with his finger. "He is going to experience a fall from grace. A permanent fall."

"Oh," said the warden. He still looked dubious, though. "I hope ye're sure, m'lord. Because, like I says, it ain't just me that'd be sorry if it turned out otherwise. Yer friend Dr. Collett—"

"Mr. Fell,"the duke said with a touch of impatience, "I'm not interested in whatever little scheme you and John have got going."

"It ain't so little," the warden said rather proudly.

The duke's upper lip curled. "Grandiose scheme, then. The point is the same. Ballenrose is finished. So trot along home to that cheerful prison of yours and go about your business."

"Well . . . if ye're sure, m'lord . . ."

"I am."

"Then I'll say good day." He sneaked another look at Clare. She hitched her skirts up, crossing her legs above the knee. Sweat sprang up on his forehead. "Good day t'ye, m'lady."

She shuddered as the door closed behind him. "God, what a revolting creature."

"Which didn't keep you from flaunting your attractions for him," said the duke, picking up his fork.

"I thought it might be amusing to watch him squirm."

"Was it?"

Clare shook her head, her mouth full of herring. "No challenge to it. Don't ever expect me to lie with someone like that the way I did the king's brother."

Buckingham considered her from beneath lazy, half-lowered lids. "But if I asked you to, you would."

"Of course I would," she said after a moment. Then she pushed her plate aside. "What makes you so certain it will only be a matter of days before Ballenrose's fall?"

"This is Monday. Tonight we leave for Cliveden to visit your sister. She's had a week in that cell with her new companions. From what you told me, I expect we'll find her ready—nay, eager to talk. Don't you?''

''Yes.''

''You don't sound convinced, my dear,'' the duke observed.

Clare shrugged prettily. ''Frankly, I'm surprised she's held out this long. She's never shown the least backbone before.''

''Sometimes people do surprise one.''

''Are you thinking of her?'' Clare asked, mouth curving downward. ''That Molly Flowers?''

''What makes you think she surprised me?''

''You cannot have expected someone of her class to be so self-sacrificing as to run away once she learned what you'd done. After all, she was married to Ballenrose. Even with him disgraced, she'd still have been a damned sight better off than she was in that prison.''

''A minor miscalculation.'' The duke shrugged it off. ''The end result will be the same.''

''You don't think he will find her now he knows who she is?''

''I've known who she was all along, and it hasn't helped me. And what if he does? By that time, thanks to your sister, I'll have made news of the wedding public—along with the new Countess of Ballenrose's true identity.'' He dabbed his mouth with his napkin. ''Do you know, I'm growing rather grateful to her for disappearing. It's been enjoyable to have these last months in which to savor my eventual victory.''

''Not to mention having savored me.'' He made her wait before he acknowledged the sally with an arch of his brow. She chose an apricot from the porcelain bowl before her and bit through the thin skin. ''George. Once this Ballenrose business is finished—you'll get rid of Agnes then, won't you, once and for all?''

''Get rid of her?'' he repeated.

''Send her away from Cliveden, I mean.'' He didn't

answer, and she went on. "After all, you've no further use for her, have you? Now that you have me."

He reached across the table, took the apricot from her, took it in his mouth, and finished it in one swallow. "I get rid of everything once I've no further use for it, Clare," he said, a bit of juice running out of the side of his mouth. "Rest assured of that." Then he fished out the apricot pit and set it on the edge of his plate, smiling enchantingly.

From the top of Farringdon Street, Smithfield Market stretched to the east like some great tawdry prostitute lolling in the midday sun, all bright and glittering but promising much more than she could deliver. Anthony stabled his horse at a public house with the peculiar name of the Dog and Feathers, and took a pint of bitter ale from the stocky, aproned barman. He drank it in the small low-walled courtyard while he considered the task that lay before him and contemplated where to begin.

He hadn't been here since he was a boy, sneaking away from his schoolbooks to take in the forbidden spectacle of the market. "Full of riffraff," his mother had sniffed, declaring it off limits, and the phrase had fired his imagination, made him curious to see just what riffraff might be. On his very first visit, neatly dressed in a velvet doublet and knee pants—he might have been ten—he'd been set on by a gang of boys who bloodied his nose and stole his purse, which held three new shillings. But right up to the moment he'd been attacked, he'd had a marvelous time.

The boys were still here, cocky as ever, crowding round a stone fountain and hurling insults at all who went by. So were the wooden stalls heaped with goods that as a boy he'd found irresistible: gleaming fish with their heads on, rainbow ribbons and laces, gewgaws, trinkets, fruits and vegetables, ducks and chickens that squawked in frantic excitement from their flimsy cages, rabbits that didn't move except for their noses and bright darting eyes.

He drained the ale and set off down the Long Lane, walking slowly. It was hard to picture Mary Catherine here, difficult to see her as one of these woman clad in cheap gray dresses, with broken fingernails and eyes that moved more quickly than those of the rabbits, gauging him as he passed by. The air rang with their voices, with hard quick patter and the songs they sang—"Buy my soaps, fine fresh soaps!" "There's linsey here, three yards the shilling!"—to draw customers in. A girl went past selling raisin-nut biscuits, their egg-brushed tops shiny as pennies, and he thought, ah, so this is where she got her taste for them.

"Ye, there! Is ye lookin' or buyin'?" a shrill voice demanded. He turned toward the fruit stall beside him, saw a small thin-nosed woman who looked a busybody if ever there was one.

"Both," he said, and reached for a bunch of green grapes.

"Don't touch the merchandise," she snapped, snatching it from him, weighing it on a tip scale. "That'll be five pence."

"Seems a bit stiff," he observed.

"Wot's wrong, can't ye afford it?" she demanded, sneering.

"I just wonder how the rest of your customers can."

"Oy, don't ye worry yer head about them." He gave her a shilling. She gave him back a handful of coins and watched, lip curled, to see whether he counted the change.

He didn't, just slipped it into his purse. "Have you ever heard of a girl named Molly Willoughby?"

"No. Is that all ye're buyin'?"

He pointed to a pile of peaches. "Two of those. She had another name too. Molly Flowers."

The woman's hand hovered over the peaches. Then she plucked two out. "Nay, never heard o' her neither. Tuppence more. Is that it?"

"A penny a peach—you ought to move your stall to High Holborn."

"Aye, well, ye ought not to pester workin' folk wi' yer questions. Good day."

Two stalls down, a wrinkled old man selling ribbons was chuckling as Anthony passed. "Heard Sarah givin' ye the devil, young laddie,"he said with a wink. "Charge ye steep fer them peaches, did she?"

"Steep enough," Anthony told him, grinning. "Want one?"

He shook his gray head. "Can't eat 'em. No teeth." He proved it, displaying his gums. "How 'bout some fine Flanders lace fer yer ladylove? Or I've silk ribbons—here, look at these. As good as ye'll find anywhere."

"I'll have two yards of the lace . . . and some information, if you don't mind."

"Not if I've got it." He sliced through the lace with his shears.

"Did you ever hear of a girl named Mary Catherine Willoughby? Molly Willoughby?"

"Willoughby . . ." He paused, folding up the lace. "Willoughby? Sounds familiar . . ."

"She used another name too. Molly Flowers."

"Oy, Molly Flowers!" The old man nodded. "O' course. May's girl, that would be."

"You know her?" Anthony's heartbeat quickened. Surely he wouldn't be that lucky so soon.

"Oy, so I did, once upon a time. Molly Flowers. Pretty thing, she was. Yellow-haired, I seems to recall."

"That's her. When was the last time you saw her?"

"Gor, it would be years 'n' years back." He shrugged. "My memory ain't wot it used t' be."

"But you've not seen her lately."

"Nay, nay. Seems t' me . . . seems t' me there were some sort o' trouble around her, back when Sarah's son Andrew were on city watch." He wagged his head. "Faith, 'tis all too long ago. I can't say for sure."

"She went to prison. To the Fleet," Anthony told him.

"Oy, pity. Such a sunny little thing she were. That's one shilling, threepence."

Anthony paid him. "Are you sure that's all you can remember?"

"Wait till ye're old as I am, young laddie! Ye'll see."
He gave him the lace, pinned up neatly, then said suddenly, "Ye wants t' know more, ye might ask Billy Buttons. Seems t' me Molly Flowers used t' have the stall beside his."

"Billy Buttons?"

"The tinker. On yer right, half a dozen stalls down."

Anthony frowned. "A tinker, eh? I've nothing on me to pay him to sharpen."

"Ye might offer t' stand him a pint at the Dog 'n' Feathers," the old man told him, winking again. "That ought t' get him talkin'."

"Thanks," Anthony said.

He strolled down the lane to the rickety stall where a huge red-faced man hunched over a grindstone, turning it with his foot while he plied a carving knife to its edge. Sparks flew and settled on his leather apron, bulging across a belly that had seen more than its share of ale.

He finished the knife, tested it on his thumb, and gave it to the customer who waited. Mopping his face with a kerchief, he looked at Anthony. "Somethin' I can do fer ye?"

"That looks like thirsty work," Anthony told him, nodding at the wheel.

"It is." He tucked the kerchief away.

"Could I buy a pint of beer for you at the tavern up the way?"

"Why would ye want t' do that?"

"I'd like to ask you about the girl who used to have the stall next to this one. Molly Flowers."

The tinker considered him for a moment. Then he got up from his stool and nodded to a nearby fishmonger. "Watch the stall fer me, will ye, Micky? Be back in a nonce. Come along, then." He crooked a finger at Anthony and headed for the Dog and Feathers. The ribbon seller winked as they passed.

"Pint o' bitter, Bart," the tinker told the barman inside the tavern. "On this gentleman here."

"The same for me," Anthony said, pushing coins across the bar. The tinker took his mug to a table, sat down, and had it drained before Anthony could join him. "Another?" Anthony asked.

"Long as ye're up," said the tinker.

Anthony brought it and sat across from him. The tinker drained the second mug just as quickly, licked foam from his lip. "About Molly Flowers," Anthony said.

"Ye're gettin' more forthright," the tinker noted. "The last one beat about the bush fer nigh on an hour."

"The last one?"

The tinker raised a finger to the barman, who grinned as he brought yet another mug and asked, "How many did ye get out o' that one, Billy?"

"Ten," said the tinker. " 'N' a dozen off the one before him."

"Bit o' luck, yer havin' the stall next t' Molly's."

"Ye can say that again, Bart." He drank that beer too, then looked at Anthony. "Buy me one more 'n' I'll tell ye wot I told them. The fact o' the matter is, this is gettin' right old."

"What did you tell them?" Anthony asked, nodding to the barman.

"That I ain't seen Molly since the city watch carted her off nearly three years back."

"Is that the truth?"

Billy whistled. "My, ye is forthright. It'll cost ye another beer for implyin' I lied."

"Keep them coming," Anthony told the barman. "Did you know her well?"

"Well enough," Billy said, swallowing.

"Why was she arrested?"

Bart, bringing another round, snorted. "Fer not givin' in t' Andrew Stiles."

"I beg your pardon?"

"Oy, he's got much nicer manners than the last one, ain't he, Billy?" the barman asked, laughing.

"Aye, he's a real toff."

"Why was she arrested?" Anthony asked again.

"Ye can look it up in the city records," Billy Buttons said. "Disturbin' the peace were the charge."

"I know that. But what did she do?"

"How many's that, Bart?" asked the tinker.

"Six," the barman said, tallying glasses.

"Here's yer six pints' worth, then. Andrew Stiles were pickin' on old Tom Peabody, 'n' Molly came to his aid." He eyed Anthony over his glass. "The other fellas didn't ask about that."

"Who's Andrew Stiles?"

"Sarah's boy—Sarah that runs the fruit stall," Bart put in. "He's dead now. Got stabbed in a brawl."

"Who's Tom Peabody?"

Billy Buttons tapped his forehead. "A nutter."

"Why was Stiles picking on him?"

"Because Stiles was a nutter too."

Anthony took a swallow of ale. "What kind of person was she?"

The tinker blinked at him. "Gor, ye do ask queer questions. Wot kind o' person are ye? Wot kind am I? She sold flowers. She looked after her aunt. She stuck up fer Tom Peabody when she should've kept quiet."

"Were she and Peabody close?"

That earned another snort from Bart. "Nobody's close t' Tom."

"I don't know about that," Billy Buttons said judiciously. "Seems like he's got plenty o' company there in his head." He stood up. "I've got t' get back."

"One more question," Anthony told him. "If Molly Flowers was in trouble, whom would she go to?"

"Now that her Aunt May's dead?" Billy shrugged. "She'd come t' me, I reckon."

"And she hasn't?"

"Nay. She hasn't."

"Thanks for your time," said Anthony.

"Thanks for the beer. Ta, Bart." The tinker lumbered out into the sunlight again.

Bart came for the glasses. "Billy feels bad he didn't do more for Molly that day," he said quietly. "We all do. But no one expected Andrew would arrest her. 'Twas a lark, that's all. Tom wouldn't fetch the watchmen water, that's wot started it." His voice held a thick Irish burr. "Then when her Aunt May went to hospital 'n' died with Molly still in prison, Billy took that hard. He 'n' May were sweethearts, I heard, once upon a time."

"There was no other family?" Anthony asked.

"None I knew of. Just May 'n' the girl."

A dead end. "How much do I owe you?"

"Fifty pounds," said the barman, then laughed. "Just pullin' yer leg. Two-shillings-ten."

Anthony paid him and walked to the door, fighting back a swell of sadness. The market swarmed with people, buying and selling, coming and going, dreaming dreams of idleness and ease. Was it any wonder Molly Flowers had jumped at the chance to rise above all this when Buckingham plucked her out of her miserable prison cell?

An old man dressed in rags shambled by, sticking close to the sides of the houses, mumbling to himself. Despite the noon heat he wore a tattered fur hat pulled low over his ears. "Hey, Tom!" a fat woman in the doorway to a baker's shop called, waving.

"Tom Peabody?" Anthony said impulsively. The ragtag figure turned, gave him a shy, childlike smile. "Could I ask you about Molly Flowers?"

The smile vanished abruptly; the man tugged the hat even lower and started to run, hobbling and pathetic. Anthony caught up to him in two long strides, touched his arm. "Leave me be! Leave me be!" he cried, hiding his face with his rags.

"I just want to know—have you seen Molly Flowers?"

"I don't know her! I never seen her!"

"Hey! Hey, there!" the fat woman shouted. "Wot're ye doin' to Tom?"

Anthony turned to her. "I wasn't going to hurt him. I just wanted to ask him a ques—"

"Can't ye see the poor man's daft?" she interrupted crossly. "Bloody toff, on yer way!" Anthony turned back to Tom, and saw only the trail of a ragged pant leg as he disappeared around the corner of the Dog and Feathers.

Best let it lie, he told himself, while the woman shook her fist at him and cursed beneath her breath. Mad old Tom Peabody didn't lack for advocates today. For an instant he imagined Mary Catherine as she might have looked three years past, defending the ragged beggar against the city watch. I'll wager she was splendid, he thought, mouth curving in a smile. Then he remembered that he hated her, and the image fled.

32

"Piers asked me again to marry him today."

In the long shadows of twilight, Molly sat with her legs crossed, leaning back on her hands with her head tilted up to the sky. "You'd like him, Aunt May. Oh, he's foreign, I know, and I imagine most of the folks at market think he's out of his mind. Maybe he is, a little. But he's good, and he's kind. His heart's in the right place, as you used to say. If things had been different . . ." She paused, leaving that thought unspoken even to her aunt's ghost. "Anyway, you would like him. Do you know what roses are up to now? Six pounds the crate, can you believe it? Piers says the shippers tell him it's been a frightful damp summer on the Continent. Hard to believe, isn't it? It's been so lovely here."

The first stars twinkled above her. Beneath her palms Molly felt the earth of the potter's field, still holding the warmth of the sun.

"All of this is Tom's Peabody's fault, I suppose, when you come right down to it," she told the night silence. "If he hadn't been so cheeky to Andrew that day, I wouldn't have been in gaol for Buckingham to find me." For that matter, if you followed that reasoning, the line of blame went back further still, to the day she spurned Andrew Stiles's advances. Or to Sarah, who'd brought Andrew up to be so bad-tempered. Or to Sarah's husband, who'd gone and got killed in the wars and made her so bitter . . . or to the kings who called men to battle. "Well, that's a fool's game," she murmured. "It's just history, isn't it? The way of the world. Might as lief trace it all the way back to Adam and Eve."

What would people think if they knew she came out here each evening to talk to a woman who'd been dead for years? "Probably that I'm daft as old Tom." But why shouldn't she come, if it gave her solace?

The lights of the city shone far below her, reflecting off the placid surface of the Thames. St. James's Palace, the Esplanade, Westminster—her life in those places seemed so distant now, more distant than the crescent moon that glided overhead. It might have all been a dream—but a dream she wouldn't soon be forgetting. She curled her hands over her belly, having saved the best news for last.

"I felt the baby move today, Aunt May," she whispered. "At least, I think I did. It isn't easy to tell, when I've got no one to ask about it but you. It was the queerest thing—like a little fish was swimming inside me, going around in circles. I was stripping roses, and it shook me so I stuck myself on a thorn. I haven't done that in years."

The night breeze brushed her face, soft as her sigh. "I already told you, if it's a girl I want to name her for you. If it's a boy, I don't know." A boy, tall and strong and black-haired, with eyes as blue as twilight—oh, God, she couldn't bear the reminder. Please, God, let it be a girl. "It won't be easy for her, I know, not having a father. But I'll do my best, just the same as you did for me. I can teach her to read and write, so she can make something of herself. And I won't let her make the mistakes that I did. I'll teach her . . ." What? Not to believe in fairy tales, in happily ever after? What sort of life was that? "I'll teach her not to be a fool," she finished firmly, "and that things aren't always what they seem to be."

A dog was barking somewhere in the distance. Molly stood up, only a little awkward with the changes in her body, and pulled her cap down over her ears. "Whist!" said a voice at her side.

"Jesu!" Hand at her throat, heart pounding, she turned and saw Tom Peabody, wrapped in his rags. "What a start you gave me!"

"Dogs," he hissed. "Can't ye hear 'em? Time t' hie yerself inside!"

"I was just going."

He nodded, tattered fur hat bobbing. "See that ye do." He paused, cocking his head at her. "Ye're lookin' different, Molly Flowers. Is ye puttin' on weight?"

Suddenly she wanted so badly to share her news. "I . . . I'm having a baby, Tom."

"Is ye really?" In the moonlight his worn face lit up. "Won't I be jiggered. Yer Aunt May'd be pleased."

"Aye, so she would."

"Well, good luck t' ye, Molly. Mind ye keep yerself hid." He started toward the prickleberry trees, then stopped. "Oy, I near forgot. There was a fellow askin' about ye at the market t'day."

Molly caught her breath. "You didn't say you'd seen me, Tom, did you?"

"Nay, nay. Told him I never even heard o' ye, just as ye said."

Relieved, she pulled her cap off, ran a hand through her hair, tucked it on again. "That's good, Tom. Thank you. You know you mustn't ever tell anyone that you've seen me."

"Oy, d'ye think me a fool? I knows that. Ye 'n' me, we've got t' stick together, don't we? We're the only ones." He nodded sagely. "The only ones that got away, that's ye 'n' me."

"All right, Tom. Good night."

"Good night, Molly Flowers. Mind yer step now, 'n' listen fer the dogs. Ye'll always know by the dogs." He patted her hand, then raised his head and cocked it, listening. " 'Tis quiet now. That means he's gone. 'Tis the blood on him that makes 'em howl so. He can't never get all the blood off, I reckon, try as he may.''

Molly suppressed a shiver. "Who, Tom? Whom are you talking about?''

"Why, the Stalker, o' course. Who else?'' He lowered his voice. "Ye must've smelt the blood on him when when he came fer ye.''

Molly thought of the way Hugh Stalker had looked at her back in the Fleet when he came to take her out of her cell. As though he'd eat her alive. And there had been a smell on him, she remembered it clearly. A metallic smell, thick and rank. Even then she'd thought it strange. "Tom—''

Something lunged at them out of the darkness, a figure, tall and black, so menacing in its silent attack that Molly's heart stopped beating. Only Tom's desperate cries brought her back to her senses: "It's him, lass! The Stalker! Run fer yer life!'' He took off for the prickleberry thicket. Molly, grabbed from behind, reached back with her nails and clawed the man's face while she kicked his kneecap as hard as she could. He grunted, his grip loosening, and she slipped from his grasp, fleeing after Tom as fast as she could. She heard his footsteps pounding after her across the soft earth, knew he was gaining, and abruptly changed course, skirting the tangle of trees for the alley that led onto Fetters Lane.

Just ahead of her, a dog threw itself against a board fence, barking frantically. Molly grabbed for the latch of the gate as she flew by. Just as she'd hoped, the dog went for the man who pursued her; she heard it howling in fury, heard muttered curses and the sounds of a scuffle as he wrestled it off. Tom's words echoed in her head: *'Tis the blood on him that makes 'em howl so.* Spurred by terror, she ran faster still, ducking behind the row of stalls that marked the start of the market, silent and empty at this hour of night.

She thought of heading for the Dog and Feathers—at least there would be people there—but that was all the way up the Long Lane, and she wasn't sure she could make it that far before he caught up to her. Not in bare feet, anyway, and running on cobbles. The dog was still barking, but even as she paused, panting, to listen, its clamor broke off, as abruptly as if its neck had been snapped. She gathered her skirt in a loop, tying it above her knees.

She peered over the top of the stall that hid her and saw him, a tall black figure standing at the top of the lane with the moon behind him. He stood very still, as if he were listening. Could he hear her heart, the pounding of the blood in her head? She held her breath, watching, waiting, and saw him swivel his head as though he looked straight at her. It so unnerved her, she backed into a pile of empty crates and sent them clattering to the ground. He started forward, and the chase was on again.

Keeping behind the stalls, dodging rubbish and mud, she made a dash for the fountain. Sometimes vagrants gathered there after the market closed; with any luck they'd be out tonight. Up to now, the desolation of Smithfield once the buyers and sellers went home had always suited her purpose, but at the moment she'd have given anything for the safety of a crowd.

He was still coming, tracking her steadily, ignoring the racket he made as he crashed through the bushels and crates and discarded refuse of the market's daylight denizens. The fountain loomed up in the moonlight, utterly abandoned. For the first time it occurred to Molly that she might not escape.

She circled the fountain in the shadows of the stalls, still heading for the Dog and Feathers, for the comfort of stouthearted Bart and his customers. But what if Bart recognized her? Brought up short, she stopped running. Glancing over her shoulder, she saw him at the fountain, tall and grim. The faint breeze carried the hiss of his short, labored breaths. The sound made him real, not a dark, faceless phantom, and chilled Molly's blood. Throwing all stealth aside, she tore across the open field to the sorting shed.

The key to the padlock was in her purse; she fumbled for it as she ran, had the shackle open in a split second. Once inside, in the sweet-scented darkness, she slammed the door shut behind her, thrust the lock through the inner staple, scrambled to the table for her shears. Their cold weight comforted her hand. To slow him down, she pushed a skid of tin buckets up to the threshold, then sank back into a corner, waiting, shears clutched tight in her fist.

The door rattled on its hinges, settled, rattled again. Then suddenly the whole shed shook, thin wood splintering as the door gave way beneath a burst of force. The buckets went flying, stems and water sailing through the air. The skid thudded into the table and bench, overturning them with an ungodly crash. Molly screamed as the figure lunged at her—she slashed out with the shears, slicing into a tangle of cloth, rearing back to strike out once more. But he caught her arm, held it tight. "Aiming for the heart again?" he asked, and the flood of relief she felt in realizing he couldn't be the tongueless Stalker was subsumed by a deeper horror as she recognized his voice. The shears dropped from her hand.

"Anthony."

33

He heard the weapon fall to the floor with a dull clank. "Who did you think it was," he demanded, "your friend Buckingham?" She didn't answer. He gave her arm a sharp twist, shoving her back against the far wall of the shed. The air inside was heady with the scent of flowers, as though some fabulous garden bloomed unseen in the darkness there. "Answer me one thing," he told her, feeling her shrink from him. "Just tell me this: why did you run away before your little play was finished? Didn't Buckingham tell you he needed proof of the wedding to ruin me?"

She didn't speak for a moment, and he shook her, hating her for what she'd done to him, hating himself even more for the way his blood caught fire at her closeness, making his manhood tighten at the feel of her skin beneath his fingertips. "Because," she spat at him at last. "Because I was sick to death of you, both of you, and your bloody games."

"He's looking for you, you know."

"Aye, I know. But he won't find me. And you won't tell him where I am, will you? Because you're right; it would be your ruin to be wedded to the likes of me."

"I am wedded to you, you stupid girl!"

She laughed at him. "So what? Go on and divorce me. That's what you rich folk do when you tire of your wives, isn't it? Buy yourself a bloody divorce. I won't fight it;

I've had enough of the aristocracy. You can say we never slept together. That's grounds, isn't it? And so far as I care, we never did.''

Her words cut him to the bone, pierced him with a pain made all the worse by the way his flesh was aching for her even now. "Liar," he said, the word strangled and faint. "You can't deny what we shared."

"Hah! If I could playact that bloody Buckingham's niece for nigh on two years, I could sure as hell playact my way through one night with you!" He caught his breath, hands tightening on her arms.

"Bitch," he heard himself say, and raised a fist to strike her, to silence that harsh, taunting voice. She stopped him, her hand on his arm.

"Get out of here," she hissed. "Go back to where you came from, before I tell you more truths you may not want to hear."

He let his arm drop, moving away from her in the darkness. He felt bereft and shaken, stung by her touch, betrayed by his memories. All thoughts of punishing her had fled; he wanted only to be gone. "Jesu knows how I ever thought I loved you," he mumbled, marveling at his own foolishness.

Her laughter rang out again. "Aye, and the devil knows how you ever thought I loved you!"

"Damn you," he whispered. "Damn you to hell."

"Go on, get out," she said again, and the cold cruelty of her words doused the last spark of fire within him. He blundered toward the doorway, stumbled through blindly, breathing hard in the warm summer air . . .

And heard, from the shed behind him, the soft sound of weeping, mournful and forlorn as the cry of a dove.

He turned back, striking his flint, holding it aloft, and as its quavering light spilled into the shed, he saw her kneeling in a corner, face hidden in her hands. "Mary Catherine?" he said.

"Leave me alone." She curled into a ball in the midst

of a carpet of crushed, broken flowers. "Just leave me alone."

Despite himself, he took a step toward her. "Mary Catherine—"

"I'm not Mary Catherine!" she cried. "I never was! My name's Molly, just Molly. Don't!" He'd reached out his hand. "Don't come near me. Don't touch me."

"My God," Anthony whispered as the truth struck him, iron-hard, like a bullet. "My God, you didn't know, did you? You really thought you were his niece."

Molly hunched over, hugging herself, fighting desperately to keep up the facade that would save him, send him away from here filled with such hate for her that she'd never see him again—for the pain of seeing him, loving him, was so great that she thought her heart would break apart. "Of course I knew," she spat at him, wiping her eyes with the back of her hand. "What kind of fool do you take me for? We were in it together, we planned the whole thing—"

"The hell you did. He didn't tell you until you went to Buckingham House to tell him we were married. And *that's* why you ran away."

"You're daft," she said, and laughed, but now, in the light, he could see how that forced laugh cost her. The flint was burning his fingers; he scanned the shed for a candle, saw one stuck in the neck of a bottle, and lit it, setting it on the floor.

"Mary Catherine—"

"Molly! The name's Molly!"

"I don't give a cat's bloody damn what you call yourself." He pulled her up from the ground, turned her to face him. She looked away, brown hair falling over her tear-swollen eyes. "What's the matter with you? Did you think I wouldn't love you anymore if I found out who you were?" She said nothing; he shook her shoulders. "Answer me, dammit! Did you honestly think so little of me as that?"

Her breath escaped in a sigh. "No. No, of course I didn't."

"Then why the devil did you run off?"

"Because . . . I was afraid you *would* still love me."

Perplexed, he loosened his hold. "I don't understand."

She turned away from him, staring at the ground. "He was going to use me to ruin you. I couldn't let that happen."

"Don't you think you might have consulted me?"

"No! How could I?" She set one of the benches upright and sat down on it, bone-achingly weary. "I knew what you'd say."

"I'd say let him ruin me and be damned!"

"Exactly. But, Anthony . . ." She paused, searching for the words that would make him see. "It wasn't just our lives in the balance. It was all those other people you've tried so hard to help—my kind, *my* people. The ones in the Fleet, and St. Bart's—what do you think would become of them without someone like you?"

"My god, Mary Ca—my God, Molly. What I've tried to do for them hasn't been any more than a drop in the ocean!"

"No, but at least you're trying! At least you're doing something. Don't you remember what you said to me on our wedding night? That we would be the conscience of the king. That Charles and the others would listen to us because of who we were—you the Earl of Ballenrose, I Buckingham's niece." She bowed her head. "Who do you think would listen to us now?"

"I don't know. No one," he admitted. "But, dammit all, that can't be helped."

"Yes. It can. There's more, Anthony." Molly stared at her hands. "He traced my real mother, found out who she was. A . . . a streetwalker named Nell Scutley. She was knifed to death on St. Katherine's docks when I was two. Can't you see—"

"And my great-great-great-grandfather was a scoundrel who won the money to buy his knighthood from Henry the Seventh by cheating at cards," he broke in impatiently. "What difference does that make? I don't care about the past. We are talking about the future, *our* future."

"We haven't got any future," she cried hopelessly. "Go away, Anthony, and just forget that you found me. Forget you ever knew me."

"Jesu, Molly, that's like saying . . . like saying I should forget that I ever saw sunlight. That I ever stood in a garden at dusk and smelled roses . . ." He picked one up from the ground, its stem bent and twisted. "Have you any notion, any notion at all, what these past months have been like without you?"

"Of course I have," she said quietly.

The broken rose in his hands, he sat down beside her. "You're my wife, Molly Flowers. I want you with me. The rest of the world will just have to go hang."

"It isn't fair," she whispered. "You would have to give up so much—"

"You'd have to give up these splendid accommodations," he teased, and saw her smile faintly. "Have you really been right here at Smithfield all this time?" Molly nodded. "Christ, it's a wonder Buckingham didn't find you."

"How . . . how did you find me?"

"I followed Tom Peabody from the marketplace. I wasn't going to go after him at all. I felt a right fool, trudging along in his wake all day while he wandered about. But something made me keep on. Some lucky angel, I guess." He touched her tear-streaked cheek. "And then he went to potter's field, and I saw you there on the hill. I didn't recognize you at first. You looked . . . different."

She put a hand to her head. "I cut and dyed my hair."

"So I see. It's very fetching."

Molly snorted. "It's dreadful."

Anthony shrugged. "It doesn't matter, does it? Since no one will receive us, we won't be going anywhere." That made her giggle, but still she would not meet his gaze. "I was so afraid," he said then, his voice shaken. "So afraid you might be dead. I watched them drag the river, and I just kept praying—"

"I threw myself in," she confessed. "I thought it would be best. But then, I couldn't go through with it. I bobbed up and shouted, and Piers heard me and saved me."

"Well, thank God for Piers, whoever that is," he said gravely. "What made you change her mind?"

He watched her hand creep up to her belly. "I don't know. The stars, I suppose. Only I don't believe in the stars anymore."

"Why not? Because all those wonderful romantic co-incidences turned out to be engineered by Buckingham?" She nodded. "The bastard did bring us together, you know. We owe him something for that."

"Aye—and I'd like to pay him with a bludgeon."

"Spoken like a true countess," he noted. "Just the proper touch of viciousness."

She looked at him then, her green eyes wide and fearful. "Anthony. Are you sure, really sure, that this is what you want?"

"More sure than I have ever been of anything in my life." He put his arm around her, pulling her close. Then his mouth touched hers.

The kiss was softer than moonlight, more gentle than starlight. "Oh," Anthony groaned as she melted against him, settled into the hollow of his shoulder, "oh, Christ, how did I ever think that I could live without you?"

"I don't know . . ." She returned the kiss eagerly, passionately, holding his face in her hands. "I do love you—"

"Not half so much as I love you." He kissed her throat, her hair, let his hand play over her breasts, and then groaned again. "Have they rooms at the Dog and Feathers? I don't think I can wait until we get home." His hand slid lower, toward her belly.

"Anthony," Molly said, "there's something you should know . . ."

About the child. How should she put it? She drew a breath, looking into his wise priest's eyes. "Anthony—"

Her next words were drowned in a fury of barking from just outside the shed. Tom burst inside, wild-eyed and panting. "He's out there, Molly!" he cried, pulling the rags he wore over his face. "Hide yerself, girl! Hide me!" He scrambled back behind the overturned table, cowering and quaking. Anthony crossed to the doorway in two long strides.

"Who's out there?"

"The Stalker! I saw him!" Tom hissed, reaching up for Molly's arm and trying to pull her to the floor with him.

"Who's this Stalker, anyway?" Anthony asked above the howls of the dog. Molly didn't answer. As Tom had raised the rags above his head, she'd seen, in the light of the candle, his scrawny stomach and chest, crisscrossed with thick raised scars.

"My God, Tom." She touched one of the angry red welts with her finger. "Who did that to you?"

"Who d'ye think? The doctor!"

The dog's frantic yelps faded away. Anthony came back to the bench. "There's no one out there." Molly scarcely heard him; she was remembering the twilit evening at the potter's field when Tom had first found her.

"Dr. Collett did that?" she asked, kneeling in front of him. Tom nodded fearfully. "Why, Tom?"

"As if ye didn't know! Didn't he take ye off too?"

"Take me where?"

"To his laboratory." He said the word carefully, with great dread.

Anthony saw the welts too, and whistled. "Good God! What was he trying to do?"

"T' see wot made me work," Tom whispered.

"You were sick, then," said Molly, still trying to understand. "He was trying to cure you."

"Cure me? Nay! He was tryin' t' kill me, just like he tried t' kill ye! Just like he did kill the baby 'n' yer Aunt May! But we was too smart fer him, wasn't we, Molly

Flowers? We got away.'' He winked at her. ''We're the only ones, ain't we, ye 'n' me?''

Molly rocked back on her heels. He is mad, she reminded herself. He is talking nonsense. But she could not quite conquer a mounting uneasiness deep in her soul. ''What is he talking about?'' Anthony asked curiously. ''What had Dr. Collett to do with your aunt?''

''Nothing,'' she told him. ''That is—that night when Buckingham took me out of prison, Dr. Collett went to fetch Aunt May. Only she was very sick, so he took her to St. Bart's instead, and she died there.'' Where there weren't any records of her ever having been admitted. Where the nurse hadn't remembered her. . . .

Molly hadn't really been Buckingham's niece. Dr. Collett knew that. Why should he have cared what happened to her blind, sick aunt?

And there had been blood on his coat the next morning when he came to tell her Aunt May was dead.

She put her fist to her mouth, swallowing bile, fighting to hold on to her own sanity. What Tom was saying wasn't possible; it was too inhuman.

But Collett had given her the plague; he'd told her that himself—boasted of it, even. Molly shuddered uncontrollably, thinking of the doctor's cold pale eyes.

''Do you mean to tell me,'' Anthony said to Tom slowly, incredulously, ''that Dr. Collett cut you open as some sort of . . . of experiment, while you were still alive?''

''Oy, not just me, mate,'' Tom hissed. ''There's been plenty o' others. The Stalker, he buries 'em at night, up in potter's field.''

''How did the doctor get hold of you? Where did he find you?''

''Why, I was in the Fleet, same as Molly. Three months I got, for bein' drunk 'n' punchin' a soldier. Then I fell sick o' the fever while I was in there, 'n' the Stalker came 'n' took me away.''

''The Stalker? Who is the Stalker?'' Anthony pressed.

''A great grim fellow who works at the prison,'' Tom

explained in a whisper. "Had his tongue cut out for somewhat or other. That's why the doctor uses him. Because he can't bear tales, ye see. 'N' the doctor lets him have the entrails t' eat—"

"Oh, for Christ's sake, stop!" Molly cried, covering her ears. "It isn't true! It's the madness—"

"Oy, 'tis madness, all right," Tom said solemnly. "But 'tis God's truth. I'd swear it on my life."

"You don't believe him, do you?" Molly asked Anthony, green eyes pleading. "You don't really think it could be true?"

"Tom," he said, not answering her question, "when did this happen to you?"

"The fifth o' June 1653," the old man said with dignified precision. "I remember just as if he'd carved it int' my chest wi' that knife o' his. He was already t' work on some poor fellow when the Stalker brought me in. I heard him screamin' 'n' screamin'—gor, it seemed like hours afore he died. Then he strapped me ont' a table, wi' candles all around me, 'n' he made these cuts." He pulled his ragged clothes up to show them again. "Only he'd been careless wi' the straps—'n' I wasn't near so sick by then as I was scared. Anyways, I jumped up 'n' ran. That's how I got away."

Molly had begun to cry, hiding her face in her smock. "I won't believe it. I won't. I can't—"

"I heard a paper Collett delivered to the Royal Society last year on the circulation of the blood," Anthony said quietly. "I remember thinking then that the man had to be some sort of wizard to know the things he did—if they were true." He looked at Tom again. "Why the devil didn't you ever tell anyone about this?"

"Tell anyone?" Tom echoed indignantly. "Good God Almighty, man, I been talkin' o' nothin' else fer the last twenty years! Ye tell him, Molly! Ain't I always warned folk t' beware o' the Stalker, 'n' t' mind themselves when they heard dogs a-barkin'?"

"He has," Molly confirmed. "Oh, God, he has, but we never paid him any mind. We all thought he was daft."

Tom sniffed. "Well, that's no fault o' mine!"

The thought of Aunt May suffering through such a barbarous death was unbearable. Molly closed her eyes, forced the sickening images in her mind away, concentrated on her anger instead. "If he did that to her, the butcher—"

"You can't be sure," Anthony told her, smoothing her hair.

"By God, I'll kill him with my two hands."

Tom hung his head. "I'm sorry, Molly, truly I is. I wanted t' help her. But wot could I do? He had her 'n' the baby—"

"Jesu, a little baby!" Molly cried in anguish. "How could anyone be so evil?"

"I'll see to it," Anthony promised. "I'll launch an inquiry, see that he's arrested—"

"Will you?" Molly demanded, pushing his hand away. "Before or after you admit that you've married a streetwalker's daughter? Oh, Anthony, it's no good, can't you see? This is just what I meant. No one will listen to you once Buckingham tells the world who I am."

"We have Tom as a witness—"

"Oh, aye, we have Tom as a witness." She laughed bitterly. "How do you think he will stand up against the next director of the Royal Society—not to mention all of the doctor's fine friends, like Lord Phipps and the great Duke of Buckingham? Begging your pardon, Tom—"

"That's all right, Molly," the old man said. "I can see wot ye mean."

"Who I am married to shouldn't have any bearing on stopping a murderer!" Anthony protested.

"Not in that perfect, just world you'd like to create," Molly agreed. "But we don't live in that world; we live in this one, and it's hateful and unjust and imperfect. And as I see it, I can be married to you or I can see Aunt May's killer punished. I can't have both." She looked at him defiantly, small chin thrust out. "Tell me that I am wrong." He didn't say anything, and she turned away, tears streaming down her face. "Oh, Lord, what a choice to make!"

Anthony watched her, feeling helpless and lost but not quite ready to admit they were beaten. "There must be a way . . ."

"Oy, ye'd have to catch him in the act," Tom muttered, " 'n' how could ye do that?"

Molly raised her bowed head. "If we could do that—"

"It wouldn't make any difference," Anthony said quietly. "It would still be our word against his."

"And what are we?" Molly asked in wry resignation. "A madman, a felon, and a renegade."

A sudden strange light ignited Anthony's blue eyes. "Molly. Love. If you had a choice of seeing Dr. Collett punished, or just making sure he was stopped—that he would never do to anyone else what he did to Tom and Aunt May—"

"He has got to be stopped, Anthony! Even if it costs me you, he has got to be stopped." She paused, seeing the gleam in his gaze. "What are you thinking of?"

"Dr. Collett knows the truth about you and Buckingham, doesn't he?" he said slowly. "That Buckingham engineered our marriage just to see me ruined."

"Aye," Molly confirmed. "It was Collett who drew the birthmark on the duke that convinced me I was his niece."

"If that story got out, it might well work against the duke's designs, don't you think? Public sympathy would surely lie with the victims of such a hoax, not with the perpetrator."

"I've thought all that through, believe me." Molly sighed in resignation. "It still comes down to our word against Buckingham's and Collett's."

"But what if the doctor were on our side?"

Molly's green gaze widened. "Collett would never side with us against Buckingham."

"He would if it were either that or having his murderous experiments exposed. He wouldn't have any choice."

"Ye're talkin' blackmail," Tom said, mouth pursed. Then he grinned. "I like it!"

Molly turned the idea over in her mind. "The king and the courtiers might be sympathetic to you, Anthony, but I don't think they ever would be to me."

"Well, what if we used Collett to pressure Buckingham into *not* exposing you? To force him into continuing to acknowledge you as his niece?"

Molly's eyes positively glowed. "Lord, wouldn't that be a splendid revenge? He'd be fit to be tied, the snob." Then her face fell. "We'd still have to have proof of what Collett is doing. Catch him in the act, as Tom said."

"Aye, there's that," Anthony acknowledged. "And even if we did, we wouldn't be able to see Collett punished for those he's already killed. The most we could hope for would be making sure he never practices medicine again. We'd be striking a bargain, offering quid pro quo."

"Making a deal with the devil." Molly looked up at her husband. "Do we have the right, Anthony, do you think, to take such a thing upon ourselves?"

"I'd say that depends on whether we think we can do enough good to balance out the evil Dr. Collett has done."

"Working together. You and I," Molly said softly. He nodded. "Oh, we can, Anthony! I know we can!"

Tom cleared his throat. "I was just goin' t' say—'em ones he's already planted in potter's field, there's naught we can do now to help 'em. It's keepin' him from hurtin' anyone else wot matters."

"Then we have your blessing?" Anthony asked.

"Oy, I don't understand all this talk o' dukes 'n' nieces 'n' such," the old man said shyly. "But I likes yer husband, Molly, 'n' I trusts him to do wot's right."

"He is a pip, Tom, isn't he?" Molly asked, smiling up at Anthony.

"I'd say ye'd done right well by yerself, lass."

"Not half so well as I did," Anthony said, bending down to kiss Molly's ear.

"That will have to wait," she told him regretfully. "We have work to do." A dog howled in the distance, and she shuddered. "Oh, love, we have got to stop him. We've got to stop him tonight! I couldn't live with myself if I thought . . ."

"I know," he told her as her voice trailed away. "Here's an idea. Suppose I went out there where this Stalker is and let him take me to Collett's laboratory."

"He won't," Tom said succinctly. "Not a great strappin' fellow like ye. He only preys on' em wot's frail or old or weak." He saw Anthony eyeing him speculatively and shook his head, backing away. "Oy, don't look at me! I wouldn't put myself back in that doctor's clutches for anythin' in the world!"

"Of course you wouldn't, Tom," Molly soothed him, "and we wouldn't ask you to. It will have to be me."

"Out of the question," Anthony said. "Michael Nivens will be back from France in a couple of days. I can get him to help me—"

"A couple of days?" Molly echoed. "Think how many lives could be lost before then! Old women, helpless little children—"

"It can't be helped," Anthony said stolidly.

"But it can! All I have to do—"

"Is play target for a vicious murderer and his deranged henchman. I forbid it, Mary Catherine."

"That's the only time Aunt May ever called me by my full name too—when she was angry." At the thought Molly's eyes filled with tears again. "Oh, God, Anthony, she must have been so horribly frightened!"

"Don't think of it, love—"

"I can't *stop* thinking of it! We have got to stop him." She curled her hands into fists. "We've got to stop him tonight. If you truly love me, you'll let me do this. For her. For Aunt May."

"I've only just found you, Molly," he said, not sounding at all great and strapping. "I couldn't bear to lose you again."

She took his hand, pressed it to her cheek. "You won't lose me, love. All you have to do is hide near me while I wait for the Stalker, and then follow him when he takes me to Collett's laboratory."

"But what if something goes wrong? What if he gets away from me somehow?"

"Then Tom will show you where the laboratory is. You would do that, Tom, wouldn't you? You wouldn't be afraid if Anthony is with you."

"Nay . . . I reckon not."

"And you're sure you know where the laboratory is?" Anthony pressed him.

"Gor, d'ye think I could ever forget? 'Tis close by the prison, there off the alleyway from Sydenham Square," Tom said with prompt certitude.

"You're absolutely sure?"

He nodded his rag-capped head. "Molly went t' the Fleet on account o' me. I don't know if ye knows that. But I looked out for her while she was there, just the same as I'll look out for her now."

Another dog began barking, this time much closer to the market. "We've no time to waste, Anthony," Molly told him, moving toward the doorway.

"Hold on!" He caught her arm. "What if Collett recognizes you?"

"Tom, give me your hat, and that coat you've got on." While he struggled out of the ragged clothes, Molly rubbed her hands in the mud the spilled vases had made of the floor, then wiped it over her face and arms. She put on the hat and coat, and then, as Anthony watched in amazement, twisted her face into a suffering scowl. "That ought to put him off, don't you think, long enough for you to get to me?" she asked, shuffling across the shed.

Anthony wagged his head. "You really should have been an actress."

"You must be jesting. Gentlemen never marry actresses; they only make mistresses of them."

He laughed, but there was fear in his eyes. "Be careful, Molly," he said, and kissed her. "I love you."

"I love you too." She returned the kiss. "Thank you for letting me do this."

"I didn't know I had a choice."

"You don't. But thanks. Good-bye, Tom."

"God go wi' ye, Molly Flowers."

She came back to Anthony for one more kiss, needing to feel his mouth against hers, hear his heart beating, so sure and strong. "Molly—" he began.

She laid a finger on his lips. "Hush, love. Everything will be all right. The stars are on our side." Then, without looking back, she hurried out of the shed, out of the warm candlelight into the dead of night.

34

ONE WOULD HAVE had to look hard to see the rag-clad, barefoot figure huddled in the doorway of the abandoned slaughter-house at the end of Long Lane, but Molly wanted it that way. She didn't care to have just any passerby come to her aid; it would have to be someone who was searching for a soul in misery. Anthony and Tom had taken up a post around the corner, scarce a hundred yards away, and though she couldn't see them, just knowing they were there almost kept her from being afraid.

It was a bit of luck, she thought, pulling Tom's coat tight around her, that she hadn't been able to tell Anthony yet about the child she carried. If she had, she was sure he never would have agreed to let her act as the Stalker's bait. And she had to do it, for the sake of Aunt May and all those other nameless, faceless victims who lay beneath the green grass and dark earth of the potter's field. There would be time enough to tell him when this was over. Then they would have the rest of their lives.

The city was so still, so quiet. It seemed as though she'd been curled up in the doorway for hours, hoping with half her heart that the Stalker would appear and with the other half that he wouldn't. Now she just longed for something, anything, to happen to make the night's adventure begin.

The moon had long since set; now there was only starlight overhead. Molly stretched her cramped legs as best she could and stared up at the velvet canopy of sky. There was Virgo—or was it Orion? She couldn't remember. *My education in astrology is lax,* she thought. *I will have to get Anthony to teach me. I'll wager he knows such things.*

The eager yap of a small dog somewhere nearby made all her muscles tighten. She was holding her breath, she realized, and let it out in a sigh. It wasn't the first dog they'd heard since they set watch, but it was the closest. The scent of blood, Tom had said; that was what set them off. Another dog, a hound of some sort, bayed forlornly. Even closer. Molly's heart began to pound. More than anything in the world she yearned to run to the comfort of Anthony's strong arms. But instead she waited, ears straining to catch any sign, any sound.

Were those footsteps? Damn her heart, she could hardly hear above its beating. Surely those were footsteps, stealthy and soft as a whisper. She remembered then the odd leather boots Hugh Stalker had worn in the Fleet, with their buttery soles. What Tom had said about his eating the victims' entrails—surely that couldn't be true. Or could it? *God, give me strength,* she prayed as another dog howled, sounding near enough to touch—Jesu, there it went running past her, tail between its legs. And then, so suddenly that she hadn't even time to be properly afraid, a figure stood before her, huge and silent and grim, with the sharp smell of iron clinging to his black clothes.

"Kind sir," she whimpered, stretching out her hand to him. "Oy, kind sir, can ye help me? I'm ill, dreadful ill. Please, sir . . ." She started up to her knees, then fell back against the door in a heap, with a pitiful moan. "Oh, Jesu in heaven, I fear I'm a-dyin'!" He drew away from her, and she bit her lip in terrified frustration. *God, if she failed now . . .*

But he was only searching the deserted street, looking up and down Long Lane. "Oy," she moaned, doubling over, clutching her middle, "for the love o' God, help me!" The silent giant stooped down and took her into his arms, raising her up from the ground. Molly fought back a swell of panic, forced her muscles to go limp and weak. "God bless ye, sir," she whispered. "May the Lord bless 'n' keep ye, for takin' pity on a wretch like me." The smell of him was suffocating as his arms folded around her, drawing her tight to his chest. "Where is ye takin' me?" she asked, because even the weakest victim surely would. "Where is we goin'?" The only answer Hugh Stalker gave was a sort of a hug, meant, she supposed, to reassure. "A silent angel, eh?" she whispered. "Well, I'll have t' trust ye anyways. Ye're the only angel I've got." She peeked out from beneath the tattered brim of Tom's hat and saw Hugh Stalker smile.

There was something so horrible about that broad, complacent smile that Molly damn near bolted. Stay with me, Anthony, she begged silently, don't lose sight of me! Don't let him get away. . . .

On those soft leather soles, the Stalker carried her through the city of London, through the desolate labyrinth of alleys and lanes that led toward Sydenham Square.

Though she pricked her ears for any sign that Anthony and Tom were following, she heard nothing. The silence was eerie, unearthly; along the convoluted route the Stalker used, no babies cried from upstairs windows, no mothers ran to soothe them, not even a soldier or sailor strolled by with his light-o'-love. He knows this city like no one else could, Molly realized. At this hour, the city is his, and the beat of his soft padding footsteps is the beat of the heart that pounds unseen at its core.

She shivered, and he paused, looking down at her in the faint glow of starlight. "The fever," Molly whispered, licking her lips. "Oy, 'tis burnin' me alive, this fever." It wasn't hard to make herself shiver again. Reassured, he moved on. When an unseen dog howled nearby, Molly flinched. The Stalker's grip grew tighter; he was hurrying now. Getting closer to his destination, Molly thought, forcing herself not to panic.

He stopped again. His head swiveled, turning this way and that. Then, with surprising quickness, he turned a key in a nondescript door and entered it, bending low to fit in.

There wasn't any light at all inside, only thick stale blackness. The lack of vision didn't hinder the Stalker; he moved quickly, easily, across a room or passageway. They went through another door, and then down a steep, twisting staircase, with Molly's toes and shoulders rubbing against the walls on either side.

Anthony is coming, she told herself as they reached the foot of the stairway. Anthony will be here at any moment; he is following right behind. Anthony won't let anything happen to . . . "Oh," she said involuntarily as out of the darkness there appeared four thin ribbons of light—the outline of a door. The Stalker's hand moved, jangling a bell, and the lines of light became a square as the door opened wide. Stark against the yellow candleglow there appeared the figure of a man with a pair of spectacles riding low on his long, bony nose. "Well, well, well, Hugh," said Dr. John Collett, and as her eyes adjusted to the light, Molly saw that the knife he held in his hand bore a coating of dried, crusted blood. "What have we here?"

"Oh, Christ," Anthony breathed as he turned a twist in the road. "Oh, Christ in heaven. We've lost them." The narrow street ahead split into three alleyways, and though the Stalker had been in view but a moment before, now he couldn't be seen.

"That's all right," Tom panted, trotting up behind him. " 'Tis this way. Down here." He pulled Anthony's sleeve, tugging him toward the alley to the right.

"Are you sure?"

"O' course I'm sure! There—did ye hear that?" A dog was howling in the darkness bordering the alley Tom was headed for. "Stick wi' me, Molly's husband. Ye'll see. Ye always can tell on account o' the dogs."

The hound was still baying. Anthony let himself be led down into the close despite his misgivings; he wasn't at all sure the Stalker had come this way.

"Fifth door down," Tom whispered, counting the blank entrances to the ruined houses they passed. This part of the city had been hit hard by the Great Fire seven years before, and had never been rebuilt. A faint odor of charred wood and seared brick still seemed to hang on the air.

The dog's agitated howls grew louder. Tom seemed so sure of himself that Anthony ran to the fifth house's stoop, prepared to batter the door. He'd just lowered his shoulder to attack the wood when he heard a gasp at his back. Whirling around, he saw what the old man had seen: a crop-eared mongrel pawing at the trunk of a dead elm in which he'd treed a cat.

He couldn't stop himself from grabbing Tom's shoulders. "You said he'd come here! You said the dog—"

"How the devil was I supposed to know the blasted thing had got a cat? Anyway, this is the right alley!" Tom protested. "Go on; break down the door!"

Anthony hit the wood running. It flew open so abruptly he could tell it hadn't even been locked. Inside, in pitch blackness, he stumbled over something that gave a high-pitched, unmistakably feminine squeal. "Molly?" he cried, fumbling at his feet in the dark.

"Oy, who the hell's there?" an outraged voice, this time male, demanded. Someone lunged at Anthony's knees, knocking him to the floor. He stumbled upright, swinging, felt his fist connect with the planes of a face. The man yelped, springing back. "Bloody Christ, woman, ye didn't tell me ye was married!"

"I ain't!" A flint flared at last, making Anthony blink. "But I bloody well wish I was!" said the coarse-featured woman who held it. "Oy, soldier, wot's yer name?"

The two of them, man and woman both, were half-dressed; clearly he'd burst in on them in the midst of co-ition. Anthony knew he had got the wrong house. Still, he grabbed the man by the throat. "Where is she?"

"Oy, mate, are ye blind? She's right there!" the startled fellow sputtered, pointing to his companion.

"Not her. The girl who came in here with the Stalker."

"The Stalker!" the woman went wide-eyed, grabbing for her clothes. "Don't tell me he's about!"

"I swear t' God, mate, I don't know wot ye're on about," the man gasped as Anthony shook him. "I ain't seen no one—" Anthony tightened his grip, and the man went sheet-white. "It's the truth, mate! I swear it!"

"Molly's husband," said Tom's small timid voice from the door, "I'm afeard this ain't the place."

Anthony turned on him. "How can you tell?"

"The other house, when ye went in, it had a long hallway, wi' stairs at the end."

"Dammit to hell!" Anthony burst out, then bit his tongue. The old man was already quaking. It wouldn't do to let him get any more upset. "All right, Tom." He let the man he held fall to the floor. "Let's go. Sorry," he flung over his shoulder at the hapless couple. The woman called back:

"Oy, wot's yer hurry, soldier? I'll give ye a special rate if ye like. Two shillin's!" The door slammed on her final offer: "All right, one shillin'! 'N' that includes yer friend too!"

Outside in the alley, Tom Peabody was crying. "I thought that was the place, honest I did! That there dog throwed me off—"

"Get a grip on yourself," Anthony told him sharply. "Tell me how much you're sure of."

"He'll be carvin' her up!" the old man wailed.

"Tom! Tom, listen to me! You can't help Molly by blubbering; you've got to think. Is the house on the left or the right?"

"The Stalker'll eat up her poor little baby!"

Anthony suddenly felt as though he'd been kicked in the groin. *"What* baby?"

"She told me just t'night," Tom sobbed, near incoherence with fear. "Just t'night she says t' me, 'Tom,' she says, 'I'm havin' a baby.' "

Christ, why hadn't he realized? Christ, why hadn't she told him? He ground his fists into his eyes, answering his own question: because he never would have let her go through with this if he had known.

"Tom." The old man was still blubbering. Anthony beat back the urge to give in to similar despair. "Tom, listen. Stop crying. You're the only one who can save Molly now. Where's the house? Which one is it? You've got to remember!"

"It's too late! He's got her! She'll be sliced to ribbons!"

"It's not too late, Tom. Think! You've got to. You've got to save Molly and the baby; they're depending on you. Molly saved you once; didn't you tell me that?" Tom nodded, sniffling back tears. "This is your chance to pay her back. But you've got to be brave—"

"I ain't brave!" Tome protested. "I'm scared near t' death!"

"So am I!" Anthony said, his voice breaking. "Help me, Tom. I love her so much—"

Tom's stooped shoulders went a little more square. " 'Tis the fifth house on the left," he said. "I'm as sure o' that as I am o' Doomsday. If it ain't in this alley, then it must be the next one over."

Or the one over from that, Anthony thought, hopelessness surging through him. Counting on Tom was lunacy. Still, what choice did he have? "I'll go and check," he told Tom, already off and running across the cobblestones.

"Hold on, I'm comin' wi' ye. Molly needs me."

Anthony didn't wait. He was already wondering how he would ever manage to forgive the old man.

35

MOLLY HAD HER eyes shut tight in a grimace of pain, figuring that Dr. Collett was less likely to recognize her if she kept her face distorted. Besides, if she looked about, who knew what horrors she might see? The Stalker was still holding her, but she could feel Collett's hands too, running over her body. "She's with child," his precise voice said. *"Very* good, Hugh. My dear, can you hear me?"

Molly nodded, eyes still clenched. "Ye've got t' help me," she whispered.

"That's just what I intend to do. How far along are you?"

"Four months, maybe."

Collett's fingers probed her belly. "Nearer five, I'd say. Does it hurt here?" Molly flinched and groaned, hoping she looked convincing. "I see. And . . . here?" Molly screamed. He patted her shoulder. "All right, my dear. Hugh, if you'll just set her down on the table and get her ready—"

"Wot are ye goin' to do?" Molly asked weakly.

"I am going to make all your pain go away."

"Ye . . . ye won't hurt my baby, will ye?"

"Of course I won't hurt your baby. Go ahead, Hugh." Molly felt the giant carry her a few yards into the room.

Anytime now would be fine, Anthony, she thought. No

need to let things go too . . . "Oy!" Stalker had laid her down atop some sort of flat plank table and was unfastening the coat she'd borrowed from Tom.

"Don't fret, my dear," Dr. Collett said soothingly. "I can hardly examine you properly while you're wrapped in those clothes. And you needn't mind Hugh. He can't speak, owing to an unfortunate accident when he was younger. But he's a most able assistant." Molly gritted her teeth as the giant's rude hands crawled over her skin. Suddenly she remembered her birthmark. Oh, God, if Collett saw that . . .

"I want my clothes on," she murmured, pushing Stalker away.

"Very well, Hugh, you may leave them on," Collett directed. "After all, she has a right to her modesty." Only an ear well trained to the inflections of the upper classes would have caught the sneer in his voice.

Eyes still shut tight, Molly felt Stalker take her wrist and circle it with some sort of strap, stretching her arm over her head. "That's just to ensure you won't make any sudden movements, my dear, that might disturb the examination," Collett purred as Stalker tied her other arm as well. "And now the feet . . . Very good. If you'll bring a basin and sponge, Hugh, we'll be set to begin."

Anthony? Molly pleaded silently. Anthony, where are you?

"Now," Dr. Collett said, "I'm going to give you something to drink that will make you sleepy."

"I don't want t' go t' sleep," Molly whispered.

"But you must, my dear, or I can't help you."

Tom hadn't mentioned getting anything to drink, Molly thought with rising panic. What would it be—laudanum? Opium? Dammit, Anthony should have been there by now. Once she took the bottle that was held to her lips, she'd have to trust in him; she wouldn't be able to help herself anymore. "I don't want t' sleep," she said again. "I'm afeard. Afeard o' dyin'."

"We all must die, my dear, when our time comes."

Molly licked her lips. "Is my time now?"

"Of course not, my dear. You're going to have a very long, happy life together, you and your baby. Give her the drink, Hugh." Molly started as the Stalker grabbed her chin, tilting it back. His fingers clawed at her, forcing her mouth to open; then she felt the warm slick liquid gliding into her throat.

Laudanum. She recognized the taste, bitter as gall beneath a surge of false sweetness. "Swallow it," Collett said. "Did you swallow it?" Molly nodded, close to choking as she struggled to hold the stuff in her mouth without letting him see. "Very well. Hugh, let go." The giant released her chin, and she fell back against the table. She turned her head to the side, parted her lips a fraction of an inch, and let the liquid trickle out onto the table, hidden by her hair. But she hadn't been able to keep from ingesting some of it. Already she felt dizzy, and wondered if it was the drug taking effect or just the paralysis of fear.

"My notebook and quill, Hugh," Collett said. "My dear, can you hear me?" Molly didn't answer. He pinched her arm, hard, and she flinched. "Ah. Not quite ready, I see. Forgive me, my dear. We'll wait a moment longer." She heard the scratch of a quill against parchment, heard him murmuring: "Age . . . let's say twenty. And approximate date of gestation . . . let's say the end of March. This should be interesting. Most interesting. I'm pleased, Hugh. Very pleased indeed. You'd best wash her off; I can scarcely see for all this dirt. Just the stomach for now; we'll start with that." As if in a dream, Molly felt her smock hiked up to her chest, and then the cold slosh of a sponge sliding over her skin. "Hmm," Collett mused, poking her belly, feeling her wrist for a pulse. "She appears quite healthy. No sign of fever . . . still, a miscarriage could be causing her pain. Suppose we find out, shall we? You'll want to sharpen the knives."

The bright slash of steel running against a whetstone, over and over again, penetrated the haze that surrounded Molly. Good God, he's set to begin, she realized dimly, the drug having taken the edge off her fear. He's going to cut me open. Where are you, Anthony?

"I'll begin with a horizontal slice, I believe," Collett went on idly. "Through the muscle wall to the uterus. It will be intriguing to see how long the fetus goes on living, Hugh, don't you think? That last one was quite disappointing. But this mother is in superb condition, and that should make a difference. Ready with those knives? Good. Bring a bowl for the blood. Don't look so glum, Hugh; you'll have your supper soon enough." Molly shuddered. "Good God, she's still twitching. Fetch a gag, Hugh; I'm getting quite anxious." Something stretched across Molly's mouth. She tried to fight it off, but her bound limbs felt as if they were underwater. "Odd, isn't it, how they always seem to know at the last?" Collett said, almost fondly. "The human body is the most remarkable thing."

Fifth house on the left. The words beat like a tattoo in Anthony's brain as he ran down the alley. Fifth house on the left—holy Christ, there were only four houses on that side, and then a garden wall. Back he ran toward the split in the road, passing Tom. "Wot's wrong?" the old man called after him. "This here's the alley; I knows it!"

"There only are four houses on the left!" Anthony shouted, fighting off an urge to throttle his neck.

"Four houses? Are ye sure?"

"Of course I'm bloody sure!"

"I could've sworn . . . ." That was all Anthony heard as he tore down the third alleyway.

There were five houses here, and the door to the fifth was locked. He took that as a good sign, battered it in with his shoulder. "Molly!" he shouted into the darkness. "Molly, where are you?" He fumbled for a flint and struck it. There wasn't any long hallway like the one Tom described. But then, the old man had been wrong about everything so far. He used the flint to light a rag from the littered floor, held it aloft. The place looked abandoned.

Rats skittered from the flame, darting for cover amidst the charred remains of a table and chairs.

"Molly's husband!" Tom called from the street. "Molly's husband, where are ye?" Anthony ignored him, moving through the house. Only two rooms on this floor, and a broken-down stair to the upper story. Was there a cellar? He searched for a door, cursed as he heard Tom coming. "What now?"

"It ain't the fifth house, I was wrong! 'Tis the third one!"

"Holy Jesu." The rag was burning Anthony's fingers; he let it drop. "Why don't you just admit it? You haven't got any bloody idea where she is, do you?" he shouted as he stamped out the flame.

" 'Tis the third house! I knows it!"

"The same way you knew it was that first alley? The same way you were sure it was on the left?" Anthony shoved him aside. "Get out of my way, you crazy old fool."

"I've made a muck o' this," Tom said penitently, earnestly, "but ye've got t' believe me this time! 'Tis the third house. Go 'n' see, Molly's husband! Hurry!"

Anthony hesitated, feeling bone-weary. What was the use? It had to have been half an hour since he'd last seen the Stalker. More than likely she was dead by now.

"Ye loves her, don't ye?" Tom asked.

"Of course I love her, what the hell do you think?"

"Then ye'd best go 'n' get her."

"Third house?" Anthony asked in resignation.

"Third house," Tom confirmed. "Ye goes down the passageway t' the end 'n' then down the stairs."

The door to the third house wasn't even locked. More sure than ever that Tom was wrong, Anthony stepped inside and struck his flint. There was a long passageway, with another door at the far end. Anthony moved toward it, listening, daring to hope. Was that the murmur of a voice or just the scurry of rats? "Molly?" he shouted, and from the bowels of the house heard a crash like the breaking of an earthenware bowl.

"Molly!" he shouted again, trying the door at the end of the passage. It was locked and solid. He butted it with his shoulder, but the wood didn't give. "Collett, I know you're in there!" he roared, running at the door again. It flew open from the inside, swinging toward him, knocking him back against the passage wall. He had a momentary glimpse of Stalker's face before the giant swung at him, sending him crashing to the floor with the flint. It sputtered out, and in the darkness Stalker struck him again.

The man's fists were like hammers. Reeling from the blows, Anthony scrambled away on his hands and knees, tasting blood on his tongue. He could hear the hiss of Stalker's breath, used it to take a bearing. If he could just get past him to the stairs . . .

The giant lunged at him, grappling him to the floor. His hand went for Anthony's throat; Anthony clawed for his eyes, connected, felt flesh tear under his nails. Stalker sprang back, but never made a sound. There was something eerie, unnerving about so silent an opponent. Anthony held his own breath, listened for Stalker's, then ran at him with his head lowered. He caught him in the back, near the kidney, and felt him go sprawling forward in a crash of limbs. Anthony aimed for the doorway, struck the wall, tried again. He fell across Stalker's leg, shoved it away, and kept going. This time he found the jamb and reached the stairs.

They were narrow and twisting, the treads worn in the center from centuries of footsteps. On the third quarter-turn, Anthony could see light ahead. Stalker was coming after him, breathing hard. He moves fast for such a big bloody monster, Anthony thought, just as a blow from behind sent him reeling headlong into the stone wall.

He flung out his hands, pushed backward, and brought his head up into the giant's chin, having the satisfaction of hearing it snap closed. The pleasure was short-lived; before he took a step, Stalker had him again, pinning his arms behind his back. But Anthony could see into the cellar now, and what he saw gave him a surge of furious strength. Against a backdrop of shelves and ghastly surgeon's tools, Molly lay pale and motionless, trussed to a table banked by candles set on tall iron stands, like a funeral bier. Collett stood over her with a knife.

"Don't touch her, Collett, you bastard!" Anthony warned, shaking the giant off. "Get away from her!"

Collett looked up, perplexed. "Ballenrose? Is that you?"

Behind Anthony, Stalker had paused as though awaiting instructions. "Well, go on. Get him, Hugh," the doctor said somewhat impatiently. "We can hardly let him live after he's seen this place."

Anthony tore his gaze from Molly's prostrate form, forced his pain and rage into clear, simple hatred for the unassailable Stalker. With Molly dead, all deals were off; there was no need to keep Collett alive. Once he'd finished with the giant, he'd kill the doctor too.

"Get him, Hugh!" Collett snapped. "Break his neck and have done!"

The voiceless giant grabbed a chair and hurled it at Anthony. He sprang aside, and the chair smashed into the jars that lined the shelves on the far side of the cellar, filling the air with an ungodly smell.

"My collection!" Collett cried. "Watch out for my collection!"

Grimacing horribly, Stalker lunged. Anthony leapt aside, skidding across the wet stones. Stalker threw another chair, shattering more jars.

"Dammit, Hugh, those are my brains!" Collett watched, aghast, as glass flew through the air. "You're ruining everything, and I won't have it! Finish him off now, do you hear me?"

Stalker charged, head down, like a maddened bull. Anthony feinted left, went right, but even so, the giant's huge shoulder caught him, sent him sprawling onto the floor. "Hugh! Catch!" Collett cried, throwing him the knife he held. Anthony somersaulted backward, knocking Stalker off-balance, and the blade skittered past him. They both lunged for it at once. Anthony's hand closed over the hilt a split second before Stalker's did, but Stalker slammed his wrist against the stone floor, and he could not hold on.

"Just keep him there, Hugh! I'll kill him," Collett ordered angrily, reaching for another knife. Stalker hauled Anthony up by the elbows, pinning him to his chest, then lifted him bodily into the air. He sent Anthony crashing into a bank of candles close to the table where Molly lay. They fell to the floor, and Anthony realized what the odor of the liquid in the jars reminded him of—brandy turned bad. One of the puddles ignited into jets of blue flame.

"Now you've done it!" Collett screeched at Hugh, running for the notebook he'd left on the table. Stalker stood stock-still, seemingly immobilized by the spectacle of the bright blue flames. Anthony grabbed one of the tall iron candlesticks, yanked the wax taper from its point, and rushed him. The point caught him just below the breastbone, thrusting into his chest.

Looking surprised, Stalker reached down and pulled the candlestick free. Blood spurted after it in a thick stream. "Carotid artery," Collett murmured absently. The giant turned to him, eyes wide. His mouth flew open. For the first time, Anthony saw the healed-over stump that had been his tongue; it waggled up and down with the giant's long soundless scream. When he fell, the whole earth seemed to shake.

Collett made for the stairs, his notebook tucked into his coat. Anthony started to follow, then stopped. The flames were spreading, leaping from puddle to puddle across the floor, already licking at Stalker's clothing. In another two minutes, the whole cellar would be filled with fire. Let the doctor escape. He couldn't bear to leave Molly's dead body there.

With one of Collett's knives he hacked through the straps that held her arms and legs, averting his eyes from her face. As he lifted her up from the table, the remaining jars along the wall began to explode from the heat, with loud hard pops like shots from a gun. He groped his way toward the staircase, found it, climbed it, gasping for air. As he neared the top, he thought he felt the body he held shifting. But it was only the impact of another series of explosions from the cellar below.

At the top of the stairs he slammed the door behind him, closed off the inferno, already wondering how he would ever close off his grief. He emerged from the house into a warm July night that was glorious with starlight.

"Molly's husband?" a small voice said. "Molly's husband, I got him!" Anthony looked down, looked away from the stars, and saw Tom Peabody sitting on the ground—or, rather, sitting atop a body that was sprawled on the ground. "I tripped him," Tom said proudly. "Never even saw me, he didn't. I did it for Molly. Is she all right?"

"She's . . ." Anthony couldn't say it, felt as mute as Stalker as he pulled his cloak around her lifeless body. Tom's upturned face went pale as the moon.

"Oh, Lord, I've lived too long," the old man whispered, "seen too many things—"

"I didn't kill her," Collett rasped, his face in the dirt.

"Shut up!" Anthony said, and kicked him in the teeth. It felt so good he did it again, would have kept on kicking had not the body he held in his arms stirred and whispered his name.

"Molly?" he said in disbelief.

"Anthony." She raised her hand, stroked his face. "Knew you'd come. But you surely . . . took your time about it."

"Molly!" He kissed her, crying, felt her heart beating against his hand. "Oh, God in heaven, Molly—"

"I *said* I didn't kill her," Collett noted superciliously.

"He told ye t' shut up, didn't he?" Tom asked, and pulled the doctor's hair.

"We got lost," Anthony tried to explain to Molly.

"I got us lost, he means," Tom put in shyly.

"It doesn't matter," Molly whispered.

"When I saw you lying there . . ." Anthony shuddered at the memory. "I thought you were dead!"

"He gave me a drug—laudanum." She shook her head to clear it. "I spit most of it out—"

"There's no harm done," Collett insisted.

"Shut yer bloody mouth," Tom told him, and turned to Anthony. "Where's the Stalker?"

"Down below," he told him. "Dead."

"Oy, there's a bit o' good news, eh, Molly Flowers?"

"Molly Flowers?" Collett echoed. "Molly *Flowers?*"

"That's right," said Anthony, holding her close. "Your final victim was my wife."

Collett tried to push up from the ground, but Tom wasn't budging. "Here, now, Ballenrose. If you know who she is, I'd think you'd count it a favor to be rid of her! A commoner, a felon—"

"You just don't get it, do you, Collett?" Anthony demanded. "You really believe all those people you butchered didn't matter, had no worth, just because they happened to be poor."

"You're the one doesn't get it," Collett retorted. "The Duke of Buckingham intends to use your marriage to ruin you! Believe you me, you'd be better off with her dead."

"Tom . . ." Anthony began.

"Aye?"

"There's a notebook inside the good doctor's coat. Would you get it out for me?"

"My pleasure.'

"Get your hands off me, you filthy old man!"

Ignoring Collett's protests, Tom retrieved the book. "Here ye go, then."

"Thank you, Tom. Tell me, Dr. Collett. Do you have enough confidence in your elite beliefs for me to make this book of your experiments public?"

"I . . ." Collett paused, swallowed.

"I didn't think so," said Anthony, and Molly smiled grimly. "It's Monday night, isn't it? Tuesday morning, really. Molly, love, if you're sure you're all right . . ."

"Oh, I am," she assured him. "And you're crazy if you think I'd miss this."

"Good. Then suppose we all take a ride in the country. To Cliveden. It's time we paid a call on the Duke of Buckingham."

36

Dawn was breaking in the eastern sky as the coach climbed the rolling hill toward Cliveden, just as it had, Molly realized, on her first journey there so many months ago. She'd thought the place heaven then, and her new uncle the most wonderful man in the world. Well, she'd grown up since then, learned that, as the poets said, not everything that glittered was gold. Though her heart was heavy with regret for the cost the lesson had exacted, she was filled with peace too. The storms were finished. This dawn truly marked the beginning of a new day.

On the seat opposite, Tom Peabody snored and shifted positions, his drooping head finally coming to rest against Dr. Collett's shoulder. Hampered by his bound hands, the doctor tried to shrug him off and only succeeded in landing Tom's head on his lap. "Good God," he muttered, squirming toward the side of the coach. "Get him off me!" Tom snored on obliviously. It was probably the best sleep he'd had in the past twenty years.

Molly's own head was resting exceedingly comfortably on Anthony's shoulder; turning to look at him, she saw him smile, his arm tightening around her. Collett's presence had made their reunion less than intimate, but that was all right too. There would be time enough for everything she longed to tell him, share with him, once this meeting was over. Once this was finished, they'd have all the time in the world.

Anthony's hand crept toward her belly, gently resting there. Molly smiled. "I shall never forget the look on that poor Bess's face when you introduced me as her new mistress."

"Bare feet and rags and all." Anthony laughed.

"Not to mention my hair." Molly put a rueful hand to her cropped tresses; pale gold roots peeked out from beneath the dyed brown.

"She liked you, though," Anthony said with satisfaction.

"She liked seeing you happy. I heard all about how difficult you've been these past months—not to mention the appalling increase in your intake of brandy."

"Bess told you all that in the time it took to bathe you and change your clothes?" he asked incredulously.

"All that and much more."

"Such as what?"

"Oh, a load of drivel about how wonderful you are."

"But you didn't believe that."

"Not a word of it." She kissed him. Dr. Collett made a small snort of disgust. Tom belched in his sleep.

The carriage clattered onto the drive, rousing the sleepy gateman. "Who goes there?" he called to the driver.

"Dr. John Collett."

"Oy, go ahead."

The tall iron gates opened. "Kind of you to lend us your name to gain admittance, Collett," Anthony said cheerfully. The doctor growled in reply.

Molly, scanning the windows of the upper stories, saw a bit of movement behind one curtained casement. By the time the carriage pulled to a stop, Lady Katherine was waiting at the front doors.

"Mary Catherine," said the pale, ghostly duchess as the footman helped Molly down. "How lovely to see you."

"It's just Molly now, milady." Behind her, Anthony

was hauling Collett out of the coach and rousing Tom from his nap. Lady Katherine never batted an eye. "We've come to see your husband."

"I'd rather hoped you would," said the duchess. Behind her, the nervous butler was buttoning himself into his livery.

"His grace is in his rooms, m'lady," he stammered. "He gave explicit orders not to be disturbed."

"Did he?" said the duchess.

"Aye, that he did. 'N' his door'll be locked."

"Ah," said the duchess. "No matter. I've got the key." She produced it from the folds of her filmy gown. "No need to look so surprised," she told the butler. "I *am* his wife." Then she beckoned to Molly and the others. "Won't you come this way?"

"This is some place ye've got here," Tom noted as they mounted the white marble stairs.

"Thank you," said the duchess. "I don't believe we've been introduced."

"Oh. Forgive me," said Molly. "Lady Katherine, this is Tom Peabody. Tom, the Duchess of Buckingham."

"Please t' meet ye," said Tom, with a gallant bow.

"And you know Anthony. Lord Ballenrose, Lady Katherine," Molly went on.

"It's been a number of years," the duchess said softly, turning to Anthony. "But we've always been companions in grief. I've often hoped—often prayed—that you didn't blame me for poor Magdalene's death."

Anthony shook his head. "I never did."

"Anthony and I are married now," Molly said shyly.

"So I gathered. How pleased King Charles will be to have the feud between our families finished at last."

Molly glanced at Anthony. "Actually, Lady Katherine, there's something you should know. I've found out I'm not really your niece at all."

"I know that," the duchess said. "I always did. That silly cow Frances could never have produced a daughter as smart as you. Who cares? I like you." She put the key to a door, turned it, and flung the door open, singing out, "Good morning, George!"

"What the bloody hell—" Startled out of a sound sleep, the duke sat up, blinking, looking oddly comical in a white nightshirt and cap. "Kate, is that you?"

She went to the windows, threw the curtains open to let in a flood of light. "It most certainly is. What a glorious day! You have visitors, George."

"Visitors?" He pushed back the nightcap, shielded the sun from his eyes. "Close those bloody draperies!"

"George?" In the bed beside him, a shape stirred sleepily, raising motes of dust that danced in the bright shafts of light. "George, what is it?"

"Rise and shine, Clare," said the duchess, yanking back the bedclothes to reveal her naked niece.

The duke snatched the sheets up again. "For God's sake, Kate, we're not decent!"

"*There's* an understatement," said the duchess, "though I'm a trifle surprised to hear you admit it. These are guests I just knew you couldn't wait to see. Lord Ballenrose—"

"Ballenrose?" the duke echoed, baffled.

"—and his wife."

"His *wife?*" That got the duke's attention; he leapt from the bed, revealing pale, rather spindly legs beneath the edge of his shirt, and caught sight of the cowering doctor.

"John, are your hands bound?" he demanded as he grabbed for his breeches.

"George," Collett said miserably, "there's been a bit of a problem."

The duke had his breeches on by now, and with them some measure of dignity. "Nothing I can't handle, I'm sure. Congratulations, Mary Catherine, on your return. I'll be placing that notice in tomorrow's newspapers."

"Oh, I don't think so, Uncle George."

"How can you *bear* to have her call you that?" Clare asked, shuddering as she clutched the sheets to her chest.

The duke was cocky now, contemplating Molly. "Just what, pray tell, do you imagine will stop me?"

"Self-interest," Molly told him. "It's the only thing that ever motivates you, isn't it? You'd do well to remember that, dear Cousin Clare."

Buckingham laughed. "And how precisely could it be in my best interest not to tell the world about you?"

"If you do, I'll be forced to make public the truth about how you plucked me out of the Fleet to masquerade as your niece. I rather imagine you'd find it quite embarrassing to have your little scheme exposed."

"Not to mention," Anthony put in, "the risk of criminal charges."

"What criminal charges?" the duke demanded.

"Well, fraud, to begin with. You misrepresented Molly's identity to induce me to wed her. I could certainly win a hefty sum in a civil case based on that. And interfering with the course of justice—"

"How?"

"You bribed Warden Fell to get me out of the Fleet before my sentence expired," Molly noted.

"And," Anthony added, "made sure he destroyed any record that she'd ever been there."

"You're clutching at straws," the duke said airily. "Go ahead. Bring your lawsuits. It will be my word against hers."

"Not exactly," said Molly. "We've got a witness. Someone who knew every detail of your plot right from the start."

The duke's upper lip curled in a sneer. "I hope she doesn't mean you, John," he told the doctor. "Because if she does, I'd like to remind you I'm aware of certain practices, shall we say, that could destroy your career and your reputation."

"That's just it, George," Collett said morosely. "So are they."

"Do you know," Anthony said, "I believe the Duke of

Buckingham has just admitted he's an accessory to murder.''

"You're crazy," snapped the duke.

"They found the laboratory, George," the doctor told him. "They've got my notebook."

"Not to mention two victims—live victims," Anthony said. "Mr. Peabody and Molly."

Tom approached Clare, raising up his ragged shirt. "D'ye want t' see my scars?" She screeched and backed away.

"I don't know exactly what you're talking about," Lady Katherine said calmly, "but I'd be more than willing to testify against my husband."

"Testify against me for *what?*" Buckingham demanded.

"Anything at all, dear," the duchess said.

"I don't think that will be necessary," Anthony told her. "After all, the duke must recognize there's far too much at stake for him to risk exposing Molly."

Clare screeched again. "But you've *got* to expose her, George! What about my inheritance?"

The duke looked at Anthony, his fine eyes narrowed. "What is it you're proposing I do?"

"Why, nothing at all. Maintain the status quo. Mary Catherine—"

"Molly," Molly said.

"Molly remains your niece and my wife. Dr. Collett will have to give up his practice—"

"I've been thinking," said Molly. "That's rather a waste, isn't it? The man does have talent. Perhaps it might be put to use as staff physician at the Fleet. Without pay. And with a decent warden to keep him in line."

"I'd sooner die," Collett snapped.

Molly looked hard at him. "You're in no position to make choices, I'm afraid."

"They've got you, John," the duke acknowledged grudgingly. "They've got me too."

"The fox," said Lady Katherine with great satisfaction,

"has got himself outfoxed. I never thought I'd see the day."

"But what about my inheritance?" Clare wailed.

The duke shrugged. "That can't be helped, my dear."

She sat up on the bed, a wild-eyed virago wrapped in a sheet. "Well, if you think I whored all over court for you for nothing, Uncle, you're sadly mistaken! What's to keep *me* from telling the truth about Mary Catherine?"

"Self-interest, I daresay," the duke told her blandly. "Even in this modern day and age, a girl who sleeps with her uncle isn't likely to be welcomed at court."

"You wouldn't," Clare hissed. "You wouldn't dare tell!"

"Not unless you left me no choice, my dear."

"George?" Tousle-haired, rubbing her eyes, the Countess of Shrewsbury appeared in the doorway. "What's all this shouting about? Are you ill?" She put her hands down, saw Clare, and froze. Her mouth opened slowly, wide, like a fish's, closed, than opened again. "My God," she said hoarsely. "God in heaven, it's true. Your sister tried to tell me—"

"Not now, Agnes, please," Buckingham told her.

"Not now? Not *now?*" The countess was winding up to full-blown rage. "Then when, you bloody pander? You filthy, louse-ridden swine, I gave you the best years of my *life*—"

"Agnes, if you don't mind, this is hardly the time or the place—"

"I stood by and watched you kill my husband, you despicable creature! I abandoned my son, my own flesh and blood, for you!"

"Live and learn, they say," the duchess murmured.

Her husband threw her a scowl. "Agnes, we'll deal with this later," he said very firmly. The countess hurled a vase at him. "Agnes!" He jumped aside and lost his grip on his breeches. They fell to his knees, sending him sprawling. Lady Agnes turned her wrath on Clare.

"And as for you, you cheap little hussy—"

"Believe me, Lady Agnes, I share your opinion of my uncle completely!" Clare said hastily, and to prove it, hit him with a candlestick.

"That makes it unanimous, George, dear," the duchess said with a beatific smile, and dropped a water pitcher on his head.

Molly was loath to interrupt their orgy of vengeance, but the absence of Jessica scared her. "Clare, where *is* your sister?"

"Dear God." Lady Agnes paused, about to fling a shoe at the duke. "Poor Jessica! He's got her locked in the dungeon!"

Anthony hauled the duke up from the floor and slammed him back against the elegant moiré-covered wall. "I'll kill you myself if any harm's come to her!"

"I'm sure she's perfectly all right," Buckingham said quickly. "It isn't as though I've been starving her or anything. It was just a little solitary confinement. For her own good, really—"

"He's got the only key," the duchess put in.

Anthony tightened his grip. "Give it to me, you bastard."

The duke fished for his purse. "I want to make one thing clear," he said, nodding at Clare. "The rats were *her* idea."

"Rats?" Molly echoed, appalled. Lady Agnes screeched.

"Just two rats," Clare explained hastily. "Two tiny little rats. And we were going to go down to check on her first thing this morning, honestly we—"

"Let's go," Anthony ordered, pushing the duke toward the door, jerking his head at Clare. "You too. And you, Collett, just in case. And by Christ, if she's hurt, I'll feed all three of you to the rats."

Back down the marble staircase they trooped, all of them, with Clare still wrapped in her sheet. Lady Katherine and Lady Agnes came too, the latter muttering the most uncouth imprecations at her lover under her breath.

Tom Peabody trailed along after everyone else, pausing from time to time to admire a painting or the heraldic shields that decorated the walls.

The passageway to the dungeon led off the kitchens. The servants readying breakfast there stared in wonder as their master was paraded past, saw the expression on his face, and quickly looked away. Lady Agnes was still cursing. Tom Peabody heisted a whole poached trout from a tray as he went by, tucking it into his coat, defiantly eyeing the scullery maid who'd been about to cover it with sauce.

But any humor in the strange processional was lost on Molly. The moment she started down the stairs to the dungeon, all she could think of was the Fleet. The stout stone walls held the same clammy, bone-chilling dampness as they led underground. Even the smell was the same, that unmistakable, unforgettable odor compounded of rot and neglect and despair. She began to pray.

There wasn't a sound coming from behind the small wooden door at the foot of the staircase. "Open it," Anthony ordered Buchingham tersely. The duke hesitated. "Open it, damn you!" The key turned in the lock. Molly held her breath. The door swung open wide.

The gloom inside the cell was impenetrable. "Jess?" Molly whispered, just as Anthony struck his flint. Three sets of twin points of light were revealed in its glare. Then, as her sight adjusted to the dimness, Molly saw her friend sitting cross-legged on the floor, grimy as any inmate of the Fleet had ever been, thin and mushroom-pale, but very much alive, with a rat perched atop each knee.

"Uncle," she said, her voice sounding rusted and weak. "Clare." Her blue eyes found her sister's, held them as she patted the creatures on her knees. "The most remarkable thing. I've discovered rats are very much like my family. Disgusting as they are, if they're all you've got, you learn to live with them anyway."

"Oh Jess." Molly ran to help her up, hugging her thin shoulders. "I'm so sorry. Forgive me—"

"There's nothing to forgive you for, Mary Catherine. Tell me, though. Is Harry Wallingford wedded?"

"Is Harry wedded?" Molly looked to Anthony. "I don't know—"

"Not the last I heard," he assured Jessica.

"There! I knew it!" she said triumphantly, and stuck her tongue out at Clare. "It was all lies, wasn't it, about Harry and that awful Alice Kenton. Just like that ridiculous story you made up about Mary Catherine not really being Uncle George's niece."

Clare hesitated. Buckingham murmured, "Self-interest, Clare . . ."

"Oh, all right," she snarled. "It was all just lies."

"Well, then." Jessica smiled sweetly. "I'm ready for a meal and a bath."

Anthony laughed and hugged her. "Hold on just one minute," Tom Peabody said, blocking the doorway.

"What now?" Buckingham asked, rolling his eyes.

"Ye're the Duke o' Buckingham, ain't ye?"

"Brilliant deduction," the duke said haughtily.

Tom pointed at Molly. " 'N' ye're his niece."

"So I am," Molly said.

Tom nodded thoughtfully. "Well, I found ye." They all looked at him rather blankly. "I found ye, Molly," he repeated. "There's a reward, ain't there? Five hundred pounds."

"By God, he's right," Anthony noted, grinning. "You owe Mr. Peabody five hundred pounds, your grace."

"The bloody hell I do."

"How in the world do you know about that reward, Tom?" Molly asked in surprise.

"Why, 'twere the talk o' the market, weren't it? Wot d'ye take me for, a fool?"

"I'm sure no one would ever do that," the Duchess of Buckingham said. "You'll have to pay up, George."

"If you think I'm handing five hundred pounds over to some ragamuffin lunatic—"

"Hey, watch wot ye're callin' me, mate," Tom warned, poking a finger at the duke's shirtfront.

"—With a fish stuck in his coat, for God's sake . . ." Buckingham went on, seeing its tail sticking out.

"What kind of fish?" Jessica asked hungrily.

"Trout. Care for some?" Tom asked, proffering it.

"Pay up, Uncle George," Clare said nastily, sloe eyes glinting.

"Aye, pay him, you cheap, no-good—"

"Lady Agnes!" Jessica said in shock, through a mouth-ful of trout.

"Pay him, George," the duchess stated firmly.

"All right, I'll pay him!" Buckingham said in disgust. "Anything for some bloody peace and quiet!"

Tom bowed politely, moving out of the doorway. "After ye, yer grace." The duke stomped past him up the stairs.

Molly took Tom's arm as they followed the rest of the party back to the kitchens. "What will you do with all that money, Tom?"

He scratched his chin. "That'll take a bit o' thought, I reckon. Get myself a suit o' clothes, first off. Nothin' flashy like yer uncle wears, though. Good sturdy linsey-woolsey, that's for me. Maybe wi' a bit o' lace at the throat."

"That won't cost more than ten pounds," Anthony noted. "What about the rest?"

"Put it in me pockets, maybe," Tom said, grinning. "Walk about the market listenin' to it jangle. Oh, 'n' buy a mess o' bones off Eben Campbell for all the dogs in Smithfield, for keepin' me safe from that Stalker all these years."

Anthony kissed Molly's ear. "We'll buy some too," he said.

EPILOGUE

St. James's Palace, London,
August 1, 1673

"Your majesty." Ice-blue skirts in her hands, Molly made a flawless curtsy to King Charles, not hampered in the least by the unmistakable swell of her belly.

"Lady Mary Catherine." The king drew her up by her fingertips, smiling with delight. "How positively splendid to see you again! My court has been impoverished by your absence." He paused, black brows knit. "Where exactly were you?"

"France," Anthony said from Molly's side.

"France?"

"Yes, your majesty. On our honeymoon."

"Your honeymoon. Ah. But I thought . . . I'd rather gathered the impression that Lady Mary Catherine was missing."

"Since my wife's uncle did not approve of our marriage," Anthony said smoothly, "we decided to elope. Alas, the message we left for milord Buckingham never reached him. Naturally, he was distraught at Molly's disappearance."

"Molly?" said the king.

"A childhood nickname," Anthony explained. "My wife prefers it."

"Ah. Well, then, Lady Molly, welcome back! I gather you made good use of your honeymoon, eh, Anthony? A little heir coming along, I see!'' Winking, he elbowed Anthony in the side.

"Excuse me, Charles darling.'' Louise Keroualle was tugging at his sleeve. "I simply must ask Lady Mary Catherine—is that the latest fashion from Paris?''

"This?'' Molly patted her pale-gold hair, cropped shorter than her ears to remove the last traces of dye. "Absolutely. Do you like it?''

"It's very . . . well, daring. Don't I wish I had the courage!''

"Not to mention the face,'' Charles murmured.

"I beg your pardon?''

"Nothing. Nothing at all. Well, Anthony! I take it you and your new uncle-in-law have buried the hatchet, so to speak? Since you've both come to my little *soirée* this evening—''

"Oh, is Uncle George here?'' Anthony turned, saw the duke just entering the reception room, and waved, calling loudly, "Uncle George! Over here!''

Looking infinitely pained, Buckingham began to thread his way through the press of courtiers. "I'm pleased to say Uncle George has come around to the notion of our marriage quite nicely,'' Molly told the king, biting her cheek.

"I'm ever so glad. These silly feuds between my nobles truly do distress me. I was saying as much just last night to Louise, wasn't I, Louise?''

Louise Keroualle was still staring at Molly's head. "Don't they even *curl* it?''

"My husband isn't fond of curls,'' said Molly.

"Oh. I see.''

Buckingham had reached the king's dais. Anthony clapped him soundly on the back. "Uncle George! So good to see you again!''

"Your majesty.'' The duke bowed to the king. "Madame Keroualle. You're looking more lovely than ever.''

"You're too kind, your grace.'' She might be the king's

mistress, but that didn't keep Louise from simpering at the handsome duke.

"I was just telling Anthony," Charles said, "how glad I am that you and he have become family. There's no bond on earth so strong as blood."

"There certainly isn't, is there, Uncle George?" Molly asked, slipping her arm through his. He growled between his teeth.

"And best of all," Anthony said brightly, "now that Uncle George and I are allies, we can work together for the good of the kingdom. Can't we, Uncle George?" The duke made an indeterminate noise. "And may I tell you, your majesty, where we'd like to start?"

"If you must," Charles said resignedly.

"A complete overhaul of your majesty's prisons," Anthony pushed on. "Starting with the Fleet. If it please your majesty, I thought you might replace the warden there with a most able gentleman I've found. He's here this evening, as a matter of fact. Michael!" He gestured to Michael Nivens, who was talking to Jessica on the far side of the room.

"Your majesty." Jessica curtsied, pulling Michael forward. "Mr. Nivens has the most fascinating ideas on prison reform; you really must hear them!"

"What, here? Now?"

"No time like the present, isn't that right, Uncle George?" Anthony asked heartily.

"I've never known you to take an interest in prison reform, Lady Jessica," said the king, looking puzzled.

"I've become quite interested in the subject of late, your majesty, and I just know Michael will make a splendid warden!" she said warmly.

The king turned to Buckingham. "You do concur in his appointment, George?"

"I . . ." The duke winced; Molly was pinching his side. "I do."

"Well, then, let it be done," Charles said grandly. "See to it, Anthony."

"Thank you, your majesty. There are a few more matters I'd like to discuss with you if you have a moment." He ticked them off on his fingers. "Lower rents for the poor. Court reform. Increased revenues for St. Bartholomew's Hospital—"

"Yes, yes," said the king, his eyes somewhat glazed. "Write up some proposals, why don't you, my good man? I'm sure that with both your and milord Buckingham's signatures on the bills, you'll have no trouble getting them through the Parliament."

"I'll do that, your majesty," Anthony said, and bowed. "But if I could just mention one more thing—"

"Isn't it time for dancing?" the king asked with an air of desperation. "Do let's have some dancing! Come, Louise!" He signaled to the musicians and escaped onto the floor.

The duke narrowed his eyes at Anthony. "If you think I intend to put my name to a parcel of bills that will only result in my taxes going sky-high—"

"Lord Ballenrose!" Portly Lord Phipps came up to Anthony, pressing his hand. "Just heard about your marriage, my boy. Congratulations! Good to have you on our side, isn't it, George?" He smiled and moved on.

"Or you on mine," Anthony murmured, and smiled at Buckingham. "I'll have copies of those bills to you in the morning for your signature. Surely a bit more in taxes is preferable to a lengthy lawsuit for fraud?"

"It's bloody blackmail!" the duke sputtered. "How far do you intend to push me, Ballenrose?"

"Just as far as I can." The duke stormed away as Anthony called to him, "Good night, Uncle George!"

Molly's laughter bubbled over. "Oh, Anthony. I almost feel sorry for him."

"*I* don't," Jessica said. "Come on, Michael. I want to hear more about your ideas for the Fleet."

"Jess." Molly caught her arm, pulling her back. "Isn't that Harry Wallingford over there? Shouldn't you go talk to him?"

"I said hello when I came in." Jessica looked at Michael, who was talking to Anthony, and her blue eyes glowed. "I never really noticed before how boring Harry can be. I mean, he doesn't have any purpose in life, does he? Not like Michael."

"No, he's not a bit like Michael," Molly agreed, inwardly suspecting that before the year was out, the Duke of Buckingham would have a commoner for a nephew-in-law.

With a cheery wave, Jessica led Michael away. "They look well together, don't they?" Molly asked her husband fondly.

"That they do." Something caught his attention across the room. "Uh-oh. Cousin Clare's here. Say, aren't those your sapphires she's wearing?"

"Victors can afford to be generous," Molly told him. "I let her keep them. Why not? She'll need all the dowry she can get with a reputation like hers."

"And no man will ever marry her for her sweet temper," he agreed with a grin, watching as Clare, dark eyes flashing, turned a scornful shoulder on the earnest young lord who'd been floundering to pay her a compliment.

"I wish her well, though," Molly said softly. "Just as I wish Lady Agnes well now that she has gone back to live with her son."

"Young Shrewsbury must be an extraordinarily forgiving chap," Anthony said with a frown. "To take her in after she's spent years as the mistress of the man who killed his father—"

"Didn't you tell me once you admire someone who puts loyalty to the family above all else?"

"I never said I don't admire him. I just doubt that I could do the same."

"Well, I am glad for him," said Molly, settling her skirts. "I think the desire for revenge is the most destructive emotion there can be."

Anthony arched a brow. "Was that barb aimed at me?"

"Of course not, darling." She paused. "Do you think,

though, that you could ever forgive Buckingham for what he did to Magdalene?''

"Forgive him?'' He shook his head. "No. No more than you can ever forgive Dr. Collett for what he did to Aunt May. But let my grief rest, bury it, and get on with my life—that I can and will do.'' He smiled at her and offered his arm. "So, wife, shall we dance?''

"I'd rather we went home to do our dancing,'' Molly told him. "If you don't mind.''

"Not at all,'' he said, and kissed her so soundly that a murmur went up from the crowd.

"And they're married, if you can believe it,'' Molly heard Louise Keroualle hiss to Lord Dacry's mistress.

She laughed and returned Anthony's kiss. "Let's go.''

Hand in hand, they started toward the receiving-room doors. Halfway there, Anthony stopped dead. "My dear God in heaven.''

"What is it?'' Molly asked, craning to see above the heads in front of her.

"Lady Katherine is here.''

"You're jesting!'' But the crowd parted, and Molly saw the Duchess of Buckingham, looking frail but ethereal in a pale silk gown. As she watched, she witnessed something even more amazing: the duke, catching sight of his wife, took leave of the delectable young viscountess with whom he'd been flirting and hurried to Lady Katherine's side. He guided her to a chair, signaled for wine, ordered a footstool—"Why, he's being positively solicitous!'' Molly whispered in astonishment. "What in the world do you suppose is going on?''

"I'm sure I don't know,'' Anthony murmured back, "but were I to venture a guess, I'd hazard it's occurred to his grace that there is only one means of making certain all his worldly goods don't someday pass to the former Molly Willoughby of Smithfield.''

Molly's brow furrowed. "What means is that?''

"Begetting himself a legitimate heir.''

"Dear God.'' Molly bit her lip as the duke proffered

his wife a plate of sweetmeats. "I don't know if we have done Aunt Kate a favor or not!"

"It's bound to be preferable to being holed up at Cliveden with the whole world thinking you're mad." Anthony laughed aloud as Lady Katherine rejected the sweetmeats and sent her husband trotting off for something else, dutiful as a potboy at the Dog and Feathers. "Anyway, it looks as though she's enjoying herself."

"I should almost like to stay and watch this show!" Molly laughed, too, at Anthony's crestfallen expression. "I said 'almost,' didn't I? Let's be gone."

They rode back to Ballenrose Hall beneath a black velvet sky stitched with stars, seamed through with pale gold moonlight. Molly leaned her head on Anthony's shoulder, her hand clasped in his hand, reveling in the sweet tranquil ease of their silence together, anticipating the passionate pleasures of the night yet to come.

"Wait," Anthony told her as the carriage drew up to the front doors.

"Wait? Whatever for?"

"A surprise. to celebrate the evening's success." While she watched, he leapt down from the coach, peeked inside the house, and then returned for her, lifting her into his arms.

"You've already carried me over the thresh—" Molly began, and then stopped as the front doors opened, as she saw the long hall banked with vases of roses—hundreds and hundreds of roses, of every color and kind: great fat damasks, overblown mosses, thick-petaled Provences, sweetbriars, even tiny dog roses, all pouring their perfume out onto the air. There were roses all along the staircase, roses hanging from the landings above, roses twined around table feet and draped over chairs . . .

"Oh, Anthony." She stared in wonder at the glorious profusion, the sheer gluttony of flowers. "You must have bought up every rose in London!"

" 'N' then some," Bess said, beaming proudly at her

master. "That friend o' yers, mum, that Piers wot brought 'em, he said he ordered two whole shipments from Spain."

"Piers ordered roses from Spain by *himself?*"

"That's wot he said, mum."

"Well, I'll be damned. I guess he meant it when he said he was managing well enough without me," Molly said ruefully.

"Oy, aye, mum," Bess rattled on, not noticing her mistress's chagrin. "Ye know, he ain't half bad for a foreigner, really. Handsome, too, in a foreign sort o' way, with that yellow hair 'n' them big shoulders o' his."

"Has he got big shoulders, Bess?" Anthony asked, tongue in cheek. "I never noticed."

"Oy, he's built ever so nice," Bess said, and her master laughed. "Well, so he is, 'n' why shouldn't I say it? Asked me t' the Queen's Fair wi' him next Thursday, didn't he?"

"And you're going?" Anthony demanded.

Bess nodded. "Why shouldn't I? Earned myself a day off, didn't I? It ain't the be-all 'n' end-all o' my life, ye know, t' be waitin' on ye."

"And here I thought it was. But what will your mother say, Bess, when she hears you're stepping out with a foreigner?"

"If she's got a peg o' sense—which she ain't—she'll be glad enough t' see I've found a fellow wi' a head for business," Bess said comfortably. "Why, look at her, married for forty years t' a stableman. Mind ye, I love Pop, honest I do, but these days a girl's got t' have some ambitions for herself. Why, I—"

"Excuse us, Bess." Anthony shifted Molly in his arms. "But if it's all right with you, I'll take my wife upstairs."

Bess shrugged. "If ye like. Bring up some supper, shall I?"

He'd started toward the stairs, threw over his shoulder, "We'll let you know. We'll ring."

Molly was laughing against his chest. "Sorry," he whispered, "I didn't mean for my surprise to involve a discourse from Bess on her family."

"I didn't mind. I'd be ever so happy if she and Piers made a match of it."

"I wouldn't be," he said glumly. "I'd have to hire a new maid."

"That's my job now."

"Oh. Well, then. Here's to Bess and Piers!"

As he carried her up the staircase, the hem of her skirts brushed against the banked roses, surrounding them with their sweet musky fragrance. "It's a wonderful surprise," Molly whispered, her arms around his neck. "Though dreadfully extravagant. They'll all be dead as doornails in two days."

He laughed and kissed her throat. "What a romantic notion."

"Still," Molly acknowledged, "it doesn't make them any less beautiful now."

"On the contrary. It makes them all the more beautiful to know their splendor is fleeting."

Molly cocked her head at him. "I always thought you had a priest's eyes, but I was wrong. They're poet's eyes instead."

"I only wish I had the soul to go with them." He tightened his arms around her, heading toward their bedroom door. "I would write such glorious verses to you if I could—"

" 'If ever any beauty I did see,' " she whispered, quoting from Donne, " 'Which I desired, and got, 'twas but a dream of thee.' "

"Exactly," he said, kicking the door shut behind them and carrying her to the bed.

He laid her atop the satin quilt and fell beside her, pulling her bodice down to bare her breasts, kissing them hungrily. Molly sighed her pleasure, reaching for him, feeling his manhood hard beneath her hand. He groaned and slipped his hands beneath her skirts, caressed her knees, her thighs. They parted to his touch, welcoming him; Molly caught his shoulders, urging him onto her, into her. "Wait," he whispered. "Slowly—"

"We can go slowly later." She raised her hips to his, coaxing, beguiling.

He laughed and gave in, thrust inside her, filling her completely. Molly wrapped her legs around his, drawing him nearer as he began to move. "The oldest dance in the world," she whispered.

"It is still the best." He drove harder, deeper. Molly caught her breath, the wonder unfurling inside her, familiar now and yet each time new. Anthony arched above her; she rose to meet him, and they came together with a swiftness that gave an added tang to their passion, left them clutching one another and panting while Molly's cries of fulfillment still rang in the air.

"Gor, that was good," Anthony said then, rolling onto his back with a thud. "Or should it be 'Oy'?"

"Hush!" She laughed, a finger to his lips. "Do you want this baby to grow up sounding like a street urchin?"

"There are worse things in this life than street urchins. I should know; I'm married to one." He caught her finger and kissed it. "What are we going to tell her about all this, anyway?"

"Him. The truth, I suppose."

"She'll never believe it."

"No, I don't suppose he will." Molly giggled. "Why should he? I scarce believe it myself sometimes."

"Believe it." He rolled toward her again, pulling her into his arms. "And believe this. I am going to love you for as long as the stars shine."

"Only so long as that?" she asked, pouting.

"All right, longer." He kissed the pout away. "Shall I ring for supper?"

"Later," Molly whispered, returning the kiss as the fire flared up between them, warm and bright as starlight. "In a little while."

① SIGNET (0451)

Journeys of Passion and Desire

☐ **FOREVER MY LOVE by Lisa Kleypas.** Their fiery embrace sparked love's eternal flame ... Beautiful Mira Germain was only eighteen when she made her bargain with the wealthy, powerful, elderly Lord Sackville, and she tried to keep her word, even when she met the handsome Duke, Alec Faulkner. But in Alec's arms, desire was more powerful than any promise or pledge. ... (401263—$4.50)

☐ **WHERE PASSION LEADS by Lisa Kleypas.** Only the flames of love could melt the barrier between them. Beautiful Rosalie Belleau was swept up in the aristocratic world of luxury when handsome Lord Randall Berkely abducted her. Now, she was awakening into womanhood, as Sir Randall lit the flames of passion and sent her to dizzying heights of ecstasy. ... (400496—$3.95)

☐ **LOVE, COME TO ME by Lisa Kleypas.** When strong and handsome Heath Rayne rescued lovely Lucinda Caldwell from an icy death, she little dreamed what a torrid torrent of passion was about to claim her. This dashing, sensuous Southerner was unlike any man she had ever known. He came to Massachusetts a stranger and conquered all the odds—not to mention her heart. ... (400933—$3.95)

☐ **A LOVE FOR ALL TIME by Bertice Small.** A breathtaking hot-blooded saga of tantalizing passion and ravishing desire. Conn O'Malley is a roving Irish rogue until he meets heiress Aidan St. Michael, the loveliest enchantress he ever beheld. When a cruel scheme makes Aidan a harem slave to a rapacious sultan, it will take all of her superb skill in ectasy's dark arts to free herself for the only man she can ever love. (159004—$4.95)

Prices slightly higher in Canada

Buy them at your local

bookstore or use coupon

on next page for ordering.

⊘ SIGNET (0451)

ROMANTIC ADVENTURES

☐ **AURORA ROSE by Anne Worboys.** For her sake he would kill a man and lose his heritage. For his sake she would marry someone she despised and travel to the lush, yet forbidding, unknown of distant New Zealand. Their energy would build a strong new country, full of hope. But their ruthless desire for each other would destroy even those they held most dear. (162110—$4.95)

☐ **LADY OF FIRE by Anita Mills.** Their love was forbidden ... their passion undeniable. Beautiful, young Lea was the most passionately pursued prize in Normandy. Three handsome and eligible men wanted her, but she gave Roger FitzGilbert, the most forbidden, her heart ... until they surrendered to the floodtide of feeling that swept away all barriers to love. (400445—$3.95)

☐ **FIRE AND STEEL by Anita Mills.** Proud, beautiful Catherine de Brione vowed never to give her heart to the handsome, daring Guy de Rivaux whom she was forced to wed. She was sure she loved another man, who had captivated her since girlhood. But against a backdrop of turmoil and intrigue in 11th Century Normandy, Catherine found it hard to resist the fiery kisses of the man she had wed.... (400917—$3.95)

Prices slightly higher in Canada.

Buy them at your local bookstore or use this convenient coupon for ordering.

NEW AMERICAN LIBRARY
P.O. Box 999, Bergenfield, New Jersey 07621

Please send me the books I have checked above. I am enclosing $_____
(please add $1.00 to this order to cover postage and handling). Send check or money order—no cash or C.O.D.'s. Prices and numbers are subject to change without notice.

Name_____

Address_____

City _____ State _____ Zip Code _____

Allow 4-6 weeks for delivery.
This offer is subject to withdrawal without notice.

Ⓞ

PASSION RIDES THE PAST

☐ **SAN ANTONIO by Sara Orwig.** In America's turbulent old West, Luke Danby, a tough lawman, vowed to exact revenge upon the vicious bandit who had raided a wagon train years ago and murdered his mother. But his plans turned to dust when Luke met his enemy's beautiful daughter Catalina ...
(401158—$4.50)

☐ **THE GATHERING OF THE WINDS by June Lund Shiplett.** Texas in the 1830s where three passionately determined women sought love's fiery fulfillment—Teffin Dante, who was helplessly drawn to the forbidden man, Blythe Kolter, who lost her innocence in the arms of a lover she could neither resist nor trust, and Catalina de Leon, who could not stop her body from responding to the man she wanted to hate. Three women ... three burning paths of desire....
(157117—$4.50)

☐ **SONG OF THE BAYOU by Elinor Lynley.** Beautiful Susannah fell in love with the bold, handsome planter who was her father's enemy. But their forbidden love kindled into wildfire passion in the sultry Cajun nights.
(401980—$4.95)

☐ **TO LOVE A ROGUE by Valerie Sherwood.** Raile Cameron, a renegade gun-runner, lovingly rescues the sensuous and charming Lorraine London from indentured servitude in Revolutionary America. Lorraine fights his wild and teasing embraces, as they sail the stormy Caribbean seas, until finally she surrenders to fiery passion.
(401778—$4.95)

☐ **WINDS OF BETRAYAL by June Lund Shiplett.** She was caught between two passionate men—and her own wild desire. Beautiful Lizette Kolter deeply loves her husband Bain Kolter, but the strong and virile free-booter, Sancho de Cordoba, seeks revenge on Bain by making her his prisoner of love. She was one man's lawful wife, but another's lawless desire.
(150376—$3.95)

Buy them at your local bookstore or use this convenient coupon for ordering.

NEW AMERICAN LIBRARY
P.O. Box 999, Bergenfield, New Jersey 07621

Please send me the books I have checked above. I am enclosing $_____
(please add $1.00 to this order to cover postage and handling). Send check or money order—no cash or C.O.D.'s. Prices and numbers are subject to change without notice.

Name_____

Address_____

City _____ State _____ Zip Code _____
Allow 4-6 weeks for delivery.
This offer, prices and numbers are subject to change without notice.